Praise for Meredith Duran's novels of scandal and seduction in nineteenth-century London—"romance at its finest" declares *New York Times* bestselling author Liz Carlyle!

A LADY'S LESSON IN SCANDAL
A July 2011 Top Pick of *Romantic Times* magazine and one of All About Romance's Desert Isle Keepers!

"Compelling, exciting, sensual, and unforgettable . . . a nonstop read everyone will savor."

—*Romantic Times* (4½ stars)

"The fascinating and compelling characters, the vivid imagery and dynamic prose, the wonderful romance—it was all I can ask of a romance [novel.] Meredith Duran just keeps getting better and better."

—All About Romance

"Delightfully honest."

—*Library Journal*

"Well-developed lead characters and a perceptive portrayal of a poor woman's reaction to the lush lifestyle of the nobility highlight a top-notch romance."

—*Publishers Weekly*

WICKED BECOMES YOU
A May 2010 Top Pick of *Romantic Times* magazine

"So much fun. . . . Charming and deliciously sensual from beginning to end."　　　—*Romantic Times* magazine

"Witty, often hilarious, sensuous, and breathlessly paced . . . [an] engaging mystery-enhanced escapade [with] charmingly matched protagonists."　　　—*Library Journal*

"The book to beat for best historical romance of the year. . . . Sexy, inventive, and riveting, it's hard to put down and a joy to read."　　　—All About Romance

"A fascinating, passionate tale . . . you won't want to miss."
　　　—Romance Reviews Today

"Rousing . . . delightful. . . . *Wicked Becomes You* enthralls with particularly likable characters and a heartwarming romance with deeply affecting emotions."
　　　—SingleTitles.com

WRITTEN ON YOUR SKIN
An August 2009 *Romantic Times* Top Pick . . .
Nominated for the *Romantic Times* award for
Best Historical Romance Adventure

"Remarkable. . . . Meredith Duran is one of the shooting stars of romance."　　　—All About Romance

"Mesmerizing . . . a glorious, nonstop, action-packed battle-of-wills romance."　　　—*Romantic Times* (4½ stars)

"Wildly romantic."　　　—Dear Author (Grade: A+)

"Everything a great historical romance should be."
　　　—Romance Junkies

MEREDITH DURAN

AT YOUR PLEASURE

Pocket Star Books

New York   Toronto   London   Sydney   New Delhi

Pocket Star Books
A Division of Simon & Schuster, Inc.
1230 Avenue of the Americas
New York, NY 10020

This book is a work of fiction. Names, characters, places, and incidents either are products of the author's imagination or are used fictitiously. Any resemblance to actual events or locales or persons, living or dead, is entirely coincidental.

Copyright © 2012 by Meredith Duran

All rights reserved, including the right to reproduce this book or portions thereof in any form whatsoever. For information address Pocket Books Subsidiary Rights Department,
1230 Avenue of the Americas, New York, NY 10020.

First Pocket Star Books paperback edition April 2012

POCKET STAR BOOKS and colophon are registered trademarks of Simon & Schuster, Inc.

For information about special discounts for bulk purchases, please contact Simon & Schuster Special Sales at 1-866-506-1949 or business@simonandschuster.com.

The Simon & Schuster Speakers Bureau can bring authors to your live event. For more information or to book an event, contact the Simon & Schuster Speakers Bureau at 1-866-248-3049 or visit our website at www.simonspeakers.com.

Designed by Jill Putorti

Manufactured in the United States of America

10   9   8   7   6   5   4   3   2   1

ISBN 978-1-4516-0695-9
ISBN 978-1-4516-0701-7 (ebook)

For Steph,
for innumerable reasons—"friendship"
being too pallid and commonplace a word
to begin to describe them.

Author's Note

When Queen Anne died, in 1714, the English crown passed to her second cousin, George of Hanover, who had been born and raised in what is now Germany. (Anne's half brother, James Stuart, was not eligible to inherit the throne because of his Catholic faith.) The accession of George I was marked by a dramatic shift in political power. The long-reigning Tory party saw many of its greatest leaders arrested and forced from office, and in the general elections that followed, the Whigs assumed almost complete control of the government.

Believing that their faith, powers, and privileges were threatened by the new king and his allies, many English Tories decided to take up the Jacobite cause and champion James Stuart's claim to the throne. Across England, 1715 was a year marked by treasonous rumors, riots, and repressions . . . and, ultimately, war.

AT YOUR PLEASURE

Prologue

Faster.

Adrian had abandoned the lathered horse a mile behind. He ran now, his feet no sooner striking the ground than lifting again, all his instincts and memories combining to aid him, directing him sure-footedly and safely over the darkened field where he had played as a boy and later loved her as a man.

Faster.

The lights of Hodderby, which had flickered in the distance for long minutes, grew brighter. He could see now the draperies thrown back, the windows blazing like torches. Behind them moved darkened shapes, perhaps looking out, one of them Nora: she was watching for him. She was strong. She would hold out. He would not be too late.

Faster.

He stumbled and the pain speared up his side, so that all at once, he grew aware of his breath sawing razor-like in his throat—the burning in his chest—the ache in his shoulder that had not yet healed; the throb in his ribs where his father had struck him. On the ship they had chained him to keep him in place, claiming that they did it with love; they were saving his life from ruin, they said. His brother had clapped him on his wounded shoulder and laughed at his expression—and then, when Adrian had hawked spit across that smirking mouth, had cursed and kicked him like a mongrel dog.

"You will thank me for that one day," his brother had said by way of farewell. Wiping his jaw, he had added, "I will have your apology then."

There would be no apology.

Faster.

Out of the dimness of twilight emerged a group of people in festive finery, men and women stumbling into each other, their wine-drunk laughter light in the cool autumn air. The girls wore bracelets of flowers braided round their wrists and brows; the flowers were orange blossoms, bridal flowers, purloined from a wedding.

Not hers, he told himself. *Not yet. She will not bend for them. She will wait for me.*

The group, seeing him, called out greetings. He had no breath for a reply. He was flying now, flying toward the manse. *Faster,* he thought. *Faster.*

1

Nora was sitting at her dressing table, her maidservant Grizel braiding her hair for bed, when she heard hoofbeats on the road without. For a moment her heart swelled with relief: *David,* she thought. Her brother had finally returned, and she could surrender his cares to his own keeping. Thank God for it: they had worn her to the bone.

The next second, the maid crossed to open the window. Peering down, she gasped. "King's riders, my lady," she said over her shoulder.

Nora felt the blood drain from her head.

King's riders, approaching by night with no message sent ahead to announce them: the only conclusion was that they meant to take the household by surprise. Their mission was not a friendly one.

Somebody had betrayed her.

"My gown," she said as she rose. "Lace me quickly. And leave the window open."

As she impatiently submitted to Grizel's nimble hands, she heard the household stirring back to life. Dogs barked in the inner courtyard. Tack jingled and a horse whinnied. Low voices rose on the cool night breeze, impossible to discern. She caught three distinct timbres, and then a fourth. Her chest tightened. "How large is the party?" she asked. "Could you tell?"

"I saw . . . eight, nine mounts?"

"So many?" Nora cast her mind back to the letter she had received last week. Since the riots at Oxford, the government had recalled the old act, passed before the Civil War, that allowed the king's agents to search any house suspected to harbor traitors. But to come this far into the Lancashire wilderness, with so very many men . . .

Evidently they felt certain they would not leave this place empty-handed.

She took a deep breath. *No cause to fear,* she told herself. As Grizel's hands fell away, she squared her shoulders. In the standing mirror in the corner, she saw herself: small, dark, half-lost in the shadows of the room.

It would not do. She lifted her head, trying for a prouder look. These visitors would behave as her manner instructed them. Best that they see a grand lady, deserving of respect.

"What can they want now?" Grizel whispered.

Turning, Nora found her maid twisting a lace cap in her hands. Her anxious gaze begged for reassurance.

Not for the first time, Nora felt a stab of anger. Her brother's mad schemes had endangered every soul in his care. At a time when heavy rains and failing crops should have riveted his attention to his estates, he conspired instead in French palaces, and exposed every throat in this house to the axe.

The thought was disloyal. She forced it away. David had no choice, after all. When her majesty had died and the German had come from Hanover to take the throne, their father's enemies had been waiting. They had whispered lies into the new king's ear. In the end, Father had been impeached, stripped of his title, and driven from England.

Neither Father nor David could be expected to tolerate such insult. As her brother often said, only dogs and cowards licked the boot that kicked them. And if the Colvilles did submit . . . who was to say that next, these lands would not be taken from them, too? The crown had already seized their more far-flung holdings, but Nora's late husband had labored to ensure that Hodderby and its environs were spared.

Now that her husband was dead, the Whigs no longer had cause to treat the Colvilles kindly. Before David could tend to these estates, he first must ensure that they remained his to protect.

As the panic ebbed, she began to think more clearly. Why, of course—nobody had betrayed her. The king's men did not come because they had learned of David's activities. More likely they came because this household had once belonged to her father, who had fled to the Jacobite court. They came on a mission of simple harassment.

"I cannot guess why they have come," she lied to the maid. "But I am sure there is good reason for it, and no cause for our anxiety."

"Yes, my lady," murmured Grizel. She did not sound convinced, but no matter. So long as the men did not know about David's affairs, there truly was nothing new to fear.

Unless, of course, it occurred to these visitors to dig up the cellar floors . . . or seize the stores of wine. The double-chambered barrels concealed more than canary and port. They housed enough gunpowder to demolish a fortress—or this house, if handled roughly.

A knock came at the door, causing her to jump. Surely they would not come straight to her rooms? Such boldness would bode very ill.

"Come," she called.

At least she sounded calm. That was a good beginning.

The door opened to reveal the steward, Mr. Montrose. He looked harassed, his white wig sitting askew on his heavy brow, revealing a wisp of gray hair beneath. "My lady," he said breathlessly. "I beg your pardon, but Hooton says a party of riders has come—they are demanding entrance—"

"On whose authority?"

"My lady . . ." He faltered, swallowing loudly. "They carry a writ of Parliament."

She refused to show how these words chilled her. "Then we have no choice. Permit them entrance and tell Hooton to make them comfortable." She bent her head so Grizel could pin up her braid.

"But, my lady—"

She looked up. Montrose was wringing his wrists. "What? Speak, sir."

"My lady, the party is led by Lord Adrian."

Grizel's hand slipped. A pin stabbed Nora's scalp, but she barely registered the pain. Montrose could not mean . . .

"Lord Adrian?" Her voice no longer sounded calm; it came out rough and choked, though she felt nothing, nothing at all but a prickling disbelief. Surely she was dreaming. Surely he could not mean—

"Ah, forgive me," Montrose stammered. "I forgot myself. I mean the Earl of Rivenham. He is Rivenham now."

My God, she thought. Then this was a mission of vengeance, indeed.

David, what have you done to me?

How could you leave me alone to face him?

They were installed in a small parlor with cups of buttered ale. Adrian watched his men assort themselves, settling with unaccustomed hesitance into chairs around the fire. The dark-paneled room seemed too fine for muddied leathers and woolens, but the stench of the journey, horse and smoke and sweat, quickly overwhelmed the sharp, clean scent of wood polish.

He was glad of it. He remembered that scent, the special mix made of aromatic balsam and the wax from Hodderby's beehives. In the stone entry hall, too, he had been caught off balance by memories. The old butler, Hooton, still answered the door, now with the aid of a cane. The unicorn tapestry next to the stair, the echo of his boots on the stone—the sense of familiarity had cut through his fatigue like a blade, spearing him straight in the gut.

It had made his manner colder than required. He had no complaint against the household, only the master—who was absent, Hooton had stammered. But Lady Towe was in residence.

There was another unwelcome surprise.

But irrelevant, he told himself.

He went to the window and looked out over the darkened parkland. A distant flicker of light in the trees caused him to tighten his grip on his goblet and lean closer to the glass. As a precaution, he had left Lord John Gardiner and a handful of outriders to stand watch from a quarter-mile away until he determined that their reception at Hodderby would be peaceful. Either the fool had disobeyed his orders and lit torches, or someone else was lurking in the wood.

It could not be David Colville. Not yet. Reports had placed him in Calais two days ago.

Perhaps the lady of the house had been expecting a midnight visitor. Did she look out some window upstairs in search of this light?

For her sake, he hoped not. Her presence here was not, in itself, suspicious; it was only logical that after the death of her husband, she had returned to her family home. But if she was involved in this plot, he would spare no concern for her. He would do what he must here, no matter the cost.

As he stared into the darkness, it came to him that another man in his place might feel a measure of dread. In his youth, he had been a friend to the man he now hunted, and to the woman abovestairs . . . more yet. Another man might well feel distaste for the current necessity.

Another man, finding himself at Hodderby again, might recall the boy he had once been, in this place—idealistic, impassioned, full of hope. A fool worth mourning, perhaps.

But Adrian felt nothing. That moment in the entry hall had been brief and unwelcome. It was over.

Sometimes he wondered at this numbness. More often it proved quite useful.

The door opened; leather creaked and throats cleared as his men rose. He took a long drink of his ale, swallowing before he turned.

The Dowager Marchioness of Towe entered the room. Adrian chose instead to focus on the man at her elbow. Here was an amusement, he thought: to find the old steward, Montrose, still on his feet, still fat as a Turk, triple chins aquiver with self-importance.

The maid that followed them carried a lamp. As the marchioness halted, the girl lifted it to show her ladyship to the company.

He was prepared for her, but his men were not: one of them sucked in an audible breath. The marchioness was too dark and small, her black brows too heavy and her jaw too bold, to qualify as beautiful. But her body was a spectacle: it would have done a barmaid proud, even in this prim gown the color of blood. The lamp's glow painted the ripe curve of her bosom and the fullness of her cheek. It drew crimson sparks from the rubies she wore at her throat.

Since it was pressing near to midnight, she would have been abed upon their arrival, or ready for it.

Those jewels had been donned mere minutes ago, to remind her visitors of her station.

She would have done better, of course, to disarm them by appearing sleepy-eyed and tousled, in a lace robe that slipped off the shoulder, wearing slippers with no heels, the better to emphasize how small, how negligible, she was.

But she had never been skilled at such games. As a girl she had scorned them. Later, after her marriage . . .

For whatever reason, she had grown quiet as a nun. *No wit,* the court's verdict had run. Adjudged to be rustic and tedious company, she had made no effort to persuade London otherwise.

Adrian had never disputed the other courtiers' judgments. He shared no opinions at all on the question of the marchioness.

In the inconstant light that rippled from the sconces along the walls, she was taking a moment to spot him. He waited, ignoring the curious glances from his men when he did not move forward to greet her. Despite her silence and the fortune around her throat, she looked to them, no doubt, harmless: a petite siren's body paired with a girlish face, given to blushes, dominated by large, round eyes.

As her gaze found his, her shoulders stiffened. For a brief moment, her alarm was obvious.

Yes, he thought. *You know better than to expect kindness from me now.*

He offered her a slight bow.

"My lord Rivenham," she said. She abjured curtsying

for a brief bow of her own, the dip of her head showing him the shining crown of her black hair. The face she lifted was unreadable to him, but he had grown accustomed to that; over the past six years, in crowds, across rooms, it had looked to him, when he had happened to look, like the mask cast to commemorate a dead woman. Attractive, albeit in an unusual way. But lifeless.

He knew enough of her late husband to guess at the cause. For her sake, Adrian supposed he was glad she'd been widowed.

"My lady Towe," he said. There was no call here for courtesies; they had determined that, tacitly, during their encounters in town. "Your steward will have told you the purpose of our visit. We will require lodging and provisions."

She stared at him. The light did not provide an exact view of her eyes, but they were gray, penetrating and clear like her voice. What London mistook for coldness was, in fact, a powerful self-possession. "I understood you come to make search of the premises. What provisions could you require for such a simple task?"

"I am glad to hear it will be simple," he said. "As to the question of provisions, if you do not understand the requirements of a traveling party, your steward no doubt can explain it to you."

By her impassive expression, the jibe did not register. She turned to confer in a low voice with Montrose. Adrian grew aware of the whispers of his men, who had perceived the undercurrent but had no hope of understanding it.

"The stables have room enough for your horses and your men besides," she said. "If you—"

"No," he said. "We will stay in the house."

She remained silent.

"We will require two private chambers in addition to the lodging for my men," he continued. "One of the Marquess of Barstow's sons accompanies us. Lord John will be arriving in the morning." The boy had whined the entirety of the journey; let him have a taste of a night watch, and a true reason to complain.

She took a step toward him, her maid with the lamp hurrying to follow. "I thought you had come to search the house," she said in a cutting voice. "If you mean to seize it, and my authority as well, then pray do me the favor of announcing it plainly."

He allowed himself a slight smile. Once, her bold speaking had fascinated him. He had imagined it the product of a mind that ranged freely and a spirit that quailed at nothing.

But her boldness was nothing so brave. Like a mule, she would persist stubbornly in her duty, never questioning it, until she dropped dead in the harness.

Indeed, for all he knew, her brother had put her to work in his plot.

The thought darkened Adrian's mood. He felt a dull throb in his shoulder, an old wound, gifted long ago by her brother, that had never healed entirely. He had ridden twelve hours or more today, through rain and wind, and he was more exhausted than he'd thought: his body was sore and so was his temper.

"Plainly, then, madam, in language you will understand," he said. "I come to do the king's bidding. I am his agent in this matter and you will treat me as such. That is your only duty: obedience."

Over the crackling of the fire, he heard the sharp breath drawn by her maid. But she never moved.

"Very well," she said after a moment. "Montrose, you will instruct Hooton to find places for these men in the east wing, and see their horses stabled. Your lordship, if you would be so kind"—her sarcasm was delicate—"may my household be given to know how long we will be graced by the king's agent?"

"That I cannot say." As long as it took, he thought. David Colville had been asking after ships in Calais. This piece of stupidity he would soon compound, for his arrogance would not allow him to remain hidden once in England. He would imagine himself capable of overpowering a small contingent of soldiers. Soon enough, he would make an appearance at Hodderby.

"I see." The marchioness hesitated. "Then perhaps you will wish me to absent myself. I can withdraw to a cousin's estate—"

"Oh, no." It was coming to him that he could not have planned this ambush better: she would make an excellent lure for her wayward brother. Indeed, once David Colville learned the identity of his sister's guest, rage might lead him directly to the front door. "Forgive me for not making myself clearer. For the remainder of our stay, this household will not stir beyond the grounds."

She took the lamp from the maid and lifted it, as

though to see him more clearly. Instead, she showed him herself: her owl's eyes, wide and pale and startled; the thick black brows that a vainer woman would have plucked; the grave line of her bowed lips, and the pulse beating too rapidly in her throat. "I—you cannot mean—but that sounds as though we are under arrest!"

"So it does," he said. "Effectively, so you are."

2

"Stay a moment," Rivenham said as Montrose ushered out the soldiers. "I must speak with you."

Speak with me, Nora thought with a hysterical flicker of humor. Once, those words had meant everything to her. *I must speak with you,* he had whispered that day in the meadow, right before he had laid her down amidst the sweet-scented grass. He had pushed his face into her hair, so his damp breath warmed her throat. For the first time they had spoken of love.

He had been no more than twenty, she a year younger. Children, really.

What a wild, foolish, stupid child she had been!

Yet, for so long after her marriage—for so many endless nights after that first glimpse of him in London, with some woman on his arm touching him as though he were hers, while his eyes passed by Nora as though she were invisible—for so long she had burned to hear him say those words to her again. To know that she was needed; that she could give him what no other woman could; that he loved her yet.

But time had made her wiser. She knew now that a man's need for a woman was no special compliment. Men had endless needs. Her father, her brother, her late husband—all of them impatiently had required her attention day after day, year after year. She had grown wise enough not to be flattered by need. She had learned to be grateful, instead, for silence and indifference.

As she sat by the fire watching Lord Rivenham prowl the room, she was proud to find no curiosity in herself regarding his need to *speak* with her. Indeed, she took his words in the same manner that he had spoken them— coldly.

"How large is your household?" he asked. "Count those who sleep in the stables."

"Forty-eight souls," she said.

He nodded. His hand passed lightly over objects as he paced: the glass-fronted cabinet of china; the japanned vase that sat atop the small table by the window; the velvet-cut arras cloth that stretched along the wall. He looked out of place in the rough clothing of the road: high boots of brown leather cuffed above his knees; dark breeches, dark waistcoat, a black wool jacket that flared out to reveal the glint of his sword hilt as he turned.

He looked like a barbarian, and she loathed not only his questions but his very presence here. How easily he had decided, at his own convenience, that he no longer wished to ignore her! Worse, she had no choice but to accede to his decision, for he came from the king.

"I will allow you twenty people," he said. "The rest, all who are not necessary for the running of the household, will be dispatched to their villages for the remainder of our stay."

The order fired an anger that astonished her. It was not her way any longer to submit to tempers, but it took great effort to keep hold of her composure now. "There is no one who is not necessary to this household. Else I would have dismissed them already." Moreover, most would have nowhere to go: after a summer of floods that imperiled the crops of corn and wheat, no household would welcome them.

"Then your decision will be difficult," he said.

"So will your breakfasts and suppers," she said, "and your laundering as well."

The corner of his mouth lifted in acknowledgment as he turned toward her. She found herself resenting even the way he moved: with a sort of liquid grace that had won him a host of admirers, all the way up to her majesty, who had favored him especially for dancing. The Queen's Delight, they used to call him in London. Her majesty had loved nothing better than the attention of talented, pretty men, and Adrian had always been that: tall and broad-shouldered, fashioned in lean, taut lines, with silver-pale hair and slumberous green eyes.

But *pretty* no longer described him. He looked weathered now, hardened, in the way of soldiers who slept in the open. Beneath the broad bones of his cheeks, his face hollowed; the set of his jaw conjured grimness, and his neck was corded with muscle. His eyes remained as thickly lashed as a woman's, but as he regarded her now they glinted with the sort of malicious intelligence that women were not allowed to claim.

He looked like a handsome stranger, and not a kind one.

"You will find a way," he said. "All across the kingdom, the Marchioness of Towe is reputed for her housekeeping."

But not for much else, his tone implied.

Unblinking, she stared at him. She knew the low regard in which the court's more glittering circles held her. Was she meant to care that his shallow, vain, foppish friends thought her cloddish?

Perhaps he did not allude to the court's judgments, though. Perhaps he meant to wound her with an older reference. She could still recall the day she had railed at him in the wood. *I am to tally accounts and stitch seams until I am gray,* she had raged. *Counting bottles of port and overseeing the making of soap—if I am lucky enough to survive the childbed. What woman should look forward to marriage? Why celebrate such an end?*

Childish complaints. But she still might have avoided that end, if only she had never met *him.*

The thought echoed in her head, growing ludicrous. No woman of sense would envy a spinster's uncertain lot. She took a long breath to calm herself. *Reputed for her housekeeping.* The mockery seemed sharper by the moment, but she would not give him the satisfaction of seeing it register.

To her relief, he turned away to resume his inspection of the room. "When did you return to Hodderby?" he asked.

She sat back. She had returned as soon as she had been able, but her path had not been direct from London. Her mother-in-law had insisted on detaining her in Hertfordshire for three long months after Towe's death, putting her every morning to prayer in the chapel, bidding her beg God for an heir, until finally it had become clear even to the old woman that Nora's womb was empty.

The Marchioness of Towe is reputed for her housekeeping. But for all her efforts, for all the bitterness she had swallowed to do her duties smiling, she had failed at the most important task of a wife.

The failure had not gladdened her, but there had been a strange justice in it, one that philosophers might have appreciated.

She cleared her throat. "Why do you wish to know?"

He paused before a portrait of an ancestor, stiff in an Elizabethan ruff. She watched him study the painting with growing anger. *Do not pretend such interest in it,* she thought. *You have seen it before.*

"I didn't know you had returned," he said. "It interests me."

"My decision to return interests you? Where did you imagine I would go?"

He smiled slightly. "What interests me is the fact that I did not know of it. Did you come in secret?"

She stiffened. "I did not. I came near to five months ago, with no small party of outriders. And why should it surprise you? Is it *your* call to keep track of me?"

"*My* call?" He turned toward her, lifting a silver-blond brow. Once these Gallic mannerisms of his had lent him a fey air. But now that his face had become a man's, the effect seemed more calculated and intimidating. "No, of course not. But you have always interested me, my lady. Perhaps you recall it."

Her skin prickled as though someone had walked over her grave. His tone was a horrible mismatch to his words. He alluded for the first time in years to matters long past, but he did so lightly, mockingly, as though their shared history were a joke he had heard in a tavern.

She laid a hand to her cheek and felt the heat there. This evidence of her blush enraged her: it suggested he had some power over her yet. Worse, it showed to him that he might.

"You know my father is not here," she said. "I fear the new king has sent you on a fool's mission."

He did not reply to this. "You say you came five months ago."

After a moment, she nodded. Had her answer suggested something to him? She cast her mind back, but could think of nothing significant about April past, save that Parliament had finally set in motion the impeachment proceedings against her father. But Father had already fled to France by then. He was innocent of wrongdoing—a faithful member of the High Church, and a true servant to his country—but with his Whig enemies come to power under the new king, the verdict against him had not surprised anyone.

"I would have come sooner," she said, "but after Lord Towe died, I remained with his mother for a time."

"How dutiful," Rivenham murmured.

It did not sound like a compliment, and she felt herself bridling again. How odd, after so many years, to converse with him in this way. From love to silence to hatred, with nary a word between.

One of his long-fingered hands settled on the back of a chair as he faced her, his heavy signet ring catching the firelight. Four years ago, the death of his elder brother had made him the earl. Some whispered that he had expedited this process by smothering his brother with a pillow as the man lay witless with fever.

Nora could not believe the rumor. But it did play uneasily through her mind that the boy she'd known had never longed for power, whereas the man he had become seemed to glory in it. Why else had he cultivated the late queen's favor, petitioning to play her diplomat at George of Hanover's court?

"I suppose you must have given thought to the other questions I will ask," he said. "Shall we save trouble by skipping directly to your answers?"

She pushed a hand over her brow. His manner was so strange, this scene so unimaginable, and the hour so late, that she felt a momentary, giddy wonder: perhaps she was only dreaming.

"Speak," he said sharply.

She pulled herself straight. "You forget yourself!" She was not one of his servants. "I have no choice but to allow you to stay in my home, and to search it as you will. But his majesty cannot command me to tolerate your insults!"

A brief silence passed, in which he did not move. And then she saw his fingers loosen slightly on the back of the chair, and it came to her that before this moment, he had been . . . braced for something.

Why? What cause had *he* to find this meeting uncomfortable? He had ignored her with effortless skill for six years now. Was he angered by her refusal to be cowed?

Or did this meeting seem as impossible, as mad and strange, to him as it did to her?

"Forgive me," he said slowly, as though the words of apology tasted foreign, and required special care in the pronunciation. "It is late, and my manners suffer from the road. I assure you, madam, that this occasion is no more agreeable to me than to you."

She swallowed. They were dancing nearer and nearer to the heart of the matter now. "Why are you here, then? Why has the king sent *you*?"

He stared at her, still impassive. The long clock in the hall began to chime, its low, mournful notes marking the death of the day. "You were better to ask my intentions here," he said. Some weight in the words bade her to take it as a warning. "Do you know where your family is?"

What sort of trick was this? Everyone knew where her father was. In the newspapers, in the coffee and chocolate houses, his flight to France had sparked a thousand speculations. "Lord Hexton has . . . gone abroad."

He did not react. "And your brother?"

She felt a sharp thump of panic. Why did he ask after David? "He has gone north to hunt. The grouse are in season."

"Indeed? An unusual time to absent himself."

She stared at him, unable to reply, but understanding

his skepticism perfectly. The harvest was upon them, but it would soon become a season of death if the rain did not cease. Corn and wheat could not survive such wet, and without them, men did not survive the winter unless they were wise enough to have planted sufficient oats and potatoes besides.

But Lord Hexton had never been one for farming. He had saved his strategies for court politics, and left his son to worry for the crops. David, in turn, had counted on the weather, and on the wealth in their coffers to purchase what stores they lacked. But the strongbox stood empty now, its contents having been spent on weaponry. Meanwhile, the tenants came to her each morning, their eyes shadowed by sleepless nights, concerned for the children they must feed.

"It is September," she said. "The grouse are thick on the ground. When else should he hunt?"

Rivenham gave her a measured, cold smile. "With whom does he hunt, then?"

"With friends."

"Which friends?"

"Any number of them. My brother is not one to forget old affections."

The jibe slipped from her without conscious intention. She felt her heartbeat stutter.

Adrian—no, she could not think of him so; she would only think of him as *Rivenham*—gave her a strange half smile. No longer the Queen's Delight, he; now that George of Hanover had taken the throne, he had become the king's own blade.

"You understand," he said, "that I am not one of those friends."

Her breath caught. So quietly he spoke, but there was something cold in his face and his eyes.

For all the times that the sight of him had made her burn, she had never before been afraid of him.

"Yes." Her voice barely carried the word. She wet her lips and tried again. "I would never think otherwise."

"Then my plain speaking will not shock you," he said. "I am here because of your brother's dealings at Bar-le-Duc. Apparently the grouse are thick there as well."

Who had told him that David had been to France?

Or was he only acting on a suspicion?

She tried for a puzzled frown. "You confuse my brother with my father, sir."

"Your father is another matter," he said with a shrug. "He remains safely ensconced in the Pretender's court. Your brother, on the other hand, left James Stuart six days ago. He sails for England now."

She sat very still, praying her expression did not betray itself. How did he know these things? The last letter had been in code, and she had burned it directly. *Who had betrayed David?*

Rivenham sat down across from her, his eyes never leaving her face. "It amazes me how well you guard yourself. I can tell nothing from your looks anymore."

Anymore. Such a small word to make her breath stop.

He leaned forward. She began to tremble as his hand settled against her cheek. The pad of his thumb nudged up her chin.

His touch was warm and light, but he might as well have held her in a grip of iron. She could not move. She stared into his eyes, green as emeralds, with the light of the fire dancing across them.

"I can help you," he said. "If you trust me. Permit me to help you now, Nora."

Her lips parted but she caught back the first syllable before it could escape. *Adrian,* she would have said. He had spoken her name and it unleashed in her throat the feel of his, the sharp vowels, the tripping conjunct. *Adrian, Adrian.*

Now his palm, rough with calluses, cupped her cheek. A whimper lodged in her chest. This touch was a shock for which she could not have prepared. Her dumb flesh did not recognize or care that the man touching her so tenderly was her family's enemy. It reacted only to the dim memory of affection—to how sweet, so sweet it had been, to be touched with care.

She sat frozen in mortification as tears pricked her eyes. She had supposed this awful need had been crushed out long ago. She had thought herself wiser. Older. Beyond this hunger. Self-sufficient and untouchable.

"Tell me," he whispered. "What is David's aim?"

Her heart stopped. The next second it resumed with a thud, a painful blow that made her chest burn.

He had spoken her name deliberately, to provoke and disarm her. He meant to trick her into indiscretion. Into betraying her own brother!

He would put her brother's head on the block.

She recoiled from his touch, biting the urge to curse

him when he sat back with no visible reaction. The hurt she felt was sharp, soul-deep, and it touched off a mortified rage. *Why* should she care if he meant to manipulate her? Six years! She was a fool to expect anything different! Children grew up. Men did not spend their lives mourning a trifling diversion that had begun and ended with one summer.

"You see nothing in my face," she said, low and harsh, "because there is nothing to see but bafflement. You speak a passel of lies fed to you by some mistaken idiot or malicious liar. I suppose I should not be surprised that you believe them: a fool's mission requires a fool to lead it."

He sighed and rubbed his hand over his face; when it lowered, she saw for the first time how weary he was.

Good, she thought. She wondered how far he had ridden today, how fiercely he had pushed his men, in his eagerness to destroy what remained of her family.

"A shipment of arms was intercepted off the coast four weeks ago." He waited a moment, during which she dared not breathe. "When put to persuasion, the captain spoke your brother's name."

Horror clawed through her. Could David have been so careless in his arrangements? "Lies! Someone, some enemy of my brother's arranged for this—"

He snorted. "So will go his defense, no doubt." He pushed to his feet. "I will take it, then, that you are ignorant. If I am wrong, and you involve yourself in the pretender's cause, then consider my gentle approach to be the courtesy you demanded from me earlier. So long as you make no trouble during my time here, you will be left alone."

Briefly she wrestled with her tongue. Nothing was to be gained by baiting him.

But when he had almost reached the door, she leapt to her feet. Her venom could not be suppressed. "We are to be strangers, then? I am glad of it!"

He stopped but did not turn.

She stepped toward him. "You see, I dislike very much your cat-and-mouse games. They seem so womanish to me. I had thought better of you, but it was my mistake."

His head turned, showing her a three-quarters profile. "If we are strangers," he said flatly, "it was by your choice, madam."

"Choice?" She took another step toward him. "What *choice* did I have in it? Oh, but I see—this is how you comfort yourself for what you do now. No doubt you think this charge laid on you by the king makes a sweet revenge for your wounded pride!"

A muscle flexed in his jaw. He turned, his green eyes hard as they speared hers. "Pride has no place in it. I am here to arrest your brother on suspicion of treason and take him to London for judgment. *That* is my charge, and be damned to anyone who stands in my way. So take comfort, madam: if you had no choice then, you *certainly* have none now."

The door shut, closing her into midnight's silence.

3

braver or prouder woman would have turned down the posset that Grizel brought to her that night. One sniff and Nora knew there was a sleeping tonic in it. But she had never cared much for her pride, and if she had, that one touch in front of the fire would have shredded it to ribbons.

She did not love the man Adrian Ferrers had become, but she was not unaffected by him. His touch stirred a part of her that she would rejoice to disown: to cut out with a knife, if only she could. This unwise and wild part of her had led to every mistake she'd ever committed. It had kept her unhappy in her marriage, where other women would have learned contentment. It had lured her to mad dreams and despair.

She had thought it vanquished, but it awoke at the sight of him—as it always had.

She drank the posset to the dregs and went into her solar to wait for its effect. By the window seat she kept a variety of instruments: her brother's barytone stood in a handsome stand, and her mandolin and lute and tambour hung from pegs above. She took down the lute and strummed a soft tune as she stared into the featureless night.

But music made its own thoughts, and after some minutes she realized with a black start where her fingers had led her: this plaintive tune she plucked had been accompanied in old times by Rivenham's clever fingers on the mandolin.

She replaced the lute and paced back into the bedchamber, where Grizel sat reading Psalms. The maid looked up, a question in her eyes, for her mistress was not accustomed to roaming at so late an hour. But any explanation would be an ill one.

Nora climbed into bed and drew the curtains, sealing herself into darkness before she lay down.

Even the silence seemed charged with significance. After all, Rivenham listened to it as well.

She laid her hand over her eyes. Would that she could darken her memory so easily as her sight! The way he had spoken to her tonight . . . it made her grateful he had never spoken to her in London. To look into his face was to remember a time when he had viewed her as a wonder. The expression in his eyes, those many years ago, had seemed to confirm all her hopes and dreams. Having corrupted her own brain with tales of warrior queens, of lady pirates and adventurers who had slain dragons and traveled the world and brought kings to their knees, she had seen in his love the proof that she was no ordinary woman. For her, anything would be possible.

Tears slipped through her fingers. Their hot progress down her temple reminded her of all the nights when she had struggled and failed not to weep. Silently she had curled at the edge of the mattress, trembling lest her husband turn in bed and feel the dampness on her pillow, for her tears had angered him immeasurably, and in his anger he had not been kind.

How long did it take for dreams to die? She had thought herself beyond this girlish grief. Her fate had not been so cruel. Indeed, she might be counted fortunate. David was already planning her next marriage. What more could a woman wish for than her own household? This time he had proposed a cousin, Cosmo Colville. At least Cosmo did not seem brutish. He likely would not require her company in London, either. He did not believe it was a woman's place to play hostess in political circles, and—as he had once told her—he found it *becoming* that she was no diplomat.

His estates lay in a rainy, dark stretch of Yorkshire where the wind-scoured soil yielded little of beauty.

She would rot there until she died.

She took a sharp breath, forcing her thoughts away from this end, but they strayed directly back to Rivenham.

A woman is no less than a man, he'd told her once. *My mother might have been a general, were wits the main requirement.*

He had worn an unpleasant smile as he'd spoken— one that had made her hesitate to understand his words as a compliment. *And I?* she'd asked. *Would I have been fit for a general?*

His smile had gentled then. Lightly, he had traced the curve of her cheek. *I can imagine no alternative for you. You are destined to conquer the world just as you are.*

That touch . . . how fervently he had seemed to believe his words . . .

The posset was unfurling through her, softening her brain. Misery loosened its grip a little, allowing a new restlessness to come over her. She stretched out her arms, measuring the width of the mattress. The carved oak posters supported a domed canopy of peacock velvet embroidered with golden leaves and scarlet rosebuds. Three men might have lain beneath it, their elbows never touching.

This, surely, was the sweetest boon of widowhood: to have this space for herself. A hulking man who took up thrice the room his body required; whose heavy limbs fell across hers like weights to suffocate her: where was the comfort in that?

She reached out to finger the lace that trimmed the bed curtains. Although she had lain with him, she had never slept at Adrian's side. They had lacked opportunity. He had come to Hodderby as her brother's guest, which in itself had been extraordinary enough: though their lands adjoined, his family, the Ferrers, were Catholic, and Catholic nobility did not often mix with outsiders. A chance meeting in London had led David to befriend him, after which there was no question but that he must pay a call, for only a day's ride separated their holdings.

She had thought him uncommonly handsome at their first meeting, but handsome men had not inter-

ested her. Having watched both her mother and elder
sister die in childbirth, she had lived in terror of the
prospect of marriage.

But Adrian Ferrers, a Catholic, was no candidate for
wedlock. And so his presence had not called for caution. That first night at dinner, when he had spoken of
Continental philosophers, of foreign places and strange
sciences, she had eagerly joined the conversation . . .
And though David had laughed, Adrian had listened to
her; he had listened carefully, and given such charming,
thoughtful replies . . .

Her eyes opened.

The curtains were drawn back to show sunlight flooding the room, sparkling across the mother-of-pearl inlays
in the heavy oak wardrobe.

For a moment, she was as confused by the sun as gladdened by it. Surely the night had not passed so quickly?
She had just closed her eyes. These possets always mud-
dled her wits . . .

Praise God it would not be another day of rain.

A shout came through the window. A man's shout.

Rivenham. It all came back to her in a moment. She
slipped from the bed and rushed toward the window.

Two men were practicing combat in the packed drive,
one dressed in rough-spun wool, the other in a suit with
fine embroidery. Steel rang out as their swords crossed;
the rough-spun man danced backward, shouting a taunt
that ended in a laugh as the dark-haired fop cursed and
pursued him.

When the fop's face came into view she recognized

him as Lord John Gardiner. She remembered the boy as a vain, idle creature, always looking down his nose. Shortly before her departure from London, he and his father had sat down at her husband's dining table with the condescension of conquering emperors.

Her husband's sycophancy had encouraged their airs. It had been clear by then that Queen Anne must die of her illness. Towe had been making a frantic search for new friendships that might preserve his power in the coming era of Whig rule. Nora had sat frozen, watching him grovel through nine courses of rich dinner fare, while Lord Barstow had toyed with his fork and smothered yawns. Lord John had spoken in his father's stead, a torrent of sly insults that had made Towe's face whiten.

But her husband had conceded to their every demand. He had borrowed and begged and robbed his own tenants to pay for the Gardiners' friendship. Shortly thereafter, in the Parliamentary debate regarding her father's impeachment, that friendship had yielded a single boon. Lord Barstow had argued that the traitor's kin should not be punished too sorely for his sins. *May we not teach these wretched souls the value of mercy? May we not show them a true example of Christian kindness, so at odds with the wicked model of their father?* In a self-congratulatory mood, the Whigs had agreed, allowing Hodderby and its environs to remain in David's possession.

Her husband had been pleased by this evidence of the Gardiners' favor. But he had not lived long enough to test their continued affection. As for Nora, she had only seen Lord John once after that day. Evidently she had not greeted him warmly enough. *What will it take for the Colvilles to learn their place?* he had drawled. *You look me in the eye when you would do better to thank me on your knees.*

Her knuckles throbbed with the force of her grip on the windowsill. Such company Rivenham brought to her house!

She took a deep breath to calm herself, and then another. The late-summer day had dawned cloudless, and a cool breeze came off the nearby field of rapeseed, carrying a pungent scent that prickled in her nose like pepper. At least there would be no rain today.

More raucous laughter rose from below.

Come to search the premises, had they? These men were gamboling like boys on holiday!

But of course they were. Searching the house was only the pretext for their visit. In truth, they had come to ambush her brother. Rivenham had said as much.

Her grip loosened. Last night, in her anger and panic, his admission had sounded like a threat. Now, in the bright light of the morning, she saw it differently. He'd had no need to tell her his true intent.

Could he have meant to warn her?

She spun toward the open door. "Grizel!"

Her maidservant appeared, a cup of tea in hand. "My lady? Will you drink?"

She waved away the cup. "The tenant whose son broke his leg two days ago. John Plummer, was it not?"

"Aye, the Plummers," Grizel said. "John and Mary, son by the name of William. Last winter the arm, and now the leg: that's the clumsiest boy God ever designed."

Nora smiled. "Do they still live near the apple grove on the eastern border?" The river Hodder had flooded two years ago, displacing many of the tenants.

Grizel nodded. "Now same as then."

"Then fetch me a new quill." Nora crossed to her writing desk. That apple grove was where she found the correspondence that did not come through the post—and where she left her own secrets, when she had cause to share them.

Lord Rivenham had told her that she could not stir beyond the grounds of Hodderby. But the grove lay within them.

The telescope took Adrian by surprise.

He laid a hand on the finely grained beech wood, stroking it once before lifting the machine from its pedestal. The inlaid brass was brightly polished, the dial well oiled.

He wondered how it had won pride of place in Lord Hexton's library. She would have had a difficult time explaining to her father how it had come into her possession. The glass had been crafted in Bohemia, to Adrian's specifications in conference with Mr. Newton. The beechwood body and brass fittings had been assembled in France. He had spent two quarters' allowance on it and consequently lived a hard winter at La Flèche, dependent on the goodwill of his fellow collegians to keep him from freezing after his store of coal ran out.

He'd given it to her without a moment's thought for its loss.

So full of wonder she had been, back then. To see it spread over her face when she'd first looked through the telescope had been like to seeing the sun rise for the first time in his life.

Oft she had looked at him with the same expression. Perhaps the boy he'd been had even deserved it. In those days, his hands had been unstained, his sleep untroubled.

One could envy the pleasures of innocence, he thought. But the fate of innocents—how easily their gullibility led them to slaughter—that was worth no envy. For the sake of his soul, he should pity those who trusted in the goodness of the world to safeguard them. But when he thought of the boy he had once been, pity was harder to feel than contempt.

He had trusted her completely. What fool did such a thing, and then dared to mourn when betrayed?

"Find something?"

He looked up. Braddock, twisted at the waist atop a short ladder that rested against the bookcase, watched him quizzically.

I have found a piece of foolishness, he thought. She should have destroyed the instrument. It would have been safer for her.

The woman she had become . . . he would have sworn that woman would destroy it very easily.

"Nothing of note," he answered. Because he did not like the feel of the instrument in his hands, the solid, undeniable weight of it, he returned it to its stand. The odd feeling he put down to fatigue. He had not slept well last night. This place, more than most, inspired twisted dreams. "And you?" he asked Braddock. "You've been poking at those books long enough to learn to read."

Braddock gave him a wry smile. "What do you reckon?" He leapt off the ladder, landing easily despite his bulk. Ruddy and dark, he was the son of a wherryman who had earned his living steering boats on the Thames. This made Braddock an unlikely man at arms, but surefooted on any surface, with skill to navigate so long as there were stars.

His complaints were not so useful. "Here's a waste of our time, searching," he went on. "A nice pantomime, when where we should be waiting is Dover, to hunt the bastard down like a dog."

Adrian lifted a brow. "Barstow's son said much the same over breakfast this morning."

Braddock grimaced. "Now you wound me, you do. To sound the smallest bit like *that* puling milksop—"

"Then distinguish yourself by using your brain. The cause here is not war but the prevention of it." The recent Riot Act had gone far to quiet the disturbances that had swept England during the spring, but Adrian had taken note of the mood in the towns they had passed on their journey here. At the taverns, in the coffeehouses, an ominous silence had greeted their appearance, and he had seen more than one man pass his wineglass over water before offering up toasts to the king.

These silent tributes to the pretender did not trouble Adrian so much as the boldness with which they were essayed. The kingdom was a powder barrel in want of a spark.

"Slaying a man in the street would not be restful to the public mood," he said.

Braddock gave a sigh. "Aye, I suppose. So we sit here in wait of him like a cat at a mouse hole. Simple work, if a mite slow."

Adrian shrugged. This task was simple for those under his command, but for himself, there was danger in it. He understood that better, even, than the king did. George Augustus was shrewd, but he was not English. One day he would learn to divine the murky undercurrents of Parliamentary politics, but at present, his logic and intuition often combined to point him down the wrong path.

The king himself recognized this weakness, and depended on English advisors. He had asked certain men in Parliament to choose a reliable man to corral a traitor. *Let it be a man of stature,* he had said, *with the authority and the willingness to complete the task peaceably or bloodily, as the situation requires.*

He had not realized that his advisors' recommendation of Adrian was an attempt at political assassination. Somerset and Lord Huthwaite in particular disliked the prospect of a former Catholic drawing so close to power. Should Adrian fail to capture David Colville, they would ensure that his religious history shed a particular light on his failure. Soon, *he* would be the one to whom the whiff of treason attached.

He had safeguarded himself as well as he could by securing Lord John's company in this work. The boy's doting father, Barstow, was cousin to Somerset and friend to Huthwaite. Should anyone allege wrongdoing on Adrian's part, they would have to incriminate Lord John, and thereby antagonize Barstow as well.

Still, that was not surety enough for comfort. Adrian's own people posed him troubles. His younger siblings lived but a day's ride away, at Beddleston. Adrian had fortified that manor, but lacking an army it would not stand against a prolonged assault, particularly if those who worked his lands, so many of them Catholic, turned against it. Moreover, should they rise, their rebellion would be blamed on their master. And this said nothing of his innumerable cousins across the northwest, or his sisters who had married within the Catholic faith, whose husbands' treason, if they pursued it, would taint Adrian and all those he sought to protect.

The easiest and most convenient course lay in making a spectacle of his loyalties. He would deliver David Colville to the Tower—publicly, with loud fanfare. Then, in good time, with this Jacobite nonsense extinguished, he would deal with his detractors. Make a private peace, if the terms suited him—or a private war, depending.

He found himself looking at the telescope again. Impatient, he passed a hand over his eyes. With so much hanging in the balance, he should not be loitering over curios. Here was no mystery, no wonder, only a piece of a past best forgotten.

What chafed him, then, in the sight of this instrument so boldly displayed?

Once upon a time, surely, he had known his own mind. But he could no longer say what lurked in his own depths. Other men looked to their emotions, but his had gone into slumber. They looked to God as well, but he had abandoned his faith and felt no welcome in any church.

Cold logic was his only guide. It had served him well on his rise, and he knew its rules well enough. It did not allow for mercy or curiosity.

Or regret.

"Hey there," said Braddock. With a frown, he made for the mullioned windows that overlooked the rolling parkland. "Who's that out in the trees?"

Adrian retrieved the telescope and joined him. A small figure in a shapeless cloak was disappearing into the woods.

He lifted the instrument to his eye, flipping the dial and adjusting the lens.

A rough cloak of undyed wool. A basket on one arm. "A woman," he said, "adjudging by her size."

The woman paused to glance over her shoulder. Her pale face briefly filled his vision, and he bit back his curse. She looked nervous, as well she might.

He lowered the telescope. "Make a count of the household," he said grimly. "I want to know exactly how many people are under this roof *at this moment*. Once you've counted, make sure that number does not change."

"Aye, m'lord. Will you take a man with you? Henslow's a sharp tracker."

"No." He needed no help to track the Marchioness of Towe. He had chased her through those woods so many times in his youth that he would have been able to catch her blindfolded.

For a brief moment he wondered if the skill would be his advantage, or his undoing.

God damn it. He shoved the telescope at Braddock. "Put that away," he said. A wiser man would have added, *Burn it.*

The apple trees were finally coming into season, leaves bright and glossy. But the deluge of the past few weeks caused new fruit to grow but sparsely. As Nora climbed the gnarled limbs, her skirts knotted at her waist, she touched each apple she passed. Still small as nuts, they felt softer than they should.

In the subtle man-made hollow hidden by the join of branch and trunk, a letter waited. Her urge was to open and read it immediately, but such business was more wisely done in a locked room with a fire burning within reach.

She eased out the paper and tucked it into her bodice before putting her own letter into the nook. Then, crouching and setting her hands on either side of her feet, she swung to the ground.

The thump of earth beneath her feet startled a laugh from her. She paused in the dappled sunlight, allowing herself a moment without worry, a smile for the simple pleasure of jumping down like a monkey. Gradually she was teaching herself this trick: to find beauty in small things. When she'd had a husband's name to bear, and his honor to uphold, and the world watching and judging her, these little freedoms had been unimaginable. But now, for a brief period—even amidst so many uncertainties—she was free.

She took a deep breath of the apple blossoms. So the fruit would not be plentiful this year. It would make next year's bounty all the sweeter, would it not? In the meantime . . . oats and potatoes would serve.

She picked up her basket and turned down the path toward the Plummers' cottage. The sun was gentle on her face, and the wind sighed through the trees. Overhead, a circling hawk cried out. She felt safe in these woods, protected by the land, even with the Earl of Rivenham's presence hanging like a shadow.

If villains in London were conspiring to rob her family of this place—to strip the Colvilles of all their ancestral rights—then how could she object to her brother's efforts to oppose them? She would live on oats until she died, if it so required.

No sooner did the thought pass through her mind than she heard hoofbeats rapidly approaching. Her heart in her throat, she ducked behind a tree and pressed herself against the rough trunk.

The horse drew up nearby. For a moment she heard only its puffing breath and the jingle of tack. Then came Rivenham's dry voice: "You dropped a roll."

She bit her lip. There was no choice for it but to step into the open.

The horse was chomping on one of her manchets.

She forced herself not to look onward toward the tree she had climbed, but if she had dropped bread there as well, it would be as good as a flag in drawing his attention. "Your horse flatters my cook," she said as calmly as she was able. The gelding had made quick work of the roll and now stepped forward to nose for more.

"He's generous in his judgments," said Rivenham. "I am not."

She looked up. The sun was shining directly behind his head, obscuring his expression. "You forbade me to leave the grounds. Surely you recall where our lands end and your own begin."

His silence made for an ominous reply. The letter seemed to burn where it pressed against her breast. She reached into her basket for another bun and deliberately threw it a good distance away from the horse.

"Minx," Rivenham said softly as his horse fought to reach it. He swung off his mount. Now she could see his expression, and it surprised her: he was smiling.

A quick, troubling throb moved through her. The wind wandered past, plucking a strand of his blond hair from its queue, waving it across his lips. Six years ago his hair had barely brushed his jaw, an effect of his time at French schools with Continental customs, where men went fully shorn beneath their wigs. In London, his courtly curls and powders had disguised the changes in him. But now he faced her bareheaded, undisguised in broad daylight, and she could see how the sun had burnt his skin too many times, tanning it to an unfashionable shade, the more shocking for the brightness of his hair. New lines feathered the corners of his eyes. There was no softness to him anymore: he had been baked and hardened like clay.

But his smile remained the same. Slow to spread, it developed into something sly and playful and somehow knowing: a smile like a wicked invitation, or a suggestion murmured in the dark.

Suddenly she felt dizzy. This smile, his easy posture, the woods breathing around them . . . Perhaps they had slipped back in time, and in another moment he would reach for her and draw her into his arms . . .

And she would relive, all over again, the greatest mistake she had ever made.

"You look happy," he said, even as her heart turned to ice.

"I am glad to be out of the house," she said flatly. "Your men render it uncomfortable to me." You *render it uncomfortable*.

"Why is that?" He reached for a low-hanging leaf, fingering it idly. "Has one of them given you offense?"

"Your very presence is an offense. You come to persecute my family—am I to welcome that?"

He let go of the branch. The leaves shivered audibly. "Were you politic, you might pretend to welcome it."

Yes, perhaps it would be wiser to cultivate his kindness with false shows of friendship. But here, in this wood, she could not bear to pretend. Before she had met him, she *had* been happy; there had been no cause for false smiles or lies. Here in this wood he had lured her into betraying herself, and afterward everything had changed.

She had made herself vulnerable for him once. She would not do so again.

"I am not politic," she said. "I never have been."

He lifted a brow. "True enough. And so what are you doing out here, impoliticly?"

"One of the tenants is ailing." She lifted the basket. "I go to visit."

He glanced to the basket, then back to her face. "How convenient for you."

Under his steady stare, she fought the urge to shift and fidget. "I have watched you wear this look before," she said. "In London, when someone was making an argument you found foolish, you made men stammer with this stare. But there is no argument to win here. I am truly only delivering food."

He slackened the rein, allowing his horse to reach the manchet. "You watched me in London, did you?"

Why had she admitted that? It was these woods, she thought. Surely they worked some sort of twisted magic on her—and on him as well, for he took a step toward her now, saying more quietly, "I watched you as well. But I never saw you looking."

The words stopped her breath. *I watched you.* His presence now, his gaze upon her, felt like a hot, delicate touch all along her skin. She hoisted the basket, desperate to have something, anything, between them.

"The first time I saw you afterward," he said, "you flinched when he touched you. And it was all I could do not to gut him where he stood."

She searched for her voice and found nothing. Even her balance suddenly seemed effortful to maintain.

"And then, for a time, I wondered if it was not you I should kill," he continued, very low. "For if you had the courage to bear him, then it could not have been cowardice that drove you to spurn me."

It had never been cowardice. He *knew* it had not been cowardice. "I had no ch—"

"You will be glad to know that hatred of you was a madness I overcame." Still he spoke in that soft, deadly voice. "I remember the night I conquered it: you danced the saraband in wine-red velvet with the Duke of Ormonde. You stumbled, and someone near me wondered if you were with child. I found it easier, thereafter, not to think of you at all."

The light was too bright in these woods; it pricked her eyes to tears. What bitter irony lay in his remark! She remembered that night too well. Faced with her husband's contempt and the court's sneers, she had felt despair wrapping her soul in weighted chains. Everything had seemed black to her. One kind word from him would have meant . . . everything.

But not now. She was no longer that weak, frightened, friendless girl.

She took a sharp breath. "Yes, well. It served you very nicely not to think of me. What would your fine friends have thought, had the court discovered you once confessed your love to the woman they ridiculed?"

The corners of his mouth tightened. "Indeed. A proper fool I would have looked, to prate of my affections for a woman who had gone so willingly into her very happy marriage."

The injustice of it struck through her like fire. "Yes, God forbid! And God forbid you had decided to offer me your *friendship* instead. I suppose that, too, would have mortified your pride!"

"No." He looked her squarely in the eye. "It would not have served either of us, would it?"

In the silence she fought to hold his regard—and to hold on to her anger, too. He spoke truly: they could not have been friends. Her husband would never have allowed it.

"And at any rate," he said, "I was never your friend, Lady Towe. And you were never mine." The ghost of a smile chased across his lips. "Never mine," he repeated lightly. "Indeed."

He gathered back the reins, pulling his horse's head around. "Tell me," he said in a different, more impersonal voice, "what you are doing in the woods."

She tried to breathe past the knot in her throat. "I told you—"

"You have a twig in your hair," he said. "A leaf stuck to your skirt. You've been climbing. Why?"

She gripped the basket harder. His harsh manner sent a flutter through her stomach: no longer did she speak with her former lover. Now she answered to his majesty's agent. "I thought to collect fruit for the Plummers. Their boy's leg is broken."

He laughed, an unkind sound. "Do you think me an idiot, or are you become one yourself? A difficult question to judge."

He spoke to her like a peasant caught poaching on the master's lands. "Mind your tongue, sir!"

All at once he was in front of her, his hand closing

like a vise on her elbow, his face like stone. "Mind *your* tongue," he said. "I will admit to a small, godforsaken corner of my brain that remains intent on the notion of sparing you discomfort during the coming days. You may call it errant idiocy or you may call it nobility, but something within me *does* protest at the notion of consigning a woman I once loved to the flames. For that is what a woman suffers for treason, Leonora: only once in a very great while is Parliament kind enough to grant her the axe, and I assure you, there is no kindness in Whitehall at present for the children of the former Lord Hexton."

He let her go. When she nearly stumbled, she realized she had been pulling, pulling at his grip, and her flesh ached where he had held her.

"No one compels you," she managed. Her lips felt numb. "No one forces you to do this to us. Do not pretend you do not enjoy it! You have waited years to make my family pay! To make *me* pay!"

His smile was a terrible thing. "Pay for what, Nora?"

Her throat closed. Yes, pay for *what*? He had spoken of marriage so often, but never once had he approached her father for her hand. What cause for complaint did he have against her family for wedding her elsewhere?

"For the pleasure of it," she spat. "For your wounded vanity at the way my brother beat you within an inch of your life."

"I recall that," he said in a bored voice. "He does an excellent job of thrashing a man who does not lift a hand to oppose him. But no, you misguess my motives. You, more than anyone on this earth, should understand what I mean when I say I am driven to this task by *duty*."

Duty: that was the ideal she had defended, once, when refusing to run away with him. *If my father forbids our marriage, I will go with you. But it is our duty to speak plainly to him first.*

She felt something hot rising in her, scalding away everything but hate. How *talented* he was at drawing barb upon barb from a history that she had once viewed as the sweetest chapter of her life.

"If you wish to lock me in my rooms," she said, "to keep me indoors against my will, do not expect *me* to play the jailer. Find the guts to turn the key yourself!"

"And so I will," he said immediately, and held out his hand.

She looked at it wonderingly. He expected her to touch him now? To sit behind him on his mount and willingly be taken to her prison? "I would not put my hand in yours for all the king's gold!"

Instantly she recognized it for a childish remark. At least it afforded her the satisfaction of seeing him scowl.

He swung back onto the horse. "Then your preference is for rough handling?" he asked from the height of his saddle. "Very well. You may try to run, if you like."

She stood rigid. "I will deliver the basket first."

"One of my men will deliver it."

He was not going to concede. Her anger swelled. She set down her basket. "You will have to bully me, then." She spread her arms, showing him her palms. "Come, give me bruises to show my maidservants. Let them see how the king's justice is done."

"Do not test me," he said quietly. "I will give you something more than bruises. If I lay my hands on you, Nora, you will regret it extremely."

"How like a man," she cried, "to threaten with his fists! I have lived with a brute before, sir; I have nothing to fear from you that I have not survived before——"

Her voice broke as he leapt off his horse. She told herself she would not retreat, but as he stalked toward her, she betrayed herself with a quick step backward.

His grip closed on her shoulders and she tried to jerk free. "*You* are cowardly," she spat, "to abuse a woman half your strength——"

His mouth came down over hers.

4

He backed her into a tree, not gently. Nothing in his manner asked for permission as his body pinned hers in place. This could not be happening.

It *was* happening. His hands slid through her hair, gripping her head as his tongue penetrated her mouth. The taste of his mouth was sweet, bilberries and sugared tea; he had broken his fast before riding out. She sagged into the rough bark, surprise giving way to alarm as she realized her own helplessness.

Worse yet, she was not numb to him, not indifferent at all. Her body remembered the way of it. His mouth on hers awoke hot sparks in her blood, currents that knocked her heart into a hard rhythm.

I cannot allow this.

But he held her motionless, taking all choices from her as his mouth stroked hers. She found herself fighting her own bodily instincts, against which her wits had no purchase. Her hands: what to do with her hands? They remembered gripping his shoulders, sliding down the bulk of his upper arms, cupping his elbows, feeling the hard flex of the muscles beneath his skin. They wanted to retrace that path.

Instead she made them into fists at her sides, but then her eyes disobeyed her. They closed and the world contracted to his heat against her, the stroke and play of his mouth, the fragrance of the apple blossoms and the touch of the sun.

She did not love him anymore! But it made no difference: the smell of his skin had not changed. It kindled old hungers; she was still on her feet but felt as though she were falling. His kiss was so skilled. She remembered now that rude revelation when Towe had first kissed her: she had known in a moment that there would never be a comparison to Adrian's mouth. What could ever rival it? Her flesh felt riveted to his, alive to it, intuiting the muscled contours beneath his clothing, the dense breadth of his thighs, coming alive bit by bit. Her body had always known the language of his; she had learned it in the manner of a native recovering the mother tongue.

Panic twisted with a deepening hunger. The longer he ravished her with his kiss, the more she remembered of how it had been between them, how sweet and hot and drugging, and she grew weaker, years of accumulated, repressed longing breaking free to crush her all at once.

His hand slipped free of her hair. Her breath faltered as he traced the line of her cheek. His touch seemed . . . tender. Not a stranger's. He touched her confidently, as though he remembered as clearly as she what she had liked;

and patiently, caressingly, as though this touch meant something more to him than lust.

His knuckles brushed down her throat, the lightest whisper over her collarbone, down to her bodice, the lace that veiled the tops of her breasts.

A groan slipped from her. Once, long ago, here in the shade of these trees, he had put his mouth to her nipples and sucked. She wanted him now to do so again.

As though he heard her thoughts, his mouth dipped to find the top of her breasts.

The note.

In another second he would find the note!

Dread commanded her. Her fist came up and slammed into his ear.

He released her as though scalded.

His lips were wet from hers, his eyes green as the leaves behind him. Locked in his hot look, she felt herself flush, then go cold. So close she had come to forgetting herself! If he had found the note . . .

Dear God. She was no girl any longer, and this man was not her tender lover. The only promises he made to her were threats.

"You must confuse me with someone else," she said, her voice broken. "One of your London women." There had been so many of them. They had seemed to keep him well entertained. "I have no interest"—oh God, what horrifying words to recognize as a lie—"*no interest* in playing whore to my jailkeep."

Something flashed over his face—disbelief, she might have said. But it was gone as quickly as it had appeared.

He looked away, showing her his profile as he drew a long breath. A humorless smile twisted his lips as he looked back to her.

"Your tongue is too sharp to belong to a whore," he said. "You would leave your clients bleeding."

She tried to steady her breath. Her blood still hummed. "I doubt that. For a woman's words to wound would require a man to *listen*, first!"

The moment the remark left her she recognized it as a mistake—a strange thing to reply to his insult.

His expression altered, becoming thoughtful. He studied her a long moment in which her face grew hot and she finally glanced away.

"Have men used you so roughly?" he asked. "Did I use you so roughly, Nora?"

She ground her teeth, her skin crawling. Why had she said such a thing? Did she wish him to *comfort* her? To assure her that he *had* listened, in those long ago days when they had spoken so freely together?

Worse yet, to know he was pondering her words, that he had given them enough thought to produce his own interpretation—this knowledge made her shudder from a strange mixture of humiliation and . . .

Pleasure. *Could* it be pleasure? God above, was she so desperate that she should be gratified for a moment of his neutral consideration?

She forced herself to speak—stiffly, hoarsely. "I will not be treated with disrespect by you. I will not allow you to—"

To treat me as you might any other woman.

Her eyes closed. There was the truth of it. When he had kissed her in years past, it had been with love. But now he turned so quickly from anger to kisses because these were simply the ways in which men handled a woman—*any* woman. Love had nothing to do with it.

Why, *why* did that wound her? What profit had she or any woman ever gained by a man's love? Disgrace or marriage: these were the only outcomes. Neither had suited her.

Her silence discontented him. He made some noise of disgust and turned away to attend to his mount. She watched him with a misery that did not abate. His body was fashioned beautifully, tall and strong, with long legs muscled from sport. Men were not the only creatures governed by base appetites. He had reminded her so today.

If only his body had belonged to some other man—one who did not remind her, so strongly and so painfully, of all the dreams for herself that had not come true. Then she might have pondered disgrace with him. Her body could no longer betray her. Only her soul would be jeopardized by the pleasures of his embrace.

The prospect made her mouth go dry, and her misery pitch higher.

Not he. Never again.

He pivoted back and ran a disinterested glance down her body. "My mistake," he said, as if his survey of her had convinced him of it. "I offer you my apologies, madam. It will not happen again."

The fresh pain that lanced through her made her realize that she had been hoping for a different answer—a denial of the words she'd not even spoken aloud.

Those women in London were nothing to me, she had wanted him to say. *You were different, Nora. You were special.*

God, what a fool she was!

"Will you ride, or will you walk?" he asked.

She shook her head. "It makes no difference," she said dully.

Adrian held the gelding to a walk as they exited the grove. Emerging from the dappled light into the blaze of the midday sun, he felt as though he were coming awake. The feeling was akin to a drinker's regret after a night spent too deep in his cups. His head ached, and he raged at his own stupidity.

Nora—*Lady Towe*—rode pillion behind him, her shoulder nudging his spine with each stride. Her thigh pressed against his lower back, full and soft beneath her skirts.

A violent feeling leapt through him: loathing for her and for himself. There was something ridiculous and abominably comic about the bodily appetites. That this stubborn, prideful termagant could be his weakness— that her temper might spur him to passion—when he had forgotten a dozen clever-tongued beauties the morning after bedding them: was this a recipe for self-respect?

She had rejected him time and again. How many lessons would it take to educate him?

The horse loosed a snort and shook its head in protest. He relaxed his grip on the reins, fully in accord with his mount's opinion of him.

When his majesty had put this task to him, he'd agreed at once. He knew the danger of failure, but not accepting held a greater risk. *One wonders that he scruples to hunt Jacobites,* his enemies would have whispered. *Perhaps he still harbors an affinity for popish causes.*

Since his childhood he had watched his family be harassed and punished for their faith. He had been forced abroad by laws that denied English Catholics an education, and in his years of absence, a younger brother and sister had come into the world and died as strangers to him. He had missed years of his family's lives. For a time, after his return, he had managed to accept this. Trusting to the goodness of the world like all innocent fools, he had hoped for contentment.

But then Nora's family had done him a favor. They had shown him the cost of his naïveté. They had taught him very neatly how a Catholic, no matter his station, might be abused and discounted with no fear for repercussions.

His own father, who had seemed like a giant to him as a boy, had counseled him to flee like a mouse in the night. *You fool,* he had spat. *Think you we can afford such enemies? Know you nothing of the world? Our safety lies in keeping unto ourselves!*

Adrian's mind had changed then. He would not spend his life skulking for fear. He would not place his head in the yoke and meekly labor on, content to be abused and ignored as a popish idolater.

He would pursue power instead. He would amass enough of it to ensure that nobody ever again thought it safe to spit on the Ferrers.

The first step had been to conform to the High Church. He had waited until his father's death to do it. His brother had reviled the decision; his mother had given him up for damned. He had held fast against tears and threats, with no moment of doubt, and he had profited by it greatly. Before her death, the queen had promised to see him made Captain of the Gentleman Pensioners—a position of no mean power, last held by the dukes of Beaufort and St. Albans.

Her death had foreclosed that future. But he was not dissuaded. Having gambled with his soul, he would not rest until he realized his ambition—and the matter of David Colville could be as helpful in that regard as dangerous. Bringing new shame upon the Colvilles would cement the friendships of those in Parliament who had brought about Lord Hexton's downfall earlier this year. And then there was the simple fact that the Colvilles' land adjoined his own. Any disturbance of their making would provoke and trouble his own people sorely.

What reason to scruple, then? This task recommended itself in all aspects. Even had Adrian foreseen that *she* would be here, it would have made no difference to him. He had achieved indifference to her in London. Why not here, too?

But here was where he had loved her.

Here was where she came alive.

Encountering her in the woods, Adrian had seen beneath the mask that London life had forced upon her. Flushed, breathless, her black hair coming loose of its pinnings, she had stepped from behind the tree and his breath had gone.

In that moment, she had seemed a girl again. And for a fleeting length of heartbeats, he had felt . . . alive. Vibrantly, ferociously aware.

Womanish. She had called him womanish, and it blackly amused him to realize she was right. When he had come down from his horse, she had cringed in expectation of a blow. But striking her had never entered his mind.

Cold logic, he reminded himself.

It faltered in her presence.

Her voice came at his ear. "I must see to the running of the household, Lord Rivenham. I cannot do so from my chambers."

How coolly she spoke after kissing! It showed how his memories could not be trusted. He remembered soft sighs, soft lips, warm hands, laughter.

He also remembered how such interludes had ended: furtively and hastily, in fear of discovery.

He had always been only a diversion to her—a temptation and distraction from the men whose opinions mattered most, and from the role she was determined to play for them. That had been made clear enough, the day he had arrived at Hodderby to ask for her hand, and found her father and brother waiting, forewarned by her—and forearmed.

He still wondered if she had watched from a window above as David Colville had tried his hand at murder.

She spoke again. "I must—"

"One of my men will attend you in your duties," he said. "But your days of roaming are over."

That seemed to satisfy her, for she made no further protest. The only noises now came from the buzzing of bees and the wind whispering through the tall grasses through which they rode. A butterfly danced across their path. Above the pink sandstone face of Hodderby, the sky was so brightly blue that it seemed to ripple and shiver.

"I will consent to an escort," she said at length—as though she had a choice in it. "But he must not interfere with my decisions regarding the management of the estate."

A laugh slipped from him, no humor in it. "And have you thought on the cost to be exacted from your estate by the war your family is plotting?"

He felt her stiffen but she made no reply.

Her silence was its own form of rebellion. Another man *would* have struck her.

He was fit for this task, was he not? Or was he a great joke? Having abandoned his own faith, he found himself flummoxed by a woman of idiotic devotion. One might understand the appeal of such devotion—it might have proved very convenient and comfortable—if only it were to him.

But it had never been to him. She had let him walk into Hodderby with a marriage proposal, knowing that her family intended to see that he never left it alive.

Ah, well. He had loved and then detested her for the selfsame cause: the ferocity with which she did as she must for those whom she loved. Now he was going to have to break her of that trait. That was *his* duty. He should try to find pleasure in it. It wasn't as though such wickedness would cast his immortal soul into peril: he had lost any chance at heaven long ago. No matter God's churchly affinity, Adrian did not imagine that He approved of apostates.

He reined up in the courtyard and turned to help her down. But she had already slipped off the saddle. As she walked away, she did not look back.

Alone in her closet, the locks turned, Nora smoothed out the letter with shaking hands. The message was brief, written by someone who had no idea that her house now hosted the king's men: tomorrow, under cover of darkness, a party would arrive to collect the arms and weaponry David had amassed.

She had waited weeks for such news. The stores of gunpowder hidden amongst the wine were an ever-living threat to the safety of all beneath this roof. But what cursed timing! If only chance had brought them three days earlier . . .

She fed the note to the fire. It curled and blackened, filling the air with a peculiar, sweet scent that made her sick to her stomach.

She had no idea who would compose this party designing to appear. David had kept her ignorant of the names of his conspirators. But unless they retrieved her letter—and sometimes it took days for them to do so— they would enter unprepared for the welcome awaiting them. Blood would spill. They would die, and Rivenham and his friends would not require further evidence of her brother's guilt: if caught, David would go straight to the block.

Or David's men would prevail. Then Rivenham and his men would be the ones to die.

She sat heavily into a chair.

It should make no matter if Rivenham was killed.

But—yes, of course it should. She put her fist to her lips, pressing hard. If Rivenham died, news of his death would reach London eventually. *That* would bring more trouble. She had every reason to care about *that*.

She shut her eyes.

Adrian.

The flesh was weak, but it was not dumb. It had its own animal intelligence. In her husband's bed her body had felt like dead clay, but it had come back to life this morning in the apple grove.

How had she forgotten such pleasure? It invigorated the senses and enlarged the lungs. Riding through the meadow, the air had tasted richer and the brush of his worsted jacket against her bare wrist had riveted her whole awareness. Even her silent, inward turmoil had felt bittersweet to her.

She lifted her head to look into the fire. *I could seduce him,* she thought. Putting aside her own considerations, she could win him to David's side—or, failing that, she could distract him from his aim.

She pushed to her feet and grabbed the fire irons, stirring the flames to ensure not a scrap of writing had survived. To lie with him . . .

The very thought weakened her knees.

She stared at her hand clenched so tightly around the irons. Once it had been white and unblemished. Now her knuckles were red, her cuticles ragged, and the veins on her hand stood out prominently. She was no longer a girl. Yet her flaw remained the same.

She had always been a wanton for him.

Nothing, not her father's rage or Adrian's abandonment or her husband's blame, had been able to transform her.

She cast down the irons, making an angry clatter against the stone. Why lie to herself? If bedding him benefited David, then it would be an accidental profit—and not one on which she could depend. Rivenham had not come here for her: he had made that clear enough.

O vanity! How it had once stung her. He had not abandoned his faith for her, though it had been the first objection her father had lodged against him when Nora had been forced to confess all. But he had abandoned it for his own gain. He had traded religions to please new friends.

What could she expect from such a man as that? Such a man as would abandon his church would be able to take a woman to bed at night, then rise at dawn to run her brother through.

Who could mourn such a man if he came to a bad end? Better *he* fail than others who fought for nobler ends, and for ideals loftier than mere material advancement.

His German majesty means no good for our nation, David often said. *His heart is in Hanover. He does not even speak the tongue! For England's sake, we must oppose him. For our family's sake as well . . .*

She wrapped her arms around herself, hugging tightly.

If she could not assume that her letter would be received by the men who meant to come here tomorrow night, then she must assume they would come as planned.

The only way to avert catastrophe lay in disabling Lord Rivenham and his men. If they were unable to oppose David's friends, then blood need not be spilled, and both sides could be saved.

All at once, she knew how she would do it.

The only question that remained was who would save *her* if Rivenham realized what she had done.

5

All afternoon Nora found reasons to delay what she must do. The thought of speaking to him again was enough to unsettle her composure, and so she attended instead to every other matter requiring her attention.

With one of Rivenham's men in tow—a wiry, silvering soldier by the name of Henslow, who followed her with his jaw set hard against the indignity of his assignment—she exited the house to make her rounds of the outbuildings. The coal house and bake house were in a tumult due to the sudden increase in demand on their stores. She ordered the release of more grain despite Montrose's protests.

In the washhouse, she took spiteful pleasure in instructing the women not to worry too greatly about stains in the clothing of Hodderby's uninvited guests.

Outside the kitchens, in the small house garden, the gardener and his lads were covering roots while the cook's assistant picked the last of the summer's cabbages. Others tended to the lines of peas and lettuce and beans that would soon come into season.

Let the sunshine last, Nora prayed. She stood a long moment in its mild warmth, gazing on the busy work before her, listening to cows low in the distance and the idle, cheerful talk of those tending the vegetables. Hodderby was a grand, largely self-sufficient estate; one day was insufficient to review all its operations. Tomorrow she would go to the apiary, to gauge the stores of honey and beeswax; the herb garden, which yielded the ingredients for medicinal tonics; the spinning sheds and the apricot and peach orchards. It would be time to take inventory of the larder, too.

Apart from her worries of the weather, it was no burden on her. Even before her marriage she had overseen Hodderby in the way of a mistress. It had always given her a feeling of satisfaction.

But this position would not remain hers overlong. David must take a wife. And she must marry again as well. David had assured her that she would be no small prize once James Stuart sat the throne. She would be daughter and sister to his chief councillor . . .

She sighed. *Then why can we not wait until that happy day?* she had asked David. But he did not understand her reluctance to remarry. He had disliked Towe's cruelties greatly, but in the way of men, he imagined that the other pleasures of wifehood had atoned for it. *I see how happy you are with a household to manage,* he'd said with a frown. *Surely you long for a home of your own.*

But a house was not always a home. Never in Lord

Towe's households had she uncovered the same kind of pride in governance that Hodderby afforded her. It was such a different thing to care for a place because somebody had acquired you for just that purpose—and, on the other hand, to care for the place where you had been born, nurtured, and loved.

She took a deep breath of the rich, fermented air. It was not only the thought of leaving Hodderby that made her innards rebel. This morning's mistake had resurrected some primal element within her, fierce and demanding. To put herself into Cosmo Colville's hands—and his bed—seemed, all at once, intolerable.

I deserve better—such a dangerous, mad thought for a woman to entertain. But was it so wrong to look for passion in a marriage? If she could feel such response to the man who had come to arrest her brother . . . good heavens. Surely she could feel something like it with some other man?

She was resolved on it: she would tell David that Cosmo would not do.

Hoofbeats interrupted her reverie. She walked around the house, Rivenham's man on her heels, to discover a messenger being admitted through the front door.

She followed him inside, then down the hall, and watched him disappear into her father's library.

He emerged not a minute later, and she stepped aside to give him passage, blackly amused at how he nodded to her as though she were his equal. In a minute or less, it seemed, Rivenham had managed to communicate to this stranger what little respect was owed to the Colvilles.

The renewed anger strengthened her. She went to the library and did not bother to knock before opening the door.

Rivenham was seated at the end of the room, behind the desk where her father had written letters and speeches and reviewed accounts, and occasionally had summoned her for a lecture—and once, on a very dreadful day, had cursed her as a jezebel and a strumpet, the ruin of her family.

She disliked the things that stirred in her to see Adrian Ferrers lounging so easily in the chair of a man whose son he conspired to destroy. Contempt and rage should have been foremost. But the light flooding the mullioned window behind him lit the pure, pale gold of his hair and cast vivid shadows beneath the finely carved bones of his face. In his studious pose, he was beautiful as an archangel . . . or as the devil's facsimile of the same.

He was looking through correspondence that had just been delivered, too immersed in it to take notice of her. Instead, another man spoke from the corner.

"Lady Towe." Lord John Gardiner rose to his feet, making her one of those pretty, overcomplicated bows that court fops favored. "At your service, madam."

Lord John was as slim and neat as a whippet, elegantly turned out in green brocade and lace, his white wig freshly combed. The ladies at court thought his blue eyes beautiful, and so did he. He was no more at her service than the king of Poland.

Still, she smiled. Her aim required a mannerly show. "Lord John," she said. "What a pleasure to see you again."

His answering smile looked malicious, but that was merely his way; she could not tell if there was any particular design to it at present. "Likewise," he said. "The court has suffered most sorely for your absence. We hardly know where to find our amusement now."

"Sir." The quiet, hard word came from Rivenham.

It had immediate effect, causing Lord John's lips to tighten. He opened his mouth, no doubt to apologize, but she spoke quickly to forestall it. She was not in need of protection; cattish words gave her no trouble, and it was not Rivenham's place to protect her anyway. "I am sorry to hear that," she said to the boy. "I suppose it takes some wit to produce one's own entertainment. Are you often bored?"

Lord John blinked. A flush rose on his cheeks. She held his eyes even as she began to wonder at herself. In London, she had never bothered to make ripostes to tacit insults, and the boy's evident surprise mirrored her own.

As if that kiss in the apple grove had infected her, she felt hot and edgy, full of wild potentials. This was not London but her home, the one place where her worth was open to no man's dispute. She would not abide insults here.

Yet to indulge her new mood would not serve her. Of all times, it was now, with these men in her house, that she must depend on good sense for guidance. She made herself turn away from Lord John toward Rivenham— bracing herself as though to lay her eyes on the sun.

She would not look at his lips. She would not recall how they had touched her today.

She would recover her deportment and control.

Manufacturing an amicable manner, she said, "I saw the messenger, Lord Rivenham. May I ask if he brought correspondence for me?"

"No, he did not," Rivenham said, not looking up from the paper in his hand. "Did you require aught else?"

His manner was cold, as though he had forgotten the kiss, or been utterly unaffected by it. She ignored the strange emotions this idea inspired, a mix of envy and resentment and anger. How fortunate he was to be able to remain unmoved!

"I require nothing," she said lightly, "only, if it were possible, I would appreciate news, and company."

The surprise he must surely feel did little to alter his expression. But the wariness that followed it—she saw that clearly enough in the way he carefully lowered the letter to the desk.

On a deep breath, she mustered herself to continue. "If you are to stay under this roof for so long, then we may as well coexist peaceably. Don't you think?"

Lord John did not like this. Coming up behind her, he said, "We are not here to entertain you, madam—"

Rivenham's brow lifted. Like magic, the boy once again fell silent.

She had seen Rivenham work these spells on men before. It was something to do with how calmly he comported himself, how closely he observed those around him, and how economically he used his words—so that when he did speak, others held their breath, anticipating something of import.

But as the silence extended, she realized with a start that Lord John had misinterpreted his master's look: that lifted brow was not a challenge to him but a silent query to *her*. Rivenham was silently asking her what accounted for this abrupt change in her manner.

She felt the blood rush into her cheeks at the intimate thought: *I know how to read his face still.* For what else was intimacy but this—the private knowledge of a person?

Uneasy, she turned away, pretending to study the books that lined the shelves against the wall. Some of them, the older ones, had chains to fasten them in place, and these hung uselessly from their spines, like the broken wings of birds.

"There is very little news of note from town," came Rivenham's measured reply. "But if you will sit, I will share all of interest."

Lord John's snort spoke volumes of its own. "Oh, yes," he said, "and let us call for tea as well. Is this a salon? Lady Towe, we might not have found aught yet to interest our king, but have no doubt that I believe you know *exactly* where we might look to find otherwise."

She glanced to Rivenham as she sat, but he seemed to have lost interest in defending her; he waited expressionlessly to see how she would reply.

Very well. She met Lord John's hostile gaze. "It would be unmannerly to contradict you, sir, but I fear your suspicions are mistaken. Of course, if you believe you have missed something, you must always feel at liberty to look again."

Rivenham smiled slightly. She found that smile puzzling, until he directed it without warning at her, and then it became something else: something too akin to a moment of uncanny understanding.

He liked her wit.

Just as quickly his smile faded, and he looked back to his letter.

He did not want to like her wit.

She understood his discomfort exactly.

She looked down to her lap, where her hands were twisting. Her breath was coming faster, as though she had done something daring or arduous, when in fact she hadn't accomplished anything yet. She must sit here awhile longer before she posed her proposition to them, and even then, with Lord John sulking, it might not work.

Clearing her throat, she tried for a way to smooth over the boy's affront. She would appeal to his apparent belief that he knew more of her than she did. "Forgive me if my words caused offense, Lord John. We have met before, so you will know I am not the most . . ."

"Politic," was Rivenham's dry suggestion.

She did not dare look at him. "*Politic* of women," she agreed. "I fear my tongue often miscarries the intention in my brain, which was only to say that, despite the circumstances, it is pleasant to have polished company, particularly after the long months of seclusion."

The boy settled like a chicken whose feathers were falling back into place. "Well," he said, and sniffed—then sniffed again before rooting himself in a nearby chair. "I am not one to criticize a lady," he said, an outrageous lie.

She had heard him criticize any number of ladies in the past. "Lord Rivenham, do tell us the news."

She divined suddenly why Lord John's mood had been so sour from the moment of her entrance: he, too, had received no mail, and must wait to hear the tidings like a boy with his elder.

Rivenham shrugged. "Very little of political import—apart from the fact that Louis XIV is dead, and the duc d'Orléans has become the regent to France's new boy-king."

Both men's eyes swung to her, while she swallowed her gasp before it could escape.

This was disastrous news. The duc was no friend to the Jacobite cause. Worse, the child-king's health was notoriously poor. If he died, then by the terms of the Treaty of Utrecht, d'Orléans himself would take the throne—but he would need England's support to enforce his claim. Otherwise Spain's King Philip would no doubt seize the French crown.

With d'Orléans as regent, France would now be a friend to England, then. So much for the fleet it had promised to support James Stuart! The court at Bar-le-Duc must be in turmoil.

"Aside from that," Rivenham continued, his regard never leaving her, "it seems the Duke of Atholl is King George's newest and dearest friend. He swore his loyalty most publicly at a levee last week."

She felt sicker and sicker. David and all his allies had counted on Atholl's aid.

"And in lighter news, Mr. Pope is still enjoying unanimous celebration," Rivenham finished smoothly. "No other auteur can rival his popularity."

"Bah, Pope," Lord John said. "Another one of these papist recusants. I say we put them all to a sword. See then if they remain so pious."

Rivenham looked inclined to ignore this remark. Nora saw no reason not to join his effort. Political conversation was not a safe topic; that much was clear. "I very much enjoyed Mr. Pope's *Rape of the Lock*," she said. "But I confess—for I doubt it speaks well of me—that my favorite of his poems remains the first they say he wrote: 'Happy the man, whose wish and care / A few paternal acres bound . . .'"

Rivenham gave her a wry smile. "'Content to breathe his native air / In his own ground.' My lady, I think you would do better to admire poems about wanderers who find contentment in foreign lands, and never dream to return."

A flush of confusion warmed her. He was alluding to her brother—and delivering warnings in the language of flirtatious, courtly banter.

Lord John did not appear not to have perceived the subtext. "Peasant life? I for one am glad he moved on to more elevated subjects."

"Oh?" said Rivenham. "Such as a great battle begun by the theft of a lock of hair?"

Lord John rolled his long-lashed eyes. "I refer, of course, to his translation of Homer. I never bothered with *The Rape of the Lock*."

"Homer? That is new," Nora said hesitantly.

"Yes," replied Rivenham. "It would please you, I think. The language is plain but deeply moving." He glanced speakingly at Lord John. "There are no false ostentations in it."

Her smile escaped her, widening without her permission. Not only had he hit exactly upon her preferences but he had managed a sly insult to Lord John at the same time. "That does sound lovely."

But when he kept looking at her, she felt her smile falter.

Of course he knew her preferences: they had shared their love of poetry once, and in his face she saw him remembering it now.

Some magnetic current passed between them. She could not look away. Her pulse began to race.

Rivenham's expression darkened. He glanced back to the note in his hand, and she felt as though she could breathe again. "Also," he said, his voice flat, "some hubbub regarding a paper presented at the Royal Academy. An alchemist claims to have produced an incalescence of mercury and another mysterious substance which he will not divulge, the projection resulting in pure silver."

"But how extraordinary," she said. "I wonder—may I see the letter?"

Rivenham passed it over. "You still study alchemy, Lady Towe?"

The words seemed to leave him reluctantly. She felt Lord John's curious gaze cut between them. "Not recently," she said as she skimmed the relevant passage. Her husband had not liked the pursuit, thinking it too near to witchcraft when practiced by a woman.

The letter held no true details, only a layman's rough summary. She handed it back.

"Alchemy!" Lord John looked caught between intrigue and disapproval. "What business has a lady in such dealings?"

"Why, I think a lady best suited to it," she said. The slight sharpness in her voice was for a man now dead, who had not appreciated her logic. "Are not women's bodies the very crucibles of transubstantiation? They take a seed and make a child of it: what else can that be but alchemy?"

Rivenham laughed. It was a beautiful sound, low and husky, and it brushed along her skin like fingertips, making her shift in her seat. "First blood to the lady, Lord John."

Lips thinning, the boy inclined his head in acknowledgment.

All at once she could not bear to remain here a moment longer. To have Rivenham laughing at her cleverness, lauding it to another man—to feel, even for a second, this camaraderie and connection—seemed infinitely more dangerous than her explicit purpose.

She rose, and the men rose as well, their courtesy ingrained. "I must resume my business," she said, "but I wished to invite you both to take supper with me tomorrow. Let it never be said that the Colvilles do not treat their guests with courtesy."

"If Lady Towe wishes to play the hostess, I see no harm in it. Let her entertain us! God knows I languish in such rustic climes."

Adrian nodded. For fully an hour now, Lord John had been complaining about his refusal of the marchioness's invitation.

To explain why he found it suspicious would entail truths he had no interest in sharing. But he felt great skepticism at the prospect of Lady Towe uncovering in herself the desire to preside over an elegant table laid for her brother's persecutors.

"Ware of poisons," he murmured, only half in jest.

The boy's laugh held a derisive edge, which faded when Adrian met his eyes. "Your fancies run wild, Rivenham."

"No doubt." Adrian returned his attention to packing the leather bag on the bed. On his return from catching Lady Towe this morning, he had found the great hall filled with farmers who disliked the long arm of the king in their fields—unwilling, on the eve of an uncertain harvest, to sacrifice even a single sheaf of grain to the tramp of careless hooves. Braddock had stood in their midst, sword drawn, threatening them with harm if they did not disperse. These Londoners had no notion of how to reason with men who knew their own dignity and rights and guarded them fiercely.

It would be a fine piece of irony if his own men, with no help from David Colville, sparked an insurrection in the northeast.

The Colville men had ever been careless of their domestic administration. Adrian's request to their steward for a detailed map of the holdings—one that might suggest routes for his men's watch that would avoid the tenantry—had been answered with a blank look. These maps did not exist. He saw no choice for it then but to go to Beddleston. In his library were accurate charts of the whole area, drawn by his brother and himself not seven years before. It was only half a day's ride, and the prospect of walking his own land also drew him strongly.

He might have sent someone in his stead. But the prospect of a few hours' distance drew him as well.

He needed to clear his head and restore his equilibrium. A survey of everything he strove to protect would achieve that nicely.

"You may compose sonnets for her if you like," he said as he buckled the bag shut. "Hold a dance in the gallery, invite all the housemaids. Only keep her inside the damned house, and keep the tenants out. I will be satisfied."

"An easy task," Lord John drawled, "if you but let me oversee it. Tenants come armed with pitchforks, not gunpowder and steel. And I am not as accustomed as you to scaring ladies into the wilderness. Even Medusa can be charmed."

Medusa. That had been the wits' name for her at court. In a world of courtesies and artifice, her reserve—and her manner of looking a man directly in the eye without smiles or flatteries to soften her regard—had not endeared her to new acquaintances.

"Do not underestimate her," Adrian said.

Lord John snorted. "Think me a fool?"

A promising question. Adrian considered the boy, who lounged on the sofa in a satin coat, his boots atop a small mahogany table meant for tea services. Fashionably slim, his face powdered thickly, his wig dressed in full curls, he looked as out of place in the dark environs of Hodderby as a hothouse flower in the kennels. Jeweled rings glittered on his fingers, which he twisted restlessly; at his elbow sat a goblet of canary wine purloined from Hodderby's stores.

Adrian would give him this: for a man so woefully out of his element, he did a damned good job of making himself comfortable.

In the silence, Lord John's color had begun to rise. Now he removed his boots and sat up. "Think me a fool?" he demanded again.

Adrian's turn to snort. A child's vanity in a grown man's body made a bad combination. "I think you accustomed to London," he said, "and London ladies. The marchioness cut no great figure among them, but here she has friends aplenty. The loyalty of every man on these lands is hers, and their pitchforks outnumber our swords ten to one."

The lad looked truly astonished. "Peasants," he said. "If they lift their hands to us, they lift them to the king!"

Barstow had done his son a disfavor by sheltering him so wholly. "You are accustomed to the south," Adrian said. "In these far-flung parts, the king is more legend than fact."

"That sounds like treason!"

Nearly he laughed. Such callow idealism might be put onstage for money. "You must inform them so," he said, "if you are unwise enough to find their tines at your throat."

"They would not dare," Lord John said. "What? The prospect of such impudence *amuses* you?"

He shrugged. It was not his business to disillusion Barstow's naïve little fledgling. Life would manage that on its own. "Stay alert," he said. "That's what I mean."

After a moment, Lord John decided to be mollified. He sat back again, drawing deep of his cup. "You will be back by tomorrow night?"

"If not before." He hefted his saddlebag. "I leave you all twenty men. Were the sentries on their marks?"

"Yes, yes," the other man said irritably. "I made the rounds of their posts not two hours ago."

"Good." Still Adrian hesitated. This unease was baseless, he told himself. There was no cause to expect David Colville until the sennight was out. As for Colville's tenants, he did not truly adjudge them likely trouble. By and large, they were High Church, and had no deep reason to sympathize with their master's quarrel.

And yet, as he looked at John Gardiner, his instincts rebelled. To leave this painted piece in command of Hodderby, with full authority over the household, Nora included . . .

Nora. His mouth twisted. The marchioness was none of his concern.

"I bid you good even," he said.

Lord John waved his cup in lazy farewell, his rings sparking in the firelight. "Good riding to you."

Nora had planned on every eventuality but this one: that Rivenham would not come to supper. When she had descended to the parlor and found Lord John awaiting her alone, she remained calm, assuming Rivenham still lurked somewhere in the house. He would eat his supper eventually, even if not under her supervision—and she trusted her women in the kitchen to make sure he received with it the necessary libation.

It did her no credit, but some dark, wretched part of her had been relishing the prospect of witnessing its effect on him. She had drunk deeply of this poison once for his sake: now, unwittingly, he would do the same for her.

But he did not appear at the table. What a pity he could not join them, she'd remarked to Lord John. Her servants were already taking trays to the rest of his men; where might they find Lord Rivenham?

"Ten miles south," he'd said with a bored smile. "He has gone to visit his estates."

Oh! How pleasant for him, she'd replied rather breathlessly. And when would he return?

"I can't say," Lord John had replied, but suddenly he had been watching her closely. "Does my lady have some cause for concern?"

She had held her tongue after that, excavating what rusted skills for flirtation she possessed, forcing herself to smile at his condescending remarks. He complimented her gown, a cobalt silk mantua embroidered in gold, then recalled for her, with astonishing accuracy, how many times he had seen her wear it in London, "when that weave was still fashionable." She sat across from him and batted her lashes as though it was her greatest pleasure to host his insults in her dining room. All the while, as the sun slid lower out the long western windows, her heart beat faster and faster.

Now true darkness was falling, spreading like a bruise across the sky. Was his speech slowing, or was that her imagination? Had he just smothered a yawn? "I heard tell," Lord John said, blotting his mouth with a napkin, "that your brother and Lord Rivenham were great friends once."

He should have been unconscious by now. Had she misjudged the dosage? Meconium, the juice of the opium poppy, was a dangerous substance: too much and a man might not wake again. "His lands adjoin ours. In such circumstances, friendship seemed a good policy."

He studied one of the many rings on his fingers, giving it a thoughtful twist. These rings were a particular affectation of his; she recalled some rumor that he named them after court beauties, and that some silly girl, Lady Mary or Lady Sarah, had wept last spring when she discovered herself demoted from diamond to sapphire. "Yes," he drawled, "but these Catholics generally keep to themselves."

The distaste in his voice caught her off guard. She had never heard anybody speak of Rivenham so. Fear and fondness were the more regular tunes. "He conformed many years ago," she said slowly.

"But not before his great friendship with your brother."

She felt a new wariness come over her. "What of it? My family is not Catholic."

"Indeed not. Only that the irony is striking, don't you agree? Your father and brother are fled to France to kiss the Catholic pretender's arse, while the old friend who aims to correct their notions has only recently abandoned his love for the Pope . . ." His malicious smile slackened suddenly, and he rubbed a hand across his forehead.

His insinuation had come clear now, and it amazed her. "You mistrust Lord Rivenham's loyalties?"

Without the drug in him, his burst of laughter would have cracked against her ears. Instead it trailed limply from his throat, ending in a sharp breath. "You were ever too direct, madam. Nobody in London could call you a *charmer* . . ." He shook his head hard. "Forgive me," he muttered, a courtier's mannerly reflex, with no real consideration behind it. "But I feel quite . . ."

His eyes fixed on the glass, halfway to his mouth. His pupils were the size of pinpricks.

Now his gaze lifted to her. "Why, you . . ."

He collapsed like a puppet with cut strings, flopping face-first into his plate of rare beef.

She sprang up from the table and bolted all the doors save one—the entry to the servants' passage.

A single lamp sat burning inside the narrow, windowless corridor. She lifted it and hurried down the spindly stairs into the coolness of the subterranean kitchens. A scullery maid and the cook shot out from a nearby door. The little maid looked frightened, her eyes huge in her pale face; she would not have been informed of the events in motion.

But the cook, Mrs. Fairfax, was calm, her hamhock arms folded beneath her bosom. "They're locked in the larder," she said.

Nora nodded. "How long?"

"Oh, for a quarter hour now, I'd say. Appetites like

pigs; I feared they'd take too much of it, so I held back with the next round of wine."

"God bless you, Mrs. Fairfax." Nora stepped past her, giving a tug to the larder door for her own comfort. The lock held, rattling reassuringly. "Where are Hooton and Montrose?"

Mrs. Fairfax snorted. "Those two were no help a'tall. Hooton's abed with an ache in his bones, and Montrose is weeping in his room, praying no doubt for God to help him find the courage owed to a man."

Hooton's absence made sense; his health did not equip him for vigorous activity. But this timidity in Montrose worried her. When her brother was in residence, Montrose served as his secretary as well as his steward; alone of the staff, he knew the full details of David's business. "He must stay in his rooms, then. I'll go speak to him—"

"Don't waste your time," Mrs. Fairfax said. "Should he recover his spine, which well I doubt, he won't stir far, I'll see to that. And you, my lady, had best take to your rooms now, and turn the key behind you. Lord David's friends will be honorable, but you're looking very fine, and one mustn't tempt a man without cause."

Nora allowed herself a brief smile. "Very well, I will retire. But you—both of you—lock yourselves into your rooms as well."

Her solar had a broad window that overlooked the front of the property. It was here she waited, watching the tree line, as Grizel read softly from *The Adventures of Rivella*.

But her eyes were not equal to the darkness outside, and when she noticed the first rider, he was nearly to the portico.

"There they are," she said, coming to her feet.

Grizel came to join her. "I only see the one," she said. "Surely it will be a larger party?"

To move the weaponry, yes, it would require several men and a cart.

"Oh," she whispered. "Oh, oh—"

That was not one of David's men dismounting in the yard. That was *Rivenham*.

"There!" Grizel cried. She tapped the glass. "There are the rest of them—coming from Bleymouth way, they are."

Nora slapped a hand to her mouth to cover her cry. Rivenham was turning: he could not miss sight of the party emerging from the trees.

For a moment he remained quite still—looking, listening; the cart they brought must make a distinct noise, impossible to miss in the stillness of the evening.

And then he drew his sword.

Nora pushed away from the window, racing through the next room to her closet. She knelt by a polished wood chest, fumbling with the lock.

Grizel chased after her. "What are you about, madam?"

The key finally turned. She opened the lid and lifted out the pistol. It was a handsome but clumsy weapon, not meant for a woman's handling. Its aim, David had warned her, could not be trusted.

But she had no choice.

As she made for the door into the hall, Grizel cried after her, "Milady, wait!"

She could not wait. He would be killed—murdered, dead—and then, why, all her plans would be for naught, for news of his mistreatment would bring the king's full forces down upon Hodderby, wouldn't it? So she must save him. She *must*. She had no choice.

6

drian's thoughts grew grim. There were any number of harmless explanations for a group of mounted men approaching the keep after dark, but none could account for why this approach failed to raise an alarm. How had none of his men come out to discover the nature of the party?

Sword in hand, Adrian tried the heavy oak doors to the entry hall. Finding them locked, he remounted and rode hard around the back of the house for the kitchen yard.

Here the door stood open. As he dismounted, he caught sight of a candle flickering in the dimness, clutched in a slim, small hand.

The candle lifted, revealing the marchioness's face as she set it aside on a ledge. Now her other hand emerged from behind her back.

Joining hands, she lifted her pistol, making his head the target.

"Step away from your horse," she said in a shaking voice.

He heard himself laugh: a short, sharp sound expressive of disbelief. "My God." *Do not underestimate her,* he'd told Lord John. "What did you do to my men?"

"They are unharmed," she said. "They will sleep through what is coming, and their lives will be spared for it. If you wish to live, too, you will come with me now, quickly."

That weapon was heavy. She would not be able to aim it for long.

"Who are those men?" he asked. He already knew that her brother was not among them; on the ride here, he had intercepted a messenger with news of Colville's escape from an inn outside Dover. But if these were her brother's allies, why did they risk approaching Hodderby before Colville's arrival?

Something here drew them. But what?

"I will answer no questions," she said. "Time is short. Do you die or do you come with me?"

He dropped the reins and stepped sharply forward. She made a convulsive flinch, but held her ground.

He could take the pistol by force. But guns had unpredictable temperaments, and a stray shot would expose his position to the approaching party.

He took another step, mirrored by her measured retreat. She seemed confident with the weapon, surprisingly strong, and too comfortable aiming it between a man's eyes.

The sense of absurdity evaporated, leaving a clear, forceful anger that made his lungs expand. "Your trip to the apple orchard," he said. "You were arranging for our murder." And he, like a green fool, had attended instead to her tousled hair, to the sweet shape of her mouth and the taste of her tongue.

His contempt was all for himself. Her skill at enmity outstripped his by far.

"If I wanted you dead, I would not have bothered to fetch you," she said, "or to drug your men besides. Obey me and no harm will come to you."

He offered her a smile that made her suck in an audible breath. "You are the fool, then. Think you a sleeping man makes a less tempting target than a waking one? Your brother's friends will slit their throats like lambs on feast day."

"They will not." But the break in her voice betrayed her sudden doubt. She had not thought on this possibility before. "They would not," she said hoarsely.

He sheathed his sword so he could step through the narrow doorway. The silence within the house was like the unnatural hush of a cathedral—or a tomb. "You cannot keep walking backward," he said grimly. A staircase rose behind her, a servant's passage to the upper floors.

She jerked her chin. "Your neckcloth. Remove it and tie it around your eyes."

He saw red. "I will not."

"Do it!"

He drew a long breath. "I will not blindfold myself while enemies prowl this house with swords drawn."

"I order you!" Her voice was high now.

"Best shoot me," he said flatly. "For I do not take orders from you, Leonora Colville."

For the space of three heartbeats they stared at each other. His rage began to yield to more calculated thinking. With it came a new view of her.

Despite his own advice to John Gardiner, he had underestimated her. She held the pistol like a bandit queen, magnificent in her posture, shoulders square, chin high, every line of her defiant. Silently she dared him to mistake her for someone he might intimidate.

It was a rare man who outwitted him, and never more than once—but she, whom he had known so well, had managed it very neatly.

He did not wish to admire her. Loathing was the wiser course. But God help him if she did not remain the boldest, most sharp-witted woman he had encountered. He would never find her like again—not for courage; not for wit; not for spirit.

And she squandered all these things—she squandered *herself*—on her brother's doomed, doltish cause.

"You *will* obey me," she said. "For all it chafes your masculine vanity, Adrian Ferrers—you *will* obey, unless you doubt my willingness to shoot."

And then she lowered the pistol to take aim at his thigh.

"That will cripple me and kill me just as well in the end, only more slowly."

"Then advise me on a better aim." She sounded deadly calm. "For I mean to take one."

From the depths of the house came the sound of a slamming door. Her regard flickered away.

He lunged at her, catching her wrist and hauling it

high over her head, her fingers around the pistol trapped hard within his grip. Ignoring her shrill yelp, he used his body to drive her back into the wall. He pinned her there for a long moment, listening, over the sound of her rough breathing and his own, to the activity in the rest of the house.

A moment of raucous laughter, at which she stiffened.

The tinkling of breaking glass, and then the louder splintering of something large being upended.

"The dining room," she whispered. "They are near."

He squeezed the slim bones of her hand. She fell silent.

Now came the heavy trundling of boots. He felt her tremble. A puff of breath escaped her.

"How many?" he demanded.

When she did not speak, he hooked his free hand in her hair and yanked back her head. Her tears did not move him. He was no longer a stupid boy in love. *"How many?"*

"Forty," she spat.

In the light from the candle a few steps away, her eyes were dark holes, a skeleton's hollows. She was lying, of course. There had not been so many men as that in the group he had seen emerging from the trees. But the lie made her position ever clearer.

She was a part of this—not incidentally. She was as much a part of it as her godforsaken brother.

And by placing herself in opposition to him, she had eliminated all complexities. She had made herself fair game.

Effectively, now, she was his.

A terrible pleasure washed through him, dark as sin, hot as triumph. In the space of a breath, his careful illusions unraveled. Almost he laughed. *Indifferent?* There was *nothing* in him indifferent to her. He had waited for this turn, hungered for it.

He leaned over her, looming deliberately. "Tell me you would have shot me." It would be laid plain between them, here and now, his lack of obligation to her. No earthbound moralist would fault him for doing with her as he wished. *"Tell me."*

For a mute moment she looked back at him silently, her eyes huge in the dim light. Then, her mouth twisting, she said, "I would have."

He smiled. "Yes," he said gently. "So you would have."

His fault, he saw now, had been to dwell on the past, and the sweeter, lighter love that had once been theirs. His soul had grown darker in the intervening years—and so, too, had hers.

The woman she had become fitted his interests perfectly.

"I will take you to London," he said, his quiet voice a strange contrast to the loud thump of blood in his ears. He would force her to better purposes than the puppetry of her rotted, conniving family. She was his now to possess.

"Prithee try," she shot back—and without warning, twisted.

Her knee smashed into his balls.

He took a sharp breath through the blinding pain, but his grip, for one agonized moment, weakened.

And then she had the gun between them, pressed into his chest.

A door opened at the end of the hall. A man's voice rang out: "Who's there?"

He struggled with his hoarse breathing, watching only her. For six years he had seen nothing of her in her face, but this wildness in her now, *this* he recognized. Even at this impossible moment, everything in him quickened in response to it. Only now her wildness had fangs; now she had developed the willingness to bite.

Her mouth pursed into a bloodless line. From the quick pulse in the hollow of her throat, she was panicking, undecided.

But then she swallowed and her chin tipped up. "It's Lady Towe," she called. She met Adrian's eyes and her face hardened. "I have a prisoner."

7

Nora watched as the last of Rivenham's lackeys were dragged into the larder. "What do you mean, 'what news you wrest from them'?"

The two men exchanged a look she did not like. They had given her no names, and their accents were not local; but they seemed to know her brother well enough, and had spoken fondly, in these last minutes, of his talent for dice. Nevertheless, she felt increasingly uneasy.

None of this had gone to plan. They had dug up the cellar an hour ago, and the last of the arms had been loaded onto the cart. But they had refused to take the gunpowder: her brother had given them no instructions for it, they said, and so they lacked the means to transport it elsewhere.

With her main hope foiled, she desired them to go. But though the moon had long since passed its zenith, they yet loitered. These two in particular hewed to her side, almost as though to watch her.

She cast off manners now to speak bluntly. "You cannot linger."

"Only a bit longer," the dark man told her. He had a sharp, wolfish face and a week's worth of beard on his sunken cheeks. "Let them awake, and we'll speak to them one by one before taking our leave."

"We'll begin with Rivenham," the other added.

She looked this one square in the eye. There was a hint of Irish in his vowels, though his sun-touched hair and weathered skin made him indistinguishable from men who worked the land anywhere. "Rivenham will tell you nothing."

His mouth quirked, a smirk that quickly faded as she scowled at him. "We have our ways, your ladyship."

"What ways are those?"

"Any man will speak if the price for silence is high enough," the dark one said.

She did not like his tone. "Torture? Is that what you mean?"

He shrugged.

She realized then that he was French. His narrow face and the slight laziness of his vowels had suggested it, but the shrug solidified her suspicion. A Frenchman and an Irishman in her kitchen, speaking casually of torturing the Englishmen locked in her larder.

The word burst from her. *"No."*

Both of them stared, uncomprehending as donkeys. "Perhaps your ladyship should retire for the night," the Frenchman suggested. "We will handle the mess. When you wake in the morning, you'll find it was as though these men never came to trouble you."

She tightened the hand in her apron pocket, her grip hard around the pistol. It was no easy weapon to disguise, and with every movement she feared it might discharge. But instinct had made her keep it close and concealed, and it comforted her now. "In my brother's absence, I govern this household and what occurs within it. Your task was to retrieve the arms. The king's men will not be molested."

The Irishman loosed a scornful laugh. "Oh, ho! And what will you say on the morrow, when they wish to know the cause of their so-interesting dreams?"

"Rivenham will not leave you in peace," the Frenchman murmured.

She feared he was right. She could not forget Rivenham's remark. His voice had grown rough as he promised it: *I will take you to London.*

She understood his meaning. He viewed her as a traitor now, as much as he did David.

But a man's pride was given to violent pronouncements that his logic, in a cooler mood, would be forced to refute. And surely—surely he would never hurt her.

The thought made her bite her lip in frustration. She could not count on any such fanciful notions!

And yet . . . to let him be slaughtered . . .

She shook her head. "I am a woman. Who will believe me capable of this business? You have repacked the floor; there is no evidence that anything untoward happened here. Better you return these men to their beds, so they will wake none the wiser to their night's travels."

"These men are not fools," the Frenchman countered. "They will know they were drugged."

"And Rivenham will inform them of it if they have doubts," the other added.

She set her jaw. "Those are my concerns. I recommend you mind your own. I believe they will prove sufficient."

A brief, uneasy silence passed. The two men exchanged another look. Then the Frenchman gave an impatient wave. "Very well, we will do as you say." To his companion he gave a short nod. That one wheeled and went for the door, she assumed to fetch the others for the task of hauling sleeping bodies.

"But Rivenham," the Frenchman went on, "must be ours. You understand," he continued sharply over her protest, "that none of the others were conscious for his return. When he fails to appear, they will assume something befell him on the road. Meanwhile, you may tell them that the entire household sickened. They will have no proof to the contrary, only suspicions. So, too, with Rivenham's disappearance: indeed, their search for him will occupy several days, when otherwise they might have been in our way."

He smiled at her, pleased by the neatness of his plot.

She felt an oncoming sickness, like to make her vomit. She had thought herself so clever with this diversion. If only Rivenham had not returned when he had!

Had her brother been here, he likely would have ordered her to accept this man's proposition. But if she did, Rivenham's life would be forfeit.

She opened her mouth but her wits forestalled her. What protest could she lodge to persuade this man? He would find her concern for an enemy suspicious indeed.

An enemy, she reminded herself, but the notion held no more power over her reasoning than it had yesterday, in the wood.

And anyway—a Frenchman and an Irishman! She was her brother's sister, her father's daughter; she knew her duty. But she would not give up any Englishman to such as these!

"Rivenham is not your business," she said coldly. "You have the weaponry. Do not overstep yourself."

The man blinked. As the rest of his party came trundling into the kitchen, he stepped past her to unbar the larder door and admit his men entry.

She heard no sound of protest from Adrian, which pitched her alarm higher.

As the first of his men emerged with a limp body slung between them, the Frenchman spoke again. "Alas," he said, "I'm afraid I cannot—"

Her panic suddenly burned into anger. She walked past him through the doorway into the chill of the storeroom.

They had tied and gagged him. His men slumped around him, their limbs carelessly crossed, their sleeping faces slack, eerily vacant.

His eyes met hers over the cloth that bound his jaw. She could feel his rage like the heat of a great bonfire.

A streak of blood painted his jaw.

"My lady," came the Frenchman's call behind her.

"You wounded him?" She turned on her heel. "You attacked a man whose hands were bound?"

The Frenchman rolled his eyes. "This is not a game."

She did not like his condescending airs. Picking her way to Adrian's side, she hauled out the pistol.

Seeing it, the Frenchman halted.

"You will do me this favor," she said through the thundering of her pulses. "You will return the slumbering men to their beds. Then you will leave. Lord Rivenham will remain with me. Should anyone wish to dispute it, I will test this cantankerous piece with your head as the target."

She felt incredulous stares pressing into her. She did not look away from the Frenchman's wolfish face.

His gaze narrowed and traveled down her. It was a survey meant to assess the strength of her intention and her ability to carry it out.

The gun seemed to weigh as much as a millstone, but her arms did not shake as she raised them.

The Frenchman could not afford to abuse her. She knew that, and so did he. She was the daughter of Lord Hexton, new advisor to the rightful king of England, His Catholic Majesty James Stuart.

"We will have to lock you inside," he said sourly. "We cannot risk his escape before we are well clear of this place."

Was that meant to frighten her?

Perhaps it should. Rivenham had good cause to be unhappy with her. She might regret being cloistered with him.

But she could not back down now. "Then do so," she said. "My servants will release me in the morning."

A muttering went up from the other men. But the Frenchman, after another cold moment of silence, only shrugged. "As you wish." He sketched a mocking bow. "I do hope her ladyship will not regret it."

As did she.

It took ten long minutes for the rest of Rivenham's men to be cleared out. In all that time, she never lowered the gun nor removed her focus from the Frenchman and his minions, though her every sense screamed of the peril immediately at her side: the furious Lord Rivenham, whose eyes must surely by now have burned a blister into her cheek.

At last, the door slammed. She waited for the thud of the bar being set into place and the rattle of the lock as someone tested it. Only then did she lower the pistol. A gusty breath burst from her.

Her knees folded, taking her to the floor.

For a dumb second, she stared at the pistol. Her fingers had gone numb around the butt. Her elbows and shoulders burned from the strain of holding it aloft.

She loosened her grip, then quickly flexed and chafed her hands, forcing the blood back into them. As feeling began to return, she made herself meet Rivenham's eyes.

They were closed.

Braced as she was for hatred, the sight struck her as a shocking relief. She exhaled as she studied him, the fatigue etched on his face, the surprising delicacy of the golden lashes that lay against his high cheekbones, the long, lean line of his legs stretched out before him.

Perhaps her heart had been as numb as her fingers, for blood now seemed to flood back into it as well, causing her chest to prickle and expand.

No doubt she would regret this as heartily as the Frenchman had predicted. But she could not have lived with herself had they killed this man.

She reached for him, intending to pat down his body to find the source of his bleeding. But at the brush of her fingers against his shoulder, his eyes opened, and she froze.

His steady regard revealed nothing. His very impassivity seemed ominous. She took a nervous breath. "You are wounded," she said. "Where?"

He bowed his head, his unbound hair falling forward to obscure his face.

Of course, the gag prevented him from replying. She rose onto her knees, wrestling with the fabric where it was knotted behind his skull. Then she remembered the small knife on her chatelaine's key ring. One slice and it was done.

He spat the rag from his mouth. She tensed in preparation for curses or a threat.

In silence, he lifted his hands where they were tied behind him.

A strange laugh born of nerves bubbled in her throat. "Where are you hurt?"

"Free my hands," he said hoarsely.

Such was his natural authority that she moved to obey him before realizing that caution demanded otherwise. Hesitating, she sat back on her haunches. Her palms had not been sweaty around the hilt of the gun, but now they were damp. "Would that be wise?" she asked.

Their eyes met. His jaw hardened.

"You fear that I will strike you?" he asked. "Do you reckon I have cause for it now?"

That was not the reply she had hoped for. "There is never cause to strike a woman."

"So lofty your ideals," he said flatly. "After a woman has held a gun on a man while delivering him to his enemies—even then, you opine that the man should scruple to use his fists?"

The cold mockery in his voice made her chest tighten. "After she has saved the man's life, yes, he should scruple."

Grim humor flitted over his mouth. "Indeed, it's a situation meriting some confusion, I agree. No, Nora, I will not strike you. Cut me free."

She did not trust the casual way he used her Christian name. "Nor misuse me in any way," she said. "Promise it."

His fledgling smile twisted into something blacker. "What do you imagine I will do? Ravish you in the larder? I begin to wonder why you saved me."

She had no good explanation for it herself. Quickly, she rose and cut free the binding. Before he could speak again, she said, "Where are you hurt?"

"A nick," he said tersely. "No cause for concern."

She felt for the wet spot on his arm. Her hand came away covered in blood.

Swallowing, she used the erstwhile gag for a makeshift bandage, wrapping it as tightly as she dared around the thick muscle of his upper arm. Then she sat back. "Only another few hours," she said unsteadily. He felt so warm to the touch. The sensation lingered on her palm, which she unobtrusively wiped on her skirts. "Will it keep until then? There is no water here to cleanse it—"

"You should have let them kill me."

"*There* is gratitude!"

His sigh bespoke impatience. "Gratitude has no place

in it. I speak of strategy—and survival. There is no room for *gratitude* in the game you now play."

She stared at him. "I play no game! I was—I kept you alive to keep the peace in my brother's absence. That's all!"

"Oh? And I suppose my men were lulled to sleep by your pacific lullabies, and poison had nothing to do with it."

"Not poison," she said. "They will recover by mid-morning."

"Ah. Medicine, then? The shadows beneath their eyes gave you cause for wholesome concern?"

She huffed out a breath. "There is no need for cheek. I don't dispute that I drugged them."

He nodded once. "And so you are courting treason. Whether you do it gladly or reluctantly makes no difference."

He looked paler than she liked. She wondered if he was lying about his injury. She wondered why she should care. "We can argue this later. After—"

"You drugged the king's men so others could have free reign of your household." His voice was hard. "Why were they here? What did they recover?"

She looked away. Her lamp spilled a shivering pool of light across the rude wooden floorboards, illuminating a stack of waxed wheels of cheese. Beyond that small puddle, the darkness gathered thickly.

"Weapons," he said. "Or bullion? *Tell me.*"

"*Why* should I tell you?" She looked back to him. "Why should I tell you anything? What are you to me, sir?"

"Why, your greatest concern." His eyes held hers intently, as though he looked for something in them. "Were it otherwise, you would not have stopped them from slitting my throat."

A flush heated her. "Do not flatter yourself I did it from tender emotion!"

The corner of his mouth lifted in a half smile.

"And mayhap I do regret it!"

"Too late. You are well in it, sweetling. To wish or claim otherwise will not spare you."

The endearment flustered her. More sarcasm, no doubt. She looked down to her hands, twisting hard in the sullied fabric of her dark skirts. She felt exhausted and soiled, in need of scrubbing. "The servants will not be up for some hours yet. Better we pass them in silence."

"You know what I must do as soon as we are freed from this room."

"I know nothing of your intentions or what you *must* do—"

"I have made them very plain to you."

"—and I care nothing for them, either!" She ceased to fuss with the fabric and lifted her head to glare. "If you mean to arrest me, I suppose I *will* regret having spared your life, but at least I will be able to hold up my head on Judgment Day, and *that* is a far greater concern." Quickly, before he could reply, she added, "Besides, your death would have brought a new set of troubles onto our heads."

She expected a sharp retort—one she might have supplied herself: with the troubles already piled onto her, a new one would not have increased the load overmuch.

But he held his tongue for a long moment before saying quietly, "I have caused you a great deal of trouble in this lifetime, no doubt."

Shock rippled through her. What a strange statement! Did he mean it as an apology, or a taunt? She could not read his expression; he sat leaning against a barrel of pickled fruit, one long leg outstretched, the other bent, his forearm draped casually across his knee.

Surely his wound was not so grave. He looked too much at his ease to be in pain.

A sharp ache moved through her. She supposed it was natural to care—not for the man he was now, but for the memory embodied in his flesh, for the boy she'd loved as a girl.

And he was right: he had destroyed that girl as surely as though he'd married her to Towe himself. Nora could hardly recall her now. That girl had looked on the world as a gift and a promise. She had seen in it so many possibilities for sweetness. She had never turned to the looking glass to discover what others would make of her, or to judge what smile would best soothe them, what frown might provoke them to rage. In her reflection, she had seen only herself, her own judgments, her own hopes and grudges. It had not occurred to her that she was only a possession waiting to be purchased.

Marriage had taught her better. A woman was never her own.

"How you look at me now," he said softly. "I have seen such eyes in dark alleys, in the faces of men approaching with blades."

She felt dim surprise at being likened to midnight as-
sassins. But surely he was right, and this burning in her
heart was hatred.

"You blame me," he murmured.

No words could have surprised her more. They caught
like a hook in her chest. That he should admit to this knowledge . . . that he should sound *surprised* by the idea . . .

"Yes." The word slipped into the silence between
them. It lingered like a wisp of smoke, staining the very
air. Such stillness in the night—stillness all around, as
though the entire universe had ceased and only the two
of them remained, enclosed together in this small pool of
light, guttering, soon to be swallowed by darkness.

In this strange, hushed, intimate space, jagged
thoughts suddenly found words. There was no one here
for them to cut but the rightful victims.

"I do blame you," she said. "Whether that is just . . . I
cannot say. But . . ." How much better it would have gone
for her if she had never met him. Or if they had remained
as they had been in childhood: distant neighbors, little
better than rumors to each other. "Sometimes, I do think
you ruined my life."

He did not react. He merely looked at her. "How biblical," he finally said.

The rage that washed through her then was bright
and violent. "Joke if you like! It is no joke to me. You
destroyed—*everything*." Before she had met him, what
had she cared for men? She had been wild and free, and
nobody had taken note of her. But he had lured her into
love, and with it the whole burdensome world of woman-

hood—and then abandoned her to another man's keeping! And *such* a man—such a man as she would *never* have accepted had she had a choice in it. And she would have had a choice! Had it not been for this man in front of her, *she would have been allowed to choose.*

"You lured me with false promises," she said through her teeth. "Do you remember your pretty words? You said that one day we would dance before everyone, open and unashamed; that we would not care how loud the music was, or how many eyes were upon us; that you would be my husband, and the world would be ours. But the world was never so kind, and you never intended to marry me. You lied, and I was a fool to believe you!"

"Do not berate yourself too bitterly," he said softly.

The smile that turned her mouth felt ugly and black. "True enough. I will reserve the blame for you."

"Your father and mine had a hand in it as well."

Scowling, she opened her mouth—then hesitated. What did he mean by that?

He might have explained himself in the pause that opened. But he made no effort. He held himself motionless, still watching her, giving the impression of tranquil alertness, like a great cat poised at the mouse hole, his eyes fixed on her, ready to spring.

She swallowed a bitter taste. If he wanted to explain, he could *speak*. She would not beg him for his reasons. She did not care for his excuses anyway! She knew full well what had happened; she needed no tales from *him*.

"But I *do* blame myself," she said. "For I was a *fool* for you. Even after they told me to forget you, my brother, my father—even then, I believed you would come. I thought you would find a way, no matter the cost! Was that not stupid? Was that not the *height* of girlish idiocy? To count on one such as *you*!"

"No doubt," he said.

Like a slap, the words knocked the breath from her. It was a cruel, cruel reply.

She twisted away from him, blinking back tears. She deserved his cruelty; it was a meet reward for the stupidity of having expected better from him. "I wish you to hell, Lord Rivenham."

"Doubtless, that will be my destination," he said. "God has no love of fools, and I was no less one than you. I looked for the ways you spoke of. I waited for my cousins to fall asleep as I picked the lock on my chains. And, most foolish of all, I was certain that when I managed to return, you would be waiting—that you would have found the strength in you to refuse to consent to Towe for a week, a day, an *hour* longer."

She stared unseeing into the shadows, unwilling to speak until she felt certain of her voice. The breath she drew shuddered in her throat. "Foolishness, indeed—for I was, after all, only a girl. How highly you must have thought of me, to imagine I would manage to do what no woman can, when men have made her choice for her."

"Yes," he said. "I thought of you very highly. So you see, we are equally fools, you and I."

How unfair he was! She dug her nails into her palms and told herself to be silent. Let dead things remain dead; let the past lie moldering.

But now they had started down this road, it seemed she could not stop. The words spilled out of their own accord. "Did you imagine me a magician, then? You know how a girl is persuaded. Locked in my room, denied meat and drink—did you think I would manage to live on air for the three years it took you to return from the continent?"

"Twenty days."

In the silence, the words seemed to echo. The repetitions did not draw clearer sense from them. Twenty days? "I don't . . ."

"It took me twenty days to find you again."

Twenty days . . .

She began to quake. She would not let herself look at him. Suddenly it seemed the most dangerous thing in the world. Twenty days . . . That would have meant . . . It wasn't possible.

"I saw you seated by his side on the dais," he said, his low voice like a river, smooth and cold, pushing and carrying her toward her doom. "Dressed in green, with orange blossoms in your hair. He spoke into your ear and you smiled. You spilled your cup in his lap. He did not mind it; he laughed and stroked your head, the very picture of the doting bridegroom."

Her insides turned to ice. A tap would shatter them. *He had come back for her.*

No. No, he was lying. "Someone told you these things!"

"Who among that crowd would have dared to speak to me?" His laughter rasped. "Your father and brother would have cut out their tongues for the offense."

She shook her head. He *must* be lying. If he wasn't—if he had been there; if he had returned so soon—not hours after the wedding . . .

She bit down hard on her fist. Grizel had drugged her that day as a kindness. She had drunk heavily to compound the effect. Hours had slipped by like a dream. She had never tried to remember it with any clarity. To imagine that he had been there—close enough to see her, close enough to fly to—while she had sat on the dais, slowly dying for lack of her heart . . .

She could not bear to think that he had come back for her.

She could not *bear* to look back to the past now, to think even for a moment that it might have turned out differently.

That heartbroken girl was a stranger to her now. She would never suffer that way again.

"It makes no difference," she said. It made no difference whatsoever that he had come back for her. "It is all done now. All of it!"

For a space of time he made no sound. The pounding of her heart was noise enough. She put her hand across her breast, pressing hard, digging her nails into the flesh bared by her neckline, focusing only on this pain, so simple, no riddle to it.

And then he said, "Are you certain it is done?"

A guttural noise broke from her. She did not understand it or herself. The lamp threw his shadow onto the wall, a rippling black monster.

Are you certain it is done?

She pinched out the flame.

Blackness enveloped them. Her breath was coming faster, sharp and jagged in her throat. She felt on the edge of . . . something terrible. Something shattering. At any moment he would speak again and she would break apart.

But he did not speak. The silence thickened. It hardened between them like a wall of stone.

It could not stop the echo of his words.

Are you certain it is done?

She pulled her knees to her chest and pressed her face into them. Soundlessly her tears fell while her fingertips remembered the flame, and smarted and burned.

8

Lord John wanted to beat the truth out of her. Adrian had foreseen as much: without a husband to protect her, with her father impeached and her brother an outlaw, she no longer counted as a lady who deserved respect and kind treatment in the face of provocation.

And then, opium's nasty effects did not work to sweeten the basic rottenness of the boy's disposition.

"An unwise strategy," Adrian said, lounging comfortably as Lord John paced. Out the mullioned windows, the sky showed gray and sullen; when the wind shifted, rain spattered the glass.

The boy wheeled. "But she—"

"Will you wish," Adrian said patiently, "to explain to his majesty how you abused a woman who made her courtesies to him at St. James's?"

"But she's a poxy Jacobite! *You* were not here to see what she did. She lured me . . . she—she—"

This sputtering was comical. "Bruised your pride," Adrian said. "Not every woman swoons for a pretty pair of eyes."

Lord John dashed a hand over his brow. The bluish light lent his pale face the look of a corpse astonished from its grave. One might think he had never been required to master his temper. "Then what? Will you pretend it never happened? I suppose that would suit you! Otherwise *you* might have to explain why you absented your post!"

Adrian lifted a brow. It was one thing to coddle this lad's vanity out of a desire to spare himself the irritation of an extended argument. But he would not tolerate blunt challenges. "Go ahead," he said, rising to look down on the other man. "Make your accusation plainly. I am glad to hear what's in your brain."

Lord John came to a stop. "Accuse you—no." His hand, dangling limp at his side, made a nervous twitch, as though to grip the hilt of a sword. "No, indeed not. You could not have known, of course—"

"Better to avoid questions of what I can and cannot know," Adrian said. "I do not believe you begin to compass my abilities."

Lord John looked to his rings, their splendor muted by the sullen light; then ran a finger beneath his steinkirk to loosen it. His much-lamented headache had not prevented him from dressing up as though for fine company. "I only mean to say—"

"That you fear the marchioness had some hand in your lengthy slumber." Adrian had kept the truth of his own experience last night to himself—not to shelter her, but because he'd understood how the boy would react to such tidings. Lord John had not yet learned—and perhaps never would—that the appearance of defeat sometimes served as a very useful weapon.

"I will question her," Adrian said. "Gently, as befits a lady."

Lord John's jaw ticked forward. "Gentle won't serve. She's a stubborn, deceitful, Pope-loving bitch—"

"Watch yourself," Adrian murmured.

Lord John, meeting his eyes, abruptly sat down.

"Our concern is for the brother. Unless your focus strays?"

"No. I didn't mean—"

Disrespect, he was going to finish, but Adrian had no interest in listening to him lie through his teeth. "Force persuades a person to speak, but it cannot guarantee his honesty. Quite the reverse: it will extract confessions from innocents and lies from simple sinners, neither of which would be to our purpose."

Lord John's head tipped. Now he looked interested. "What do you mean to do, then?"

"I mean to persuade her tongue to loosen," Adrian said with a shrug. "Or rather, to let nature persuade it for me. Torture need not always involve knives."

For two days Rivenham kept her locked in her rooms, an armed guard at the door. Grizel was not allowed to remain with her, only to come in the morning to dress her, and later in the day to deliver meals of bread, cold chicken, and cheese.

Nora put on bright smiles for her maid, who looked pale and drawn. Grizel told her in a whisper how Lord John had railed at Mrs. Fairfax and Hooton; how Rivenham had dismissed half the household; and how Montrose hid in his rooms like a spineless cur when his advice might have guided the rest of the servants.

Nora told herself she should be comforted by the fact that Rivenham's men had not lifted a hand to anyone. But then, she knew the reason for it: Rivenham would not waste effort on those who had only been following orders. He would save his punishment for the woman who gave them.

She should have felt fear but she was numb to it. Her body ached queerly, as though she had suffered a great fall. Part of herself still seemed to languish in the dark of the larder, reeling from the unthinkable tidings he had shared with her.

For so long she had despaired, and then for so long she had loathed him, for abandoning her to the fate that his own actions had forced on her.

But he had not abandoned her. *He had come back*.

It changed nothing to know that now. But it would have changed so much had she known it before. To have proof that his love had been true; that he had not merely trifled with her; that he had risked as much for her as she had done for him . . .

The knowledge would have sustained her on so many nights when she had longed for an end.

Her mind did not know how to compass such knowledge, which rendered her whole history strange to her.

She stayed by her window in the sitting room and watched the gray, wet days pass.

When, on the second night, the door to her chambers opened to admit three of Rivenham's men, her tired mind leapt to the most vile possibility. Each of these men-at-arms stood a head taller than she did. They carried wine and goblets and rush-bottomed chairs, and they ignored her when she ordered them to leave. Seating themselves in her sitting room, they talked and drank as though in a tavern.

When it became clear they had no intention of leaving, she retreated to her bedroom.

That was when the real clamor began.

She lay awake listening to what sounded like pots being knocked together; to deliberate stomps and the heavy fall of fists against the door. At first it frightened her, but after a time she realized they had no intention of entering the inner chamber. Her heart calmed then, her thoughts clearing enough to fathom a guess: she had been braced for violence, but Rivenham's revenge would be subtler.

He meant to forbid her sleep.

"Wake up." The voice wove into her dreams, the color of exhaustion, darkest blue, a midnight sky without stars . . .

Choking! She coughed and pushed upright, struggling to breathe.

Rivenham lifted away the cup, his red-rimmed eyes meeting hers. "You will not sleep until you answer my questions."

She wiped water from her face with the back of her sleeve. Three hours ago, or six, or twelve, she would have cursed him in reply. Fifteen hours ago, still alert enough to master herself, she would have held her tongue and given him a glare that bespoke her disdain. But now she could not muster anything so impassioned. Fatigue combined with hunger churned in her stomach. Her heart seemed to beat in fits. She had fallen asleep sitting against the headboard, and her shoulder blades throbbed from the bruising press of carved oak.

He rose from the stool by her bed. "Collect yourself," he said quietly, and walked to the pitcher on the washstand. With movements precise, almost mechanical, he refilled the cup. His expression was serene, as though he were at some mundane task, rather than the coordination of torture.

She rubbed her hands over her eyes. Torture, yes. He had not laid a hand to her, but his unceasing questions—his denial to her of food, though he broke his fast regularly; his ruthless rousing whenever she dozed—were treatments for an enemy. To think that only twenty hours ago—awakened by him at dawn, from a sleep that had overtaken her despite the noise of his men—she had, for a moment, been *glad* to see him! He had spoken into her ear and for the brief muzzy space of a heartbeat, longing for him had run freely through her, shining like a river beneath a sunlit sky.

But he no longer cared to discuss the past. He wished only to know the purpose of the men who had paid a midnight visit to Hodderby.

He set down the pitcher, staring at it for a long moment. "Will you speak?"

Will you speak?

Will you speak?

Will you speak?

If she heard that question again, it would snap her mind. "No," she said hoarsely.

He turned back from the washstand and fixed a steady look on her. His clothing befit a Puritan or penitent, unbroken black save for the white neckcloth at his throat. A leather tie bound his silver-blond hair tightly away from his face. "I am sorry to hear that," he said. Taking up the cup, he started toward her.

His smooth advance struck some primal alarm through her. She forced her stiff legs to straighten; with a grunt, she slipped to her feet.

The floor rocked beneath her.

She grabbed hold of a bed poster, breathing hard.

"Sleep would cure you," he said.

God above, she had never been so tired. "The devil take you!"

He stopped just out of arm's reach. "Perhaps I am already in his service." He smiled slightly. "I recommend you do not count on God, Lady Towe, when I am in the room."

The blasphemy shocked her. What had he become? What monster stood before her? His face seemed to ripple before her eyes.

His hands closed on her shoulders. Sharply he said, "Sit down."

She surrendered to his urging. The bed met her, softer than a cloud, more deeply drugging than any posset. It rose beneath her like a mother's hand, cradling her. In the night, on a full moon, there was music in the grasses, soft winds that plucked the blades like lute strings. The sky above was velvet, the moon a mirror. *Look up*, Adrian whispered, *see your fair face reflected in the heavens . . .*

"Awake!"

Fingers bit into her shoulders. Sickness was boiling up in her gut. Her heart thudded like the kicks of a mule.

With great effort she pried her eyes open.

"Adrian," she whispered.

The stubble on his sharp jaw looked a shade darker than the hair on his head. That stubble had not been visible when first he had entered. Was that a trick of the oil lamps set about the room? They cast a shivering light. How much time had passed since he'd first roused her?

"Listen to me," he said, his words like ice. "Soon I will hand this charge to Lord John. I have given him instructions not to harm you, but you will not want to depend on his obedience."

Her face was wet. Why? She wiped droplets of water from her cheek. *He upended a cup.* She was forgetting things now; her very mind seemed to spin, making truths hard to hold. Objects danced around her. "Go, then," she said.

The slurring of her voice dimly surprised her. "Go," she tried again. A fist seemed preferable to this misery.

Fists were simple. One did not need to remain awake to suffer them.

His grip flexed on her arms. "Who were the men who came? What did they take?"

She blinked. The coldness of his speech, the ruthless intensity of his focus, made him like a stranger. Perhaps this was not Adrian after all but some demon come to inhabit his body—an automaton whose instructions were issued from hell. The dim light from the nearby lamp could not account for how his green eyes burned. Shadows lay over his face, and his mouth looked chiseled from stone. He looked down at her without kindness or recognition.

Again he said, "Who were those men?"

What stupid questions. Spoken often enough, words became nonsense. She looked away. Pitch blackness pressed against the window. Outside the lamp's radius, the room looked drawn in shades of charcoal. Her skirts of gray silk tabby puddled on the darker flagstones.

She was on the floor?

She tried to sit up. His hands aided her. Yes, she was on the floor. The stone bruised her buttocks; her knees ached as though she had fallen onto them. How had it happened? She did not remember leaving the bed.

"Look at me."

She flinched at the crack of this command. He palmed her cheek, sliding his fingers through her hair; only then did she realize that her head had been lolling.

In one forceful move he yanked her up onto her knees. A pin clattered against stone. Cold hanks of hair slithered down her nape. She swayed in his grip. The pain in her scalp made tears prick her eyes. Oh, to lie down . . . to sleep . . .

"Speak." A new hoarseness roughened his voice. "*Speak,* damn you."

She would speak. She must speak. "Don't touch me."

"I will cease to touch you when you answer my question."

What sort of man would persist in this odd torment? Why did he not strike her? *Strike me,* she thought. *End this.* "You are the devil."

"Yes. You have said it before."

So she had. And not only tonight, but . . . long ago, too. She remembered the argument. He had begged her to elope with him, as though there were a chaplain or priest in the kingdom who would wed a Catholic to a Protestant. But no, he had not begged . . . he had dared her, eyes laughing, mouth warm on her throat.

Come sin with me, he'd said, *in the eyes of God. Let our firstborn child decide which church has the right of it.*

Her knees gave way. She would have fallen but his fist in her hair tightened.

"*Wake up!*"

The shout in her ear startled a sob from her. Why was he so cruel?

He pulled her hair, forcing her face upward. His eyes were not laughing now. They were bloodshot. Vividly green amidst a tracery of red.

Why, he was exhausted, too.

He was only a man.

"I remember when I called you the devil." The words

seemed to float from her, drawn by an invisible hand, nothing to do with her lips. "I almost came away with you. So close."

"No," he said after a moment. "You never came near to it. You were no rebel."

She felt dim surprise. "But I was." Had he never understood this? She would have thrown over the world for him. But she had wanted, required, him to risk the same. To ask her father for her hand . . . even if only to be refused.

That was all she had needed: equal courage from him. For all the passion he had shown her, he had ever been guarded, self-contained, in company. Even her brother had not guessed what transpired between them, and in a strange way she had resented Adrian for it. His ability to pretend she meant nothing to him . . . It had troubled her. She had wanted a wildness from him to match hers.

But in the end, he had come for her. He had employed courage and boldness for her sake, but only in the end. What if he had dared it sooner?

She took a breath. "It is good," she said. "Good that you kept your head so long."

A line appeared between his brows. "What do you mean?"

"If you had announced our love . . . if you had approached my father and been denied by him, if I had run away with you . . . then where would we be now?"

His face became very still. Like a mask. "We would be man and wife."

Here, on her knees, at his mercy, the notion struck

her as a joke. "Oh, yes," she said, her voice torn between laughter and tears. "Man and wife. And dead of poverty." Their love could not have ended happily. Either way, they had been doomed. "Or alone and friendless, forsaken by everyone."

Something moved through his eyes. His hand loosened in her hair. "We are alone anyway, Nora."

Her breath stuttered. Yes. So they were. Here, in the hushed silence before dawn, those words felt weighted with profound truth.

His hand slid free of her. Slowly she eased back to the ground, sitting heavily, the inconstant circle of lamplight spilling over her knees. Now that he was not touching her, the chill air seemed to wrap around her like a shroud.

Tears stabbed her sore eyes. This great tiredness left no strength to resist them. "Yes," she said. "Alone." Cosmo would be much like Towe. Her father and David loved her, but with no true understanding of her. She was alone.

Lips touched the corner of her eye. Hot and soft. Confusion yielded to amazement, spreading through her from the place his mouth touched. His breath bathed her cheek. Her wits had no strength to interpret this turn.

But she had no strength to revile it, either. Slowly, so as not to dislodge his mouth, she set her forehead to his shoulder. The darkness there was softer.

His lips slipped up to her temple. "Don't cry," he said, barely more than a breath. "As you said: what is done is done."

She drew a shaking breath. "It is not done." Else, why did the feeling of his lips call out her soul? He was a brute, a hell-bound villain, but his kiss . . . It felt like nothing so much as a benediction.

He misunderstood her words. "Simply answer my questions and it will be done." His voice was low now, his breath warm on her ear as she leaned against him, her forehead on his shoulder. "Then you will sleep as long as you like."

She took a deep breath. He did not smell like brimstone but like a man, flesh and blood. His shoulder was solid, strapped with muscle. A woman might depend on it for support.

He had not always been a villain.

He had come back for her.

The revelation grew stranger the longer she dwelled on it. This cold man had risked everything for her, once. *This* man, whom every woman in London admired; she had seen how they fawned on him. Men feared him, if they were wise. She should fear him. She had feared him minutes ago.

His palm settled between her shoulder blades, a warm and steady pressure, as though to hold her in place. But then his fingertips trailed down her spine, patient and slow, reaching the small of her back, returning again. They hesitated, then repeated their journey.

They opened on her waist and grasped her lightly, as though she were precious.

"Make me speak." The words slipped from her in a whisper. If only he could make her. "I will not betray him otherwise." And if she did not betray him . . . she must lift her head and move away, for this man could not be hers.

He made some adjustment that brought their torsos together, then put her face into the cradle where his throat met his shoulder. His head bowed, and she felt the soft brush of his hair over her cheek. "Even though he betrays you? To put you in this position showed no love or care for you. No man who loved you would risk you so."

There were different kinds of love, then. The one on which David depended was forged of duty and blood. He counted on her as he might count on his own limbs to perform his bidding. "He needs me." She herself had needed David in the past, and he had not failed her then.

"Think, for once, of yourself."

She could feel the vibrations of his voice through his flesh. She closed her eyes, and—ah, dear God, he did not shake her. It felt blissful to lie against him. The darkness behind her lids swirled in dizzying circles.

Perhaps they were always meant to meet in darkness. Mayhap it was only daylight, and the world's watching eyes, that conspired against them.

His arms closed around her—he was lifting her, pulling her into his lap. This felt now like a dream, and she submitted peacefully as his hand around her ankles lifted her feet onto his long thighs. He sat cross-legged, cradling her as though he still loved her.

Sanity still lurked somewhere within. It kicked hard against her complacence. She could not trust him.

"You mean to kill my brother." She must remind herself of this, cling to *this* truth rather than to him.

"No," he said.

How simple the denial. She might have accepted it

and let him hold her like this until he tired of it. But she had promises to keep. She had a duty. "You will take him to London," she said into the hot skin of his throat. "Can you guarantee his safety there?"

His answer did not come immediately. "I mean to prevent a war, Nora."

"Noble," she said. "But not if the cost is David's life."

His grip tightened on her back. "Know you how many lives would be spared by averting this war your brother foments? My own people—so many of them lured by false promises and predictions—they are in no danger from their government; but if they believe they are to be killed for their religion, why shouldn't they take up arms? And then the lies spread by your brother and his allies *will* lead them to their deaths, as surely as though those lies had been the truth."

She did not know . . . She could barely think . . . She could not parse for herself the truth of what he said. It was true that David was counting on Adrian's tenants to aid in the cause . . . So many of them were Catholic; why should they not wish to fight for a Catholic king? But to call these lies . . . They were not lies . . .

She forced herself to open her eyes, to pull away a little so she could look into Adrian's face. How beautiful he was, his sharp features shadowed in the light of the lamp behind them. Her hand rose of its own accord to smooth his brow, the hollow of his cheek. Stubble abraded her fingertips. His beard had not been so thick when he was young. His shoulders had not been so broad. He felt like a man now, grown, strong.

She felt the warmth of his exhalation. "You could not sit in Parliament," she murmured. His bottom lip was full, the edge perfectly delineated, easy to trace with her thumb; it was so much softer than it looked. The deep hollow beneath it called up a strange tenderness within her. "You could not vote, nor go to London without a ticket of permission, when you kept your old faith. Those are not lies."

"No." His voice sounded ragged now. "They weren't."

She glanced to his eyes and found herself snared in an intense, unwavering look. "Then why . . ." She took a long breath, struggling to think clearly. A possibility occurred to her, wild, the stuff of dreams: imagine if she could win him to their side. Then he would no longer be her enemy. Then they could be friends, and he could hold her like this without causing her to feel like a traitor to her own blood . . . "Why should you do the German king's bidding?"

His hand closed over her own, holding it to his cheek, his grip intent. "Because he will remain the king. Because your brother's cause is no wiser than a drunkard's midnight gamble. The war he plots will be short and bloody—and he will lose, along with every Catholic in this land, no matter whether they take up arms or no."

"But James Stuart is our rightful king—a direct heir of Stuart blood. Surely you, of all people, cannot resent him for his religion!"

A low noise of scorn came from him. "What difference does it make to me who deserves the throne? I save my cares for matters that touch me directly. Think you

I abandoned my faith for some true revelation of God? No. I do what I must to protect me and mine. But your brother does not." His hand tightened over hers, as hard as his words. "He is a boy in a man's body," he bit out, "who chooses to squander on foolish dreams not only himself but also those whom he owes his protection. I am cut of a different cloth, Nora. I deal in *reality*. This country will not stand for a Catholic ruler; it will destroy any who seek otherwise. But me and mine will not be among them."

In the silence she could hear her own heartbeat. He did not look away from her, his regard fierce.

"You cast yourself as a man without morals," she whispered.

"My morals are in service to my purpose. I will keep safe what is mine. Now *tell me what those men were after*."

Some part of her felt the sting of his words, and recoiled at his return to interrogation. But the greater part of her attention reeled from a different cause: the ferocious conviction with which he spoke, and the strange, irresistible pull of his philosophy.

I will keep safe what is mine.

It spoke to the deepest part of her, that dark, tangled place that fretted incessantly over her own powerlessness; that craved so desperately to protect this place, and her brother, despite the fact that David's own actions made these aims impossible.

Her eyes focused on the sight of his hand over hers, large, powerful. She felt the calluses where his palm pressed against her knuckles. He was a swordsman. He had soldiered on the Continent for her majesty; he had played the diplomat between Queen Anne and George of Hanover. The strength in his body was but a reflection of the strength he exercised at court. He had loved her with this body that enfolded hers now. They tried to be strangers to each other, but they were not.

Once, long ago, he had come back for her. He had tried to protect her, for she had been his then.

"I was carrying your child," she said.

His grip seized.

For several long heartbeats he stared at her; she looked back at him, astonished by her own words. Could such a secret, guarded for so long, held as carefully as a wicked splinter of sharp-edged glass, be tossed free so suddenly?

The next words came just as unbidden: "I did not betray you. I told them nothing of the babe, either." She swallowed. "How could I? I was so ignorant—I did not recognize the signs. My tirewoman saw them. She realized I was with child. She spoke to my sister, God rest her soul, who went to my lord father. I never told your name, but they found the telescope you gave me . . ."

His grip was painful now. "The child . . ."

"Lost before my belly even embiggened. He forced . . ." She took a sharp breath. "Some posset. I don't know what was in it. It made me . . . ill."

"Your father," he said.

"No. Lord Towe."

"He *knew*?"

"Oh, yes." Her laugh felt jagged in her throat. It sounded strange to her, too . . . fraught. This was old news. It should not give her fresh pain. But she had learned recently how old news might set a person on her head. And to share this with him . . . after so many years of secrecy . . .

She must be mad; lack of sleep had sickened her brain. His eyes seemed to fill her vision, his gold-tipped lashes unnaturally distinct, his attention riveted to her in a way that shut out all the world. He had come back for her. For that one boon, for that act of courage, he deserved now to know everything. "My lord father said— he said I would not wed you; and then, when I refused to bend to him, he said you refused to wed me, that you had mocked his proposal, for I was not a Catholic, and had proved myself a jade and a slut, no fit wife in your eyes."

"That is a *lie*."

"I knew it," she said. "Can you imagine I believed it? Never. I heard rumor of how they beat you in the courtyard, though nobody allowed me to see it. But then they said you had left the country—they produced your own brother to swear to it." Her voice broke; she closed her eyes. "I was carrying your *child*, Adrian. They called me a disgrace. They starved me and the babe inside me. For the child's sake, what was I to do? *You had left me.* Towe seemed my only choice."

The memory of that time lived in her flesh. It overwhelmed her now, dark and suffocating, like the locks of her hair, fallen free of her pins, that snaked around her face and throat. She shoved them away, heedless of snarls, glad for the pain they caused as she ripped through them with her fingers.

But it was not enough. Her throat felt too tight. She needed air and liberty. She pulled free of Adrian's grip and scrambled off his lap to the floor.

He made no move to stop her. He appeared frozen. Only his eyes followed her as she moved.

The stone floor was cold and smooth. She flattened her palm against it, grateful for the chill. The roiling in her stomach demanded shallow, careful breaths.

Say it. Tell it all.

She curled her fingers into a hard, aching fist and made herself look at him. His pulse beat visibly in his throat. Tendons stood out on the back of his broad hand where it braced against the floor to support his weight.

"I did not know," she said. "That they had told all to Towe—or the agreement they had struck. I knew naught of it. In our bridal chamber, that first night, after he . . . had his way with me, he called for libations. I was already . . . not myself. Drunk, drugged, what have you. I took the posset he gave me." Some vicious thing uncoiled in her and made her eyes sting. "It had good effect. I never conceived again."

"God." The word slipped from him softly. When he ran his hand over his mouth, it appeared to tremble. "My God, Leonora."

"I do not think He concerns Himself overmuch with such matters. He saves His attentions for judging us in the hereafter. In this world, we must fend for ourselves."

He blinked, as though blinded. "And you . . ." He took an audible breath, then exhaled slowly. "And you wish," he said, "for me to spare your brother."

She leaned forward. "Adrian, he was the *only one* to show me kindness." *He* had slipped her bread and water. He had brought Grizel to tend to her in place of the tirewoman who had betrayed her so cruelly. He had braved their father's wrath to offer her solace when no one else would.

He had blamed himself for bringing Adrian into the household in the first place.

"David was all I had," she whispered. "The only one who helped me."

Some complex struggle was working across Adrian's face. "You should have told me."

She sighed. "To what purpose? I was married when next we met. How would it have profited either of us?"

His bleak expression admitted that he could make no reply. Fate had trapped them both very neatly.

"Besides," she said more gently, "my husband might have made trouble for you. Marriage to me enriched him greatly—by some six thousand pounds, I believe. But his pride could not have borne it if he thought you understood the arrangement he had struck with my father. He preferred you to believe him an ignorant gull than the willing husband of a slut."

He leaned forward so suddenly that she shrank. "Do not wrong yourself so."

"It is only a word," she whispered. "Of all people, you know best if its meaning is meet in my regard."

He seemed to have no answer to that. He searched her face as though desperately trying to place who she was.

She wondered if that had been her unconscious intention. Their roles in this room had been so much clearer some minutes ago.

Perhaps it was safer to remain at this distance, and return to those roles.

On a breath, she said, "Perhaps, rather than strangers, we may be proper enemies. Enemies may respect each other, I think."

He shook his head. He looked haunted, and his short laugh was ghost-soft and strange. "You are a fool," he said.

He rose and came toward her. She watched his approach in puzzlement, then gasped when he lifted her into his arms. The world tilted around her; his broad palm cradled her skull. "What—"

"Shh." He carried her to the bed, his steps smooth, his grip firm beneath her knees and shoulders. The scent of lavender rose as he laid her atop the quilts. She looked up at him in wonderment. In his face, her addled imagination now glimpsed a tenderness she had not seen in . . . years.

He leaned down so close that she could see the striations in his irises, the green fading into a ring of gold around his pupils. His breath warmed her lips as he searched her face. She held still, uncertain what he looked for, riveted by the sensation of his body's warmth. Everything in these past few hours seemed more and more like a dream. She could not attempt any longer to make sense of it.

"I would ask once more," he said, his tone very gentle. She felt the light brush of his knuckles down her cheek as he lifted a strand of hair away from her mouth. "What did those men come for?"

She moistened her lips. His gaze dropped to watch them, and a queer, hot thrill blossomed through her. She felt almost drunk.

Dream or no, this was dangerous. She pressed her lips into a hard line and drew a long breath through her nose.

"I will not betray my brother," she said. "You will have to force me by some other means."

Now his eyes lifted again to hers. "Suggest me a way."

"I cannot say one. I mean to repay my debts to him."

He showed her a brief, black smile. "As do I."

His voice held a promise of blood. She bit her lip to forestall the urge to protest of David's kindness; to demand that he spare her brother's life. She knew how it worked among men. David had shown no kindness to Adrian that day in the courtyard. He never would have supported a marriage between their families.

She must protect David, for Adrian never would.

He retreated a step but remained looking down at her a moment. Then he turned for the door.

She frowned and pushed herself up on one elbow. He intended to leave? Had he given up on his questions? But she had one of her own. "What did you mean? How am I a fool?"

His hand on the latch, he paused. She watched the line of his shoulders square.

But when he spoke, he said only, "Go to sleep, my lady. Dream sweetly,"

The door closed softly behind him.

9

The chapel was dark and narrow, hewn from stone in a time when a Plantagenet had held the throne. Adrian took a seat on the hard, chilled bench. Narrow windows of rippled glass permitted only a weak glow from the sun dawning without.

He wanted to smash something.

Something needed to shatter, bleed, and collapse.

He stared at the ornate gold crucifix that loomed over the mahogany altar, at the broken body that draped across it. Someone had put exquisite care into crafting the agony on this wooden face of Christ.

Perhaps Nora was right: God watched but did not concern Himself with this kingdom. In His son He had exhausted His interest in suffering. Now He waited indifferently until Judgment Day.

Or perhaps He did not even watch. This Jesus on the cross must be *blind* to have endured the worship of David Colville and his father.

Adrian exhaled. The events of her wedding day had been emblazoned into his brain with a searing force that no amount of time would blur. He could still recall with perfect detail the jewels around her fingers as she had lifted her wineglass. The smell of the feast, sharp alcoholic fumes mixed with the richness of roasted game. The lilting tune of the pipes playing in the gallery above. His own sensation of shock—like a full-bodied blow, an impact that somehow did not end—as he had backed out of the hall. The bite of the knife that had settled then against his throat.

He could hear the words David Colville had spoken as though the man now stood beside him.

Catholic dog, I would kill you and rejoice in it. But your life is not worth the meanest servant's effort to clean these floors of your blood.

What he could not recall was his own response—as if the great blankness inside him, like an explosion of light, had blotted out his senses.

But he had said something to prompt David Colville's parting remark.

I would see her dead before you soiled her again.

This was the brother she protected. This was the man whom she called her only help.

I knew naught of the agreement they had struck.

The memory of her soft words hammered at him. He had thought himself numb? He was rage, nothing but it. Rage . . . and horror . . . and regret.

And shame.

He made fists. He relaxed them. He breathed in and out.

There must be a way to fathom this. It had happened long ago. It was *done*. It changed nothing of what had come afterward.

So she had not betrayed him. So she had been cruelly abused. His course would not have altered had he known it. He had tried with every faculty and the last ounce of his strength to return to her. Knowing the truth now did not cast that effort in a different light, only restored to him the certainty that his effort had been just.

It did, however, clarify his shame.

He had lain with her only once. A single time, so fumbling and brief, so incandescently sweet, that it had seemed almost innocent. Blameless; a sanctified thing.

Afterward, caution had reclaimed him. He had waged a mighty struggle to keep chaste, recognizing that the danger in lying together was all to her peril, not his. Cowardly indeed of him to put that risk upon her, though youthful ardor had painted it in a different light.

Understanding now how she had been ruined by it—fathoming fully why she accused him of destroying her life—showed him the truth of that day in the fields. An embrace of transcendent sweetness now twisted in his mind into a clumsy act of violence, which had torn a bloody gash across the fabric of her life and his own.

It sickened him in waves. If he had never touched her . . . if they had always remained chaste . . .

And now he had come to ravage her life again.

He looked down at his own hands, his palms upward atop his thighs, the posture of a penitent begging God's forgiveness. But this test was man-made and had no divine resolution. Angels would turn their faces away. Only darkness lay ahead.

He did not know if an afterlife awaited him, a judgment and a punishment. Perhaps there was no hell, or any heaven, either; perhaps his body would only molder, and turn into food for worms. Men made games of religion, did they not? They made God into a reason for warfare. Who was to say that He was anything more than an excuse, an invention, a convenient cause? Adrian had never felt Him save in His absence.

Nothingness, then: no punishment for sin but death; no reward for virtue but the grave. Yet, even if there was a master in heaven, it would make no difference to his course. He would accept damnation as his due in exchange for an earthly life in which he and his were no one's slaves.

His own brother—*who had known; who had known she carried his child*—his brother was dead. Hexton was out of reach—*for now*.

But David Colville would come into his grasp, and then there would be justice.

There would be a smashing, and a shattering, and a collapse.

There would be blood.

He inhaled, tasting the musty air, the dust of centuries of penance, and spat it out.

He came to his feet. He felt nothing in this space, no divinity, no disapproval, no breath of damnation. But as a monument to hypocrisy it was unrivaled.

Here, before this blind face on the crucifix, he would slit David Colville's throat.

He started for the exit. Halfway down the aisle he heard a thought not his own, a dim voice that spoke in his head:

And who will clean the blood from these floors?

The voice sounded like Nora's.

Would he ask the mistress of this house to clean her brother's blood?

He drove his hand up his face and cursed.

But if there was no god, there was nothing to curse for this bind. Without God, there was no fate, only chance. Only flesh, and pain, and occasionally, so briefly, moments of pleasure, unexpected, unbidden—

—as when he had taken her into his arms tonight, too exhausted to heed caution.

David Colville's rotted, myopic ambitions might cost her life.

David is all I had, she had said. *The only one who helped me.*

But it had not always been so.

It had not always been so, and it would be so no longer. Now, whether she willed it or no, she would have *him.*

Her brother had forsaken her welfare when choosing his path. Adrian had seen this knowledge in her face. But she could not break from the course her brother had set for her—not even if the man died. Her principles and allegiances were not so flexible.

Indeed, her brother's death might only strengthen her resolve.

Very well. If Colville died, it would not be by his hands. Instead, Adrian thought, *he* would choose a new course for her. And he would make her walk it, though it won him her rage.

He had no illusions of what her reaction would be. In her grief, she would loathe and revile him.

But she would be alive. And she would be *his*.

10

Nora slept, and woke, and slept again. She slept for nearly a full day, dimly conscious, in the break between dreams, of Grizel's cool hand on her forehead and the maid's quiet fussing with the blankets that enclosed her.

When her eyes finally came open with the desire to stay so, another dawn glowed through the windows. She lay alone, enfolded by warmth and peace.

Only once before had she slept through a day of her life—after miscarrying the child. The missing hours had haunted her thereafter. That something so dreadful and altering might occur, and its consequences unfold, while she lay unawares . . . It had caused her to think for the first time on mortality. Surely this was what death would be like: nothingness, oblivion, as the world continued to turn, heedless of her absence.

She had felt corrupted by this new understanding, intolerably cognizant that one day she would cease. She had turned to prayer for comfort, desiring to be persuaded that oblivion was only the step before grace, the last trial before everlasting resurrection.

But prayer had not helped her. That bleakness had endured for months, if not years.

Not so now. She rose from the bed with a lightness of body and spirit. She felt as though a storm had passed, leaving great peace in its wake.

He knew everything. The past was no longer her dark secret to carry.

Out the window the day was blooming, great swaths of scarlet and gold spreading across the sky. She wanted to be in the light, with the dew soaking her slippers, grass brushing at her skirts and bending greenly beneath her feet. The locked door across the room taunted her as the birds outside sang invitations.

She went to the door and put her ear against it, hoping to hear Grizel's approaching footsteps. The answering silence puzzled her. She could not even hear the quiet conversation of her erstwhile guards.

When she pressed her ear harder against the door, it creaked and gave way.

Startled, she held her breath—certain that at any moment it would be slammed in her face and locked again.

But silence still reigned, and the door remained ajar. Tentatively she pushed it farther.

Her sitting room was empty. The far door—the door to the hall—stood open.

Was this some mistake? She dared not waste a minute. A fresh shift, her stays, petticoats, and a sack gown she could lace herself: dressed thus in haste, she crept out from her chambers and down the stairs. Nobody appeared to stop her, but she held her breath as she went. She felt like a thief stealing through the house with mischief in her heart. She felt like somebody enchanted, a princess from an Arthurian legend, rejuvenated from a magical rest of centuries.

This serenity was not to be trusted. Great matters still pressed on all sides, demanding her worry.

But joy knew no reason and did not repay restraint. She let herself smile as she passed through the entry hall. She laughed as she stepped out into the cool morning air.

The sun, rising higher, welcomed her.

The silence in the library spoke briefly and eloquently of disbelief. Adrian, his weight braced against the great oak desk behind him, let it extend to its natural conclusion. His gaze found the telescope, its brass fittings gleaming in the rising light. To think her rotted father had kept it as a prize.

He must find some other chamber in this house in which to conduct his business—some space uncorrupted by the stench of Colville men.

Lord John was the first to speak. "You must be joking." He wheeled toward Braddock. "He jests, surely!"

That Lord John solicited Braddock's opinion was, in itself, a good measure of his shock. Raised by a father too proud of his station, the boy more generally behaved as though the lower orders existed only to scrape and serve.

Braddock knew better than to reply. Though his frown clearly conveyed his displeasure, he at least understood the nature of this meeting. Adrian had called it to give not explanations but orders.

"I do not joke," Adrian said calmly. "Beestings is never safe in early autumn. Any wisewoman will tell you so."

Lord John pivoted back. *"Beestings."* His sputtered laugh smacked of scorn. "But this is absurd! Think you I cannot recognize the effect of spoiled food? No curdled milk ever left a man unconscious for twelve hours or more! I know very well when I have been poisoned, sir—" Braddock laid a hand on his arm, which he angrily shook away. "Do not touch me! You low fool who stands here mute, swallowing these lies as obedient and wretched as a mule—"

Braddock's color rose. One hand fisted at his side as he retreated a pace. He would not dare speak back to the boy, nor respond in the light of day; any public incident would ruin him and cast a black mark on his master besides.

But a midnight accident . . . Adrian considered him closely. This was not the first provocation he had swallowed from Lord John. An accident might happen very easily, and in the end, it would serve Adrian just as ill.

"Go speak to the men," Adrian told him. Best to keep them apart for now. "Inform them that it was some feculence from the kitchen which sickened them."

"I will tell them," Braddock said gruffly. He cast a dark look toward Lord John. "And should any object, I'll gladly correct 'em."

"No need. Should anyone doubt it, he may apply to me for clarification."

Braddock bowed and turned to leave.

Lord John shoved a hand through his disordered hair. His eyes looked wild. "I cannot credit this," he said when the door closed. "This is madness. You know it was no food that poisoned us. And the woman?" He dropped his hand to slap against his thigh. "That you propose to let her rove *freely*, despite the fact—"

"I do not propose it," Adrian said flatly. "I order it. Should obedience vex you unduly, you may leave this house for London—within the hour. I can spare no men, but I will give you provisions, and your horse."

The lad made a noise of disbelief. "I cannot—you cannot mean—to make that journey alone—"

Adrian shrugged. It was true that thieves and bandits peopled the high road. Most of them believed the best way to avoid a hanging was to leave their victim unable to testify. "You must not sound so discouraged. I have made the journey several times myself. All it takes is skill with a sword."

The implicit insult brought the blood back to the boy's face. He took a sharp step forward. "What next, then? What next, if I stay? Shall you invite her brother into the house to watch over us while we sleep?"

Adrian straightened off the desk. "To reply to a threat with a jibe may work in the nursery, but among men, it does not wound so much as annoy, much like a fly's useless buzzing."

"You protect a woman who poisoned us! You coddle

that traitorous bitch, when any man but a papist dog would string her up in the courtyard for his guards to teach—"

The blow knocked the boy off his feet.

Sprawling on the ground, he blinked up at Adrian, who drew a long breath, then offered a smile.

"Have you aught else to say?" Adrian waited a few moments. "No? Ah, well. You may thank your father for the backhand. I have no objections to a fist, but I understand that Lord Barstow dotes on your pretty face. Perhaps you should write him your thanks. I'm sure he'll wish to hear your other thoughts as well."

The boy's paralysis broke all at once; he scrambled to his feet and backed away. "My father will see you dead, sir!"

"If it were in your father's power, or his friends' power, I would be dead already," Adrian said. "Alas, it seems that Barstow neglected to educate you. Ask him to explain to you the sum of money he owes me, and what of his correspondence has found its way into my possession, and how this might guide your understanding of his reluctant friendship with me. I think you will find it most instructive."

Lord John made a convulsive move, a shake of the head halted midway. Now, for the first time in this conversation, uncertainty showed in the pinched line of his lips.

"You look unwell," Adrian murmured. The boy's cheek was already purpling. "Spoiled food can wreak havoc on the bodily humors, can it not?"

Lord John's lips moved soundlessly.

"Can it not?"

"Yes." The boy spat it. "Yes, it can."

Adrian laughed. "Indeed, we should be grateful that nobody died of that rotten meal. It happens every day. We must pray that it does not happen again for the worse."

The boy, learning quickly, made no reply to this threat. He was trembling visibly now—as much with rage, Adrian guessed, as with fear. He did show some small promise. This lesson in restraint would benefit him.

"You will keep your eyes and your thoughts away from Lady Towe," Adrian added quietly. She was his concern now, and none other's. "Now go find Braddock. Apologize for your insult to him. Then ask if you may help him spread the news."

Nora returned from her walk to a house fully awakened. As she turned the corner she nearly collided with Adrian, who steadied her by the shoulders before stepping back a pace. "My lady Towe," he said. "Good morning."

To see him in the light of this new day was to discover she no longer knew how to look at him. He was dressed soberly, in a dark-green coat with riding leathers; his hair was scraped away from the severe, bold bones of his face.

Nervousness overtook her. "Good morning to you." Now would come an order to return to her room, or to explain her purpose in wandering out of doors.

But all he said was "You look well. Sleep was restorative?"

She found herself at a loss. He met her eyes easily, his

expression showing no sign of what had passed between them in midnight's hush.

"Yes," she said faintly. "I am well."

"I am glad of it." He inclined his head again, a brief courtesy, and walked onward.

She turned to watch his progress in an increasing daze. Was it really to be so simple? Would he pretend that she had never told him of what had happened six years ago?

Had the news not meant anything to him?

She opened her mouth, then bit hard on her tongue. She should be grateful for his indifference. It should confirm and strengthen the harder feelings she should have for an enemy.

Yet, before he turned the corner, she called out to him. "Wait! I . . ."

He turned back. "Yes?"

She tried for a more dignified tone. "I confess I was surprised to find my chamber unguarded."

A smile tipped the corner of his mouth. "Would you prefer the guards?"

"No, of course not. But I cannot understand—" She paused, flustered. Of course she did not wish to point out the wisdom in keeping her under watch after she had drugged his company. "That is, I do wonder what you told them." She feared to encounter a soldier with a grudge.

He lifted a brow and stepped toward her. "Told them? Of their prolonged sleep, do you mean?"

"Yes."

"Why, the explanation was simple: what but spoiled

food? Beestings pudding is always a chancy dish. I hope your cook will refrain from attempting it again."

It took a moment to digest her astonishment. "You can't be serious."

"But I am."

"They can't believe that!"

"But they do."

She could read nothing in his calm expression. "But . . . why?" Why would he lie to spare her their wrath?

"That was all they needed to know," he said with a shrug. He glanced over his shoulder, then back at her. "Are you coming, then?"

What strange madness was this? Was she still dreaming? "Coming where?"

"Montrose mentioned that you were due to visit the apiary. I should like to see how it turned out."

"My goodness. I'd . . . forgotten." He'd helped to design it, in fact.

He smiled—a beautiful smile, it seemed to her, absent of any complex motive. "Did it turn out so poorly, then?"

"No," she said. "Not at all." Suddenly she felt amazed by this . . . *easiness* between them. The strange peace she had felt watching the dawn touched her again. Tentatively she smiled back at him. "In fact, it turned out wonderfully."

Bees had no liking for smoke or noise, so the apiary lay a good distance from the manor, through fields where sweet white clover grew in abundance. They walked side by side through grasses still wet with morning dew. In the distance birds hidden in the green depths of lime trees trilled taunts at them, joyful, frenetic.

"The weather looks to be holding," Nora said as she glanced at Adrian sidelong. He had kept his own counsel for the last few minutes, setting a steady pace—although slower, perhaps, than was his custom. She kept up with him easily, her skirts wadded in her fists, while his attention roamed freely and impartially over the verdant, rolling landscape that enclosed them.

"So it does." He tilted his face to the sky, then closed his eyes, basking in the light. The sight of his simple, sensual enjoyment startled and then arrested her. With his burnt gold skin and pale hair, he looked like the sun's own creature, its natural worshipper. He looked like a man who knew how to make the most of even the simplest pleasures.

Her mouth went dry. She remembered, all at once and vividly, the look on his face when he had brought her to pleasure as a girl. His intense concentration, his slow smile of satisfaction . . .

"A turn of luck," he said as she forced her eyes away.

She took a hard breath. "Yes, indeed." Such foolishness! A man turned his face to the sun and her pulse began to race. Impatience with herself made her voice waspish. "But it comes too late, of course. There's a hard winter upon us now."

She sensed his curious glance but kept her eyes on the grass bending beneath her feet. "I heard some talk of these troubles," he said. "Will you be forced to ration the harvest?"

"Will you not?" Any rains that swept Hodderby could not but pass through Beddleston as well.

"We might have been forced to it," he said, "but for a measure I undertook two springs past—an experiment, to the great displeasure of my tenants. Mr. Tull's seed drill—have you heard of it?" She shook her head. "A remarkable device," he continued, "far more economical than casting seed by hand. Of course, the tenants fear that if their hands are no longer needed for broadcasting, they themselves may soon prove redundant. I've had a difficult time persuading them to use the invention. But it increased our harvest last autumn fourfold—"

"Fourfold!"

"Yes. Which allows us some margin of comfort even now."

She could barely compass such bounty. *Fourfold!* "Is it very expensive, this device?"

"Not so much expensive as difficult to obtain," he said with a rueful smile. "Mr. Tull justly fears for his life when his appearance is announced in a district. No man likes the idea that he might be replaced by a machine." He laughed. "Perhaps I should be grateful to these rains: when we eat well this winter despite them, they will have proved, as I could not, the true uses of innovation."

"I would write to this Mr. Tull! Hodderby could profit by his machine."

"By all means. But I have his plans. If you like, my steward will consult with Montrose on designing such an instrument for you."

She opened her mouth to agree, then caught herself. This was not her decision to make. David must be consulted on any step that might roil the tenancy.

The thought made her glum. Her brother's interest proved difficult to capture when it came to questions agricultural. He had been born of their father's temperament, better suited to courtly politics than rural government.

As was Rivenham, she'd assumed.

"Why do you bother with it?" she asked.

He cast her a startled look. "With crop improvement?"

"The management of the land is your steward's concern, surely."

"Of course. But it is my land. And my people."

How simple he made it sound! "Yet, with your political interests, your business in London . . ."

"But they are all to a purpose," he said. "What use in any of it, if not for the safeguarding of what is mine?"

Yes. She knew what he meant precisely. "Beddleston is everything to you."

A line appeared between his brows. "As is Hodderby to you . . . or so I recall."

"Indeed, but—" She swallowed the rest of her words. Hodderby was not hers. It had been her father's, and now it was her brother's, and his son's after him.

Yet—traitorous thought!—David would never care for Hodderby as she did. The land spoke to her; it was part of her soul. She could not separate her love of this place from her love of family, for to serve them was to serve the land; and from possession of this land came all power, honors, and achievements to which the Colvilles so proudly laid claim.

Why, then, while the land was suffering and its people feared to starve, were its caretakers on some foreign shore, politicking and squabbling?

She wrapped her arms around her waist, disliking her own thoughts. Her father and brother did not court James Stuart for vainglorious reasons. Yes, Father had been treated wretchedly by George of Hanover's new friends; yes, he deserved justice for it. But his support of the true king served a nobler purpose than vengeance. Did it not?

"You may speak to him yourself, if you like."

She glanced up. "To—your steward, do you mean?"

He nodded.

She bit her lip. David had left Hodderby in her care on the tacit understanding that she would steer the course he had set for her. But he had been gone so long now . . .

And he had been wrong to leave.

When his people needed him, it was not to France he should have gone. Even in service of James Stuart's cause, he might have taken direction from afar.

He had chosen to go to France when he should have remained here.

"Yes," she said. "Do send for your steward. I should like very much to speak with him."

And when David returned—if it even occurred to him to quarrel over this, with so many greater concerns awaiting him—she would explain her reasoning then.

"You will like him," Adrian said. "He's a man of great learning—educated at St. Andrews, in fact."

She smiled, reluctantly flattered by this vision of her as a woman who could appreciate scholarship. "Will he listen to a woman?"

"I cannot imagine otherwise. But you will make him listen, if he hesitates."

The reply struck a strange, sweet pain through her. How nonchalantly this man assumed that she would be able to command others' respect.

No—that she *deserved* such respect.

"Yes," she said slowly, "I will."

She remembered now why she had fallen in love with him.

She wished she did not.

They came into sight of the rude wooden hut that housed the beehives. A grin broke over Adrian's face. For a moment, he looked much younger—the picture of the boy she had loved. Her heart gave another painful twist. "How remarkable," he said. "You've whitewashed the beehouse."

She nodded. "Yes. And I painted the hives yellow. I had the idea that bees are drawn to brightness—in their homes as well as in flowers."

"And has it proved successful?"

"Considerably."

"Ingenious," he murmured.

She restrained, with some amusement, an immodest impulse to agree with him. David had teased her for painting the hives, thinking it a beautification project. *Next you'll be wanting to paper them in velvet print.* But it had been marvelously effective in multiplying swarms.

"We've kept your design for the hives, though," she said. "Before I thought of painting them, I did experiment with wheat straw and bramble, but I found the swarms much diminished by it."

Mr. Harrison, the bee-master, had spotted their approach and came out to meet them. Nora had sent a boy ahead with a jug of small beer and clean lengths of knitted netting, which now waited in a small basket outside the door. Harrison picked up the jug as they neared.

"Morning, m'lady," he said, tugging his white forelock and adding a scowl to inflect it. He had seemed ancient even during her childhood, and in early years, when she'd still been permitted to play with the tenants' children, she had led daring expeditions here, one amongst a group of grubby-faced tykes creeping toward the beehouse as toward the cave of a monster. Out Mr. Harrison had come, shaking his stick and growling, and they had shrieked and run away, frantic with delicious terror.

Sometimes the memory was enough to make her wondrous that he did not still shake his stick at her approach. Next to that, his scowl was nothing.

The sight of the earl, however, prompted a different welcome from him. He recognized Adrian of old; snapped straight and then performed a proper bow that made her jaw drop.

"My lord," he said roughly. "At your service. And a right pleasure to see you, if I may say so."

"And you as well," said Adrian, smiling. "I hear you have kept in use the hives we designed."

Harrison's liver-spotted cheeks reddened. "Och, that was her ladyship's doing. But aye, there be no better yet I know." He handed them each a cup of small beer. "To the dregs, now."

"This is a superstition, you know." Adrian sounded amused. "Beer does not keep the bees from stinging."

"But it's a pleasant one, surely," Nora replied.

"Surely," he echoed, winking at her.

Her smile slipped. She turned away as she drank her own draft. This same man had shown a much harder face to her recently. Which was true, which false? She had proposed to him that they be enemies. Instead, he had decided on friendship. Why?

There was no need to divine his motives, she told herself. The rapid beating of her heart was what she must divine—and trammel. *Rivenham,* she told herself. *He is Rivenham to me, not Adrian.*

She gave her cup back to Harrison, who in exchange handed her a length of netting. Rivenham tied his mask with the ease of long practice: he had made a study of insects during his years in France, as a student of a great scientist, and in congress with that man, he had invented the hive construction he had proposed to David and Harrison on his first visit to Hodderby.

Having managed the apiaries at Towe's estate, Nora was no less practiced at the donning of such masks. But the slippery fabric resisted her fingers this morning. She wondered at herself, at how fragile and ridiculous she had become, that a man's smile might discompose her sufficiently to reduce her to an infant's fumblings.

Warm fingers closed over her own. "Let me," Rivenham said.

His knuckles brushed her bare nape. The touch of his fingers was light, barely noticeable, but she felt it in the way her muscles seemed to unravel. A warm pleasure hummed over her skin. Such delicate, careful handling: who would imagine a large man capable of it? Very gently he disentangled a stray wisp of her hair that interfered with the knot.

Was it her imagination, or did he pass that strand through his fingers before releasing it?

She set her jaw. This pitching of her stomach was a purely alchemical reaction: his presence triggered some incalescence within her, a heat that made her stupid. It was no more her fault than it was his. She must not think on it.

When he stepped away, she tried for briskness. "Very well, Mr. Harrison; show us the news."

Harrison led them into the gloomy interior, where the air grew sharp and musty from the mulch of cow dung, lime, and ashes mounded at the base of the hives to keep them warm. The boxes sat stacked three by three, each stack an arm's length apart, octagonal in shape, connected inside but open to the air only through a single aperture at the bottom. In their hindmost side, each stack boasted shutters that concealed a better view to the interior.

Harrison unlatched one of these, whispering, "They're lessening slower than to be expected, milady, but I've little hope of a new swarm so late in the year."

She nodded. It being September, the cold would soon inhibit the bees. "August was good in respect to honey," she told Rivenham. The wax now packed and stored would prove sufficient for a half year's stock of candles and ink, with a little left over for medicinal balms and the waterproofing of fabrics to be worn in the rainy months.

Still, as she bent to peer through the little window, it delighted her to see sizable combs on each level. One could never have too much wax. She stepped back to allow Rivenham a view.

"A fortuitous strain," he murmured. "One doesn't often see so many new combs at this season."

Harrison looked uneasily toward her, silently asking if he was allowed to reply. She gave a small nod.

"Aye, but I expect we'll have but one more harvest," Harrison said. "The backmost hive be ready, and I intend to take it today. But I don't hope for aught else with it turning so cold of the morning. They're to build their stores for winter now."

Rivenham nodded. "Yet the number of drones remains considerable."

Harrison's brow furrowed. "Aye," he said cautiously. "Aye, there's a point. Perhaps two more, then, do you say?"

Nora walked to the next hive as the two men conversed in low tones behind her. Rivenham's indistinct words caused Harrison to choke down a laugh. She fought the impulse to turn back, to ask to share in the joke. But the effort left her uneasy and edgy.

One did not expect the Earl of Rivenham to trade jokes with servants. But she was not surprised to discover otherwise. The boy she had loved had been able to talk to anyone. He had shared smiles with cobblers, and drawn novel thoughts from scullery maids. Mean personages who blushed and stammered in her presence had relaxed in his.

The trick, he had explained to her once, came of having been forced into strange lands while very young. *We Catholics must look to foreigners for our learning,* he'd said with a rueful smile. *By the time I was ten, I was studying abroad. Once one learns to make excuses for bad behavior in other tongues, speaking one's own language is no challenge, no matter the subject.*

But it was more than that, of course. She had realized it even as a girl. He had a peculiar ability to remain . . . *himself* . . . no matter his audience. Sometimes he was guarded; often he made no effort to promote himself. But he never altered his basic nature to please anyone—and perhaps people sensed this in him, and found him easy to trust because of it.

She dared a look at him, his tall, lean form silhouetted in the doorway, inclining slightly to listen to the bee-master.

Bittersweet longing nearly choked her.

The boy she'd loved was not gone. He stood eight paces away, in the body of a man she must fear.

Her romanticism frightened her. She could not afford to indulge such fancies. He did not alter his nature to suit the circumstances? What nonsense! He had altered his faith, had he not?

Besides—had he been a woman, he would never have

enjoyed the privilege of being true to himself. A woman's duty lay in being true to others.

As she watched, curmudgeonly Harrison clapped a hand to his mouth to smother another laugh that would have disturbed the swarms. Rivenham gestured with his chin to invite the other man outside, so they might continue their talk at unrestrained volume.

Out they went. In the solitude, her bitterness faded, leaving her strangely flat.

There was no use in longing for what she could not have. She would never be a man. Never travel the world. Never speak freely, with laughter, to those not her equal.

She would never have him.

Or a child.

She took a long breath, then bent to examine the bees. They crawled busily over the combs, and the sight of their intent industry made her feel calmer, more settled in herself.

The nearest comb looked ready for harvesting. Thick yellowish wax capped almost every cell. Harrison had said he meant to take it today, but what better time than now? It being mid-morning, most of the bees were slumberous.

Slowly, keeping her movement smooth and steady, she inserted her hand into the hive.

One step inside the beehouse, Adrian put out a hand to halt the bee-master, who was hard on his heels.

Nora stood five paces away, the entirety of her left arm covered in bees. Her expression was blank with terror.

Harrison started to speak. "Quiet," Adrian said in a low voice. Noise would incite the bees. Smoke was what he needed. He looked around, taking care to keep his movements leisurely despite the urgency driving him. There must be kindling hereabouts—

"Are you well?"

The calmness of Nora's voice struck him like a slap. As he wheeled back, his reply froze in his mouth. What he had taken for the paralysis of panic was, in fact, perfect tranquillity. Her lifting face showed him her slight smile, growing now as she studied him.

"I would not have thought you affrighted of bees," she said.

The world seemed to shift for him then—a slight adjustment that brought her, at last, into perfect clarity. In her hand, hitherto concealed by the industry of bees, she held a frame of honeycomb.

"I am not afraid of them," he said slowly. "But I confess I usually employ smoke to daze them before I take their honey."

Behind him, the bee-master loosed a gusty sigh. "Done it again, has she?"

"Does she do it often?" Adrian asked, never removing his eyes from her.

Her smile deepened even as the beekeeper replied, "She's an interfering woman. I'll have another cup of beer."

His footsteps retreated.

"Smoke is one useful technique," she said. "But the bees are not selfish. So long as you treat them respectfully, they will gladly share their bounty." Gentle irony entered her voice. "Are you sure you're not fearful, Lord Rivenham? You clutch the door frame like a man grasping a beam in a storm."

Registering his white-knuckled grip, Adrian dropped his hands. The impulse to laugh came over him; he swallowed it for fear of upsetting the hive. *You are extraordinary,* he did not say. If few people in London had realized it, that only reflected their inadequate perception.

"I assure you it's all right," she said. "I will protect you."

The dimness of the beehouse caused her hair to blend with the shadows, but the slight tilt of her head and the sly curve of her mouth translated clearly to him. She was utterly at her ease, and taking the opportunity, with a hundred bees swarming her flesh, to tease him.

The smile that turned his lips then felt as foreign as the wonder prickling his skin. He knew her, but this sense of discovery suggested there was yet more to learn, things he could not even guess at.

"Your self-possession," he said, "could be quite terrifying."

"And yet, only now you begin to seem calm." The barest hint of laughter infected her words. "I would call that perversity, sir."

"And what would you call your own show?"

She ducked her head, hiding her expression, and he felt the loss of it with an absurd sharpness, outsized to the moment but identical to the feeling that had speared through him when he had spotted her in the hall this morning.

He did not pretend to misunderstand it. He had resolved now on his course. That resolution freed his awareness of her effect on him.

He could not admire her destructive loyalty to her brother. But it was born of the steel at her core. As a girl, she had not disguised that steel, speaking boldly, daring the world to cross her. But now that she carried it concealed, it took on a new element of power, like the hidden stiletto that could save a man's life when all else was stripped from him. Adrian had never glimpsed such ferocity of will in another woman—or man, for that matter. What man would manage to endure a history of betrayal without letting it corrode his soul? Adrian had not so managed, himself. And then, men too often mistook bravado for courage. Her courage was not wasted on display.

But what a wealth of riches she offered to those who possessed her loyalties. She put her whole self into their defense and never accepted defeat. Even if her wits saw the weakness in a cause, she would sacrifice herself for the sake of honor.

David Colville would be her death.

Softly she blew on her arm. Adrian tensed, but his concern was unfounded; a good number of bees scattered, lazily lurching into the air, milling about, some finding their way back into the hive.

Her glance looked apologetic. "It is a question of patience," she said. "One must coax them to it."

He nodded. He did not have the time to coax her. An accident of circumstances had given him a final chance to have her. That chance would expire the moment her brother reappeared.

She wet her lips to blow again. The dimpling of her lips, the quick glimpse of her tongue, turned his thoughts from cold analysis to hotter strategy.

The interlude in the apple orchard suggested one way to lure her. She was by no means indifferent to him.

It also showed that she would have to be seduced—not only into his arms, but out of her own caution.

Only a single bee now remained on her arm. He stepped forward, ignoring her retreat, and slid his fingers down the warm, soft skin exposed by the cuff of her sleeve. Her inhalation was soft, but he was listening for it—and watching, too, for the slight quirk of her mouth, the shadow at the corner of her lips that suggested she bit the inside of her cheek. Six years ago he had devoted himself to study of her, collecting her every look, her smallest habits and gestures, as miraculous clues to the great wonder that was Leonora Colville.

He still remembered all of them. These signs with which she unwittingly revealed herself, these lessons he had mastered so ardently—now they became unjust advantages that would serve him well in his effort to capture her.

He slid the bee onto his own hand, then blew it to freedom.

Her attention followed its path as it lurched through the air like a drunkard. But Adrian knew her show of interest was a pretext. She was attempting to master her reaction to his touch.

He wanted her overset. "Rather stupid creatures, aren't they?" he said to draw her eyes back to his.

"No. I find them quite—admirable, in fact."

"How so?"

She gave him a frown, as though doubting the sincerity of his interest. This hesitance was new to her, and it grated him, for it suggested an unpleasant history—one in which her youthful confidence had been eroded, gradually, by men who took no interest in her thoughts.

"Go on," he said. "Do you mean to follow Mandeville, and argue that bees show how self-interest and vice might profit the world?"

She laughed. "Oh, no, I was thinking far less philosophically. Besides, Mandeville wrongs the poor bees in his verse. They are quite Christian in their industry, don't you think? Unceasing in their duties. And yet—one cannot say their docility signifies stupidity, or any dullness of sentiment. When one of their own is threatened, they rouse in unison to defend him. Even the lowliest drone might count on his brethren's support, and I think—I think there is great virtue, great comfort, in such brotherhood."

He had meant to continue to speak lightly, to entice her into ease. But the message in her words pricked his temper. "You are no drone, Nora. And unthinking loyalty is no virtue by my account."

Her mouth flattened. She locked eyes with him for a hard second. "Do not imagine my loyalty is unthinking."

He did not pretend that she had misunderstood him. "You have weighed the costs of war, then? And the likelihood of victory as well? You have judged carefully the price of supporting your family?"

She opened her mouth, then seemed to think better of argument. "Come," she said. "Let me give this comb to Harrison."

Enough politics, he decided as he followed her out. Persuasion would not sway her. Let her believe as she liked; it would make no difference to his course. Though she did not know it yet, a private battle had begun between them. To win it, he would use every weapon at his disposal, of brain and body both. Her injured feelings, her brother's life—none of it signified if victory ensured her survival.

He would save her from David Colville's folly—no matter what it took.

11

On the path back to the manor, Nora set a quick pace. A childish impulse had driven her to remove the honeycomb. She had wanted to surprise him—to impress him, even. A foolish whim! He was too skilled in turning such displays around on a woman. When he had brushed the bee from her arm, his touch had raced along her skin like a flame, unsettling her completely.

But he would not overturn her so easily in matters concerning her family. Let him harangue her as he liked; she would not defend herself. To protest that she *had* scrutinized her family's position would be an insult to them. It required no calculations to trust in her father and brother's judgments.

And yet . . . to trust her family without question was the very definition of *unthinking* loyalty, was it not?

Her irritation sharpened, now divided neatly between Rivenham and herself. She walked faster. Why, to be near him was like to linger near a plague: one constantly risked the danger of infection.

When he started to speak, she forestalled him. "You will not trick me into doubting my family!"

"I never expected it," he replied.

She kept her eyes on their destination, the path along the lime trees at the edge of the field. It irked her that he did not sound breathless, though this pace was putting a stitch into her side.

After another stubborn second, she slowed. No use in punishing herself if it did not trouble him.

She could feel his attention focused on her like a ray of concentrated light. The cause for his amicable show this morning had come clear to her. He thought to disarm her—and then, no doubt, to persuade her to admit the secrets he had not managed to wrest from her by force.

An even darker possibility occurred to her. *You are no drone,* he had said. "You pity me!" she blurted. Mortification made her face burn. After that intimate, dreadful conversation in her bedchamber, he felt badly for her, the way he might for an orphan or a beaten dog.

"Pity, no," he said evenly. "That would be very unwise."

She dared a glance at him. "Then what?"

It emerged as a strident challenge. She realized she wanted to be convinced of the truth of his answer. Anything—contempt, hatred, disgust—*anything* was better than pity.

"Puzzlement," he said. "I am puzzled by you, Nora. The change in you in London was so profound. Now you've given me a piece of the cause, but I cannot make it fit."

They reached the lime trees. She drew to a stop to face him. The secret of six years ago had been shared, and its keeping no longer burdened her. But their conversation the other night had changed nothing else, and she would not let his company persuade her otherwise.

Now, here, she would define how it would go between them.

"I am no mystery." She took a deep, bracing breath. "And you must not address me so familiarly."

The words seemed to surprise a smile from him. "The birds might object to it?"

"*I* object to it."

He took one measured step toward her. She held her ground and hiked her chin to keep her stare steady and cold. No further intimacy must pass between them.

She could not bear the false sweetness of it.

"Do you remember," he said, "the game we used to play? 'Courage,' I believe you called it."

The change of subject disconcerted her. Courage was a silly jape, a game of dares and questions, invented by David. She had taught it to Adrian that drowsy summer, and traded dares with him that no sister ever spoke to a brother. "Children's nonsense," she said. "We have gone well beyond that now."

"We went beyond it even then." The light played over his face, shadows of leaves sliding over his green eyes like a mask, then lifting away again. "But that did not stop us from playing it very well, indeed."

"Are you . . . *flirting*?"

His lips twitched. "Yes, I very well might be. As Lord John would point out, the country demands all number of pursuits to stave off tedium."

She swallowed. "Then find another one."

"Oh, but there's no harm in games, I believe, if even children may play them." His smile deepened, a vertical crease appearing aside his sculpted lips. "So here is your test of courage, Nora: admit that you doubt your brother's cause."

Anger roughened her voice. "You have no right to ask it! I would never answer such."

"Then you are a coward," he said softly.

"I am a *Colville*. Do not think to make me forget it!"

"Could I make you?" A speculative note now flavored his voice. "Is that what you fear of me?"

"I do not fear you," she said, though as his next step closed the distance between them, the quickening of her breath suggested something very near to fear. Only, to her horror, it felt too warm and drugging to be fear. It felt like . . . excitement.

She hardened her voice in the hope that her senses would follow suit. "The great Lord Rivenham," she said mockingly. "You flatter yourself if you think I fear that name."

"And his touch?" He lifted his hand, laying a single finger against the pulse in her throat as his green eyes captured hers. "Do you fear his touch, or does your heart beat faster from a different emotion?"

She stared into his face and recognized that the slight curve of his lips signified triumph. Her pulses answered to him, not to her brain. Her heart was pounding now.

Be as ice. Be untouchable! In London it had seemed so easy to produce an appearance of disinterest. She had been able to pass by him without so much as a sidelong glance. She strove now for the numbness that had allowed it. "I admit," she said flatly, "that the brain does not govern the body as well as one might wish—else all men would be saints and hell would be empty of lechers."

He lifted a brow. "So I make you a lecher." So casually he spoke, as though the possibility intrigued him only mildly.

"I did not say that!" But, God above, he might be right. The mere press of his fingertip was collecting and concentrating all the force of her senses.

"My touch will not disturb your dreams tonight, then?"

"No. *No.*" She spoke as much to herself as him, desperate to believe these words. "For where wisdom has given us medicine, virtue gives us the will to partake. I will sleep very easily." She caught his errant hand in her own, gratified by the flash of surprise on his face. He was not the only one bold enough to press a question. "And here is *your* test of courage, Lord Rivenham: did memories of me ever trouble your sleep, or did the painted ladies of the court keep you sufficiently occupied?"

The barbed question did not seem to register the proper sting. "You are of two minds," he replied easily. "You desire me to say I never thought of you, so you may sleep tonight without the aid of medicine, safe in the throes of your anger. But you also know that the ghost of you followed me to my bed every night—and now that I've admitted it, you will wish you'd never asked."

She threw his hand away from her. His honesty felt

like a betrayal. "What are you about? *Why* must you taunt me—"

She bit back the rest of her words and whirled. But he caught her by the elbow at her second step.

Her temper broke open. She laid her hands on his chest and shoved him.

He took a graceful step backward and laughed. "Now here," he said, grinning, "is the hotheaded girl I once knew."

"The devil take you! Is it not enough that you come to hound my brother? Why must you trifle with me, too?"

"Because you are no less of interest than your brother," he said. "No drone, to do others' bidding and never think of her own aims. No drone to be ignored and expected to carry on."

"Bold words! What do you propose me to do, then? Shall I once more play the strumpet with you? Such joy it brought me!"

An inward part of her winced at these terrible words even as he visibly recoiled from them—but panic was driving her. He stood so close, and now, suddenly, it was clear what hidden intention had been directing him today. It showed plainly in his face as he recovered himself and stepped toward her.

His hands captured hers, not gently. He held them when she would have yanked free, his grip as stern as his expression.

She loosed a small cry of frustration and made her fingers into fists. He pried them open with gentle but intractable force, braiding his own fingers through them.

"Stop it!" she said. "There is no use to it!" There could *be* no use to it. How could he not understand that? Why did he torment them both?

He made no reply, still gripping her . . . waiting, it seemed. He held her there beneath the lime trees for a long moment, watching her, as though his only concern now was to see what she would do.

She stopped struggling. If he was content only to hold her hands, she would wait until he had satisfied his appetite. She returned his regard with stony disinterest, putting all her effort into ignoring the feel of his hands pressed around hers.

But as the moments passed, the sensation nagged at her. With her fingers pressed so firmly against his, the boundary between their flesh grew indistinct. His hand was large, tanned, a few golden hairs glinting on his knuckles. His skin was rough with hard use, accustomed to wrapping a sword hilt with this very surety. A nervous flutter, birthed low in her belly, shivered up her spine.

What a queer thing—that holding hands, that most innocent of lovers' pleasures, should seem strange, premonitory, fraught with veiled significance that any moment might be put into words and change . . . everything.

She bit her tongue to keep it still. Let the pain act as an antidote to these stupid fancies as well!

But the temptation rode her hard to ask what he was about. He *wanted* her to ask, no doubt. With his silence, with his steady, solemn gaze, he was wooing her into curiosity that she could ill afford.

His thumb made a slow stroke across her knuckles.

"Listen to me," he murmured, his voice low and gentle as a song. "I know I have caused you suffering. How may I atone for it?"

There was a trick at court among women, a wicked little laugh that communicated every shade of scorn. But she had never been skilled in it. Her laugh now sounded more like a sob. "You cannot."

He nodded once. "How, then, may I persuade you to let me try?"

Oh, God. She pressed her lips together and shook her head. This was . . . inconceivable. Had an angel appeared, that night Rivenham had arrived in her house, to predict that the mighty earl would soon beg her to let him make amends, she would have called the creature a minion of Beelzebub.

"You said we must coexist peaceably," he continued. "I agree. Instruct me how."

"That was a lie," she said, her voice choked. "I meant to trick you to my table. You know this!"

"Truths sometimes appear in unbidden forms. I would make no strumpet of you, Leonora, but I would love you again, if you would have me."

Her astonishment seemed to take her out of her body. For a long moment, every inch of her skin prickling, she gaped at him.

"What . . . What trick is this?"

"No trick."

He was lying. This seduction was a stratagem. But his face looked so serious . . . "If not a trick, then perfect madness," she whispered. "You do not know me now. Why should you care for me?"

"I think it better said that you do not know yourself." Once again his thumbs made their persuasive stroke. "You spent those years in London as a stranger—to yourself, I think, as much as me. What if it had gone differently? What if I had shown more care for you? What if I had contented myself only with caresses . . ."

He leaned forward and placed his lips to her throat.

She gasped. His mouth was hot, soft. Her eyes closed of their own will. The smell of his skin, and crushed grass and green leaves . . .

His hands directed her own behind her back; he held her wrists at the base of her spine as his lips captured her ear, suckling the tender lobe.

"Adrian," she whispered. The darkness behind her eyes was dizzying. She opened them to stare into the verdant canopy of the lime tree, the bright pieces of sky that showed through. "We *cannot*. Simply because I was honest with you, two nights ago . . ."

"You have said the past is done." The words came softly into her ear. "Yet this desire never was. It lived even in the distance between us. When you passed me in London, your eyes downcast . . . you felt it then, and so did I. I did not require even to turn to know that you were near. But now, here, that distance is gone. It, too, is in the past. Who is to stop us now, Nora? What can touch us here?"

His mouth tracked downward, to the join of her throat and shoulder, while his fingers whispered down her spine, light blessings, melting pleasure. She fought to breathe. Such touches seemed innocent, but she knew where they led. The liquid heat pooling in her loins had no business with chaste kisses. "There is also the future," she said. "The future, and my brother's return."

His fingers stilled for a moment, then rubbed a leisurely circle on the small of her back. "If I told you now that my heart knew no greater desire than to remove you from this bind, would you believe me?"

The speech left her puzzled beyond words. She turned to look into his face and his mouth opened on hers.

Alchemy. Their lips, pressed together, crushed reason.

Some women would never know a touch like this. They would never know what they deserved.

But she knew. *Only the present,* he'd said, and like a spell, the words repeated themselves in her mind, lulling her into quiescence as his mouth took hers. Yes, she would let him kiss her. But she would do nothing to encourage him. She would wait until he was through. She would fix this moment in her mind as a guide in the years to come: the sort of pleasure she deserved from a man.

His hand smoothed up her back again, the track of his nails light but distinct. The sensation drew a shiver from her, the bliss a scratched cat must feel; she wanted to push against him, to rub into him to encourage him to scratch her again. His lips moved her own apart; his tongue touched hers and another honeyed shock rolled through her. Her hands, free now, rose to wind through his soft hair, holding him closer to her as he tasted her deeply.

She had thought of seducing him. In a cooler moment, the prospect had merited consideration—not for her sake but for David's. That calculation could be trusted, could it not? To trust it in retrospect would mean that she did not accept this pleasure recklessly, without thought.

She stepped into him, giving him her tongue, urging him to plunder her. Not for herself, but for David she kissed him; the hot sweetness of his body against hers had nothing to do with it. How much safer for her brother to have this man intent on ravishing her rather than prying secrets from her brain. Was there not even a biblical precedent for it? Esther, that most virtuous queen, had seduced a king to save her people.

His long fingers framed her face. Together they sank to the soft earth. She pushed his fustian coat off his shoulders, palming the strength of his upper arms, the bulge of muscle that flexed as though at her command. It was not enough. She reached for his waistcoat, yanking free the fastenings, and then tugged his soft wool shirt from his breeches. His sharp breath gave her a heady feeling, voluptuous triumph; beneath the hem of his shirt she discovered the hot skin of his abdomen, rippling planes of muscle distinct beneath her fingertips.

What risk was there? Her body had proved, after so many years of a barren bed, that there would be no consequences to lying with a man. And did she not deserve such pleasure, just once more? Only once . . . and for her family's sake, not her own.

She pulled the shirt over his head.

The sight of his bare upper body shocked her. It did not match her memories. Where his belly had once been smooth and hairless, solid shelves of muscle now strapped him, dividing his abdomen into striated ridges around the narrow trail of hair that led into his breeches.

An ugly scar across his shoulder spoke of violence.

Sobriety felt unpleasant and cold. What was she doing? Six years—

He reached for her, those bands of muscle rippling as he moved. With his thumb he nudged up her chin, and another shock moved through her as she met his eyes, identical to those of the boy she had loved. But this was no boy. His body testified to a history unfamiliar to her.

Whatever lessons it had taught him, he showed no hesitance or uncertainty to match her own. He cupped her nape and drew her mouth to his while his free hand trailed down her body, startling each inch of flesh it passed: her shoulders, her ribs, her hips. In turn, reminded of their due, they awakened; her very skin seemed to tighten and warm, flush with forgotten demands. He palmed her buttocks and pulled her closer yet, so her breasts crushed into his chest.

Against her belly she felt his erection. As a girl, the sensation had embarrassed her . . . and then excited her. She pulled away the slightest inch and placed her hand over him, shaping his length. His groan parted their mouths, and then his teeth lightly closed on her throat. She tilted her head to allow him better access, then gasped when he took her by the arms and pulled her over him as he reclined. His pale hair spilled over the green grass like strands of sunlight. As he looked up at her, he smiled.

No shame in that smile. No doubt. Only joy.

The past lay open between them, emptied of secrets. With a trembling finger she traced the curve of his lips.

He caught her hips in his hands and turned her onto her back, pinning her to the grass with his body. A sound escaped her, a breathy gasp he captured with his mouth as he rolled his hips against her. Then he slid down her body, pulling down her neckline and putting his mouth to her breast.

A moan escaped her. That wild, reckless girl she had once been returned to her now, possessing her body, driving out every ounce of hard-won wisdom, every shred of painfully gained restraint. She remembered now how it should be: the ferocity of his attentions; his hands and lips and tongue, the way he used his entire body to seduce her, angling himself so his knee came against the softness between her thighs, coaxing her to ride him, to buck and flex beneath him as he suckled her.

She made some noise and he lifted his head to look into her eyes. His shoulders blocked out the sun, but all around him the sky glowed lividly blue. For the space of a heartbeat, the intensity of his expression frightened her. He looked at her as though he would devour her—as though nothing she could say or do would sway him from the intention so clear in his hungry face.

But then he took a long, audible breath, and lifted his hand to cup her cheek. His eyes followed his fingertips as they traced her brow, skating down to her cheekbone, pausing there. His lips parted as though to speak, but he did not; after a moment, he lowered his face to hers, and softly he kissed her.

His weight shifted off her. He supported himself on one elbow as he sipped from her mouth. His hand slipped down her body. Cool air brushed over her calf, her knee . . .

His hot palm stroked up her thigh. Higher and higher yet it stroked before retreating. She instinctively understood the tease, and it made her twist and grow desperate again. She tried to turn into him, but the combined pressures of his palm against her thigh and his lips against hers held her in place. Her grasping fingers quested down his body, over the bumping slope of his ribs, the hard muscle banding his waist. She broke free of his mouth to cover his throat in kisses, begging silently for his hand to find its destination. She licked the bare length of his throat and knew triumph when he hissed.

His hand slipped up to cover her, pressing firmly over her most tender flesh, stroking. She turned her face into his throat, gasping as sensation built. Here was what she had forgotten: true desire. Unbearable, exquisite. No room for fear or conscience. Wanting, *needing*, to feel his mastery: be devoured, laid bare, filled, left no say in it. And yet at the same time hungering for more—hungering to wrap herself around him and hold him there forever; to sink her teeth into him and grip him when he cried out.

Her release came without warning—a violent shuddering, a convulsion so painfully sweet that tears pricked her eyes. She sobbed out a breath. So long, so long it had been . . .

As the pleasure ebbed, she forced her eyes open and looked upon a world that was shockingly unchanged.

The birds, after another moment, resumed their song.

She felt transparent, light-filled. Not fragile but newly alive. She had wagered so much for this feeling as a girl, and the courage it had taken to do so now seemed to return to her as well. She pushed herself up by her elbow and looked into his face.

He watched her with a narrow, grim focus.

As she frowned, his expression changed. He smiled, taking her face in his broad hand as he leaned down to kiss her.

His kiss seemed somehow deliberate, like a tool of distraction. Her euphoria shifted, suddenly and jarringly, to unease. The leisurely play of his lips suggested that he was not done with her by any measure. He came over her, deepening the kiss, his weight settling again between her thighs, and her body responded even as her foreboding strengthened.

There was an instrumental quality to the press of his hips against hers. He meant now to satisfy himself. And it would not be for David if she permitted him to do so.

The realization lashed through her: this quickening within her was purely carnal, self-interested. She was no Queen Esther; she did not control this desire. Her thighs parted further to accommodate the weight of Adrian's body, and the throb between her legs urged her to tilt her hips against him. The feel of him unraveled her inborn restraint.

She would not be the seducer now, but the seduced. *She* would be the one softened by this. *She* would be the one destroyed.

She ripped her mouth from his. "Wait," she gasped. "I can't."

He stilled above her. His thumb stroked her lower lip as he dipped his head to catch her gaze. "Explain to me why."

She took a long breath for strength, then squirmed out from under his touch.

He made no move to stop her. Sitting back on his heels, he waited, watchful.

To look at him, so handsome in the sunlight, full of an animal strength he would never use against her in these matters, hurt her very heart. She pushed a hand over her face. Reasons twisted in her throat, finding no good words to carry them. She could hardly confess that she feared her desire for him would twist her judgment and corrupt her resolve. That would be all but an invitation to him, who had no love for David.

"This is unwise," she said. "I need not say the reasons. I have spoken them before."

"Unwise, yes." He paused. "But inevitable, I think."

Inevitable? She did not like that notion. This current between them had once seemed born of a perfect match between souls. That it had survived so many years' separation might indicate that it was inborn: the product of the stars' configuration at their respective births. But that did not make them hostage to its magnetism. "We are not animals," she said. "We can govern our appetites."

For a moment longer he held her gaze, thoughts shifting behind his eyes that she could not decipher. And then, in a sudden shift of mood, he gave her a wicked, slanted smile. "And so too may we choose to indulge them." He leaned forward to brush his lips over hers, retreating again too quickly for her to protest. "My lady's appetites have been too long denied, and I fear it cannot be good for her health: allow me to satisfy them again."

A startled laugh escaped her. How unexpected, how strangely wonderful, to be the object of playful seduction. How long had it been since she had been wooed?

But when he moved toward her, she made a retreat that was foiled by the interference of her skirts. "No," she said. "Adrian—" His hand on her shoulder held her in place while his mouth stopped her protest. His aggressive kiss did not permit refusal; his tongue came deep inside her mouth as he pressed into her with his full weight.

Ah, God, it would be so sweet to lie with him; to surrender her cares and worries and know only the pleasures of the flesh. But her conscience was awake now. Even as she kissed him, it insisted on calculations, and marshaled her fear to aid its cause.

She turned her head aside, gasping. "Stop! You will not seduce me into betraying my brother!"

"Your brother," he said. His sharp bark of laughter brought her face around. Disbelief showed in the twist of his mouth. "This has *naught* to do with your brother, Nora. This is you and I here, and no one else."

She dug her hand into the cool grass, the soil still moist from recent rains. Had he truly lost track of the circumstances when he had laid her down here?

If only for a moment, had he looked on her not as the sister of his enemy, not as a tool for the advancement of his aims, but simply as . . . a woman?

A woman he desired.

God above, but he was well worth desiring. Fashioned with the height and strength and fairness of an angel, with the devil's talent resident in his lips and fingers, he could make a woman's breath stop to look on him.

She bit the inside of her cheek. *Concentrate.* She ripped up a handful of grass, scattering it. "Do not separate our causes. My brother and I are one and the same."

He laughed again, but it was an easier sound now. "By God, I say you are not. For I never tumbled your brother in the grass, and I think you will find he confirms it."

The urge to smile back at him amazed her. These were weighty matters; why did she suddenly feel so light?

"Only two days ago you locked me in a room to interrogate me," she pointed out. "Why should I trust your intentions?"

"Because I give you my word," he said. "On all I hold dear, I swear to you that my intentions here are in every way ignoble: they have nothing to do with the welfare of the kingdom or with the vows I swore in service to the king." He rolled onto his knees and came closer to her, planting one hand by hers, leaning forward so their faces nearly touched. "Seducing you is its own reward," he murmured.

Her face burned. He looked at her as though she were Venus rising from the waves—as though she did, indeed, have the power to make a man forget country and kingdom. God save her; what woman could resist such a lure?

But she caught herself even as she canted toward him. She was wise enough, at least, to know her weakness. It looked her in the eye now, blond and beautiful. "I cannot do this," she said quietly. "I'm sorry."

A line appeared between his brows. He looked away, over her shoulder.

She bit her lip against the urge to speak further. The best thing now was to put distance between them. She began to scoot backward, but just as quickly, he grabbed her arm.

"Wait," he said, still looking over her head.

"Loose me. I am resolved."

Suddenly he was on his feet, dragging her up as well, while his free hand went to the place where, of a custom, he wore his sword.

That single movement made her blood turn to ice. She wheeled to look in the direction that had caught his attention, but he did not allow her leisure; swearing, he pulled her toward the trees, lifting her bodily when she stumbled.

His intensity infected her; fear thumped through her blood as he drew her into the shadows of the grove. Behind the shelter of a broad trunk, he paused to withdraw a blade from his boot. The dagger was plain but well kept, the tip wickedly curved. "Run, if I instruct you," he said in a low voice.

"But—"

"Listen," he said.

And she heard it.

She turned with him to look south.

A party of riders was coming over the crest of the hill, making haste toward Hodderby.

They carried the Colville colors.

"No," she whispered.

David.

12

⁓

"I imagine I gave you a good start," said Cosmo Colville cheerfully as he took the seat opposite Nora in the parlor. From the cup in his hand came the strong reek of port. "Never dreamed my letter would go awry. I'd written you of my visit a fortnight ago."

"The surprise was a happy one." Nora kept her eyes on the needle as she drew it through the embroidery hoop on her lap. No doubt his appearance had cost her ten years of her life; those minutes she'd stood trembling in the wood, certain she was about to witness bloodshed, unable yet to make out the face of the man leading the riders, had seemed to last for centuries. She had entertained a vivid, nightmarish vision of David riding down on Adrian, sword drawn.

Worse, with the number of riders on the horizon, and Adrian unarmed, her fear had not been for David.

God! What madness possessed her? Why had she thought it safe to lie down with him? How had she forgotten the danger of his caresses? It went far beyond the question of conceiving a bastard. Passion was a thief that could steal away her heart. She had surrendered it to him once and paid a terrible price for it. Was she such a fool that she would court that punishment again?

It had not been David riding down that hill. But one day very soon, it would be. If she were *fortunate*, Lord Rivenham once again would meet this sight without so much as a blade to defend himself.

"You are quiet," Cosmo remarked. "No doubt it has been difficult, entertaining the king's men."

It was far too easy. Adrian's company was like music, and she had not the strength to close her ears.

"Not so difficult," she said. "But there is no joy like the company of one's blood." Her loyalties were decided for her. Why could she not hew to them gladly? Did she wish her brother dead?

No?

Then cease to play the jezebel!

Cosmo showed her a gleaming smile as he lifted his glass to her. "Very sweetly put, cousin."

She forced an answering smile. It puzzled her that Adrian had welcomed her cousin with all appearance of goodwill. Cosmo's three men-at-arms—a small number, admittedly—now gamed in the great hall with Adrian's soldiers, as friendly as natural confederates. It made no sense that Adrian had allowed this . . . unless he knew there was naught to fear from Cosmo's men. Yet why should he think so? Cosmo's loyalties ought—she had *believed* them—to lie with David.

"You come from London," she said casually, spearing the cambric once more. She was no great hand with embroidery, but it proved a useful occupation when one's nerves might otherwise cause one's hands to shake. "How fare our friends in town?" *And are your friends the same as ours?* she added silently. Had Cosmo only come to call on his cousin? Or—she had no choice but to consider it—had he come to give intelligence to the Earl of Rivenham?

"Town is miserable," said Cosmo. "Rain and more rain, until even the shit melts and runs like water." He took a long draft of his drink. When he lowered his cup, his pleasant expression evinced no sign of the turmoil that surely must attend a man who conspired against his family.

But Cosmo had always been difficult to read. Now in his mid-forties, he retained the youthful air of insouciance, the lightness of spirit, that had endeared him to her as a child. Although her first cousin, he had always seemed to her more of an uncle—the kind of favored elder who appeared, once in a rare while, to play tricks with a coin, or deliver a doll fresh from France.

Even now that she was a woman, and encouraged by her brother to see him in a more husbandly light, she felt the child's urge to look to him for wonders and tricks. It unsettled her all the more, then, to see his regard rest upon her now with the narrow, speculative flavor of a man considering a potential bedmate.

She broke the look to examine her needlepoint. He was not unattractive; his strong build, his lean waist and deep blue eyes, would capture any number of women's hearts. She wished he would look to them, then, and reserve for her only a platonic affection.

I will not marry this man, David.

Her grip tightened around the needle. How would she defend her refusal? How would she explain that David's own persecutor had charmed her flesh into rebellion?

Ah, God, his touch set her alight. If she concentrated, it seemed that she could still feel the pleasure rolling through her like honey . . .

"I would fain have brought a present," Cosmo said. "It leaves me loath to break our tradition. But I fear my time in the capital was too brief to allow for such pleasures."

I am no longer a child in want of presents, she thought, but did not say. It too plainly invited a saucy rebuttal. "What business had you there, if I may ask?"

"Why, what but commerce," he said, brushing a slim hand over the pigeon's wing curls of his periwig. "And, of course, a host of tedious politicking. Our new king hails from a coal-rich region; he wished to hear of our mines in the north, and what methods we may suggest for Hanover's. But forgive me; such details are too cloddish for a lady."

Delicately she tested his allegiances. "Is our new king's main concern for Hanover, then? One might wish he cared foremost for the improvement of England."

"One might wish," Cosmo agreed, settling back into the leather easy chair. He had changed costume since his arrival, and sported a rich suit of yellow satin fringed with brown lace. It was uncommonly luxurious for him.

She imagined that he had worn this same suit when treating with the king.

She did not like that he had chosen it for his first supper in her house. It bespoke some intention to impress her.

"You agree, then?" she asked. "You believe his loyalties remain in Hanover?"

His teeth flashed again, though she would not have called it a smile: it looked too much like a dog's baring of fangs. "My dear coz, what would you have of me? Shall I read the mind of our king? I can tell you that he showed a great interest in my holdings, and that his offer of friendship, if I do not flatter myself, seemed heartfelt. Now, instruct me on Rivenham's presence here. He says quite plainly that he waits for my cousin's appearance. Has David aught to fear from him?"

Her needle fell still. She stared at the lopsided violet flower that was all she had to show for this long, miserable hour. Did Cosmo truly not know David's business? Or was his show of ignorance designed to ferret out whether *she* was privy to David's activities, in which case, he might then speak openly?

"I should think," she said carefully, "that there must always be cause for concern where a king has taken interest."

"Ah. Yes." He set his cup down on the small table beside his chair. "And not just the king but the king's man." Nodding at his own words, he rotated the cup, causing it to scrape. No doubt he intended to strike a thoughtful appearance, it never occurring to him, or indeed to any man, that what they scraped, a woman would have to polish later. "I have heard the Earl of Rivenham likened to nightshade," he said. "He never visits a place without laying roots that poison the host."

His glance seemed sly somehow. She sat straighter. Cosmo did not know what had passed six years ago. Her father and brother never would have told him. Whence this look, then? "Lord Rivenham's presence alarms you?"

"Alarm?" Cosmo blinked. "Perhaps the wrong choice of words, coz. Lord Rivenham's presence commands my . . . respect, better say. There are those who dislike having to answer to a turncoat papist—great men, who had the power to ensure that Rivenham's fate matched your father's. But they underestimated him, you see. He did not waste his time kissing her majesty's skirts, as did your lord father. Instead he played the suitor between Anne and her cousin George. Now, as the new king dotes on him, he prospers. Yet his enemies never diminish. I will respect such a man, undoubtedly . . . but not love him, I think. And indeed, Rivenham is far better at inspiring hatred. I assure you, his enemies still nurse their grudges most keenly."

She searched Cosmo's face. This speech did not paint any clear sense of his own allegiances. But such ambiguity must be a choice in itself—a significant one.

"You mean to walk the middle ground." The road of the coward who would refuse to commit himself until he saw which way victory lay. "You will take no side in these great matters upon us."

He let go of his cup and folded his hands together in his lap, a neat, prim posture that annoyed her. "If I were to exercise such restraint, you would rightly be glad of it. It would advance your welfare, too."

She stabbed the needle into the cloth and cast it aside. "I cannot imagine how my welfare would be concerned in it." No decision had been reached regarding a marriage between them. "Your presumption—"

"Be grateful for it." His voice was suddenly cold. "You sit in a vipers' nest, Lady Towe, and the vipers are stirring. A fortnight ago, the Earl of Mar raised the Jacobite standard at Kirkmichael. The Duke of Argyll has taken command of the army. It will be war in the north, and these Scottish affairs have a way of spilling into Lancashire. One wrong step and your guests will bite you to death. You are, after all, your father's daughter."

She sat frozen for a moment. "It has begun, then."

"Yes." He retrieved his glass. "I cannot say if Lord Rivenham knows it yet. The news of Kirkmichael was fresh yet in London." He took a long drink. "Hark, it seems I did bring you a present after all: *wisdom*. If you wish to survive, you must trust in me. We leave this place tomorrow, together."

Leave? Abandon Hodderby? "Cousin, my brother himself gave me the care and keeping of this estate—"

"Plans have changed," he said. "That is what I am come to inform you."

Suddenly she could not abide the smugness of yet another man, instructing her to cede her will and free thinking to him for her own protection. She rose. "I will not say it again, sir: I am *none* of your concern. Nor is Hodderby!"

He looked up, mild surprise in his face. "But of course you are. You are my betrothed."

For a moment she felt sure she had misheard him. His arrogance amazed her. "I am not and will never be." Had any doubt remained, his manner here would have ended it!

He came to his feet, frowning. "Can it be that your brother did not tell you? My lady, we finalized the contract before his departure."

"No." David would never have taken such a step without consulting her. He could not dispose her without her consent. "I have signed no contract!"

He shook his head, looking mystified. "A small formality—one your brother gave me to believe you would be eager to remedy!"

Her hand closed on the back of her chair as the floor seemed to shift beneath her. This feeling of betrayal was too sharp to compass in words.

"Listen here," he said more gently. "This is all of a plan, cousin. As Hodderby was never entailed, it will make your brother's marriage gift to us. Should his fate resemble your father's, should his . . . *adventures* go awry, then we, you and I, will wed directly. Between the two of us, we will keep these estates in the family. *That* is the central concern, is it not? *That* is the cause of our marriage."

His reply had the ring of truth. Yet if Cosmo's claims were true, then David had fixed her marriage with no care for her consent. The notion swam through her like a toxin, turning her stomach.

She tried to reason with her growing panic. If David had done this, it was to safeguard Hodderby. Of that, she *must* approve.

But must *she* be the sacrifice that safeguarded it?

Cosmo misread her face. Stepping toward her, he said, "Do not misunderstand me. You know my love for your brother. Can you doubt it? He and I hatched this plan together—should it come to the worst."

Some strangled noise escaped her. It stopped him dead. Putting his hands behind his back, he rocked on his heels, eyeing her as though at any moment he expected her to scream or collapse.

She turned away from his prying eyes, staring blindly at the china cabinet that sat in the corner. How had David committed her without consulting her? What had possessed him?

Her cousin's voice came from behind her, tentative. "The journey left me famished for a proper meal."

If she opened her mouth to reply she would shriek like a madwoman. She had given David every support! She had suffered against her will his journey to France. She had let him persuade her to countenance the gunpowder, though even now it sat like death beneath her feet, ripe to kill them all. Not a single cause had she given him to keep these plans from her.

Was she to be sorted and disposed with the same careless handling as his guns?

"Cousin." Cosmo's voice was brusquer now. "I am hungry. You would do well to call Lord Rivenham and Lord John to the table."

Bile churned in her stomach. Already, she thought, he led her like a husband.

*   *   *

Adrian had called his men to gather in the great hall, around a long, scarred table where Colvilles had feasted when Hodderby was yet a hunting lodge. The atmosphere was primitive; rough-hewn stone buttresses supported a ceiling lost in darkness far overhead, and torches fixed in recesses spilled a violent light across the uneven flagstones.

This chamber had witnessed the strategizing of war parties in times when bloodshed had been the mark of manhood. It was not a room for hesitation or scruples, and his mood allowed for none. He felt ablaze, as though victory was already his.

He fully expected her anger once she discovered the whole of it. But by then, she would have no say in its outcome. Hatred was the privilege of the living, whose minds could be changed. And he would change hers. Eventually she would understand that he'd had no choice in it. Even in this civilized age, the games of kings did not allow mercy for women who aided treason. She would be made to see how Adrian's actions had spared her from sharing her brother's fate.

Around the table, his men took their seats restlessly, drumming fingers and tapping feet. Over the past five years, he had enlisted each of them precisely for the qualities that made these past few days such a trial. A soft bed, a warm fire, regular meals—had these men craved such, they might have followed their fathers' footsteps, becoming cobblers or craftsmen, wherrymen or tailors. But to a man, they had rebelled at their families' legacies.

His enemies sneered at his followers' motley genealogies. It did not bother Adrian. He understood the advantage of tradesmen's sons turned soldiers, having experienced firsthand what unique zeal was born of being told, again and again, that one's nature made one unfit for one's appetites.

Lord John entered last, sullenly, his right eye swollen to a slit. He took a seat slightly apart from the other men. For all that his father had spoiled him with indulgences, he had been born with a backbone; he took care to fix Adrian with a defiant look as he whipped out his knife—though his courage then failed him, for after a moment's hesitation, he put himself to trimming his nails.

Braddock caught Adrian's eye and loosed a speaking snort.

Adrian allowed himself a smile. "Grooming," he said. "You would do well to master the concept."

Braddock, understanding him perfectly, ran a hand over his scraggly beard and chuckled.

Without further preamble, Adrian lifted the letter he'd received on his return to the manse this afternoon. "Lord Mar has raised the Jacobite banner at Kirkmichael," he said.

Silence fell.

"He leads a progress to gather recruits. Parliament has authorized additional troops to be mustered to Fort William to answer him. The Duke of Argyll has taken the command."

Mutters rose from his men. "Action?" Henslow inquired.

"As of yet, very little," Adrian said. "A failed attempt to seize Edinburgh Castle."

Braddock whistled. "Seize the castle? There's hardihood."

Peters, short and deceptively slim, guffawed over his cup. "Or lunatic stupidity."

"The latter," Adrian said. "The castle guards were waiting—forewarned by the wife of a conspirator's brother, who overheard his plans. The rebels were killed."

Snickers all around, building into guffaws. It suited these men's notions of the rebels to imagine them undone by a gossiping housewife. Only Lord John, at the far end of the table, retained his composure. Laying down his knife, he looked across the company with open contempt.

Adrian kept an eye on him while waiting for the laughter to subside. "A pretty picture, no doubt," he said as his men quieted. "But if four men died every time a housewife gossiped, the toll would quickly steepen. Our job is to end the matter, and let the women turn back to their needlework."

Nods traveled the table.

"I know that your patience has been sorely tested," he went on. "Counting sheep and walking the lines is no fit test of your mettle. You will notice two men missing from your ranks: Lovatt and Dutton stand guard in the bailey, where I have quartered Cosmo Colville's men-at-arms. His visit interests me. It suggests some intent concerning his cousin, David."

Anticipation thickened the air. Someone scuffed his boot against the stone floor. Henslow coughed. But every man's eyes rested rapt upon him, and no one spoke now.

"David Colville must be captured alive," Adrian said. He gave them a moment to absorb this, to adjust their expectations. "But as his arrival draws near, I find I have no care for the condition in which you deliver him."

Comprehension was quick to develop in their faces. Henslow smiled. Braddock nodded. Lord John, scowling, leaned forward as if to object. He alone knew the precise terms of their instructions: to deliver David Colville in sound health to London for interrogation and trial.

But Adrian had decided to adjust those orders. He himself would discover what answers might be pried by pain from David Colville's lips. He, not some stranger in London, would learn first whether any of these answers happened to touch on Lady Towe. And if they did . . . why, he would adjust them as well.

As for the explanation for his delay in delivering Colville to London, that would be simple: he planned to ensure that David Colville's health would be ailing upon his capture. The man would require time at Hodderby to recover from his wounds.

"Indeed," Adrian continued, "I encourage you, in delivering him to me, to abandon your natural restraint."

That inspired a grim round of laughter. None of these men had been chosen for a merciful disposition.

"And how, pray tell, may we be so certain that he will come to Hodderby at all?"

Lord John's surly tone drew several sharp glances.

"His men operate in this area," said Adrian. "Did you not know?"

A snort came from Henslow's direction. The boy's good eye narrowed. "Oh? I suppose you have some proof?"

With a sharp curse, Braddock made to rise. Adrian laid a hand on his shoulder to forestall him.

"Lord John asks a fair question," he said, "and is owed a fair reply. Yes. I have proof."

When the following silence made it obvious that he did not intend to share this proof, Lord John colored. Adrian could see the wheels of his mind turning, directing him back to the night he had passed unconscious—a night that might well have counted as proof, had the cause of it not been dismissed as spoiled food.

"I see," the boy said in an ugly voice. "So, his men are hereabouts. His cousin. And his lady sister, of course." He took up his knife again, standing it by its point to give it a spin. "A pity my lord Rivenham forbids others to question her. I believe my knife could make her sing quite sweetly." He glanced around the table, seeking support for this proposition.

The boy was damnably green. His own manner had alienated those who otherwise might have agreed with him.

Adrian waited for Lord John's attention to return to him. Then, very deliberately, he smiled. "Hark, sirs: this man appears to nurse some doubt regarding my interrogation."

"Only that I do wonder," Lord John said sharply, "whether it was an interrogation, or something more luxurious. It was in her bedchamber that you . . . *spoke* with her, was it not?"

Braddock slammed his palm onto the table. "Look here, *boy*—"

Lord John exploded to his feet. "I am not your *boy*!"

"Indeed," Adrian said, "do not provoke him. Can you not see Lord John's bruises? A difficult day it has been for him. Let us indulge him, then; let us hear what devices his imagination has wrought."

"If nothing else, it will entertain," muttered Peters.

Lord John slammed his dagger into the tabletop. The steel shuddered, pinging. "I will not be mocked! I will be addressed with respect, as befits my station!"

"But by all means," Adrian said. "Sirs, show Lord John the respect he is due."

As if on cue, the men loosed their choked-back laughter.

Lord John stood gawping for the space of a breath; then he snatched up his dagger and spun on his heel. His stalking exit only heightened the mirth around the table.

Braddock leaned toward Adrian. "Shall I follow?" he asked in an undertone.

Adrian nodded. "But lift not a hand," he said. "For all that he's a fool, he's his father's fool, and Barstow requires his return in one piece."

A blind man would have known that something ailed their hostess. Her distress seemed to consume the available air in the room. Against the backdrop of Indian curtains of scarlet and gold, she sat silently, her supper plate untouched, her face pale. Here was the mask Adrian remembered from London: the brave blankness of a tragic heroine.

He did not think it was their interlude in the meadow

that accounted for her gloom. Or perhaps he indulged a weakness by telling himself the cause must be otherwise. Having touched her again—having felt the beauty of her willing flesh, and the triumph of watching her defenses tremble and yield to him—he could not imagine a force on earth that might stop him from having her again.

But her distress might suffice. To his own displeasure, he could not detach himself from his awareness of it, though it would have done him better to focus solely on her cousin, whose idle remarks might prove revealing if carefully attended. Concern was a mistake. Compassion for her would not serve his aims. Far wiser to use her weaknesses against her than to wish to protect her from them.

He could not afford to protect her from them. Loyalty, duty, courage—these were what he must exploit in her.

Could Cosmo Colville be the cause of her distress? Perhaps Adrian had surmised incorrectly, and the man had brought news not of her brother's approach, but of some other misfortune.

He watched them for clues: she, wooden-faced, and Colville, ruddy and jolly, a man with no cares . . . or a man pretending with great effort that he had none. He drank deeply, laughed loudly, and traded increasingly vulgar quips with Lord John, who had begun the meal in sullen silence but had been steadily drowning his reserve in glass upon glass of canary.

"But there is no place sweeter than home, surely," Cosmo was saying to the boy. "No matter the wonders of town life."

"You Colvilles must have dirt in your very blood," the boy replied. "I cannot fathom any comparison that would find London lacking! It would take a great want of taste."

Colville seemed peculiarly deaf to the boy's jibing. With a grin, he turned toward Nora. "What say you, my lady? Have we dirt in our blood, or will you support my contention that Askham Manor would awe even the brightest young spark?"

Her attention remained fixed on her plate. "I could not argue it either way. After all, I have never been to Askham."

The footman was ready to refill Adrian's glass. He covered it with his hand. Some tension that he did not understand infused this exchange, and he required all his senses for it.

"Ah, true enough," Colville said, his gaze lingering on his cousin with something more complex than affection. "I had forgotten. Well, I promise you it will not disappoint—though I suppose that even Askham will profit from your gentle ministrations."

The implication slammed into Adrian as a hammer might. Only as a wife would it make sense for Nora to administer her cousin's household.

Nora's expression betrayed no surprise at Cosmo's remark. Evidently she had kept more secrets from Adrian than those concerning her brother.

She had kept this secret even as he pleasured her in the meadow today.

He sat back, releasing a harsh breath. One pointed glance brought Braddock from the corner, where he had been attempting to play footman.

"Fetch your late-come guest from the high road," Adrian told him quietly. "Install him in my rooms and keep him in wine."

With a nod, Braddock slipped out.

Lord John was asking the obvious question. "Is there to be a happy event, then?"

"I am the most fortunate man alive," Colville affirmed. He reached out to take his cousin's hand and she shifted subtly away.

If Colville noticed this rebuff, he gave no sign of it. "The betrothal contact has been drawn," he continued. "Only the date remains to be determined." He turned to Adrian. "In fact, my lord, we touch on the true cause of my visit now. I think you will agree that in these uncertain times, and with the nature of the disagreeable task upon you, Hodderby is no fit place for the marchioness. I mean to take her to my estates, where she will shelter among family and friends."

This news did not surprise Adrian. Should David Colville wish to retake Hodderby, it would profit him to have his sister removed from the premises. Otherwise she would prove a worry in combat.

Adrian considered his choices. The easiest would serve. "By all means," he said. "The marchioness must not be inconvenienced by these matters."

Nora stiffened. He glanced into her eyes and found them wide and startled. The next moment her lashes fell, and all that remained to guide him was the color blooming in her cheeks.

What this flush betokened, he could not decide. Had

she expected him to oppose her cousin? Or to accuse her, before the company, of behavior ill becoming a woman promised in marriage?

If so, she overestimated his care for propriety. He would have put his hands on her today had she been engaged to marry a king. Her misunderstanding of him, however, was all to his advantage.

"We will leave at once, then," said Cosmo. "We cannot wish to inconvenience you. Your hospitality has been generous."

"*My* hospitality." Nora spoke coldly. "Hodderby is not Lord Rivenham's estate."

Colville mustered a thin smile. "Indeed, indeed."

Hodderby would be no one's estate but the crown's, once David Colville was done. The family had been unusually fortunate to retain a slice of their ancestral estates when Lord Hexton had been impeached. They would not be so fortunate again.

Nevertheless, Hodderby would remain hers. Adrian would make sure of it.

"But you must stay for a few days," he said to Colville, investing his words with congenial invitation. "Recuperate from your long journey."

"Most kind," Colville said, "but I believe one night will suffice." Beside him, the bride gave a telling jerk: she had not known of this plan for rapid departure. "Your trunks can follow us," he added to her, as though her concern were merely for her wardrobe. "You understand: with the news from Scotland, we cannot trust the roads to remain quiet for long."

This haste was intriguing. It suggested that David Colville lingered somewhere very nearby, biding his time until his sister could be cleared of the keep.

Adrian did not bother to repress his smile. *Tonight.* His instincts had never spoken more loudly. *It is tonight, or never.*

He sensed Nora's eyes on him. Catching her look, he lifted his glass to her.

Some inscrutable emotion crossed her face. She looked into her own cup, but did not raise it in reply.

Unfazed, Adrian turned his glass toward Colville. "A toast, then." Good cheer roughened his voice. Anticipation grew all the sweeter as the end drew near. "To your safe journey."

"And to Lady Towe's, of course," Colville added.

Adrian drank without speaking. After tonight, Lady Towe's safety would not be any Colville's concern.

13

*P*ast midnight. Nora walked in silent, measured steps down the cold stone corridor, her cloak bag clutched under her arm. Such precious freight must be carried with care, for within this bag lay the articles of estate, the rent rolls and ancient deeds of land, the Bible that attested to family marriages and deaths—none of which could be left behind to chance.

For hours she had wrestled with herself over this course. At the table, she had held her tongue when Cosmo spoke of marriage, forbidding herself by a fierce will to quarrel in the presence of enemies. Then, when Adrian had ceded so easily to Cosmo's plan to remove her from Hodderby, her own foolish grief had almost crushed her. Evidently he had not found their interlude in the meadow worth repeating. On the contrary, it seemed to have proved to him that she was more trouble than she was worth.

But these men, both of them, could go to the devil! In his absence, David had entrusted *her* with Hodderby's care. If he had formed some new plan thereafter with Cosmo, then he should have shared it. But he had not, and she would not take her cousin's word for truth. She would not abandon Hodderby—and she would not marry Cosmo, either. Indeed, she was done with men entirely! What a more peaceful life she would lead freed from their deceptions—and from the casual violence with which they betrayed a woman's hopes. Idiotic hopes, unforgivable hopes—they sprang up like weeds and flourished without permission . . .

She took a sharp breath and forced her attention to the present. Her decision had been made. There was no use in dwelling on aught else.

The arrow-slit windows permitted only the barest ghostly glow to penetrate the gloom. With one hand she guided herself, her fingertips brushing over tapestries she knew like her own face, and the frames of paintings showing her forebears. Once this entire hall had been a gallery, and her ancestors' images had hung side by side with great works by Caravaggio, Rubens, and Van Dyck. But the travails of the Civil War had cost the Colvilles these treasures. Nora only knew of them from her late grandfather's tales.

Grandfather had cherished those memories of greatness. He had seen fit to press them on her as well as David. In so many ways he had shown her that Hodderby was her legacy as much as her brother's. David had known this, once. But he was only a man, and she could not blame him if he fell prey to the same masculine disorders of the mind that plagued his cousin and Lord Rivenham to boot.

No matter what any of them believed, her place was *here*. She knew a hundred places to hide on this estate, and a hundred people, plainspoken and honorable, who would shelter her. It was unjust to ask them to risk themselves, but she would find a way to reward them for it.

The floor abruptly slanted upward, signaling the threshold to the entresol that looked over the entry hall. She stepped across it—and gasped as a hand closed on her arm.

The cloak bag slipped, thumping against the floor as a hard body came up behind her. The hilt of a sword stabbed her ribs.

The hand across her mouth seemed . . . familiar.

Adrian whispered in her ear, *"Quietly."*

He made the mistake of releasing her then. She turned to face him, calculating how best to deter his interest, to send him onward so she might accomplish her escape. He was nothing in this blackness but the faint glow of his hair and the glint of his eyes.

A quick glance downward could not locate her cloak bag, but as she shifted, her foot came up against it. Pray God he had not noticed it, for it would be a telltale sign of her intention to flee.

"What are you doing?" she whispered. "Why do you prowl?"

"I could ask you the same. If you seek your cousin, you need only wait in your chambers. I wager he will soon come sniffing about them."

His voice was pitched so low that she might have imagined the growl in it. But his phrasing made her wary; it did not sound kind.

When he took hold of her arm again, the flexing pressure of his hand proved more distinct to her senses. Mere inches separated them. In the surrounding chill, her body wanted to step closer to the great warmth coming off his.

"You are armed," she said.

"Yes."

She thought she saw the flash of his teeth, though it was no remark to inspire a smile. She tried to pull away. His grip tightened.

A shadow shifted in the corner of her vision. When she looked, it was already gone.

"One of my men," he said. "They walk the house tonight."

"To what purpose?" A horrific idea suggested itself. "Mean you to slay my cousin?"

His soft laugh raised the hairs on her nape. This strange cheer in his manner alarmed her; he all but vibrated with wild energy. "Would you weep for him if I did?"

These were not the words of a man resigned to Cosmo Colville's wishes. Had his merry routine at dinner been but a show? "You gave him permission to take me!"

"I lie very well."

So. That answered one question. The other yet remained. "You cannot mean to harm him."

"Oh, I have murder in me," he said softly. "Generally it requires provocation. Do you wish to marry him?"

The casual tenor of his voice, so mismatched to his words, made her wary. She did not know what answer might count as the provocation he required.

"What are you about?" she asked slowly.

"You were mine in the meadow this morning. It was not by accident."

She was grateful for the darkness as she felt her face flame. "This morning was . . ." *Magical,* she thought. *A dream.* Some stolen moment not meant to exist in the waking world.

A mistake.

"It should not have happened," she whispered.

"You do not lie nearly so well as I." How strangely pleased he sounded. She did not recognize this man who held her in the darkness. "Be honest now." His hand closed over her hip and she sucked in a breath. "Be honest," he murmured.

His tongue traced the curve of her ear.

She shuddered and turned away. "Not here," she said hoarsely. "Stop it."

"I mean to make you mine."

Though his mouth was hot, the words sounded cold. His statement held no pleasure, no passion; he spoke a flat promise to her.

For a moment, she quailed. If he wanted to drive her away, he could not do so more effectively than by threatening to take his full liberties without her say.

But the fear faded almost instantly. What a queer, curious idea: she knew him too well, even now, to imagine he would ever use her brutally. "Adrian . . ." *What devil rides you tonight?*

But caution checked her words. His answer, she sensed, would not leave her any easy exit.

She reached out, avoiding his sword, brushing over

the stiff leather of a fighting man's waistcoat, to find his hand. That she discovered it clenched into a fist startled forth a tenderness she did not understand. This intuitive knowledge of him did not bear scrutiny, but she yielded to it as her fingers wrapped over his knuckles.

"You are the villain here by accident," she murmured. "I will fight you, but I will not fear you."

"Then God help you, Nora," he said softly. "For I mean to show you no mercy."

That such words should strike joy in her made as little sense as her instinct now to lift her face, or her lack of surprise when his mouth touched hers.

His arms came around her and she felt the full evidence of his readiness for bloodshed: not only the hilt of his saber, but the rude butt of a dagger strapped to his thigh. Such proof should have chilled her. It was her family, her cousin, that he armed himself against.

She was a wicked, depraved creature to want him more for it. She tightened her arms around him, pulling him as close as he might come—not close enough; she wanted no space between them. As a girl she had craved only this, to be loved without scruples or surcease, to be loved violently and against all good sense. She had not realized that the price would be to love him in the same fashion, and to pay a higher cost than he did.

But now the knowledge made this hot kiss seem all the more wondrous. It was bound to end. It always ended. But until it did, would that every walk in the shadows, every long night of self-doubt, had such blissful dangers as its reward.

His mouth broke from hers. "Come," he said, taking her by the shoulders, turning her and urging her forward. *To his chambers.*

Her mouth went dry.

Could she do this? Could she lie with him? She had known it for a mistake this afternoon, but now, in the giddiness of midnight, although her stomach soared with a mix of fear and anticipation, she could not locate her doubts. "I don't . . ."

But she forgot the rest of her words when he directed her toward the stair.

His chambers lay above, not below.

She dug in her heels. "Where do you take me?"

"To the chapel," he said.

The fluttering in her stomach sharpened, now flavored more by panic. "But why?"

"A very good reason," he said. "That is where marriages are performed."

For the space of a shocked heartbeat she waited for his next remark, which would clarify this joke.

But all he said was "Come."

He was not asking.

She swallowed the sudden wild urge to laugh. "Come? To—be married, do you mean?"

"Yes, that is what I mean." His voice was cool, evidencing no trace of shame at his brazenness nor any concern for the turmoil his proposition raised in her. "I am removing you from this unhappy bind. Your brother's troubles will concern you no longer."

Now her laugh did slip out. It sounded savage. So, he

would not let Cosmo take her against her will; instead, he would take her himself! But how *kind* he was to free her of this *obligation* of her brother! How kind, indeed, to inform her of her impending marriage!

Twice now in one day she had learned such happy news. Had any woman ever been blessed with so much tender, solicitous *consideration*?

"You are mad," she said. But she sounded breathless when rage would do better. "I will not marry you for aught!" If only she might smite every man in the human race who had ever told her a single instruction for her benefit! "Simply because I trifled with you in the meadow—why, any slut might instruct you what store to set by *that*!"

In the brief space of his silence, she felt her temper yield to the stirring of hope. "I know you wish to spare me," she said more softly. "But this is not the way, Adrian. I—you and I—I cannot tell you what all is in my heart for you, but now, as matters stand, there is no clear way to see—"

"And so I see for you," he cut in. "In time you, too, will come to understand. Now I must bid you come. I am sorry for it, Leonora, but I will carry you if I must."

Disbelief splintered into shock.

He truly did not care for her consent.

With the pressure of his hand, he tried to marshal her down the steps.

She drew back her fist and slammed it into his ear.

He hissed out a breath. As his fingers flexed on her arm, she hit him again—one great shove toward the stairs. Perforce he released her to catch himself, and she did not wait for him to recover. Sprinting past him, she flew down the staircase.

Five steps' advantage, then four: she heard the light fall of his foot as he bounded after her. She would have cursed him—*you arrogant, conceited, Lucifer's spawn*—but she saved her breath for flight. Lifting her skirts, she took the stairs two by two, reckless with her footing, giddy with some hot intoxication that might, soon enough, prove to be fury.

He called to her, rough words, indistinct, as she leapt the last length of stairs. Marry her, would he? She had been trapped before, *because of him*, and she would see him in hell before he worked this trick on her! She was done with surrendering choices!

She spun away from the main entrance, for there was no escape outside in the moonlight, on terrain where he could easily outpace her, where his men waited in watch of her brother . . . Oh, he had planned very well, had he not, to capture every Colville of interest to him!

A hidden door stood behind a tapestry. She knocked aside the dusty cloth and struck the door with her shoulder, the pain welcome, blending into and heightening the violence inside her. Let him try to find his way in the blackness! This interior passage twisted like a snake, the stone flooring uneven; it had been paved long before the erection of the walls that now enclosed Hodderby, a remainder of the old lodge that had stood when the houses of York and Lancaster had split apart the kingdom centuries ago.

She sprinted silently, knowing by memory when to turn. The cramped corridor curved, and she ducked as she approached the sudden drop in the ceiling, invisible in the dark. The door, now distant behind her, thumped at Adrian's entrance. Another sharp thud and a curse announced his encounter with the buckling slant of the ancient masonry.

Good. She hoped he bled.

Her course dead-ended at a new door. She threw it open.

The ancient hall blazed with light. Rivenham's men looked up from the end of the room. The dice rolling between them reached the edge of the table and skittered onto the floor, loud in the silence of their surprise.

"Hold!" called one as they shot to their feet. She pulled shut the door and was running again, left now with no choice but go exactly where she should not.

Down again the path dipped, through air that grew cool and dry. Did she truly mean to do this? One wrong step—gunpowder was unpredictable—

She slowed and put out her hands, feeling her way between the casks that cropped up all around her. Splinters of oak stabbed her palms. *Carefully, carefully* . . .

"Nora."

His voice echoed off the low ceiling. Like a tightening noose, it halted her.

At the far end of this chamber, a bolted door opened into the stable yard. But she could not risk leading him through these barrels. He had no idea of the dangers they contained.

He spoke again. "If it will comfort you to know you ran . . ."

Comfort?

". . . then by all means," he said. "Run."

She would show him *comfort*! She reached into her pocket, the bottom of which she had slit open in her solar. He was not the only one carrying a weapon. She had planned well for her midnight departure. The hilt of the small knife strapped to her thigh butted into her grasp. The trembling of her fingers infuriated her. She tightened her grip until pain stabbed through her knuckles.

Damn him.

Damn him for making this choice for her!

His hand closed on her arm.

"This is the only way," he said.

She dared not struggle. It had been reckless to lead him here. "The only way to . . . what, Lord Rivenham?"

Her voice sounded strange to her, low and unnaturally calm.

"Listen well," he said. "I see two ways for it: I kill your brother myself—here—and thereby spare you the chance to follow his treason. I save your life thereby but earn your enmity for eternity."

"Yes," she whispered. "So you do."

"Or I refrain from authoring his death, and you, doing your best to aid him, thereby author your own. No Colville will find mercy in London."

His grip was tightening; he was trying to turn her toward him, but the position of the casks between them put him at an odd angle that prevented him from exerting the full force of his strength.

She could not fight, lest they upset the barrels around them. But with every muscle in her body she strained against his grip, and the effort frayed her words. "You did not speak of my brother on the stair. You spoke of marriage, and I will not have it."

"But you will," he said very softly.

Goose bumps rose on her skin.

"Your brother will not touch you," he continued, his words still low, as though he sought to lull her into believing them. "As a Ferrers, you cannot be touched. You will be safe, and so, too, this place you love: I swear it to you."

Her scoff seemed to explode, echoing around them. "Such charitable motives!"

And she drove her knife into his arm.

To her shock, he did not cry out—or release her, either. A small hissing breath escaped him. His free hand gripped hers, twisting hard, until she gasped from pain and the knife dropped from her numb fingers.

A cask toppled as he dragged her backward into the iron grip of his arms. She flinched—but naught happened, save that his mouth came against her ear.

"I see that you will make a most interesting wife."

14

The bride was bound and gagged. The parson was drunk, and had been kept so since Adrian's men had purloined him from the high road a day earlier. At first terror-stricken at being separated from his party, the clergyman had found calm in a sizable bribe. It now resided in his dusty pockets, the former contents of which had sealed his fate: Jonathon Masters of York was one of those innumerable clergymen who did a brisk trade in illicitly distributed marriage licenses, properly stamped, affixed with the seal of the Royal Arms, conveniently lacking only the names of bride and groom.

Adrian's men had detained three other holy men before finding one so well equipped. The only surprise was that it had taken so long: the trade in such certificates was a much-favored way to support the godly lifestyle.

The clergyman slurred out the words now from the Book of Common Prayer, his voice rising in counterpoise to the bride's furious grunts. Braddock and Henslow, flanking the parson to encourage him, presented stern countenances only occasionally prey to smirks: alas, the parson's faculties at present were not equal to the language of his office.

When Masters paused to hold out the book a distance from his face, squinting quizzically at the riddles it presented, Adrian shifted impatiently. "Skip to the vows," he said. "I do not require a jobsworth."

The parson lowered the book, blinking. "Well, if it comes to that, your shig—your signatures will shuffice."

Reaching inside his valise, he produced a dog-eared folio that he settled atop the altar. Next he produced a bottle of ink—its spillage prevented by a quick, lunging intervention by Braddock—and a quill, which he offered up with a lopsided smile that bespoke pride in his own resourcefulness.

"Never without it," he said. "Good many a-marry on the road."

Henslow snorted. Undoubtedly these proceedings had taken on a comical note, but Adrian's current mood did not allow for humor. He wanted this completed—in all regards. And then he wanted Cosmo Colville off this property.

The quill was in want of sharpening. His signature emerged illegibly, the thick ink smearing with a drop of blood that had escaped the makeshift bandage—his own neckcloth—with which he'd bound his arm. The wound was not deep; he would need to teach her better to defend herself.

He wiped his palm on his leather waistcoat and signed again, writing his name at a much larger size.

He turned to Nora, whose glare looked forceful enough to permanently displace her eyes from her skull. For a moment he paused, struck by the finality of this moment: from now forward, this woman was his.

The smile that grew on his lips did not please her. Her eyes narrowed, threatening him silently.

"You will forgive me," he said. Eventually.

He meant it as a promise to her, even as she furiously shook her head. Now, here, he would right the injustice done them six years ago. After this night, no man would be able to unmake his claim to her.

Picking up her bound wrists, he forced her right hand around the pen and drew her name himself. Her nails turned into his flesh, digging viciously.

"God save me when I untie you," he murmured.

Her emphatic grunt, in his reckoning, signaled agreement.

He returned the quill to the parson. "Now you will sign and notarize this page," he instructed, "stating your name, your direction, and your posting. Should any of the other happy couples registered herein require some proof of their union, they may apply to the Earl of Rivenham for the record of it."

The parson frowned. "I don't—" And then scandalized understanding twisted his mouth. "You can't mean to keep the registry!"

"I can," said Adrian. He nodded toward the page. "Now attest yourself, and then Braddock will see you comfortably provisioned for your journey to Preston. An escort will ride you off at dawn."

The parson chewed his lip. "And—and if someone should ask me of this? The bride's d-d-demeanor?"

Adrian tightened his arm around his wife's waist. When he looked into her face, she bent her head to avoid his eyes. The small mole on her right cheek stood out lividly against her pallor.

"Why, speak the truth," he said. "While a heavenly vision in the composure of her features, she seemed somewhat . . . indisposed."

"Indisposed," the parson repeated, nodding in the manner of a man set to memorization.

"But not for long," Adrian said softly, for her ears alone.

He had taken her knife.

He had forced her hand at the registry.

He had picked her up and carried her out of the chapel like a war prize.

And now he took her into his rooms—rooms that *she*, against her will, had been compelled to allot him—and strode directly into his bedchamber, where he knocked aside the bed curtains and settled her atop a dark quilt of embroidered silk that she should have cast into the sty before lending to this blackguard's use.

A futile jerk of her wrists confirmed, yet again, that the knots there had been tied with skill. He knelt by the bed, forcing her to twist her neck to an uncomfortable degree to keep him out of her vision.

"You play mute disdain very well," he said.

She stared fixedly at an oak bedpost carved into a cascade of flowers and fruit. The mattress sagged as he settled beside her. The scent of cloves rose from the bed linens beneath them. She went rigid to avoid contact with his body.

His touch on the tender skin of her inner wrists made her flinch. A moment later the bonds about her wrists loosened and slipped away.

She twisted at the waist and punched him.

The blow was sound, a solid crack across his cheek. Her numb hand did not register its force, but her forearm ached like a struck bell.

His impassive reaction gave no satisfaction. She struck out again.

He caught her fist before it landed, his grip hard.

Very well, then her skull would make a weapon! She hurled herself at him.

He leaned back, forcing her head into his chest, then gripped it against him as he fell backward onto the mattress. Her belly came up against his. She scratched for his eyes and brought up her knee, driving for his balls or his gut, but in one broad hand he caught her thigh and twisted out from beneath her, flipping her onto her back and placing his knee over her legs.

His hand at her wrists pinned her flat.

A silent scream rasped in her throat, hot and rapid; there was not enough air to feed this conflagration of rage inside her. She jerked at his hold, but under his narrow regard, the fruitless struggle to free herself seemed like a new humiliation.

She fell still, loathing him. The bandage he'd tied around his arm galled her, proof of her stupidity. She should have stabbed him in the throat!

At least he wore the mark of her nails now. A long, vicious scratch ran from the corner of his eye to his mouth.

His face grim, he hauled her upright and pulled her to the edge of the bed so her legs dangled into air. His hand, which still trapped her own, began to massage her, coaxing the blood to prickle painfully back through her fingers.

She bit hard on the gag and stared fixedly at nothing. She was alone, she told herself. She was anywhere but here. This was a dream; it would pass. She had not just been forced, *again*, into marriage—this time by the very man who had first lured her to dream of wifehood. No, she could not compass such a betrayal. That *he* of all men should treat her only as a *woman*, as all men treated women—as a witless creature born only to do men's bidding, at men's convenience—

That parson had been fraudulent. This could be undone.

"You were right to call me a villain," he said quietly. "But you were wrong to think that only the circumstances cast me as such."

Riddles. He should speak them to someone who cared. She was deaf to him.

"I am as much a villain in my nature as a common thief on the high road," he said. "Did you not know it?"

His words framed a confession but he spoke it shamelessly. He did not sound sorry at all.

"Here is what makes me a criminal, Nora. Righteous men conceive of an end and pray for righteous means to obtain it. But criminals do not look to prayer for their hopes. They place no faith in chance. When they see an end, they risk everything to obtain it—no matter whether it is theirs to risk or no."

She heard him loose a breath.

"I have loved you for a very long time now, you see."

For a mad moment her very blood seemed to leap and pulse. Tears came to her eyes. She shut them to crush the tears away. *He loved her?* Words were nothing, unmarried to action!

"For the remainder of my life, no matter what course it runs, I will not regret this night. I did what I must, by what means were available. I knew the opportunity to have you would not come again, and I have loved you too long now to hesitate."

The words burned through her like fire. She ground the gag between her teeth, longing to scream, to strike him, to *curse* him for speaking words of love. A pox on him! What scurvy love was this, which stripped her of her honor and choice? His love meant nothing to her. She would not *allow* it to mean aught. It was diseased. How *dare* he speak such words to her now?

"A villain's love is not a comfortable thing," he said. "But I promise, I will endeavor to make it a pleasure to you."

He released her hands, sliding his own up her arms, slowly but without hesitation. She willed her flesh to feel nothing. She would have slapped him again but it would only provoke him to put himself atop her. Instead she made her hands into fists, her fingernails digging for blood. Bloodshed seemed fitting.

His fingers moved against her nape and then the gag loosened. She spat it out, loathing the taste of wool, uncaring of whether her spittle touched him or not.

The idea inspired her rage. She twisted toward him and spat in his face.

His eyes met hers. Shadows gathered beneath them. Her spit trailed down his cheek.

She did not *care* for his exhaustion!

When he still did not move, her temper seized her tongue. "Wipe your face, jackanapes. Or would you prefer that I slap it off?"

To her disbelief, he laughed softly. "You may try."

Try? To hell with him! She lashed out with her palm.

He caught her wrist and turned his mouth into it. His teeth closed on her skin, and his tongue made a hot stroke over her pulse.

Her breath shuddered out in a loud gust. She stared at him, appalled—not only by him but also by herself. This fury felt like a movable creature stretching inside her skin, expanding now into a violence to which his mouth seemed the answer.

Her body had learned too well that lesson in the meadow. It still answered to the instruction of his flesh.

She wanted to claw his face bloody!

She wanted him to bite her harder.

And *why not?* He had hurt her, tonight, in the sharpest and most deadly way possible: not with his body but with his mind, outwitting her, stripping her of her ability to decide for herself, to lay her own course. He had herded her like a dumb animal, a sheep, a dog.

But this was no new injury. Other men had done it to her before. She had already endured one marriage begun by force. She understood exactly what her future held now.

So, why should he not hurt her with his body as well?

"Better to bite out my heart," she said.

His face lifted and she saw his mask of indifference dissolve. His nostrils flared, and a muscle flexed in his jaw. "No," he said. "I mean to keep your heart for myself."

The laugh that spilled from her now would have done a scornful court beauty proud. "You will not have it. Not after tonight. You betrayed me—"

"I saved you," he said evenly. "And if I betrayed you to do so—so be it. There can be no betrayal where there is no affection."

When he reached toward her, she threw herself backward. The carved post knocked into her spine. "Do not speak to me of affection! You corrupt knave—love does not allow for such poxy treatment!"

"There's a pretty ideal," he said. Could nothing shatter his calm? "But I think you are not so blind in this matter as you would wish to be. If you put your own safety first, I believe you will see how this marriage might benefit you." He paused, considering her squarely. Then the line of his jaw firmed, as though he had resolved himself to some unpleasant decision. "I protect what is mine. And you are a danger to yourself, Leonora. Hate me if you like, but I will not permit you to risk yourself. I will bear your hatred easily so long as you are safe."

As his eyes held hers, the silence between them seemed to crackle. She grew suddenly, painfully aware of the mattress beneath her, and the door that stood closed beyond it, and his muscled body, not an arm's length from hers.

She threw the words at him: "Will you force me in this, too?"

"No," he said more quietly. "I will do nothing to your displeasure."

"Then atone," she said desperately. "For this whole affair displeases me. It is not too late! A marriage may be annulled—"

His expression did not change, but he placed his hand over hers. His light grip carried its own message: she was caught. No argument remained to be made of it.

She snatched her hand away. "Then you will not touch me at all!"

His head tilted. Leisurely he studied her, as though viewing a puzzle he had all the time in the world to solve. "You told me that you would have played the rebel, long ago, only I never made it possible. You craved wildness then . . . and I think you still do. I think you have enough of a taste for it to pursue your own pleasures. I do not think you truly crave to be a martyr for your brother."

His words lashed her. Of course she did not crave martyrdom! But what kind of woman would it make her if she permitted this private reluctance to become an excuse for turning to her brother's enemy? This desire Adrian stirred in her was already dishonorable—all the more so after tonight's crime. If she betrayed her brother for it, it would spell her damnation! "I do not call it martyrdom to desire to see him well!"

"I cannot promise his health," he said gravely. "But the choice I posed to you in the entresol was true. I will not be the man to author his death."

"That does not suffice! You work against him—"

His hand over hers tightened. "He works against himself. He invites his own end. But if he only saw sense, he could find me useful."

She caught her breath. "What . . . what does that mean?"

"It means precisely as I say. I have no small power with the king. But if I should meet your brother in battle, it will not go to his betterment."

She searched his face, his eyes so intent upon hers. Was he offering to help her brother, should it come to his peaceful capture? "And if you do not meet in battle? What then?"

"Then my power may be of use to him."

This was a veiled promise at best—and she would be a fool to trust aught from this man after what he had done tonight.

Only . . . only if Adrian did speak truly now . . . if he did care for her . . . then if it should come to the worst— if David should be caught—then what would he lose by speaking for her brother?

Would it not suit the Earl of Rivenham's station better to ensure that his new brother-in-law was not beheaded before the town?

In which case, was not this marriage of some advantage after all?

Her own thoughts frightened her. How easily she made Adrian's arguments for him!

He reached out. With one hand he captured her braid and brought it over her shoulder, running his hand down its length, drawing it into a rope that spanned the space between them.

She resisted the gentle tug he gave. Breath held, skin prickling, she waited to see what he would do.

He did nothing. He merely watched her. But the gentle play of his hand on the ends of her hair began to sap at her like poison.

"I cannot trust you," she whispered.

The regret in his slight smile was only a show. It must be. "What cause have you to trust me?" he said. "It falls to me to persuade you."

"You will not succeed in it."

"You may be surprised." Again he made the barest tug on her braid, urging her toward him. He murmured, "You may learn to enjoy me more than you imagine."

She leaned back in resistance, trying desperately to reason her own best action. They were alone in his bedchamber. He was laying hands on her. His intention was clear, though he'd claimed he would not force her.

I mean to make you mine.

The echo of those words made her dizzy and hot. She swallowed hard, appalled by herself. The worst of it was, he did not *play* the enemy. As she resisted him, he made no effort to compel her nearer; indeed, he leaned forward to maintain, not increase, the tension on her hair.

She could not understand him. If he was a villain, let him behave as one! Her reluctance had infuriated Towe; in London, her coldness had enraged a dozen leering courtiers, who proved willing to proposition her but vicious upon her refusals. Yet Adrian remained perfectly still, that gentle tug on her hair conveying not a command but an invitation. His thumb stroked thoughtfully across the curling ends of her hair as he watched her.

The silence grew hushed and thick.

A small shock moved through her. Why, they were married. This was her husband now.

She was married to *Adrian*.

A shuddering started inside her. How could it be that this nightmare followed so exactly the lines of a once-cherished dream? This man at arm's-length . . . she had longed once to marry him. He was not some stranger. He *knew* her. He called up feelings within her that no one else had ever stirred.

She could not forgive him.

But she still could not fear him. And she could not cease wanting him, either. Even now, her body awoke to his presence.

Chills danced through her stomach. Her confusion felt sickening. For honor's sake she must oppose him. Where was her strength? She remembered the one time he had lain with her. *It will not hurt again,* he had promised. But he had never had a chance to prove it. And it had hurt, terribly. Every time that Towe had come to her bed . . .

"The look on your face," he said quietly, "suggests you think no happy thoughts."

Her jagged emotions sharpened her voice to a knife's edge. "Why should I look happy? What cause have you given me for happiness tonight?"

"None yet," he said. "But half the night remains."

The promise in his voice struck a thrill through her. It angered her, this rebellion in her flesh. "I have spent such nights with a husband. I found no joy in them, I assure you."

Briefly his expression darkened. He leaned forward and caught her hand again, stroking his thumb over her knuckles.

"There is a large universe of difference between those nights and this one."

He spoke the words calmly, no boast or bravado in them. How certain he was that he would please her. And in the meadow, she had glimpsed the cause of his certainty. Only by her last straining effort had she stopped him. The feel of his hips against hers . . .

The ragged rhythm of her own breathing startled her. Was she no better than an animal? How could she long for a man who had trammeled her will just as thoroughly as Towe had done?

I *long.* I *long for him. It is* I *who do this:* I, I, I.

A knot formed in her throat, and her stomach dipped as though at the start of a fall. She had never longed for Towe. And it had made no difference that she hadn't. Her will had played no role in that union. But this one . . . *she had longed for it,* though others had forbidden it of her.

And now Adrian's silent invitation made obvious that there was, again, a part to play for her will. *Hers.* Not her father's, nor her brother's, but *her* will, *her* desire.

A strange panic twisted through her. She fought the revelation dawning inside her. After all, he had not given her a choice in this marriage! What did it matter if he now showed care for her consent?

"You could have made me happy," she said rapidly. "Once you could have. Once—to be married to you would have been . . ." She shook her head, not wanting to put words to it. "But after tonight, Adrian—what you did—with no right . . ."

A flush prickled her cheeks. She felt . . . awkward with herself, increasingly flustered, for suddenly it felt as though she was arguing with herself as much as him. *What is your will?* This question she had longed forever to answer and live by, it was so much more dangerous that she had thought, for what if her will were not to the liking of her loftier ideals? What if she were hungrier, more greedy and less virtuous, than she had imagined? She could not shake her awareness from the spot where his hand gripped her hair . . .

"Tonight I sinned," he said. He wrapped her braid around his palm, drawing nearer though she had not moved. "Let me now atone."

"I do not wish it," she managed. Oh, God, that was what she *must* say.

"I can do nothing against your consent," he said. "Only, ask honestly of yourself what it is you desire— and tell me your answers frankly, from now forward.

Every part of me, Lady Rivenham, now serves at your pleasure."

He laid down her braid, and for a baffling moment she wondered if he could be done with her. But then he lifted her hand. His eyes on hers, he closed his lips around her index and middle fingers, sucking them into his mouth.

Her breath hissed from her. His tongue painted soft strokes to her middle knuckle, his teeth closing gently on her fingertips, and her mouth went dry.

She broke away from his gaze, staring blindly at the bed curtains, at the woven rush matting on the floor. *Stop,* she thought, but could not say. Her thudding pulse crushed the word.

He released her fingers and pressed a hot kiss against her palm. "A simple test," he said, his voice hoarse. "Did my kiss displease you?"

The answer pealed through her mind like a clarion. She felt choked by the effort not to speak it aloud. She could not, would not consent. After what he had done, she *could* not.

Was muteness, was silence, to be the cost of her honor, then? Would she strangle herself to preserve her self-regard? And if that regard also required that her will and desire be crushed, this time by *herself* . . . what then?

"If silence is your reply, you must instruct me in how to interpret it." The bed ropes groaned as he moved nearer.

She closed her eyes. She could not look at him. She could not oppose him as well as herself.

He said into her ear, "I never intended this night to be short. But I will gladly make it into a night and a day—and perhaps I must, for I will not proceed without your reply."

Her face flamed. She dug her fingers into the quilt. Hidden in his everyday words was a sly and shameless promise to make her speak of things that modest folk left unsaid. But he would not be modest. He would not let her remain unmoved. He would do things to her that she had only dreamed about, during long, tossing nights . . .

A stifled sound escaped her. "David—if you will help him, if you promise—"

His lips touched her cheek and the words fell from her. God, his mouth was the sweetest drug; on her death-bed she would require nothing else to recall to her soul the possibility of heaven.

"I have said I might," he murmured. "But is it not a curious thing, that one's conscience so often wars with one's desires? How can we put yours to sleep? Shall I speak my promise again?" His tongue curled over the lobe of her ear. "Only tell me what to say," he whispered. "Shall I speak of your brother, Nora mine?"

No.

His hand slid around her nape, closing there. "You must instruct me," he said. "I cannot trust my own wishes at present." His voice grew rougher. "You see, I have rehearsed this hour, this very moment, a thousand times and a thousand times more since last I lay with you. Trust me when I say that you do not wish me to heed my own desires, Nora: they are too impatient and too hun-gered to guide me wisely."

His hand cupped her nape: that was all. And yet, his words—the raw intensity in them—brushed over her like a thousand hot mouths. They left her skin flushed and swollen with want.

A thousand times and a thousand times more.

A new heat burned over her. It felt like *anger.*

David. What *of* David? Must all others' needs ever come before her own? Must she forever trammel her appetites? I *long.* I *want.* I.

I want this man.

What lay between her and this man was older than her brother's troubles by far. What did David have to do with this moment? What more did she owe her family in regard to this man? What price had she *not* paid to them for this love?

She turned violently toward Adrian, pushing him by the shoulders, forcing him down toward the quilts. Crouched over him, she froze.

As though she had been blind until a moment ago, the sight of him beneath her struck her like a shock. *God, he is beautiful.* His grave eyes were green as grass, steady, unsurprised, rapt on hers. His pale hair had come unbound; it tumbled across the dark quilt, and beneath her trembling fingers, it felt soft and cool to the touch. His cheeks were rough, the line of his full lower lip smooth and hot. His long limbs sprawled across the bed, his leather trousers outlining the sculpted muscles of his thighs. One upturned palm exposed his tanned, hairless inner wrist, a sight somehow jarring, vulnerable.

Her throat filled. His absolute stillness communicated an invitation: he offered this body to her; he lay beneath her and let her look on it because it was hers now to take.

A dream, she thought, *this is a dream.* Adrian Ferrers, beneath her on the bed . . . speaking to her of love after enduring the bite of her blade. . . .

What was he to her? A villain indeed . . . but what else?

This riddle felt painfully, impossibly large; she could not think on it. She knew what must happen now. She would put out this fire inside her as quickly as possible. Reason would play no part in it. Her doubts she would wrestle later, when the flame was quenched, when she was cold. "Do not speak," she said, and leaned down to press her mouth to his.

He deserved a bruising kiss. His broad hands grasped her head and held her there as he took his punishment. Their tongues tangled; he tasted of whiskey and hot, restless dreams and years of longing; of the sweetness of youth, and the darker, more complex pleasures of maturity. He tasted dangerous. She could lose herself in this taste. She could forget all the ties that bound her, leaving only her hunger to guide her.

He took her by the arms and rolled her beneath him, his propped elbow sparing her his weight as he ravished her mouth. She opened her mouth wider to him, glad when his hand found her knee and parted her legs to allow him to settle between them. Quickly, let him be quick, before her doubts found her again. She rocked into him, encouraging him with her hips, sighing into his mouth when his hand found her breast and began to stroke and squeeze her through the layers that separated them. She wanted to be overcome—not with his words but with his body. His words invited thought; his body issued only instructions, which her own accepted joyously.

But when she tried to remove his coat, he caught her wrist and checked her. His kiss gentled; slowly his mouth moved over her cheek, down her throat. His hands slipped behind her back and he pulled her upright.

Her head fell into the crook of his shoulder. She breathed deeply of him, squirming to keep contact with the flat muscle of his abdomen as he pulled her onto her knees, so they knelt body to body.

His hands were moving on the lacings of her dress.

She jerked her shoulders. "Stop," she said. "You need not undress me." Once, she had lain nude with him— but she had been a girl then. And once, too, her husband had bared her, but her body had changed by then, and it had been . . . unpleasant in the extreme. "You needn't," she said. He could lift her skirts easily enough.

Adrian drew away to look into her face. She did not like the thoughtful quality of his regard. She pressed her lips together and took a hard breath through her nose. "You *needn't*," she said. "Be quick."

He leaned down to kiss her mouth. "No," he said against her lips, "I needn't. But for those years, those endless nights, when I made a picture of you before me . . . I would know the reality."

Dread coiled in her belly. "I have . . . changed," she

whispered. Towe had mocked the size of her breasts, which had grown fuller and more pendulous in her maturity.

This warning went unheeded. Adrian's lips grew more intent yet, now on her mouth, now on her neck, brushing the top of her gown, softly biting, his tongue tracing a spell over her flesh.

A sigh slipped from her. Her eyes drifted shut beneath the hot track of his lips. She understood how sugar felt as it dissolved into water.

Her bodice parted and sagged from her shoulders.

She froze.

His hands urged her to turn. Stiffly, resentfully, she followed his direction, her skirts making her movements more awkward yet. Now would come her stays, then her shift . . .

Hot kisses on her bared shoulder blades distracted her. Strings popped audibly, and fabric ripped. Her stays went flying over the side of the bed. Her knife followed.

Adrian slid the ripped shift off her arms, then bodily lifted her so she faced him again.

She could not bring herself to look into his face. She focused instead on the vicinity of his chest. That he remained fully clothed made this moment all the more mortifying.

A finger at her chin tipped up her face, but her eyes remained fixed on his body.

"This," he said roughly, and his knuckles trailed lightly down her throat, making a path along one collarbone before passing along the outer swell of her breast.

She felt her nipples pucker, and now his finger moved to touch one of them, resting there, striking a sharp throb between her legs.

He had not finished his sentence. Was she so much more ungainly than he'd supposed? Time had been kind to him where it had thickened and loosened her. She took a shuddering breath and forced her eyes upward.

His lips were parted. He was watching his own finger as it circled her nipple. He looked . . . younger, almost as if he saw something . . . wondrous . . .

His eyes lifted to hers, and her breath caught. Some hot, fierce emotion burned in his face, and she could not mistake it for aught but triumph.

His palm closed over her breast. He bent to kiss her, giving her the fullness of his tongue. "No dream," he said, very low, "no memory, could suffice."

A queer feeling came over her, sweet and amazed. His head lowered; he took the tip of her breast between his lips.

The heat of his mouth swam through her. She clutched his soft hair and his palm pressed on the small of her back, holding her steady as he suckled her. When he bowed her back again, she curved as pliantly as the stem of a flower. His hands moved beneath her buttocks, lifting her; a tearing noise as her skirts ripped, and then he was baring her below as well.

She spread her arms across the span of the mattress, lifting herself, inviting him to do as he would.

He kept utter silence as his mouth moved down her body, but the ferocity of his kisses, the feverish sweep of his hands over her calves and thighs, lent the hush a charged, intent quality. Her thighs fell apart at his urging.

He put his mouth between her legs.

A rasping noise escaped her. She bit down on her knuckles as his tongue penetrated her, then retreated. He found the small, aching spot where her desire pulsed and licked her there, again and again. She looked down her body, saw him crouched between her legs, holding her thighs apart, and the pleasure that rolled through her seemed to lift away the top of her skull.

It frightened her. She twisted beneath him. "Enough—" she managed, but when she would have closed her thighs, he sent a hot, intent look up her body that made her freeze. His face looked deadly serious.

He gripped her thighs and opened them wider.

Gasping, she lay back, bucking beneath him now, sensation darting through her and building in jolts, concentrating into an aching throb. She was too empty; she found the smooth curve of his muscled shoulders and squeezed, demanding, urging him up her body.

"Please," she gasped, pulling at this cloth that kept him from her, wanting the hot press of his skin along hers. She yanked harder, and now he heeded her; he sat up and threw off his clothing, divesting himself in quick order, his eyes moving along her again and again, as though she might vanish from him; and then he was back above her, and she hissed out a breath at the branding heat of his flesh against hers. She wriggled beneath him, adjusting herself, wanting his weight to crush her harder; there was nothing, no satisfaction, to be had like his solidity, the tension in his corded neck, the biting kiss he gave her as he adjusted his hips and his cock came up against her.

She lifted her hips and felt the blunt, nudging pressure of his penetration. As he pressed into her, the discomfort grew sharper, and then, suddenly, eased into a burning almost pleasurable—and then entirely so as he began to move.

Her hands slipped to his buttocks, urging him as he pushed into her; she turned her throat to his mouth, and used her nails to encourage the pressure of his teeth. He sucked on her neck, and then took her mouth again. Hunger gained on her and took direction of her hips, so she rose and fell with him, filled, conquered, wilder yet than he; in a mad moment she tried to turn him so she could mount him and take this slow, steady rhythm into a faster, harsher pace. But his hands caught her wrists and brought her arms over her head, pinning her in place as he took her.

She opened her eyes and found his fixed on her, his face a harsh mask. He leaned down to take her mouth and she bit his lip. The kiss turned savage and his restraint finally broke. He thrust into her faster and faster, and finally the delicious tension in her belly coalesced; she seized around him, crying out into his shoulder. His hips rolled once more against her, and then again, and then he, too, shuddered and fell still, his hand slipping from her wrists to cup her face as he exhaled into her throat.

He rolled to one side, taking her with him, his arms

wrapped around her, his mouth on her ear, and now on her shoulder, lazy, now interested, charting the course of her collarbone.

She felt herself trembling. His hand stroked her back now as though to calm her, then closed on her nape, clasping her firmly. His heavy thigh lay over hers.

"Sleep," he said. "You are weary."

She was the last thing from weary. Even now something low in her belly stretched and yawned. The breadth of his muscled thigh, the feel of the sparse hair there beneath her wandering hand, the density of his chest, were enough to renew the echoes of her climax.

The flame within her had not been quenched. In giving it full license to burn, she had also fed it fresh fuel.

My God, she thought. *What have I done?*

15

It was Adrian's wont to rise before dawn, and rarely had he such good cause for it as now: he had ordered his men to save for him the pleasure of expelling Cosmo Colville from the house.

But though his eyes opened before the light had begun to edge through the window, the prospect of Cosmo Colville's reaction could not entice him to bestir himself. Not when he had, next to him on the bed, her hand laid lightly over his chest, a wonder.

She slept deeply. Her hand was small where it curled atop his chest. He placed his own over it, covering it more tightly when he felt how the coolness of the room had settled into her skin. Her fingers were slim but not soft; her ragged cuticles betrayed how quickly she had left behind the soft routines of court life. Her body beneath the embroidered quilt lent it more beauty than it deserved, shaping it with the slopes and valleys of her curving flesh.

Last night he had been struck dumb by her. What he

had not felt in the chapel, the breath of grace too pure for earthly corruption, had fallen across him in this bed. For the briefest moment, beholding her naked, he had wondered at himself, feeling almost unmanned—reluctant even to touch her, lest the history collected in his skin, the dark deeds in his bones, somehow bring her to ruin.

But he was only a man, not a saint; and even divinity could not restrain for too long the baser hunger in him, the need to possess her rearing so ferociously that only her eyes, fastened wide and luminous on his, had recalled to him the strain of sanity required not to crush her; to use her thoroughly but not forcefully; to ensure that her sleep now remained undisturbed by the bruising of his grip.

He looked upon her for long minutes, seeing more and more to wonder at: the shades of her hair, changing from purest night to the shadows of evening, cobalt to inky black, and the faint tracery of veins beneath her pale skin. He felt as Saul must have done when a great light burned the scales from his eyes—newly exalted by the sight of the world, liberated again to true vision. Her wrists were slim as saplings' branches. The curve of her arm might have taught grace to birds in flight. But her calf over his weighed solidly, a sweet provocation, and the plush give of her thigh was the sweetest submission he had ever known.

The fear stole over him like the first breath of night, at first a subtle chill on his nape, and then a spreading, sharpening cold that made his gut contract and his breath come short.

She had spoken truly. He had sinned against her by

forcing her into wedlock. Did she know how easily she might punish him for it? Her slim, small hands held his future now, and with a single twist, they could shatter it.

A logical man—the man he'd supposed himself to be—never would have touched her, never would have given her such power over him. As his wife, her actions were his. Her treason would be counted his treason. Her mistakes could end his fortune—his family—everything he had fought to build and safeguard.

Yet . . . with her, he was no logical man, and so this was not the true source of his fear.

He had told himself that he could bear her hatred so long as she was safe. Yet it came to him now that her esteem was also . . . beyond price to him. If he had sacrificed the chance to recover her love—if she never found it in herself to forgive his crime, if her hatred was all that remained to him . . .

She would nevertheless be safe. For that alone, he could entertain no regrets. But as for himself . . . with all her hatred and none of her love, he could see no way to prosper. Truly, he would be destroyed.

At last, he removed himself from her side, moving slowly lest he wake her, pausing in his retreat to clear the hair that crossed her eyes, and to press his lips to hers— just once, for if this morning never started, then the night ahead would never come.

He was not a patient man. The urge to woo her, to begin the persuasion of reconciling her to this marriage, pressed him hard. But he would give her the span of the day. He would wait until darkness to seduce her again.

He marshaled his discipline, forcing his thoughts toward other matters as he dressed himself. But at the door, he could not help but turn back.

The first ray of sunrise had crossed her bare arm. As he watched it spread, coloring her like honey, his wonder condensed into a weight in his chest. He remembered now why men prayed; why earth-made miracles caused them to cast their eyes to heaven in search of reassurance that their great good fortune would not be snatched away.

On a long, shaken breath, he stepped out of the chamber.

Nora woke alone to a morning fractured by a nightingale's distant melody and, closer at hand, the sharp slap of her maid's slippers across the floor.

She pushed herself up on one elbow, turmoil rising instantly within her. He had forced her . . . He had said he loved her . . . He had seduced her despite herself. And she had been willing.

He was not here.

She was relieved.

She was . . . disappointed.

Dear God in heaven. She could not bear to look into her own mind just yet. "Grizel," she said.

The maid gasped and wheeled back from the far end of the room. "Oh, my lady—" She rushed forward, one hand clutching her cap to keep it in place, and fell to her knees beside the bed. With clammy fingers she enfolded Nora's hand and carried it to her breast. "Was he cruel to you?"

"No," Nora said slowly. Or did she mean *yes*? His body, his attentions, had been the furthest thing from cruel. But the manner in which he had secured her—that had been cruel indeed.

As for the manner in which she had received his attentions—the ferocious, joyous, terrible hunger that had driven her, and that he had satisfied so expertly, again and again—what did that say of *her*?

She realized that Grizel's speculative gaze was wandering the rumpled sheets. This bed loudly spoke that the night had not been chaste.

Blushing, Nora pulled free of the maid's grasp. "How did you know to find me here?"

"But where else would you have been, after such words? I could hardly credit them—the whole house is on its ear. Mr. Colville lifted his voice; he threatened to cut his lordship's throat; only his lordship invited him to do so, and then Mr. Colville got very quiet. But how did it happen, madam? When did he marry you?"

This breathless recital left Nora in a daze. "Mr. Colville? But how did he—and how did *you* learn of it?"

Grizel leapt back to her feet. "Oh! It is true, then! And as for how I know—why, he called us all to the great hall, he did, and pronounced the news—"

"All of you?" Nora slipped off the bed. "The whole household?"

Grizel hesitated. "Was he wrong to do so, my lady? I did grow worried when you made no appearance—"

Nora held up a hand for silence. These tidings unsettled her extremely. Calling her household to order while she had lain asleep upstairs—it was not simply high-handed, but part of his larger strategy. He had bedded her last night and made certain this morning that the entire house knew enough to testify to it.

Such cold-blooded calculation! How could she match it with the hot tenderness of his kisses?

She put her arms around herself, feeling suddenly cold. "I don't . . ."

I don't know what I should feel, or what I must do.

This was not a sentiment to be shared with one's maid. "I need to bathe," she said. "Arrange for it."

"Aye, my lady. Here, or in your own—" Grizel stopped. "That is," she said more cautiously, "will these be your chambers from now forward, my lady?"

"I don't *know!*"

The words burst from her too sharply. "Forgive me," she said. "I am—I have yet to decide on these matters. But I will bathe in my own chambers."

At least, she thought blackly, he had spared her the right to make *that* decision for herself.

In the midst of her bath it came to her with a start that she had abandoned the cloak bag in the entresol. Her frantic inquiry of Grizel, who had helped her to pack it, yielded a quick reassurance: the contents had been returned to the steward for safekeeping.

But on such a day, Nora could not take assurance for

certainty. After dressing, she went to confirm for herself that Montrose had secured the deeds.

The door to her steward's office stood ajar. She entered, expecting to find him at solitary work, but he had company: her new husband sat at the desk while Montrose hung about his elbow, solicitously attending Adrian's inspection of some document.

Glancing up, Adrian offered her a lazy smile. "Good day, lady wife."

While it was a proper greeting for a husband to offer, in the context of these strange events, it seemed as much a challenge as a welcome. "Good day," she said, but felt too uncertain of herself to smile.

Moreover, her steward's reaction puzzled her: as she stepped inside, he recoiled from Adrian's side. Had he not heard news of the marriage? How had he avoided Adrian's *announcement*?

She followed his glance downward.

Her cloak bag sat open by Adrian's feet.

The documents spread before him assumed new, shocking significance. He was inspecting the deeds and rent rolls! No wonder Montrose looked at her with hangdog eyes!

"Those are not for you," she burst out. "What business have you with those?"

"I suppose that depends," Adrian said, leaning back in his chair. "Where did you mean to take them?"

"Away," she said. "To safety. They are no business for outsiders!" She cast a sharp look toward Montrose, who busied himself in a close scrutiny of his own hands.

"And where did you think to find this safety?" Adrian asked.

If the softness of his question was intended to convey a warning, it worked the opposite effect. His presumption was stupendous; she would not be cowed in her correction of it. "That does not concern you! A soused parson might give you possession of me, but he cannot put Hodderby into your hands!"

He laid down the ancient parchment and stared at her. "Indeed. And yet, still I wonder: to whom did you seek to carry this proof of Hodderby's possession?"

Oh, ho. Did he think he had gained the right to know everything in her brain? "You may deprive me of sleep again, if you like. You may demand the answer after two or three nights of my misery. But I promise you, you will receive the same answer as you did before. It does not concern you!"

He lifted a brow. "It was no demand, only a question. I hadn't imagined that the answer might be so interesting as to merit your circumspection."

"Demand or no, you overstep yourself. Merely because I—" She cast a glance toward Montrose, unwilling to speak so plainly in the steward's presence.

Adrian understood. With a nod to the man, he said, "I will finish here."

Montrose rose.

"I have not given you permission to leave," she said sharply.

The steward divided a miserable glance between them. In a flash of bitter, black humor, she foresaw how it would go next: Adrian's imminent nod would send her steward stumbling out, his quick exit further undercutting her authority.

She did not wait for it. *"Go,"* she said.

Montrose fled, tugging the door closed behind him.

In the opening silence, she turned away from Adrian's laconic regard and went to the window. The sight of orderly fields could not soothe her, but the rain dappling the glass, and the gray sky overhead, matched her mood perfectly.

On a deep breath, she tried to collect herself. This marriage was a fact. What she said next would be crucial to how it developed. She had held her tongue a thousand, thousand times with Towe, but she could not learn to break her own spine again.

Not for him.

Not for a man who managed, despite her own best efforts of resistance, to make her long for his presence when he was absent.

Towe's opinion had never mattered to her. But to crush her own will and spirit for Adrian's sake—it would destroy her. She would never recover any measure of independence.

"Do me the favor of completing your remark," he said behind her. "I expect to find it instructive."

His composure pricked her own temper sorely. She turned on her heel. "I let you have your way in the marriage bed," she said through her teeth. "That does not mean you may trammel me in aught else. I am still the mistress of this household, and in its service I do not answer to you!"

"Trammel?" He rose, his chair scraping over the stone. "And *was* it a trammeling, then, that I delivered in that bed?"

She retreated a pace, her hips colliding with the sharp ledge of the windowsill. "Leave that be," she said, for his intent expression now threatened, with the promise of touches and kisses, to undo her purpose here. "We must come to an understanding!"

"I believed we had come to one," he said. "With my mouth on your quim, you seemed agreeable to the prospect of mastery. Shall I remind you of it?"

A strangled sound escaped her. He should not speak of such things. He was—more than wanton; he was pagan! In his face as he walked toward her now she saw his intentions very clearly.

He would take her here, in her own steward's office.

"Stop!" She threw up a hand to halt him—physically, if need be—but the gesture was unneeded, for he did pause, just out of reach.

The stamp of his features, the new tension in his face, did not require interpretation. An entrant now might have scented it in the air, this lust that leapt between their bodies and stifled her wits. The longer their eyes held, the looser felt her bones and joints.

She swallowed hard. "I did not come here to trifle with you. I did not come here expecting you at all! You have no right to interrogate my steward—"

"So many interrogations," he purred. "You seem enamored of the exercise. I do wonder, Nora, where your imagination takes you."

Her mouth went dry. It would be a girl's mistake to

think his effect on her boded well for their future. Instead of wondering at the desire she felt for him, she should deplore it as a singular weapon he alone held against her. "I must—" She paused, wanting her voice to be steady. "I must have your respect, Adrian. I must feel—I must feel as though I am not only a woman to you, but a person, a . . ." Her fists knotted in her skirts. It did not require his baffled silence to know how nonsensical she sounded. She shook her head, too dispirited to continue.

"Go on," he said quietly.

She remembered suddenly their conversation in the beehouse. Then, too, she had hesitated, and he had prompted her. He was not . . . indifferent to her opinions.

He was not Towe.

"I am your wife," she said slowly. *God above.* How strange it seemed. "But I am my own, as well. I must remain so. Do you understand what I mean?"

"I believe so," he said, just as slowly.

She took a deep breath, knowing her next words were an open invitation for his mockery. "Then . . . can you think of *my* needs? Can you . . . respect them, as much as your own?"

"But your needs are precisely my concern here," he said.

Hearing in these words a lewd double meaning, she felt her heart sink. But then, studying her, he frowned and turned to fetch the stack of documents. "Hark," he said as he turned back. "The tallies of your harvest. The number of dependents who rely on those stores, and the names of families whose yields may not suffice for the winter months. I was calculating with your steward what aid you and yours might require. As I told you, Beddleston has more than it requires."

This speech left her dumbfounded. She had not imagined such a motive. This was nothing but a kindness, for what difference did it make to him how Hodderby fared?

I have loved you for a very long time, he had said.

Wonder prickled through her. Perhaps . . . perhaps he meant those words.

Ah, God, but were these not the most dangerous words to hear from him? For now he had put them into her brain, they would lurk there forever, waiting for moments such as these to seduce her into forgetting what he had *done* rather than said.

"That is a most thoughtful and generous offer," she said softly. "But you should have put it to me, not to my man."

He laid the documents back on the table. "So I intended. But before I offered, I wished to make certain that Beddleston's stores could meet your whole need. Otherwise it would be a churlish thing to hold out hope to you for nothing."

She hesitated, torn between pressing her point again and the more immediate question, to which she surrendered with a sigh. "And what did you discover? Can you supply our requirements?"

"Happily, yes. No one need starve in the coming year."

The news overwhelmed her. Pressing her lips together, she nodded once. Not knowing what showed in her face, she turned away from his close regard and stared blindly into the fields.

This was . . . an unexpected boon, indeed. Until this moment she had not realized what a great weight these harvest worries had put upon her.

His footsteps approached; his hands closed on her shoulders, massaging them.

It felt then as though something inside her broke open. A shiver passed through her.

This was how she had imagined it would be between them, so many years ago. Tender consideration. A partnership of equals.

She felt cast into a dream. *A dream.* He had come here hunting for her brother. This dream would not end happily.

"I have every respect for you," he said quietly. "But where lies disrespect in my offer of aid? Your worries are mine own now, Nora."

What a seductive idea. His hands felt blissful. She recognized the tension she had carried only as it began to ease away under the strength of his grip. A man in love might indeed make a woman's worries his own.

But she could not surrender *all* her cares to him. "My brother's welfare does not worry you," she whispered.

His hands paused. "Must we revisit this question?"

That he needed to ask boded ill. Could she not make him see what an impossible position he had made for her, in seeking to remove her from her *bind*?

She laid her hand over his where it closed on her shoulder. "Where is my cousin Cosmo? As his host, I find it odd that he has not offered his felicitations to me."

"Your cousin felt the need to start his journey very early. He conveys his best wishes to you."

She shrugged out from his touch and turned on him. He had come so close that her body brushed his; she was trapped between his chest and the deep ledge of the window. He made no move to retreat, forcing her to hike her chin to meet his eyes.

"You mean you ordered him to depart," she said calmly. "Yes, I believe we must revisit these questions of my family. This matter will not vanish merely because we wish it."

Lightly he ran his thumb across her lower lip, so she tasted the salt of his skin. "And so you do wish it? There, at least, is a start."

She would not be distracted now by caresses. "This land is precious to me. These people . . ." She took a breath. "But they are all of a part with my family. And this estate you propose to grace with your generosity—it is only mine to care for so long as its master is absent. If I accept your aid, it will be in my brother's name."

His eyes narrowed. "You choose now to speak of matters where silence might serve you better."

"Is that a warning?" She would not look away, would not so much as blink. "Am I to hold my tongue when its tune does not please you?"

With his thumb remaining at the center of her lip, his hand turned to grip her cheek. He stared down at her an unspeaking moment. "I would have thought you knew me better."

"I know you think of my welfare. But what you cannot imagine is that I value my honor as much as you do your own."

His mouth twisted. "I see you do misunderstand me—for I find that questions of honor are better left to those who lack more pressing concerns to occupy them. And where your brother is concerned"—he made a scornful noise—"there is no honor to speak of. Any man who asks a woman to run his risks for him—"

"So you say," she cut in. "But saying it does not make it so. I say differently, you see."

He regarded her silently. It seemed he had reached the end of his willingness to argue. "Then what do you propose?"

"I know not. But of one thing, I am certain." She knocked away his hand. "You may collar me like a dog. But I will not heel, Lord Rivenham."

Sliding past him, she walked quickly out of the room.

16

Nora half expected Adrian to pursue her. When he did not, she found herself wandering the halls like a ghost in search of a haunt.

In her refusal to be distracted by his wooing, she had thought to salve her pride and teach him a lesson: he had married her indeed, and he had given her pleasure she could not deny. But he had not won her heart. Even if it inclined to him, she would not hand it over if the cost was her own self-regard.

But as she walked the house, she began to wonder at the wisdom of provoking him. Twice she encountered Adrian's men—and both times, their low conversations ended at the sight of her. She sensed some new mood among them, tense, expectant.

Perhaps, instead of reproaching Adrian, she would have done better to play the blushing bride, and woo *him* for what information he might be persuaded to share.

So unsettled, longing to cast off such worries, she

went into her solar and lifted her lute from the wall. The bench by the window afforded a good survey of the parkland, and she could not shake the intuition that Adrian's men very soon expected to see something of interest there. Taking a seat, she put herself to the methodical task of tuning and tightening the strings, then launched into a melody.

Every time the wind shifted the trees, she caught her breath. But her hands never faltered.

She had run through all her favorites and turned to less familiar melodies when a voice came behind her. "'Old Sir Simon the King,' is it?"

She turned to find Lord John hovering in the doorway.

"I do admire that song," he said.

Deliberately she let her hand slip, drawing out an ugly, discordant sound.

This subtle message went ignored. Looking right and left, Lord John stepped inside. When he drew shut the door, she grew wary, and set aside the lute to rise.

He sketched her an ornate bow, the formality ludicrous. "My dear lady," he said. "Are you well?"

The concern in his voice seemed so unlikely, and therefore nearly alarming, that she looked down at herself to find the cause for it—a wound she had not noticed, perhaps, or a snake at her feet.

"I am well," she replied, looking up with a frown. "Are *you* well, sir?" For if he had discovered a better nature, surely it had required a very hard knock to his head.

"Well? No! In truth, my mind is very uneasy. Such untoward happenings!" He took a step toward her, his hands outstretched as though to grasp hers. Startled into stepping backward, she locked her own hands behind her back, and breathed a sigh of relief when his fell.

"I feel responsible," he said. He flashed her a significant look—his lower lip plumping to produce a peculiar expression that struck her as something between anger and petulance. But when he spoke again, she realized she had misread it: he was trying to manufacture a look of guilt. "I cannot but feel that the blame is mine." Turning away, he tucked his hand into his waistcoat, striking a solemn pose for his ruminative gaze out the window. "I, no less than Lord Rivenham, was given charge of this mission. Thus, though I took no hand in it nor knew aught of it till it was done, I must bear part of the blame for your misfortune."

She realized then that he spoke of her new marriage. Her surprise was short-lived; on its heels chased suspicion.

"You must not trouble yourself," she said. This sham was to some purpose, though she could not imagine what. Indeed, she wasn't certain there was any use to knowing the answer. That the boy imagined himself Adrian's equal in command bespoke a powerful imagination. Whatever aim he had in mind, chances were it was equally fantastical.

"You bear it with dignity!" His voice dropped. "But I wish you to know, dear lady, that you have my support."

Support for what? The remark cast a lure that she had no intention of taking. She waited until the silence forced him to turn around in search of her reply.

She offered up a smile. "How kind," she said. "I will bid you good day."

"But you need not put on a brave face with me!" Now he approached again, and because she would not be driven to sidle away like a frightened mouse, she had no choice but to let him take her hands. "I understand, you see. I know that you share an uncommon closeness with your brother."

The prickle down her spine felt like a warning. Whence had David entered this game? "I do not recall that you have met my brother, Lord John."

"No, alas! I have not had that pleasure." His solicitous expression betrayed no awareness of how unlikely it was that he might describe the man he hunted as an acquaintance worth knowing. He squeezed her hands. "But I had it from your cousin that you are most devoted to him."

She did not recall such matters being raised at the table last night. "You spoke with my cousin before he departed?"

Lord John nodded. "Poor soul! How distressed he was to leave without a farewell to you. In anguish he guessed you would think it a betrayal—"

"No," she said. "I never saw it so."

His cornflower-blue eyes widened. "But of course! I told him just the same. 'How now betrayal,' I said, 'when she will understand precisely the tyranny that was wielded to expel you!' But he could not be calm, my lady! He begged of me—and I gladly gave him"—here he paused long enough to lend a peculiar emphasis to his next words—"my promise. I vowed to look after your best interests in his absence as I might for my own sister: as tenderly, as solicitously."

He still grasped her hands, but such was her amazement that she barely noted the awkwardness of it. If only she were in London now, she might have told a tale that set the court on its ear. Nobody who knew him would cast Lord John in the role of protector—least of all his sister, a wealthy widow of thirty, who when not in one man's bed was being directed by her family to the next one, the better to whisper their messages into ears gentled by her caress.

Double-tongued speeches and deceitful friendships were the court's stock-in-trade. Lord John shone in that setting, but she never had. Her next words were too wooden to match their message.

"That is generous," she said.

He hesitated, visibly cautious now. "But perhaps I misunderstand your situation?"

She felt increasingly dizzy. "I begin to think I do not understand the situation so well myself. How do you see it, sir?"

"Why, that this marriage was not to your liking," he said slowly. "How could it be, when your first loyalty must be to your dear brother?"

His question pointed toward too many traps to count.

Her smile felt stiff on her mouth. "You have considered my brother a criminal, Lord John. To ask me if I am loyal to him seems a question with teeth."

He studied her intently. "Yes, I suppose it does. Will you take it amiss, madam, if I speak plainly? I do not believe you were planning a marriage at supper last night—at least, not to Lord Rivenham. I find this changes my view of things. I begin to reconsider who be the criminal here, and who be the victim."

Her foreboding returned, sharper now, drawing her stomach tight. "Oh," she said softly. Here was plain speaking, indeed. This boy was trying to entice her into some confederation against his master, her new husband.

She would rather treat with a feral boar. At least then she would be able to predict with some certainty when the creature would turn on her.

Gently she pulled her hands from his grasp. "I am grateful for your kindness," she said. Walking past him, she pulled open the door.

A sound came from down the hall—a laughing exchange, one of the voices Adrian's.

Lord John paled. "We'll speak more anon," he said. "Good day, sweet lady!"

He slipped past her, out the door.

Nora returned to her window seat, taking up the tune once more. She was out of practice, but her fingers remembered the notes well enough to proceed without her direction.

What manner of mischief was that mooncalf designing? She would not trust him for the world. But his talk had sown seeds . . . and now they began to sprout in her mind.

Why had he spoken to Cosmo? Had he recognized in her cousin a common enemy to Adrian? Could it be that the two men had jointly conceived some plan?

If so, could she blame Lord John for hinting it to her? She was David's sister, Cosmo's cousin, an unwilling bride. Where in those roles lay any cause for this uneasiness she felt at the notion of a plot against Adrian?

If even Lord John, who disliked her, thought her a natural ally—then what did it say of her that she worried instead for her husband?

Traitor: so David might have called her for it.

A footstep came behind her. She did not bother to look but made the tune in her hands run faster, concentration her pretext for failing to speak. The disquiet inside her was swelling; it ached like a bruise. She did not understand herself. Had Lord John intended to broach some private message from Cosmo? What if he meant to come over to her brother's side, the better to spite Adrian? How would she account to David for her failure to encourage Lord John in such matters?

I could not trust him, David—no, nor Cosmo either!

And how should I have trusted Cosmo? If there was indeed a betrothal between us, you should have informed me of it!

Perhaps there had never been a betrothal, though. Perhaps Cosmo had lied.

Then I was all the more right to suspect him. And of course I could not trust Lord John.

Behind her came a sweet chord. Her fingers stumbled briefly. The music of the mandolin rose like laughter, a light and bright counterpoint to the throaty tune she plucked.

She glanced over her shoulder. Adrian sat on a stool, his attention on his hands, which flowed over the strings with unlikely grace for their size. A lock of his hair had fallen loose and snaked like a length of sunlight along his cheek.

She turned back to the window, swallowing hard against a sudden feeling of tears. Lack of sleep accounted for this ridiculous reaction. An unwanted marriage undertaken at midnight might overset any woman.

Yet, as she forced herself to continue to play and his tune twined with hers, the music made her throat fill until she could not swallow. It was so easy to play with him. She still understood, after six years, as by instinct, how her fingers must improvise to aid his approaching runs.

And oh, their song! Caution and foreboding faltered before it. It seemed to leap between them, twisting and braiding into something far greater than its parts. The music caught her in its grasp; it lifted away the sorrow and turned her mood; a sense of wonder filled her at the graces Adrian performed on his strings, a feeling of laughter that made her own fingers fly faster.

This was music: not idle pastime or distraction but a force of its own, exalting. It swept through her and called up her soul, pushing the laugh out from her lips. A part of herself woke and saw hope where minutes ago had appeared only darkness.

She closed her eyes and gave herself over to the melody.

Finally, long minutes later, she strummed the last few bars. As the song ended, so did her joy. Her hand slapped over the courses to stop their vibrations. The lute's hollow body thumped.

I am no traitor.

It was not for him that I disliked to marry Cosmo. You told me to keep Hodderby safe. I could not do that from afar!

Adrian's hand covered her. She watched his fingers braid through hers over the fingerboard.

How could she excuse, how could she reconcile to herself, the feelings this touch stirred in her? As though all her old dreams had resurrected, in the moment before she made herself remember why she must loathe it, his touch always felt like a miracle.

"You still have a talent," he said.

She would not be wise to compliment him. But this was only the truth. "As do you."

In the long space of his silence, she struggled with herself. To stand up and walk away? To wait here, in a pause that seemed invitation to further folly?

He spoke before her mind decided itself. "I am no scholar of honor. But I would fain find a way to safeguard yours. Yet, when I ask myself how to do it, I find no answer."

A sigh slipped from her. Of all things he might have said, he had hit on a remark that did not allow for anger or fear. And what other defense did she have?

Gently he removed the lute from her grasp. She watched him return the instrument to its peg. "Why have you come, then?" she asked. "For I cannot cede my honor, Adrian."

He looked at her over his shoulder, a thoughtful and measuring glance. Then he stepped again behind her, kneeling, putting himself out of her view as his hands found hers again.

"I have come to tell you something," he said in her ear. "But the road to it is winding. May I beg your indulgence?"

The strange request from this strange posture, spoken with a tentativeness foreign to his character, left her no choice but to nod.

"These lands to your west"—his breath warmed her lobe—"they were ever my home. Because of them, I understand what Hodderby means to you."

She nodded. She had never doubted that.

"And this place," he said, "this isle, this kingdom: this is where I felt I belonged. The language I first spake was bred of this soil. The blood of my family is mixed with the blood of English kings."

"Yes." The Ferrers were an older family than her own.

She felt him set his forehead to the crown of her head, and heard his inhalation—as though he sought to breathe in the scent of her. "But so long as I kept to my forefathers' faith—a faith which had been bred of this land no less than its plants and cattle—I found no welcome here," he said. "In my own home, Nora, I have been a stranger, though I never realized it until I went to France. Only on those foreign shores did I finally feel what it might be to belong."

This was a view of his time in France that he had not shared with her six years ago. Then, he had spoken of his education, the sights he had seen, the characteristics of continental courts and peoples. And she had been hungry to travel vicariously through his accounts.

To hear him speak now of what he had *felt* then—this was an intimacy that her younger self had not known to crave. It was like balm to some sore and tired part of her that had been educated by intimacy's absence. For all the many nights at her late husband's table and in his bed, when his cold silence had pressed like a fist against her lungs, she now held her breath and waited eagerly for more, though she knew she should not.

"It was a sweet thing," he said at last. "I will not disguise it. To speak my name and see no black recognition . . . to admit my faith and find a brethren's greeting instead of suspicion and hatred . . . Perhaps I was softened by this pleasure, corrupted by it, for I grew so accustomed to it that I could not imagine its loss. Spoiled, should I say—"

"No." It hurt to hear his doubts of himself—especially when they crossed so sharply with the truth. "There is no sin in wishing to find welcome."

He lifted their joined hands to her breast as his arms tightened around her, making an odd embrace, almost prayer-like. His mouth touched the side of her throat. The most fleeting kiss. By the time she caught her breath, it was already over.

"But to chafe against unwelcome," he said, "to believe the world should accept me however I formed myself, and to complain when it did not—that is the dream of a child, not a man."

Had she imagined his lips, a moment ago? Her skin burned at that spot. "No," she whispered. "Do you not see, Adrian? It was ever a cause for my admiration—how certain you were of yourself; how you never diminished yourself, never altered, to please or suit another. But somehow . . . somehow you pleased all the same."

"And yet, I did alter. Did I not, in the end? Faith apart, you found me changed."

She swallowed. Was this some veiled apology? He was no longer the laughing boy of yore. He had murder in him now, as he himself had said. He had done a terrible thing to her. His younger self would not have done it.

But she could not resent him simply for the sin of having changed. Forsooth, she herself was no longer that wild young girl she had once been, so unafraid and so bold.

She did not want to speak words that abjured him. But she could not hold silent, either. "Perforce we all alter," she said haltingly. "Time . . . batters us. Perchance we must change or die."

Now, no doubt of the sensation, his lips turned into her hair, and his hands loosened over hers, his thumb drawing a casual stroke down her inner wrist. For a moment they breathed together in the silence, her body tightening and trembling like a drawn bow, anticipating where his lips would move next.

Slowly, so slowly, his right hand moved to her waist, lightly stroking her hip, while his left hand remained atop hers. And into her ear he said, "You are kind."

Or a fool. She had no will to withdraw from his touch. *I have loved you for a very long time . . .*

"But there was a choice for me, you know," he continued. "I might have stayed abroad. France welcomed me very gently. Only . . . I could not forget where I belonged."

She bit her lip and drew a hard breath through her

nose. But why restrain agreement? "Nor could I have done. I—I know the claws sunk by the call of home. Were I ever to have had such a choice . . ." Were she to have found herself in a world where all her young dreams might have come true, where every choice would have been hers, where adventure and glory had attended her . . . she might not have stayed, either. "We are bred to our soil."

"Yes." The word was harsh, expelled on a breath. "Bred to our soil: and yet, when here I returned, I felt myself a foreigner. What a homecoming, to return to that place where one finds himself always a stranger! It came to me then to wonder what cause I had for love of England. I found no gentle welcome here, Nora."

No, he had not.

His soft laugh sounded dark. His knuckles traced a leisurely path up her ribs, then back again. "But I needn't speak of this to you," he said. "You know better than anyone what cost my religion exacted. It touched you, too— more cruelly, mayhap, than it ever did me."

His warm lips pressed against her temple. The simplicity of the kiss fractured something inside her. Her throat closed; she felt on the edge of tears. Where his words were leading, she could not guess, but she felt, in their roughness and the increasing pressure of his hand massaging her waist, what it cost him to speak.

She would have answered him, but all possible answers threatened her. *Yes, we paid a high price: my father treated you cruelly, and abandoned me to Towe because you had touched me. Yes, you learned a cruel lesson at the hands of my kin. And so did I.*

But she did not need to speak, for he had followed her thoughts. His cheek came against hers now. He laid his palm flat over her belly.

"Had I been other than I was," he murmured, "a son of the High Church, a son of some other man, then you and I would know no arguments. We would have children now. A strapping boy of five years—"

"Stop." She closed her eyes. She would not see this image he conjured. It pained her in her very marrow. "Such fantasies are for fools. You are who you are." She would not have wished him otherwise, even when her suffering had been sharpest.

What a truth!

It rang through her like a bell. In its echoing aftermath she felt shaken and . . . suspended, poised on the edge of something momentous.

"And now you are speaking as I do." The barest trace of humor skated through his words. "You resolve to be immune to all but plain truths."

She tried to turn toward him but his arms tightened, holding her in place.

"I made plain truth my guide," he said. "After I lost you, I saw what faith had cost me and I could not envision a greater loss. And so I turned away from it. I would not live as a stranger in my own land. But that cost me, too. I had lost you, and now, in the loss of my faith, I lost my family as well. Even as I profited from the fruits of my new resolve—even as the queen showed me favor and the court began to curry favor with me—those of my blood turned their faces away."

She had wondered of his family. Never in London had she glimpsed him in the company of his kin. "I am . . . so sorry."

"Do not be. Do not be sorry for a cowardice your soul would never permit." Now he did turn her, so they knelt together in the afternoon light. "Do you not see?" His callous palms framed her face. His green eyes looked so earnest. "Had I realized in France what course my return would take, I still would have come back to England. It was home that I could not abandon—home, which remains after all else falls away. As to my family . . . I regret not the loss of those who would abandon me. I regret very little. There is only one person whom I have known to remain true in the face of such tests. And that is *you*."

His speech robbed her of breath. She laid her hands over his, pressing hard. He leaned toward her and their mouths met.

This kiss took her away from herself. Slow and soft, his lips and tongue ravished her. Such sweetness in tasting him. It would be so easy, amidst such kisses and such words, to forget that he had ridden roughshod over her, and taken by force what his words and touch now addressed so seductively.

Where was her fear, then? It was lost in his kiss. When her grip tightened, his thumb stroked once beneath her lower lip, as though to acknowledge it, or—mad thought—to reassure her: *Yes,* said his touch, *it is this way for me as well. How can you doubt?*

When their lips parted, he rested his forehead against hers, and spoke looking into her eyes. "Your loyalty is not to me. Well do I know it, Nora. But that only strengthens my course. You alone . . ." He traced the line of her cheek, his finger following it like a whisper to her jaw. "You alone," he whispered, "among every creature in my knowledge, will never let go of what is yours, no matter how it pains you. And so I know I cannot ask for your glad cooperation." Now he hooked his finger around the curve of her ear. "I cannot demand your submission. I can only hold you, and pray I keep you safe, and spare you, by force if need be, from the consequences of what I admire in you most."

Staring at him, she felt a flicker of amazement. How he looked at her! Most men reserved such regard for saints. "You think of me too highly." Soon he would find a clearer view.

He smiled slightly. "No. You think of yourself too low."

Something in her swelled at those words, something foolish and infinitely young: it was her pride. *Yes, you are right; this is who I am,* it said. How wondrous it seemed to hear such a verdict, how unbearably sweet to hear affirmed and lauded that which other men had scorned as flaws, as obstinacy, as vanity and willfulness.

He kissed her again, his hand brushing down her body, cupping her breast. The weight of his grip lent the kiss a new edge of possessiveness that awoke her caution.

To yield to his view of her was to accept that he tried to rule her from charitable and loving impulses. But she could not grant such motives to him without also accepting his rule.

She broke from his mouth. "I wish you would not praise me," she whispered. "If kindness is your aim, it would be kinder to tell me a way to hate you."

"Perhaps," he said. "But kindness is not my aim here. And well you know it."

With the flat of his palm on the small of her back, he brought her to him again. Now his hand grew busy, stroking the cloth over her nipple as the gentle address of his lips warmed her in waves. In fevers one felt like this: sluggish, helplessly adrift in a warm, pulsing haze, unable to rouse oneself. When his lips dropped to her throat and he sucked the tender skin there, her eyes fluttered closed. She heard her own stuttering breath, the small sounds of her building pleasure. The place between her thighs clutched and ached.

"I promised myself I would leave you be," he said against her skin. "For the day, at least."

In her daze, she could think of nothing more cruel. His wandering hand now slipped from her breast, but an adjustment of an inch would satisfy her again. She made her own adjustments, running her hand down his abdomen, then farther yet, until she found with her hand the rigid shape of his cock.

His body did not desire restraint.

"And will you leave me be?" she asked hoarsely.

His laughter was soundless, a warmth along her neck. "Not all decisions are mine, love."

The words stroked through her like a caress. She grasped his shoulder and tipped herself backward, drawing him over her, trusting his hand at the small of her back to protect her from hard contact with the floor. Silent and graceful, he followed her down, pulling her collar aside to set his mouth to her bare shoulder. A small breath escaped her, a sigh that felt almost wistful.

The solar was small, the walls bare but for the instruments, whose polished mahogany bodies shone overhead in the sun. The rude stone floor made no romantic bed; the muffled voices from the hallway did not permit her imagination to paint a bower in her mind. But when he slid his hand up her bare calf and took hold of her inner knee, when he urged her legs apart, the feel of her own muscles bending to his direction felt like a revelation. She could imagine no greater enchantment than this: the flooding light, and the cool air of an autumn afternoon, and the music suspended above them, and this man who kissed her now, as reverently as though his kiss were a prayer, and she were his faith, and the press of their bodies, a sacrament.

"Come," he said into her mouth. "Let me take you to bed."

In the hushed stillness of her bedchamber, he made quick work of undressing her, amazed at his good fortune when she made no protest. They stood by the bed, he turning her in his arms, unveiling her: pale skin, and full breasts with nipples ripe for sucking, a slim waist that swelled into hips to hold her by when he laid her down, very soon. Her body might have been the inspiration for a viola da gamba, the most harmonious collection of curves, producing the sweetest vibrations.

But when he stepped back to see her more fully—a breath of amazement escaping him—he noticed how her knees pressed together and a hot blush burned her face.

When she reached for her discarded gown, he took her wrist to stop her. She froze. "It is not . . . natural to me . . . to be so immodest in light of day," she said in a strangled voice.

He let go of her wrist to catch a strand of hair and curl it behind her ear. "What is immodest here, Nora?" He watched his hand drop, tracking the unblemished curve of her shoulder, skimming the slope of her breast, heavy and full, the dusky tip hardening. The sight struck something raw and hot in him, so powerful that his hand trembled a little as it passed onward to the slope of her waist.

"This is you," he said. "If to show yourself is a sin, then the sin is temptation, for any man in the world would covet you in his heart."

"Flattery." She seemed to attempt levity with this accusation, but her hitching voice did not manage it.

Nevertheless, he called up a smile for her. "I will show you flattery." He dropped to his knees before her, breathing in the scent of her rounded belly, a voluptuous goad, softer than any man deserved. The flat of his hand could span the length from her pubis to navel, above which he placed his lips, touching her with her tongue so she gasped.

The sound unhinged some piece of him that he badly

required. He paused, gripping her hips, searching for his control as he came up against a dark truth in himself. He had bedded other women, and he had done it very well, so that both of them rose satisfied from bed. But what he did with this woman was no simple bedding. The desire that moved him to it was not simply concerned with satisfaction. This hunger in him wanted to break her open so completely that she would never recover her reserve; that she would forget, for eternity, that once her body had been aught else but his.

It was not an innocent craving.

It was too near to violence for him to trust.

But this was the only love he had known, and so perhaps this was the nature of love itself, nothing elegant or pretty in it. He was learning again, after six years, why love and bloodshed seemed to poets to be natural confederates, for he would split the skull of any man who came between him and this woman.

He kissed her belly again, slowly now, feeling in the sudden tension of her buttocks that she had divined his course. Her hands fell fretful into his hair as he pressed her by the hips to walk backward toward the bed, until she sat hesitantly onto the edge of the mattress. But her fingers were squeezing a protest, tightening to draw up his head.

Perhaps some wise instinct in her divined his greater aim. A sense of self-preservation drove her to resist what would give her pleasure. But pleasure was the greatest weapon he wielded against her now in his campaign to seduce her heart to his possession.

He took her hands in his and lifted them free of his hair, then stretched up on his knees to kiss her mouth before he pushed her by the shoulder, gently but firmly, into a reclining position on the bed. With his shoulder he parted her legs more widely, so she lay exposed to him, like a feast awaiting his leisure.

"I . . . do not think I like this," she said in a high, nervous voice. But she did not close her legs. Between them, the heart of her opened like a flower, pink and scarlet, dewed beneath his touch. She bucked at the light stroke of his finger and an anxious noise escaped her, but her effort to squirm backward was halfhearted, halted easily by his hand on her knee.

He placed a kiss on her inner thigh, taking an almost savage gratification in how her flesh quivered beneath his lips. "I will teach you to like it," he said hoarsely.

He slid his hands beneath her buttocks and lifted her to his mouth. Her moan reached his ears as he tasted her. Then, as though to correct herself, she said, "You needn't—"

It was to his advantage that she thought so—to his advantage that she did not realize how her quickening breath, and the small movements of her hips, and the feel and taste of her in his mouth, gratified that black part of him that wanted only her compliance, her duty, her loyalty, her devotion, her unswerving and unconditional and unceasing surrender. God, but this dark creature in him wanted her whether it cost him the rest of the world, or even her respect, for at moments like this, to have her, to have her any and every way he could, seemed worth any cost.

Her thighs closed around him, gripping his shoulders, urging him upward, over the wondrous terrain of her body. He permitted it, letting his mouth lead the way up her ribs to the tight peak of her nipple that he took between his lips and sucked until she writhed. But she had an aim now, and moved beneath him with purpose, inching down until her hot quim brushed his cock.

Their eyes met. She still looked too much herself, when he wanted her flushed, wild, beyond herself.

But her hand between them brought him to her entrance, and then he was pushing inside her, and it was he who was lost.

17

Adrian was not accustomed to a desire for compliments. But as he crested the hill, he discovered in himself a peculiar anticipation. Reining to a halt, he waited for Nora to reach him.

She was laughing as she approached, amused perhaps by some tomfoolery of her mare. When their eyes met, she shook her head and rolled her eyes, still smiling, inviting him to share in her pleasure. Her color was high, and beneath her wide-brimmed hat, her tight cap had not proved equal to the sharp, cool wind. A wayward lock of black hair had escaped it, lashing across her mouth, then snapping behind her when the wind turned.

She glanced beyond him and her smile faded. Gripping the pommel with one gloved hand, she leaned forward. "Beddleston?"

"Yes."

She gave him a brief, wondering look. He did not need to ask the cause. Beddleston was not so large as Hodderby, nor so elegant. Yet it made an imposing sight. Adrian's fore-bears had dismantled the stones of the abbey that once had stood here and heaped them again into a wall that encircled the house and the moat. Because they had been Catholic, not a single generation of Ferrers had imagined there might come a time when such defenses proved unnecessary.

"It's a castle," Nora said.

"Something of it."

"I had not imagined it so."

"Did you imagine it often?"

Her eyes were serious by their very design, large but heavy-lidded, the color of smoke. They held his steadily for a silent moment. "How could I not have?" she said finally. "In those days . . . when you left, my thoughts flew after you."

It satisfied him to hear her speak so easily now of that bygone time. With a nod of his head, he encouraged her to spur forward down the hill.

She rode well, his wife—not boldly, for there was nothing showy in her comportment. But her very ease, the grace with which she sat her mount, made for a pretty show, one which he slowed to enjoy.

My wife.

Seven days had passed now since those words had be-come his to use, and he had spoken them more times than he cared to count—silently, to himself; to his men; and often to her—who, to his surprise, did not bridle or dispute the title. After their wedding night, she had not mentioned annulment again.

Perhaps, as had been his intention, he had wooed the

idea straight from her brain. Certainly he neglected no opportunities. His body increasingly seemed to him the only claim he could press on her that was able to keep her undivided attention. What progress he made in luring her nearer to forgiveness, he had begun now to chart by the number of her sighs when she lay beneath him, or by the hot looks he intercepted, so quickly averted, when he passed her in the hall.

Otherwise she excelled in keeping occupied at endeavors too feminine to allow his company. He had little care for others' judgments, but his own pride did scruple at following her from larder to garden, slipping in bids for her attention as she supervised her house. The bed and table were where he laid siege to her. Dining in private at the end of the day, he drew her into conversations that proceeded like horses being broken: now smoothly running, now bucking to a stop.

Those moments at supper yielded, perhaps, the most valuable clues to how he must proceed. As they spoke of poems and far-flung places and dusty histories and philosophy, he glimpsed in her pauses how she battled herself—how her laughter suddenly became, to her ears, an indictment of her character.

Every time he charmed her, her smile belatedly signified to her a betrayal of her family.

Every time her smile faltered, he returned to the question of killing David Colville—who, like his father before him, now appeared to have abandoned a woman who would not permit herself to abandon him.

There was no news of the man. Yesterday, before receiving word of the rebels' defeat at Preston, Adrian had written to the king, speculating that Colville might have gone into battle there, or perhaps ridden north to Scottish soil. *I begin to think he never intended to return to his property here, though his sister fully expected him.* He had closed the letter with a proposal to return to London, where he might be of use in formulating a policy to handle the aftermath of the upheavals.

He had not spoken of this yet to Nora.

A boy spotted them as they neared the fortified wall. Recognizing Adrian, he ran ahead, bare feet flying, yelling for the gates to be opened.

"He is eager," Nora said with a smile.

"He's a scamp, off on a pretext in search of a hiding place, for I promised to wallop him if ever I caught him again without shoes."

Her laughter sounded surprised. "But who are his parents?"

"Distant relations," he said. "Deceased."

"Do you take in many orphans?"

Her voice was teasing. But the answer was simple. "Any who are Ferrers, or related thereof."

She kept smiling at him for a moment, and then a blush rose in her face, and she ducked her head and looked away, absorbing herself in a survey of the walls they now approached. New freckles showed on her cheeks and the slim bridge of her nose. Here in the country she never wore powder.

To take her to London would be a mistake. He knew what the city meant to her, and how easily old habits were recovered. Hope might suggest that her dislike of court would draw her nearer to him, her only counsel . . . but wisdom suggested otherwise. In so many regards she remained out of his reach, and in the city, reminded of the mask she had once worn, she would find it easier to remain aloof from him.

If he could not win her in Hodderby, the place where she felt safest to be herself, then in London he would lose her—for at court, nobody was ever himself.

Perhaps *he* was never himself but with her. Or rather, with her, he was more than himself. He did not recognize this excess of emotion within him. Six years out of practice, he had yet to fathom a way to govern it.

To have her at court would pose a dangerous distraction to his composure.

Yet, he had no choice but to take her, for he could not leave her alone so long as her brother remained on the loose.

Side by side they rode across the short wooden bridge that spanned the moat. Late-blooming water violets stippled the green water. On the bank, half hidden by a profusion of wild roses, two swans loitered, their chins tucked modestly to their chests. Thence into the large, well-combed yard, where they drew up in the shade of an elder tree sprouting with scarlet berries. The passing of the wet weather had given rise to a riot of color. Stands of yellow poppy and purple foxglove hugged the walls, and the ivy was verdant where it spilled down Beddleston's weathered face.

"But how beautiful," Nora said as he helped her dismount. On the ground, she hesitated, encircled by his arms, to consider the crenellated tower that topped the great hall. "That facing is new."

She had a sharp eye. In Adrian's childhood, the tower had collapsed, killing a man. His father had ordered the stones removed, the hall repaired and roofed. For almost two decades Beddleston had lacked a tower. But without one, its vantage, nestled in the valley, lacked a clear view to the surrounding hills.

"It was repaired this winter," Adrian said.

She gave him an opaque look. "And the moat? Was that repaired as well?"

He smiled and offered her his arm. When she looked like to press him, he tilted his head toward the front doors. "Your curiosity does honor to your house, my lady. Come meet your people."

Her startled look betrayed that she had not taken note, before, of the servants forming a line by the front doors to greet her.

The brief dance of her fingers on his arm revealed her disquiet. But she drew herself upright and moved forward with him, making poised courtesies to the twenty men and women there assembled before allowing Adrian to draw her into the entry hall.

The stained glass in the entresol above shed rainbow light across the tiled hall. In a puddle of scarlet they paused to be divested of their outerwear. "No luggage," Adrian said to the porter, "only the saddlebags without." They had ridden hard today and planned to return to Hodderby at dawn. "Have my sisters and brother readied to greet us before supper."

Again he caught her curious, speaking look, but she made no comment as he led her onward.

Up the broad wooden stairs they went, she running a curious hand over the carved balustrade. The niches in the walls, once used to house torches, now supported brass urns overflowing with flowers. These, too, she touched gently as she passed, fingering the petals of roses and lilies, her gaze wandering. The stained window, which showed the martyrdom of St. Theresa, briefly caught her attention, but it was the oil portraits of his ancestors that most plainly intrigued her. Near the top of the staircase, she came to a halt.

"This is you," she said.

The painting had been made in his university days in France. As he watched her study his younger self, a bittersweet feeling took him by surprise. When she glanced back to him, he bit down an impulse to ask her if she could still find that boy in him—if she could tell him where to look.

Instead he put his thoughts to what miracles time had wrought on her. Taking her by the shoulders, letting the softness of her breasts against his chest serve as answer to any questions his rotted brain might manufacture, he kissed her in full view of those who cared to look.

Another surprise: her mouth yielded to him when he had expected her to complain for privacy. A gentle hand fluttered over his back, then gripped his waist with a strength that belied its size. She stepped closer yet, fully against him, and the kiss she gave back to him grew puzzling, flavored by something that felt closer to desperation than desire.

He set his forehead to hers. "What is it?"

She shook her head, but her hands traveled down his hip to skate, provocatively, the top of his buttocks.

He almost spoke bluntly: there was a library directly behind them and its floor or furniture could be made fit for their purpose.

But the odd quality to her silence commanded his own. For a long moment they stood together, breathing, as she leaned into him.

At last, haltingly, she said, "This place . . . I did not expect it to be so lovely."

"No?" He kept his voice soft. "Does it please you, then?"

"It feels like"—she gave an abashed tug of her lips— "an enchantment to me." She ducked her head as though embarrassed by her admission.

He gently took her chin to lift her eyes to his. "I am glad," he said. This was the place that gave all his efforts meaning. To have her here . . . no sweeter triumph had ever been his than to be able to say, "And now it is your home as well."

"Yes," she said, but some anxiety still trembled in her voice. "Yet I cannot but think, looking around . . . that this was where you thought of me." She glanced back to his portrait. "Where you slept six years ago," she whispered. "Where you rode from to meet me. As though it were . . . haunted by us."

"I rode from here a month ago, too," he said. "And how fortunate for me that I did."

He felt, heard, the hitch of her breath. She kissed him

again, then, a short and violent kiss from which she broke suddenly, slipping past him to climb the rest of the stairs.

He showed her onward to his chambers, where he watched her walk the corners of his dressing room. *Haunted by us*: her words began to make sense as he saw this room through her eyes. Here were the most prized ornaments of his history—the astrolabe on his writing desk, collected from a Turk in Italy; the *mappa mundi* that he had found at a market in Antwerp, painted on goatskins stitched to the width of a man's outstretched arms. Volumes of philosophy and rhetoric sat on the oak bookshelves. He was a man of few personal possessions, and until this moment, he had never considered what they might say of him. But to see her close examination of them . . . suddenly he realized that each held a story that he might wish to share with her; and that in sharing these stories with her, these objects would finally realize their value.

The odd, poetic thought unnerved him. Too late he remembered the one item in this room that he did not entirely wish her to see.

Her steps faltered as she spotted it. Slowly, with a hand that looked to tremble, she opened the door of the small glass-fronted cabinet that sat beside his dressing table.

The silver pomander, worked in delicate filigree, no longer smelled of her. Or perhaps she no longer smelled of the herbs that she had stored in it, once upon a time, when she had worn it daily, next to her heart.

She turned to him, the pomander clasped in her fist, her mouth thin and white, her eyes shining. "You . . . kept this?"

He could not endure her tears. "Not for sentiment," he said with deliberate honesty. "I spake curses to it more often than not." He had told himself, these many years, that he kept it as a reminder of the cost of weakness.

He wondered now if it had not taught him, instead, how to lie to himself with conviction.

She shook her head, looking as though she did not believe him, or had not heard him right. Very carefully, she replaced the pomander in the cabinet, then gazed upon it a moment longer before she whispered, "Adrian . . . why did you bring me here?"

He took a breath. There were plain answers to give: it was meet that a new wife should see her holdings; that she should know her husband's family, though those in residence be yet in the schoolroom.

But the truth was not so plain.

In order to know her, one must know Hodderby. So, too, with him and this place.

He wanted her to know him here.

To speak such words was impossible. The very prospect stopped his throat. He was not a boy to beg her to know him, or to forgive him for forcing her hand. He had bullied her into marriage to protect her life, and he would not bargain with her now in the hopes of gaining a greater reward than her health. He was no self-deluding fool: never had he imagined that stripping her of choices would win him her love.

He was at peace with this, was he not? He had practice in surrendering love: he had let go of any number of people in his life. The losses had scarred him, but they had never rearranged his innards.

Only now, here, in this moment, did he understand that it would not be the same, should she be lost again.

So what, then? Would he play the jailer for the rest of his natural life? Would he lock the bird in its cage until it forgot how to sing? What use, then, for the cage, once the song had gone?

She watched him very closely. "I am glad to see this place," she said. "Do not mistake my meaning. It . . . to be amongst everything that is you . . ." She lifted her fist to her chest. "Here, it almost . . . hurts me." She tried for a smile. "I see all I lost. Or rather . . . the full nature of what I never could have had, long ago."

"But it was not to taunt you that I brought you here," he answered slowly. "Only that it seems to me—" He cleared his throat. Explanation went against his grain, but for her, he would try. "It seems that you look upon my intentions toward your brother as willful persecution. But each of us has people of our own, Nora, and places worth protection."

She looked at him uncertainly for a moment, and then comprehension whitened her face. "But who have you to fear?" She took a quick step toward him. "You are Rivenham! Surely no one could touch *you*!"

Her hand was reaching for his. He took it, squeezing hard. "None of us is without enemies. You of all people know this. Your father was no small figure, but he was careless, and rested too comfortably on his laurels. What keeps a man powerful is his dissuasion of his enemies' aims. This task which was set me with regard to your brother—my failure is one of their aims. How would it look if I failed? I, a former recusant?"

"But—" She looked dazed, as though it truly had never occurred to her that to set a former Catholic on the trail of a Jacobite might be a task as politically perilous to the former as the latter. "There must be another way to rout them!"

"There are many ways to defend oneself." That was only the truth. "Do not mistake me: I do not speak to you from a place of fear. I merely ask you to understand that I did not conceive your brother's downfall as a piece of private malice. It was ever part of a larger contest, which I have little choice but to wage."

To his surprise, she put her arms around him, digging her head into his chest as she said in a muffled voice, "I had never thought . . ." In the pause that opened, her swallow was audible. "I was selfish. All my care was . . . for what I must give up. I never thought you had aught to lose."

But his ears had latched onto one notion in particular, and it fixated his predatory instincts. "What you must give up," he repeated softly. "Would that be me?"

Her head lifted. She reached up to cup his face, and the touch of her cool, soft hands was sweeter perhaps than any words she might have spoken. "Oh, Adrian." Her voice seemed clogged with unshed tears. But then she pulled his head down to hers, pressing her lips to his fiercely, and her kiss spoke nothing of grief. The hot hunger in it instantly kindled him.

He caught her by the waist, holding her steady as he returned like force with like. She pressed her body into his, sliding her hand into his hair with stinging violence. "Take me to bed," she said into his mouth.

This forwardness was new. He meant to encourage it. He swung her into his arms and kissed her again, using his shoulder to knock open the door to the next chamber, carrying her to the bed and setting her upon it.

He meant to follow her down, but the vision she made arrested him: hair tousled, slipping from its pins; sober dark skirts knocked over her knees to reveal embroidered stockings and slim legs. As he gazed upon them, they opened in a wanton invitation that made his entire body tighten to steel.

He exhaled. Here on this bed he had lain through so many open-eyed nights, forbidding himself thoughts of her. And here she now lay, like a sultry vision designed to lure saints from their pedestals.

"You are beautiful," he said slowly. What an insufficient word.

The smile that curved her mouth raised the hairs on his nape. When she lifted a hand to him, she might have been beckoning an army, gesturing for the destruction of cities and the embarkation of war ships, or the lowering of the moon: such was the uncanny, hot power she radiated.

"Come," she said, her gray eyes slumberous.

Hesitantly, almost fearing himself—for this was no gentle desire that roared in him—he sat on the bed. But she was not content for patience: seizing his elbow, she pulled him down atop her. Reclaiming his mouth, she wrapped her leg around his and anchored him to her.

Her confidence silenced his hesitation. He drove his hands through her hair, plundering what she offered—

nay, what she insisted that he take. Beneath him she was sinuous, wild and hot as a flame as she arched against him, her hips goading him on. In her boldness now she took him back to the time when neither of them had known caution—for he had not seduced her, six years ago, but they had seduced each other. Together, equally, they had burned.

Nora opened her mouth on Adrian's throat, tasting the salt of his skin, digging her nails into his flesh. Some wild hunger drove her, wanting a brutal satisfaction. The pomander—it had been that pomander which shattered her . . . Oh, to see it again, which she had given so long ago, and guessed destroyed. To see this place, and him within it, finally, when those many years ago, all she'd had of him were stolen hours in the wood . . .

Until she had seen him here, now, it had not struck home to her what he risked by marrying her. And yet, he had risked this enchanted place once before, too—had risked his right to it, and his welcome in it, when he had defied his family to come for her.

The risk had profited him nothing. Yet he had taken it once again when he'd wed her.

She kissed him fiercely, willing her tongue and lips to communicate what words could not. This desperation felt almost panicked. How had she not seen him more clearly? What god would not punish a woman for failing to see this man's worth? She felt seized by the strange conviction that somewhere, in some sibyl's cave on a distant shore, an hourglass with their names was trickling its last grains of sand.

She was grateful when he growled and drove his hands through her hair, grateful for the slight pain of his grip and the aggression of his mouth; it bespoke a mood to match her own. The unyielding press of his body, the unhesitant strength with which he directed her head to a more opportune angle, took her away from herself, breaking the reign of mind over flesh. Her bodily need ruled her now; her troubled thoughts fell away.

She clasped him to her, nipping his throat, the flavor of his warm skin inspiring an animal strategy. Pushing his hand away, she gripped him by the shoulders and forced him ungently beneath her. Then, shifting herself atop his body, she placed her feet on his and flexed her toes to lift herself higher. Shamelessly she rubbed against him, against the thick, hot length of his cock, but it was not enough. Twining her calf around his thigh, hooking her arms around his neck, she laid herself along him and clung like a vine. Vines were soft and easily cut, but when they set deep roots and wrapped tightly enough, they could topple even the tallest stone walls.

I am not letting you go.

He placed his leg between hers and lifted her with his thigh, but the bulk of her skirts concealed the feel of his shifting muscle. These clothes seemed suddenly to be unbearable impediments, requiring patience where none remained. Even his hand gripping her clothed waist seemed an insult to the skin beneath, which wanted only his nakedness against hers.

When she clawed at the fastenings of his shirt, he caught her hand in a hard grip and went still. She met his eyes, growing aware all at once of the rasp of her own breath, ragged as an animal's. Her face turned hot. But he looked arrested, not appalled; a slow smile took his mouth as his green eyes traced over her face. "Such hurry," he murmured.

His voice was more beautiful to her than music, low and husky, rich with promises. What a picture he made beneath her, his silver hair mussed from her hands, his white shirt disarranged, half-open at his tanned throat. "Indulge me," she said, and the throaty tenor of her words intrigued her and made her feel hotter. "Indulge me," she said again, and turned her head to flick her tongue over his wrist where he gripped her.

He made a sound like a choked gasp. "Thoroughly, Lady Rivenham."

But despite his promise, the kiss he gave her when he pulled her head down was slow and deep, a leisurely address that reached into her like the whisper of music. His fingertips trailed down the profile of her body, then slid up beneath her skirts, coaxing each part of her, each bone and joint and muscle and span of skin, as though they were new to any touch, objects of enchantment, to be wooed into waking.

His wooing lulled her. He divested her of skirts so gracefully that the movement of her hips beneath his direction felt like part of their dance. When he turned her in his arms, rolling her beneath him again, she felt as though she moved through water, deliciously weighted, surrounded everywhere by his touch, by his smell, his warmth and his eyes. He helped her to bare his chest, and the feel of it beneath her mouth as she rained kisses along his flat belly made her ache.

She knocked aside his hand when he would have helped to remove his breeches. She wanted to reveal him herself. His hips were slim, his thighs thick with muscle. Nature had designed him in long, muscular lines. She smoothed her hands up the sinewy breadth of his calves, using her nails on his thighs, and then grasped his cock, gratified by the oath she heard him bite out.

She could wait no longer, and it came to her how she might satisfy herself.

She crawled up over him and settled astride his thighs. Leaning forward to kiss him, she felt his smile as she directed his cock, and then his sigh as she lowered herself slowly onto him.

He was large, and despite her desire, it took care to accept him fully. Once penetrated, anchored to the hilt by his thick flesh, she leaned forward to kiss him. His eyelashes fluttered against hers; he took her bare hip in a steady, callous grip and urged her to rock against him, making a low noise as she began to move.

She sighed into his mouth. These noises they made were songs upon songs, music created between them. With her mouth she traced his jaw, then shaped the solid breadth of his shoulder with her lips, gasping again when he lifted his hips to thrust more forcefully.

Nothing had ever felt so right to her as this moment. The designs of his mouth along her throat amazed her;

they were full of love. Somehow he saw no flaw in anything he had done for her, and God save them both, but she finally understood why: when he spoke of *home*, he included her within it.

The pleasure built in her in fleeting sensations as he worked in and out of her. His eyes locked onto hers, and her heart swelled; she laid her hand along his cheek, riveted by this shared gaze, feeling now finally as though she saw the full truth of him, all he had done for her, the whys and wherefores of it. From now forward, anger could never again be her shield against him. She had never stopped loving him. Only now she loved him with her eyes open to all the impossibilities: to how easily and brutally she might lose him; to how neatly fate and politics had designed their romance to become, soon enough, a tragedy.

Love was no solution here. It only brought her dilemmas into a more terrible focus. But in this bed there were no dilemmas. There was only him, and she could have him now—and afterward, again—and after that, again.

Her climax came all at once: a greedy, almost painful seizing, violent, euphoric. As it released her, she clutched his shoulders and put her head into his throat. His hands ran over her back and then tightened; he rolled her over beneath him, making three deep, hard strokes before he, too, shuddered and finished.

When she slipped from bed afterward to dress, Adrian checked the impulse to restrain her. He watched her busy herself in the retrieval of clothing; mustered some sane reply when she excused herself to use the bath the servants had arranged. The door shut behind her and he lay still, trying to reason with himself.

Force did not always serve a man.

To refuse to let go guaranteed nothing.

He knew this lesson best of all. Why, even God had slipped away from him while he'd still clutched his rosary. Had David Colville succeeded in killing him that day long ago, he would have died a believer, faith scenting the blood that spilled over Hodderby's flagstones. But instead he had risen again, empty of it—though not by choice, and not with knowledge, at first, of this new emptiness in him.

The emptiness had not concerned him until he had met her again. He had felt it as a strength, not a lack. He could let go of anything.

But now he had her, his view of himself had changed. When he compassed his life now, it seemed a series of empty chambers, full of the echoes of fading footsteps and doors closing to him.

He pictured her in the fading light, the curve of her cheek, the deceptive fragility of her narrow shoulders, the softness of her lips that he had tried to bruise with his mouth that day in the apple grove. He pictured her, who stood in the next room, behind a closed door, and tried to remind himself of his lessons.

The tightest grip failed to hold the most important things. There was no use in giving chase.

But never before had he wished so fiercely to do so.

18

Nora flew upright, her heart in her throat.

The bed curtains stood open. Moonlight showed the indentation on the mattress where Adrian had lain beside her. They had reached Hodderby very late, taking to bed shortly after supper.

Where had he gone?

Her heart began to slow. What a nightmare she'd been having! She could not recall the details, only she had been in the wood, one among faceless dozens, lacking noses and mouths, unable to cry out as armed men encircled them.

Her brother's men. Yes—the same group that had come to remove the weaponry. They had raised their swords, and blood had leached through the snow—

Shuddering, she pulled the coverlet higher, then touched her face, feeling for the reassurance of lips, nose, and eyes. What a peculiar visitation. The prick of terror still felt fresh, but she remembered, too, an overwhelming feeling of anger and humiliation. In her dream, she had been as furious with herself as with her murderers.

It was not the first night this week that her sleep had been plagued so violently. Were Adrian here, she would have turned into his arms.

When alone with him, she never heard her brother's voice accusing her. No one else seemed to exist. And she wanted for nothing else, either.

She knuckled her eyes hard enough to call up sparks. What cause for fantastic nightmares when her life offered its own doomed riddle? She was in love with a man duty-bound to destroy what family remained to her. She'd spent foolish hours embroidering daydreams of a tranquil life with him, but whence tranquillity in the future that must come? If her beloved husband had his way, her beloved brother would be lost.

She reached out to touch his pillow. He had forgotten nothing of his original purpose here. Else why would he have slipped out in silence, not waking her? He walked the estates with his men, in wait of her brother. And how could she blame him for it? At Beddleston, he had told her he was helpless to change his course. If he did not recover David, his enemies would exploit his failure—

A great boom shattered the silence.

She bolted upright. The building shook.

No.

The gunpowder.

Another explosion rocked the room. She leapt to her feet as the stones in the walls groaned.

Dear God, dear God, I pray you, no. As she scrambled

for clothing, the litany repeated through her mind. She had known, hadn't she, that David's plans would come to no good? But she had done nothing, nothing but worry, when all this time it had been sitting below, a disaster in wait of the smallest opportunity—

Another blast rent the air. She caught hold of her dressing table, gripping it with all her might, waiting for the shudder to subside. How many souls under this roof? Thirty people of her own, and Adrian's men—

Where was Adrian? Had he been injured?

"Dear God, I pray you . . ." She ripped off her dressing robe and snatched petticoats and stays from the hook on the wall. With rough jerks she laced herself, heedless of comfort, tripping on the hem of her gown as she wrestled it onto her body.

The floor still trembled, a gentle but continuous quaking that might, she prayed, only be the work of her own shaking limbs, her fingers fumbling over the ties of her bodice. Muffled shouts now filtered through the walls. She tied the last of her fastenings just as the door flew open.

Sword in hand, Adrian took one comprehensive look around the room. "Are you well?"

"Yes!" She stepped toward him and he checked her with a hard, strange look, one he might have given a stranger, nothing intimate in it.

"Alone?" he asked.

She stared at him. "Yes, what else?"

Turning, he gestured with a jerk of his chin for the man at his elbow to step past him into the room. "Keep her close," he said. Looking back to her, he added, "Have you aught to tell me?"

"To—tell you?" She shook her head, confused.

He nodded once and turned to leave, sparing another word for his man: "Should it come to that, take her to the inner yard. I'll find you there."

All at once she realized where his thoughts had led him. "I know whence that came. It wasn't David!"

Both men wheeled toward her. "Where?" Adrian demanded.

"Beneath the old hall! In the barrels—" She hesitated for one cowardly moment, appalled by what she must admit, the danger and stupidity of it. "Only the top held wine. In the compartments beneath, hidden, there was gunpowder."

His man, the dark, bear-like Braddock, made a choked noise, as easily contempt as surprise.

Adrian's eyes narrowed. But when he spoke, there was no anger in his voice, only a deadly calm. "It would take a match. Can you say who lit it?"

"Nobody knew it was there—and if they did, nobody would incite it—not to Hodderby's peril—"

"Yet you knew of it," Adrian's man muttered.

The truth of his remark did not lessen its sting. Flushing, she kept her eyes on her husband—who abruptly appeared to lose interest in her. "Mind her," he bit out to Braddock, then turned on his heel.

The door slammed shut.

For the briefest second she remained staring at the door, dazed by his coldness, sick at her role in this turn.

Then her better wits asserted themselves. She spun and dashed toward the window, where by leaning out she might win a view of the old wing, which curved around from the main body of the house.

Braddock caught her by the elbow. "Stay away from the glass."

She tore free of him, who was nobody to command her—but he caught her again, his grip more punishing now. Suspicion rode openly on his face when he dragged her backward.

"My brother would not do this!" She jerked ineffectually against his hold. "It was an accident—and if it were my brother, he would not target me!"

"Glass may shatter should your powder blow again. I will look myself."

He released her and threw open the sash.

The smell of burnt powder was like a blow, removing all doubt of causes. As she covered her nose with her hand, Braddock cursed and swung back to her. "Flames," he said—and once again, the world roared and shook.

Goaded by Braddock, Nora flew down the narrow, spiraling stairway that led most directly to the inner yard. As she descended, she found herself silently reciting David's reasoning, the logic he had spelled for her when she had objected to storing gunpowder so close. Stone did not burn; stone would save them. The damage would not be great or irreversible. Fire could feed on tapestries, it could travel through wooden tables and trestles; but so long as the explosions had ceased, the fire could be stopped before it reached the main body of the manor.

And the explosions were a blessing in this single regard: nobody had slept through them. Nobody lay slumbering as flames rolled toward him.

The door at the bottom of the stairway stood open, revealing a night sky stained by flames, the color of old blood, of apocalypse and portents. She stepped into smoke-scented air. Two stablehands led blindfolded horses toward the main yard; a scullery maid and a footman rushed by with buckets of sand.

For its disuse, the old wing had not been equipped for fire, and the minutes it took to carry equipment toward the flames would require every hand available. She turned to enlist Braddock to this end—and found him slumping silently into the dirt.

Her brother stood over him.

"Come!" He grabbed her wrist and pulled her along the wall. She stumbled and he dragged her onward through the shadows.

"Wait! We must—"

"*Come!*"

Around the corner they went, into open moonlight. The perfume of crushed basil and rosemary infected the burnt air. There, in the kitchen garden, he drew up and gripped her by the shoulders. Only then did she realize she was swaying.

"Are you all right?" he asked urgently.

David looked sallow and near to gaunt, and his dark

hair stood up in corkscrew tangles. The smile he tried for her look more like a grimace. She clutched his upper arms, unable to speak. He was *here*.

He pulled her into a fierce, swift embrace. Tears pricked her eyes. He clasped her to the point of pain.

"I have horses," he said in her ear. His voice was scraped raw, as though he'd been screaming. "In the wood. Can you run?"

Her senses seemed to expand, swelling out through her skin as the strange numbness evaporated. The night was full of sounds, distant screams and cries. "Hodderby is burning!"

"There was no other way. How else could I have reached you? Cosmo told me of what that whoreson has done—"

She jerked back from him. "*You* set this fire?"

"We have no time for this!" The light of the half-moon shone coldly on his face; his eyes were black hollows as he loomed over her. "I could not leave you here to suffer that scum—"

The sliding of steel interrupted his words. But it did not come from him.

They both froze. He lifted his face; what he saw over her shoulder made him smile savagely. He thrust her behind him so suddenly that she tripped and went to her knees amidst the herbs.

"Very well," he said coldly. "This is fitting."

Adrian stood ten paces away. He wore no smile. There was nothing in his face, and that was more frightening by far.

"No," she whispered. She clawed to her feet, grabbing David's arm when he reached for his sword. "No! David—Adrian, turn away! David, fly! Go, go to the wood!"

A sharp laugh broke from her brother, a scornful reply.

Adrian spoke slowly and distinctly. "He had that chance already. But he troubled you. You will remember that, Nora."

"By God," David snarled, "I will make you regret that address. I will cut out your entrails and feed them to the swine."

The slightest, most chilling smile tipped her husband's mouth. "By all means," he said. "Proceed."

David brandished his sword and lunged.

She had seen duels before. Who had not? She had seen men ape combat in the dusty yard, or in salons for sport, or in streets from drunken rage.

But this lacked even the flourishes of a drunken brawl. As David sprang, his blade gleaming in the moonlight, Adrian made no move to meet him. His face calm, his blade lifted, he waited. And the oddity of his non-reply gave her brother brief pause—she saw it in how he hesitated.

"Farther," Adrian said, the softest goad.

With a growling noise David advanced. She cried out as their swords met, the clang of steel coming once, then again in rapid successions. Each clash made her wince; it drove her eyes shut; she opened them again, dreading blood, but neither man made his mark. As David danced retreat, Adrian lunged, but this was not a duel, no: there was nothing artful in his movement, in their intent focus as they circled each other.

These solid, heavy blows were primitive, a contest of muscle and rage.

David lashed out with a kick toward Adrian's chest. A scream escaped her.

Adrian sidestepped the kick and pivoted, his sliding steps bringing David into her line of view. Her brother's brief wondering glance gave her a start: he was wondering at her cry, at why his moment of advantage had prompted it.

Comprehension broke over her. She knew how to stop this. She knew how to prevent a death.

"I wish to stay!" she screamed. "David, leave him be—Adrian, please—I will not go with him—only leave him be—"

Neither man heeded her. David swung with brutal force, using his sword like a battle-axe to knock Adrian's aside. But Adrian recovered instantly: he had the advantage of French training, spinning and crouching in a manner not taught by English instructors.

Horror felt thick and black as mud. She would see one of them dead.

It would be David.

She would fall on his body and weep but there would be no heart left in her to break by then.

This was the true nightmare her restless sleep had foretold. There was no victory here for her, and overhead the smoke grew thicker yet. Behind them, beyond the deceptively serene facade of the west wing, the sky lightened further yet. The flames were spreading. The heart of Hodderby burned.

Her grief and panic twisted into something jagged and violent. She loathed them both—hated *both* of them—for the casual wreckage they made, for everything good and pure that they destroyed with their violent contest.

Reason left her. She looked for a rock. She looked for something to bash their skulls.

But the soil was smooth and stoneless. Hodderby's people tended its gardens well.

She looked up again. Adrian struck, quick as a snake—delivering a strange kick, a blow that swept round to catch David in the ribs and strike him off his feet. She burst to her feet, leaping forward toward David as he scrambled to recover—

Turning his sword, Adrian smashed the hilt into David's head.

Her brother lay still.

She collapsed into the dirt, grasping her brother's skull. So much blood. So much. Her palm could not staunch it. He was dead—no! A pulse beat in his throat—but his eyes did not open. "Wake up!" This blood, it did not stop. *No, no, no, no*—

A force seized her wrist and dragged her backward, her brother receding. Men encircled him, kneeling, blocking sight of his body. The men were not his friends; they handled him roughly. They must let him alone.

The vise tightened brutally around her wrist as she staggered to her feet. The men were trying to lift him.

"Do not touch him! Let him be! God curse you! Be gentle to him! Gently!"

Rough hands turned her to a new view.

The flames had spread. They crackled over the roof line. The light of hell now painted her husband's face.

He took a violent step toward her. "You *fool*! You could have been *killed*!"

She stared at him. He screamed at her? He, who had nearly killed her brother? *Had* he killed her brother?

She turned, but he caught her by the arm and hauled her back to him. *"You will look me in the eye,"* he said, and his voice was terrible, charged with rage.

She jerked against him. "Let me go! I must go to him!"

"You may go to him in hell!" he shouted. "What lunatic spirit rotted your brain? You would store *gunpowder* for him? You would let him keep it beneath your roof? You would *trust* him not to use it?"

"Stop!" She clawed at his hand, which shook her so her teeth rattled. "Stop it!"

"Would you let him put a pistol to your head for a target? Would you, Leonora? *Tell me!*"

"Let me go!" she screamed.

He did, so suddenly that she staggered. As he backed away, he spat, *"Never* preach to me again of your honor! Never pretend to me that you care for this place again! What honorable woman would store gunpowder beneath her roof—to her own peril, and to that of the innocents in her care—" He broke off, breathing heavily, and shoved his hand up his face, leaving a streak of blood, a crimson mask through which his green eyes glittered.

"Never," he bit out. "Damn you, Nora Colville. *Never again* speak to me of it."

Turning on his heel, he strode away.

As she watched him retreat, the roar in her head pitched louder yet. Sobs: these were sobs breaking from her throat, as hoarse as an animal's.

All around her, the light of the fire danced, staining the bloodied ground.

19

The day was gray, a cool gray haze that muted the colors of the land. Mist slipped down the hillsides and blotted out the valleys. The land was changing as they rode southward, but the mist did not allow for particularities of perception.

"My lord."

The road, straight and well laid, would have made for good time, if only the procession were not slowed by a woman and a prisoner. The thought goaded Adrian to urge his mount faster. Only three more days before he slept in Soho Square.

"My lord!"

The edge in Braddock's voice did not fit his station. "Speak," Adrian said. But there was no cause for it; he already knew what the message concerned.

"She begs to meet with him."

Now she begged, did she? The first day she had demanded it. Yesterday she had asked. He could not compass the notion of her begging for aught.

It grated on him.

If he kept a cold remove from her now, it was not to force false shows of humility. From the first, he had known—although like a fool he had sometimes forgotten—that the steel at her core would not bend. That morning after her exhausted confessions about the child, even at the very moment when he had resolved to make her his wife, he had known that a marriage vow would not win her loyalty. All he could do was keep her safe.

But what he had not foreseen was this weakness in himself, the fatal crack that her very presence seemed to widen. *To save her,* he had told himself as he married her, *to protect her from her own foolishness.* But to have her as his own, it transpired, was to alter himself. Like to drinking an intoxicant, exposure to her had corrupted his senses and his wit besides.

His care for her would be her undoing as well as his own. He had put his blade to her bastard brother's throat, but where once he would have pressed his point home, his hand had been stayed by thoughts of his wife. And where once he would have bloodied Colville to insensibility, instead he had lifted away his sword.

If she was an intoxicant, then her effect was poisonous. Her brother's wild scheme might have killed her, and the rest of them, too. Such feckless idiocy was better crushed in the bud than left to fester on the vine. Yet, concern for her had swayed him to mercy. It decimated the wisdom he'd amassed at high cost.

At court, a man of no wisdom made an easy feast for enemies.

He could not tolerate her effect any longer.

At least now he knew what ailed him. He lacked immunity to her. He therefore would keep himself away—for both their sakes.

The decision had brought him a cold measure of peace. He was done with complexity. David Colville rode in chains, bruised and bloodied; Adrian's fists had not been able to make him talk, which was all the satisfaction Adrian required of him. He would be dead soon enough.

Hodderby was half-gutted and closed, its servants dispersed; for a year or two, his wife would have to make do with Beddleston when in the north.

What else? Nothing. By noon the day after the fire, the horses had been saddled, the bags packed, the party on the road. From Hodderby to London was a straight line in more ways than one.

His wife rode halfway down the party, out of his sight.

"My lord." Braddock wore shadows beneath his eyes. "What shall I tell her?"

Adrian shrugged. "How fares your shoulder?" Colville had not been content to knock Braddock senseless; he had scored the man's flesh besides.

"Well enough," said Braddock. "Lady Rivenham and her tirewoman have been tending to it. What shall I tell her?"

Despite his claim to the contrary, strain showed in his voice. This was not a hard pace that Adrian had set;

yet, for a wounded man . . . or for a woman . . . it might go slower.

He reined in his horse. "She begs?" he asked evenly.

Braddock's mouth twisted. "Aye, my lord, that was the word she did use."

"If you disapprove of aught, say it."

Braddock looked to his mount, placed a hand on her neck, felt down to the breast strap, which he tested with a tug.

"She's a woman," he said. "Can't expect her to defy her menfolk."

Ah. So Braddock had discovered a strain of chivalry— but a latent one, for it had not flavored his opinions the night that Hodderby had burned. As his wound had been dressed, he had condemned his master's wife very explicitly. Adrian, steps away, had pretended to have deaf ears. To have heard the harsh words would have required him to punish Braddock for an opinion that seemed just, with the house burnt around them.

"You do wrong to imagine Lady Rivenham a mere woman," Adrian said now, flatly. "She is well capable of defiance, and any amount of cunning."

Braddock flashed him a look he did not like. It verged too closely on sympathy. "She is full of regrets, my lord. You cannot mistake her suffering, to look at her."

"I do not doubt it."

Braddock hesitated. "So . . . what answer shall I bring her?"

"Let her speak to him."

He would not play the part of Lord Towe with his

wife. His hand would not lie heavy on her save when circumstances required it. For now, she could ride where she wished. And if she wept to see her brother in chains . . . he would not allow it to make a difference to him.

The road rose at a gentle slope, carrying the men ahead into full visibility. Nora saw her husband riding tall in his saddle, his ease apparent in the loose rhythm of his body moving with his mount.

He never looked back.

He had not looked back once since leaving Hodderby.

At night, when they had found lodgings—once at an inn, twice in the open countryside—he had treated her courteously. His courtesy was polished and complete, wholly impenetrable. Already, she thought, he was his London self, wearing a courtier's face, for at court, even rage was shown through a smile. That first day and night on the road, his distance had not stung her as sharply as her own conscience. Or perhaps her miseries had been so complexly entangled that she had not been able to parse them. There was David, whom Adrian had not put down gently, and who was bound for execution, with the gunpowder as the evidence that would convict him. There was Hodderby, terribly damaged, in part by her doing. Her exhaustion magnified these griefs until she felt as though she lived in a nightmare without end.

Adrian had been right to scoff at her honor. If any remained to her, it was ragged and soiled.

No wonder he treated her so coldly now.

Last night, when he had settled her into the hostelry, in the best room it could offer, her anguish had finally overwhelmed her. "Tell me," she had burst out. "Tell me how I might atone."

"It matters not," he'd said in a very pleasant way, and then sketched her a bow and bid her good night before shutting the door, locking her inside with Grizel.

She understood the true meaning of his reply. The intuition emerged from her bones like a breath of ice, chilling her through. It mattered not, for he had given up on something . . . and that something was her.

A woman undivided might have flouted his remoteness and ridden up to his side to demand a reckoning. Having forced her hand to a marriage, now he gave up on it? An undivided woman would grab his jaw when he turned away, steer his face back to hers, and remind him of the bargain that he had forced upon her: to treat her as a wife. Yes, she had erred. Yes, her sin was great. But *she was still his wife.*

Yet, how could she be that woman? One portion of her soul strained behind her, toward the brother whose health Braddock had assured her was fair, but who was being taken to his end. The other half strained forward, to the man on the hill who had betrayed her into wedding him, who had claimed to love her—but who no longer felt even the need to glance over his shoulder to see what he left behind.

Braddock came riding up now, a smile on his face. "Good news," he said. "You may treat with your brother."

She gathered up her reins. "For how long?"

"Why, he did not say." Braddock's smile faded, as though he recognized the unlikely laxity of this oversight. He cleared his throat. "For as long you like, then, my lady."

She tried to smile. She should be grateful. David was bound to a place where he would never speak again.

But her husband's indifference could not hearten her. It sent a message to her, and not a kind one: *Do as you like. It matters not to me.*

She pulled her horse around to follow Braddock down the line. Men looked away as she advanced, their mouths tightening with dislike. She raised her chin, accepting it as her due. They might have been killed by the gunpowder. It was a miracle, but not by her working, that no one had been in the old banquet hall when David had lit the powder fuse. She still wondered that Braddock treated her so kindly. Over these last three days, he seemed to have found a measure of pity for her, and she did not think herself too good for the condescension of common soldiers. Every one of her actions felt corrupt to her now.

Her heart clutched as her brother came into sight. His head was bandaged, his eyes blackened; he slumped a little in the saddle. But—strangest of sights—he seemed in good cheer, his hand sketching an animated accompaniment to whatever conversation he traded with his unlikely companion, Lord John.

His smile awoke some sleeping beast in her. What right had he to smile? How dare he smile? Did he not realize what he had done?

Sighting her approach, Lord John touched his cap to her. "A happy reunion," he said, drawing his horse away from cozy conference with her brother.

"Not so happy," she said sharply.

The manufactured sympathy on his face did not suit him. "I will leave you," he said, and put his heels into his horse, riding around and past.

Braddock, too, pulled up short, providing her a space of privacy for which she sent him a grateful look as she rode up to David's side.

Her brother fixed her with a steady look from gray eyes very like her own—but darkened, perhaps, by an accusation. He had their mother's coloring, as she did, but in his bones he took after their father. She had never resented the resemblance before today.

"Lady sister," he said, "you look more tired than I feel. How so?"

"I suppose it is grief that wears me," she said. "And regret, and shame. Better to ask yourself wherefore you can smile."

His square jaw worked as though he chewed over his next words. "Shame, indeed," he said at length. "I have yet to come to an accounting of how you married the man who would see me dead. Even Lord John has no story for it. "

Astonishment briefly paralyzed her tongue. Rage resuscitated it. "I will teach you the cause of my shame," she bit out, "for you own a full measure of it yourself! You put Hodderby to the flames! What demon possessed you? Where is *your* shame, David?"

"This is war. There will be losses—"

"The war is *over*! Over almost before it had begun. Preston has fallen; Scotland is put down. And whence the gain from your idiocy? What army was defeated when Hodderby burned?"

"Enough!" he snapped. "Hodderby is my own! If I sowed the fields with salt, it would still be within my right!"

Oh, but she recognized this clipped tone. Their father in France had been tutoring him in arrogance. "That you have any estate to your name is owed to *me*. I persuaded Towe to lobby for your inheritance. Did you think he was eager to argue for you? *My* administration kept Hodderby running when its profits had been squandered on weaponry. Or did you imagine it was easy to maintain an estate with empty coffers?" Her laugh scraped in her throat. "If I could live that history again, David, I would give you an education. Perhaps if I could undo my efforts, Hodderby would still stand whole!"

He caught her arm. "Leo. What is this? I came back for *you*. How can you speak to me so? I set off the powder for *you*. Or was I to abandon you to his clutches? Tell me, how else was I to save you?"

She wrenched free, and her startled horse shied beneath her. "How brotherly you are," she said, reining her horse tight. "What consideration you show me! Did the same tender affection prompt you to promise my hand without my consent? How glad I was to learn the news from Cosmo!"

He scowled. "You had said you would consider him—"

"*Consider!* I did not say I *consented*!"

"But you would have." He pushed a hand over the dark stubble on his jaw, then lifted it away to show her his teeth. "But I reckon how it transpires. You grew hot for that whoreson, didn't you?"

"Hold your tongue," she hissed.

"Aye, he always knew how to get under your skirts. Twisted your brain and corrupted your allegiances, did he? By God, I should have known that dog would come sniffing again! To think he dared to aim so high—and you, Leo! Where is your honor? To go against your family—"

"I aided you," she said through her teeth, "in every way I could. I aided you beyond good sense and all reason. Consider, brother, what a reward I received for it: to watch Hodderby be ruined. You say I go against the family? Very well! I am glad to do it now. I am done with your cause, I tell you."

She reined her horse away, furious with him. But— bitterly she knew it—he was not the only one to blame here. If he had crossed a line, then she had made it possible for him to do so. She would never forgive herself the consequences.

"You're right."

The admission startled her. She turned back, eyeing him warily.

He nudged his horse forward so they sat mounted knee to knee. Reaching for her hand, he squeezed it lightly.

She looked at where he touched her, then pointedly lifted her gaze to his.

He grimaced. "Leo . . ." Now he leaned forward, cajoling. "Forgive me, sis. I was wrong to question your loyalty. And my strategy, I admit, was . . . foolhardy. But, by God—I was panicked! How not? You see . . . I'd left something very precious at Hodderby." He offered her a lopsided smile. "You may know her."

For one moment, his charm muted her turmoil. She recalled with a pang what it had ever meant to be his sister: to have his laughing attention, his support and encouragement, the warmth their father had never provided.

"Oh, David." Tears pricked her eyes. "You never should have come back. I did not require rescuing."

He shook his head. "Colvilles do not abandon their own."

"But I am a Ferrers now."

He winced. "I accept the blame for it. I should have been there to protect you. But I will atone, Leo. I will kill him for you."

Calm like ice descended on her. She withdrew her hand from his. "How easily you speak of killing." In France, it seemed, their father had been teaching him stubbornness—and cultivating his natural immunity to female opinion, besides. "But you must accept facts. My husband will not let you slip. You are for trial now, and the Tower." The very name of that place sickened her; it seemed, in her mouth, to be coated with blood.

He nudged his horse closer yet, so its head came up against her mount's flank. In her ear, he murmured, "And I tell you, Leo, I will surprise you."

She jerked back. "How do you mean?"

"I have plans."

The fervent note in his voice chilled her. *Plans!* Was there no end to his visions? "Are you mad? It is *over*! They intercepted your shipment of arms, David! And the gun-powder—you are caught! Your only hope now is for imprisonment rather than death!"

"You do not sound so mournful for it!"

"Do not—" She stopped herself, folding her lips, breathing hard. But no—why should she stop herself? "Do not *dare* impugn my love for you. I have proved it time and again."

"Love is well and good," he said sharply. "But where is your loyalty? Do I have it? *That* is what I need to know."

He spoke as though her loyalty were worth aught. How could he not see the truth? "I would move heaven and earth to spare you," she said hoarsely. "But the money I might have spent on bribes was put to your arms. And my husband—he will not even speak to me, and I . . ."

I fear I will have to watch you die.

She made herself reach again for David's hand. He did not resist it, watching narrowly as she lifted and kissed his dirty knuckles. This *was* her brother: tall, lanky, unshaven, his eyes feverish, but not, by the feel of his flesh, from any physical ailment. He was on fire for some vision she had never been able to see. She had seen only *him*—and tried to do her duty by him, to repay his past kindness as love and kinship demanded.

"You are still a Colville, then," he said.

She sighed. Such arguments wasted what little time remained to them. "Someone is caring for you," she said instead. She laid his hand back on his pommel as she looked him over. His clothing was soiled but his bandages were fresh.

He gave her a queer smile. "One wonders why they bother if they mean to behead me in the fortnight."

"Perhaps—" She could not bear to surrender all hope. "Should the king grant you mercy—my husband's order now is only to imprison you, and others have survived the Tower—"

His laughter silenced her. "Oh, dear sister." He chucked her chin. "Dear, foolish Leo. Go, ride ahead now. Dream your silly dreams, and trust in me to find a way to make you happy."

His mockery was like a slap. She held his eyes and made her voice cutting. "Love you have from me, David. But trust? It burned with Hodderby. If you die, I will mourn you for the rest of my life. But I will never tell another soul that your actions were just."

She turned her horse then and rode forward. Like her husband, she did not look back.

20

~~~

In the far corner of the taproom, a chair crashed against the floor as two men leapt up to brawl. Raucous cheers swept the room. Braddock and Henslow slammed down their tankards to join the fray; the barmaid, hovering by Lord John, abandoned flirtation midsyllable to trail after them.

Lord John heaved a loud sigh as he watched her go. "I will be most glad," he said, "to pass tomorrow night at Manston House."

It was not the first time he had observed this. Adrian himself had no pressing desire to sleep in the bosom of Lord John's family, but the manor lay direct on the path to town, so he would allow it. There were members of his party who would benefit from a good bed.

As for the Lamb's Head, it offered other advantages, most notably the low crowd to which it catered. Its innkeeper—now screaming at the brawlers, who rolled across his floor as bystanders jeered—was not much interested in his patrons, neither for their journeys nor their comfort. A year's worth of grease encrusted the table, and decades of smoke blackened the low-beamed roof. Its blowsy barmaids showed no curiosity beyond what could win them a coin, and its clientele verged closely on a mob.

It was the mob whose opinion most interested Adrian. They were but two days' distance from the capital now, and the banter that had sparked the fight provided every answer he'd required. These travelers were abuzz with anticipation of a public execution for the man who, unbeknownst to them, was locked upstairs under the watchful eyes of Adrian's men. With the uprising crushed but the majority of its rebels imprisoned in the north, the south longed for a vengeful show of its own.

Nora thought she knew what awaited her brother. She imagined, perhaps, that she would have weeks, even months, to try to win mercy for him. But his trial would be little better than an entertainment offered to the public to satisfy its bloodlust. David Colville would be dead within the month.

This is not my concern.

A table crashed on its side, showering ale across the spectators. Lord John cursed and sprang to his feet, dashing his sleeve over his eyes. "Damn these rustics!" As he lowered his hand, he jerked. "By God!" He shoved his arm in Adrian's face. "Look! Some ass's head has stolen my rings!"

Adrian lifted a brow at the sight of the boy's naked fingers. "A skilled thief, then."

"I have a mind to search this company!"

A crash went up from the other side of the room: the brawlers had knocked over another table.

"As you wish," Adrian drawled. "They seem a compliant lot."

After a moment of visible indecision, the boy hissed a breath through his teeth and yanked down his jacket. "No," he muttered, "no. Let them enjoy their misbegotten gains. And God curse them for it!" Stiffly he bowed to Adrian. "By your leave, I'll withdraw."

Adrian lifted his drink in farewell, then took a long swallow to mark Lord John's stalking retreat. For lack of larger joys, these small victories must be celebrated zealously.

The brew was dark and strong, briny like seawater. He checked himself when he would have sipped again. It was an unwise impulse to blur his mind. He would make his decisions soberly and coldly. He would relocate that place within him where choices seemed simple, unshaded by any thought of her.

He would unlearn this damned talent at seeing through her eyes.

She had wanted to speak with him earlier this evening. Had tried to stay him when he took his leave. But he had ignored her. To give her an opportunity for explanations or pleas would be pointless, painful to both of them. He already knew what must be done.

A hiss went up. "There's a fine piece," crowed some wag at the next table. He followed the man's look and a curse tore from him. She stood in the doorway, showing less sense than a dormouse. At least that creature, looking in upon this chaos, would know to stay hidden.

Instead, eyes rounding, she surveyed the scene—and then saw him, and firmed her jaw, and started into the fray.

He was on his feet instantly, despite the darker impulse that seized him: to let her taste the consequences of her actions. She was determined to set her own course and walk it without care for where it led her. Why not let her confront for herself the troubles her mulish pursuit would encounter?

But what a joke he was. He could sit here mustering indifference for hours, yet one glimpse of her broke his resolve. By God, the leers she collected as she wove toward him scraped his temper like flint. He knocked people aside, ignoring their shouts of complaint as he advanced on her. Stupid little fool! Did she imagine this rowdy lot would not take an interest? In her riding habit of rose wool, only half-spattered by the road, she looked provocatively misplaced. The fresh purity of her skin, the sleek shining crest of her uncovered black hair, the grave composure with which she endured the buffeting of passersby, even the coolness of her gray eyes acted as a goad. Adrian felt the effect himself: fragile things, delicacies that held themselves far above commonplace life, did not engender respectful admiration. Rather, they churned up a greedy sort of hunger, one that lured a man to smash what he could not have.

He shoved another jackanapes out of his path, cataloging likely trouble in the expressions of those eyeing her, nudging each other, jerking their chins in her direction. It was not only her elegance that made her conspicuous. The simple provocation of her silhouette caused drunkards to imagine that her tastes would run as coarsely as their appreciation of her bosom.

He had nearly reached her when trouble erupted. The fight spilled suddenly between them. One of the brawlers sprawled at her feet, gawping up at her. "Here's an angel!" Seizing hold of her skirts, he cried, "Angel, show me your favor!"

The filth-faced drunkard hanging from her skirts yanked Nora off her balance. Helpful hands caught her by the elbows, and for a moment she thought herself spared; but the hands instantly grew lewd, slipping to deliver a sly pinch at her breast, a firm grope to her buttocks. She whirled to swat them away, but all at once, there were too many hands to defray, and yellow, toothy grins encircled her.

The crowd lurched. Bodies packed thick as pelts crushed into her, stinking of sweat and alcohol. She elbowed free of a sweaty grip but somebody, stumbling, caught hold of her hair and snapped her backward at the waist. She cried out as she clawed at the fingers that pulled at her scalp.

They loosed her all at once; she straightened, gasping, to discover Adrian taking her assailant by the throat and physically tossing him away. Another vulgar, questing hand found her buttocks and Adrian stepped past her, laying the rogue out with a fist to the face. His arm closed around her waist; clearing a path with his elbow and shoulder, he hauled her forward.

"You," he growled in her ear, "were to stay in your damned room."

She had no breath to reply; she could only clutch him and try to keep her footing. The brawler who had caught her skirts stepped into their path again and Adrian caught him by the hair and hauled his head into an uplifted knee. Almost effortless, almost elegant, this violence; the man groaned and slumped to the side, falling beneath the trample of feet.

People began to scream and shove harder. She could not understand what had turned the mundane chaos into a stampede, but everywhere now men were fighting, and those who tried to move away were thwarted by jeerers who pushed closer to encourage the brawlers. Somebody's fist flew toward her, and before she could shriek, Adrian deflected it with his forearm. Finally, finally, she spotted the door, through which more men were piling in to join the fracas. Adrian broke through these newcomers and pulled her into the hall, where the smoky heat and noise subsided with shocking abruptness.

"Move," he bit out, letting go of her waist but placing himself behind her, directing her by the shoulders toward the stairs. "Up!"

She had wished to speak with him. To confront him. To demand plain speaking, or any kind of speaking at all. She had not realized they passed this night in the seventh circle of hell, or certainly she *would* have stayed in her room!

Face burning, her skirts gathered tightly in her fists, she hurried up the stairs. He marshaled her so closely with his body that every step brought him brushing up against her.

At the top of the stairs he seized her elbow and took the lead again, dragging her down the hall almost too quickly for her to manage. The door to her room he knocked open with his shoulder. Grizel, who had been brushing down a dress by the fire, bolted up.

"Out!" he roared.

Grizel threw a panicked look toward Nora, who managed a jerky nod. The girl gathered the dress to her chest and hurried out.

The door slammed. He leaned back against it, staring blindly into space, his breathing audible. His head turned slowly toward her, and the hard look in his face made her throat close. His silence crisped the air like an oncoming storm.

He shoved off the door and stalked toward her. She would not back away. She was not afraid of him! Only she had never seen such rage in his face—save that night he had railed at her while Hodderby burned . . .

He stalked past, stripping off his coat and waistcoat. In his shirtsleeves he looked out the window into the coaching yard. His grip on the sill turned his knuckles white.

Whatever he saw made him spin back toward her. "I would throw you through this damned window if I thought it would fix your brain!"

Her knees folded, landing her heavily into a cane chair. "I did nothing to provoke them. There was a fight—"

He drew back his fist and slammed it into the wall.

Powdery wattle rained onto the floor. Her tongue felt like lead, but a paralyzing prickle passed down her skin.

"You little *fool*. Have you no care for yourself? To walk into that room—" His laugh was ugly. "But why do I ask! *I* am the fool to wonder! Again and again you have proved your reckless disregard for yourself! What is today next to your other exploits? A grope of your bosom—nay, even a rape on the floor—would be nothing compared to your idiocy with the gunpowder. Your life is but a toy to you, is it? You gamble with it so *freely*—"

Mouth tight, he stared at her for an unspeaking moment. Then he snatched up the chair next to him and smashed it against the wall.

"Stop!" She was on her feet. "Cease this childish—"

"Childish?" he roared. *"Childish?"* He sprang toward her, and now she did scramble backward, for in his face was the fury of a marauding savage. She ducked around the bed and he lunged across it, seizing her arm and dragging her bodily over the mattress. A strangled cry escaped her as she spilled onto her knees on the floor.

He hauled her up and pulled her to the window that overlooked the yard.

"Look," he said in a murderous voice, his hands hard as manacles on her shoulders. "Behold the company which you so blithely tempted today!"

She held very still, not daring to move. The heat of his body surrounded her like a great, raging fire, and his bruising grip flexed erratically on her arms.

He shook her once. "*Look!* Behold the work of *childish* men!"

Half the brawlers had spilled out of doors. They had set upon one of the London-bound coaches, rocking it wildly as the coachman, atop the roof, screamed curses at them.

"This rabble is bound for London," he said in her ear. "Rape is a game to them—an execution a holiday. Imagine their joy if they learned your name."

Cold spilled over her. He could not mean . . . "My brother's execution? Is that why they travel?"

He snapped her around to face him. "Forget your damned brother! His cause is as dead as he! Are you so intent to follow him?"

For an unending moment they stared at each other. She could not have managed a word. Her very lungs froze for horror.

He made a noise of disgust and released her. "Christ. Tell me—have I married a Jacobite? I did not think so— but if I am wrong, prithee tell me now, so I may *wash my hands of this lunacy!*"

"No." The word came out brokenly.

"No? *No?*" Viciously he mocked her. "No, you are no Jacobite? So only a madwoman then—a lunatic who destroyed her home for sisterly love! Hodderby is ruined, Nora! Your demesne is laid waste! But perhaps you aim higher yet. Tell me, how far will you go for your accursed family?"

The blood had drained from her head. She put a hand to the windowsill for balance, but the world continued to spin.

"Answer me!" He screamed so loudly that his voice lost all color. "Did I marry a drone? Are you a lunatic? So tenderly the Colvilles care for you—how far will you go to repay them? *How far?*"

Such hatred in his voice! Such murderous anger. "I am done with their cause," she said hoarsely. "I am *done*! But that does not mean I will watch David die gladly—or that I will let him go to the block without trying to save him! *Surely* you must understand that!"

His expression went blank. And then he gave her a terrible smile. "Always a new reason," he said. "Why do I bother? There is no saving you from yourself."

Turning on his heel, he strode toward the wardrobe that stood along the far wall. The heavy piece topped his head. The violence with which he threw his weight into it—and the ease with which it began to move, scraping and bumping over the floor—frightened her further yet. It bespoke an unnatural strength, born of berserker's rage.

Once the wardrobe blocked the door, he stepped away and with cold, unnerving precision began to unwind his neckcloth. Tossing that aside, he took up his sword from where it stood by the hearth, then sat, laying the weapon across his lap as though he anticipated the use of it.

He did not look at her but stared into the flames.

Her throat tightened. She would not be afraid of him. She *would* speak. "Where is he now? Is he safe from them?"

His mouth twisted. "As safe as can be, with that mob in the courtyard. They would make quick work of him." Darkness moved across his face. "Or you," he said. "Lacking the brother, those vermin would not scruple to make do with the sister."

Dear God. She wrapped her arms around herself. "I spoke to no one."

His smile looked cutting. "How *wise.*"

The silence that opened then seemed to suffice for him. Sprawled in the chair, legs outstretched, his sword across his lap, he tipped his head to gaze on the water-stained ceiling. But despite his casual posture, she sensed an alertness about him. He listened closely to the noises in the coaching yard.

Her eyes wandered across the evidence of the rage he now restrained—the cracked wall, the broken chair. In contrast, his stillness grew the more chilling. She had to try several times to find the courage to speak.

"They must try him first, mustn't they?"

Glancing to her, he lifted a brow.

"They cannot simply execute him," she said. "He must be tried in the House of Lords!"

"Your father was impeached." He spoke as though to a dim-witted child. "The Colvilles lost that entitlement."

"But even a common prisoner is entitled to some sort of trial!"

He looked away again. "Indeed. You must remind the lawmen so, when next they consult you."

He sounded almost bored now. It wounded her. In her place, would he let his siblings be put to the axe? Would he not do everything in his power to protect them? "Perhaps I will remind them! Perhaps I will petition the king myself! If he allows men to flout and abuse our laws, perhaps he *is* a fraud, and no true king for England!"

His chin came down. He looked at her narrowly. *"Sit,"* he bit out.

But his bullying suddenly enraged her. So he regretted marrying her. A just fruit for his use of force! She had not asked to marry him! She had not asked to be placed in this bind! "Why should I sit? Are you afraid to hear me speak? Do you think someone will overhear? Or will you yourself turn me in for a Jacobite? A fine turn that will be for your courtly ambitions, to expose your wife for a criminal!"

He straightened slowly, the movement sinuous, like a snake uncoiling. "Sit," he said softly, "and shut your mouth."

"No." He might recline like a pasha, indifferent to the ugliness of which he spoke, her brother's violent end, but *she* was not fashioned from such cold clay! Damn him for bullying her into this hellish place, and then scorning her for trying for endure it! "What difference does it make to *you* what happens to me? I am a great inconvenience to you, so let my rashness be the cure! If you think me a drone, it will be a great fortune to you, no doubt, for the mob to find me!"

He exploded from the chair. In one lithe move he lunged toward her and caught her by the shoulders. "Think me indifferent?" he said. "Let me correct you, *wife.*"

A cry broke from her throat as he drove her backward, straight against the wall. His fingers flexing and firming on her upper arms, he loomed over her.

The strangeness in his face froze her to the core.

"Can you," he said, in a voice of terrible softness, "*can* you be such a fool? Can you imagine that I have witnessed, indifferently, your loyalty to a man who, but for God's grace or the devil's own luck, would have blown you to smithereens for his notion of a lark? Can you *imagine*—" A muscle ticked in his jaw; he drew a hard breath through his nose. "Can you *imagine,*" he said, "that I would not gut him from gullet to groin, were it *not* for you?"

A smile sharpened his mouth, dark as night. "Ah," he whispered, lifting his hand to catch a lock of her hair, making her flinch. "But that would be an injustice, I think." Her heart was pounding; she did not recognize this man who studied the hair that he lightly clasped. "For if I am rageful, Leonora"—his eyes speared hers— "then it is not so much for your brother, my love. The largest part of my wrath is for you." Slowly he leaned down to her mouth. The brush of his lips sent chills over her skin.

"My lovely little idiot," he said against her lips. "Having risked all you held dear to suit your brother's feckless whims—having housed gunpowder in the heart of your hold and kept silent the secret that might have killed you, and your whole household too—what else am I to feel? Tell me: shall I feel *love*? But in love lies no lesser a danger, for in such moods as this one, I find my love and rage combine."

His fingertips settled along her jaw, light as breaths as he directed her face upward. But as their eyes locked, some primitive instinct in her raised a shudder. He studied her so intently. A predatory heat infected his regard.

"And so," he whispered, "can you believe, for love's sake, that if I thought striking you would knock your brother from your brain, I would use my fist? And I would not stop until you bled, Leonora. God help me, but I would count the drops of blood I spilled as though they were years I might add to your life."

He slammed his fist into the wall by her ear.

Crumbs of wattle dusted her cheek. But she did not flinch, for his face was finally naked of its masks, and the desperation she saw in it caused her mouth to go dry and her heart, very briefly, to stop.

My God, she thought. In his face now she saw the truth: it was not rage that drove him. It was fear. He *feared* for her.

For *her.*

In that moment it all came clear. Finally, horribly, she saw what power she had over him. How easy it would be to destroy him. He, who had seemed invulnerable, had made her his Achilles' heel. *He feared for her.* Yet if in London she spoke awry—if she were ever to make good on her mad threats—on whom would it reflect but him?

He had gambled his future, the future of his kin—all he held dear—on a woman who could undo him in a moment. He *expected* her to undo him now.

And yet, if she baited him or accused him of brutality . . . she understood suddenly that he would not attempt to punish or curb her. He would strike walls and break chairs, and watch her lead the Ferrers to their end.

My God, Adrian.

Still it took courage—heart-thudding, breath-stopping courage—to grasp his face in her hands. Beneath her palms she felt the fine tremor that ran through him. Otherwise he remained perfectly still, his regard fierce, his face opaque. He had shown all of himself to her that he could; she sensed that he would give nothing more to her now.

Not willingly, at least. He had some small instinct of self-preservation left to him.

"You need not strike me," she murmured, her voice unsteady, overwhelmed by her revelation. "For if you strike out that part of me that cleaves to my own, you will strike yourself from me as well."

His caught breath spelled its own message, despite the silence of his tongue. She smoothed her palm along his cheek, into his hair. Once, long ago, she had fantasized of his force. She had dreamed that he would return, and seize her from Lord Towe's side, and carry her away. Later, so much later, he *had* seized her, and she had reviled him for it. But he had always possessed some part of her . . . even when the distance between them had been greatest.

She had loathed that missing piece of her soul as a weakness. How astonishing now to see that his weakness was the same. His weakness was *her*.

"I love you," she said. "Never doubt that, Adrian. No matter what comes, I cannot act but as my love for you guides me." She would never betray him. There had to be some other escape from this conundrum.

His face changed. The terrible blankness loosened from his features. "You will remember you said that," he whispered.

She swallowed. Such a low, growling note in his words, and she did not mistake its meaning: he was not comforting or reassuring her. He was warning her.

"Yes," she said. "I will never forget it."

His hands drove through her hair and pinned her against the rough wall. As he stared at her, she held perfectly still, her heart in her throat.

And then his hands slid behind her back, down over her buttocks, which he palmed openly, in a show of bold, shameless effrontery.

"Remember," he said, and lifted her, making her gasp. With the edge of his hip he knocked her knees apart, and stepped into the lee between them, using his body to press hers against the wall as his mouth came over hers.

He devoured her. He devoured her gasp. His hands massaged her buttocks as he ground against her, the thick length of his erection pressing insistently through her petticoats. His savagery stirred some primal alarm in her, but the force of his mouth did not allow her to turn away. Then his open mouth fell to her throat, his teeth nipping her collarbone, and with no warning he swung her away from the wall.

She clutched tightly to his shoulders as he carried her in three long strides to the bed. He spilled her onto the mattress and then planted his knee by her hip and his hand by her shoulder, crouching over her, his hair spilling down.

"Lie still," he said very softly.

She swallowed from nerves and forced her eyes shut. His hands slid up her belly to the neckline of her bodice and yanked. A sharp tug, a ripping sound; she felt the cool air spill across her breasts, bare to the world over the tops of her stays.

A low, rough sound came from him. She opened her eyes in time to see him fasten his mouth to her nipple. He suckled her forcefully, as though to punish her, but it was no punishment, it was the furthest thing from it. His wildness called to her. She cupped his head, arching into his mouth, the strong pull of his lips causing her body to grow loose and compliant.

His hand ran up her calf and knocked apart her legs. His hot, rough palm slid up her thigh, found her wet folds and parted them. With one long finger, he penetrated her.

The shock of sensation caused her to jerk.

"Be still," he said through his teeth.

She held her breath as his hand set up a slow, rhythmic penetration. His head lowered again to hers to seize her mouth. With tongue and fingers he ravished her, licking and rubbing, sucking and stroking. His hip against her inner knee urged her legs apart more widely; she felt his minute adjustment as he brought his body into the cradle of her thighs. His hand, now damp, released her tender flesh and made quick work of baring him. The heavy head of his cock slid down her slick channel; and then, in one sure, hard stroke, he thrust into her.

She cried out. He caught her arms and held them out

to either side, pinning her with his hands and his tongue in her mouth and his cock deep inside her. Again and again he thrust into her, long, hard strokes that rubbed some hidden, terribly sensitive place she had never felt before; it swelled and ached more fiercely with every pass. He muttered into her mouth, then into her cheek and hair, words she could not decipher, only—ah, God, she had never been used so hard, and her own pleasure began to frighten her. With each flex of his hips, each demand, his teeth on her earlobe, his biting kiss of her shoulder, she gasped more and more loudly, and then a grunt tore from her. She was lost to anything but the slap of his body into hers.

She surrendered to it. She gave herself over to him, let his body master hers, and at some point her wrists came free. She wrapped her arms around him, tightened her thighs' grip on his hips, and sank into his mouth like air into the fire that consumed it. Dimly she was aware when his arm slipped beneath her knee, when he hoisted her leg higher, and the depth of his penetration straddled a line between pleasure and pain that made her groan— and then sigh as her climax seized her.

The sound of her pleasure seemed to alter something in him, for he kissed her knee and then lowered it, slowing to a more leisurely pace, rocking into her gently now, lifting her hand to his mouth to kiss her fingertips, to paint and suckle them with his tongue. Their eyes met, and something passed between them, hot and tremulous. She caught his face, putting her mouth to his ear, whispering against it, "I am yours."

A gasp broke from him. His arms came hard around her, and she felt him shudder in his little death.

They lay locked together as their breathing slowed.

Silence now from the coaching yard; the evening had grown peaceful. She reached up to stroke his hair, to run her thumb along the sharp edge of his cheekbone.

His eyes fluttered opened. He kissed her softly, a kiss grave and sweet and full of portent. A shiver passed through her. The echo of unimaginable pleasure, perhaps . . . or a premonition.

May God show mercy to all whom she loved, this man as much as her brother. For in London, no one would.

21

As they drew closer to London, the roads grew choked with traffic, and the hills gave way to rolling fields neatly bordered by hedges. The sense of the nearing city began to grew oppressive. It seemed to lurk just beyond the horizon like some great, unseen monster, waiting to devour all that Nora held dear.

And yet, she found an unexpected peace in riding by Adrian's side. The occasional grip of his hand over hers, and the steady looks and occasional smiles he gave her, reminded her of the night that had passed. They had reached a silent understanding in that dusty little room, and it rose in her now like a wonder, astonishing, precious: no matter what they rode toward, they rode toward it together.

As they passed through the gates to Manston House, where they would stay this final night before reaching town, Lord Barstow came into the yard. Adrian left her with their host to attend to his men and her brother.

Barstow led her toward the house, Grizel trailing, as he apologized prettily for the absence of his wife. "My son," he said with a chiding look toward Lord John, who was walking with them, "did not give proper notice, otherwise Lady Barstow would be here to receive you. Alas, she is at Bath with our daughter, who takes the waters for her health."

Nora murmured some pleasantry, but her attention was caught by the scene transpiring by the mews. Adrian's men were helping her brother from the saddle, for with his hands bound behind his back he could not dismount on his own.

Lord Barstow, following her glance, sighed. "An unhappy sight for you, no doubt. An unhappy fix."

A woman less versed in the ways of courtiers might have heard an offer of friendship in his voice. But the closer they neared to London, the more Nora recalled of its ways. With a leaden heart she said lightly, "You are kind to think of me."

"Oh, but ever since I received my son's extraordinary tidings, I have thought of little else," Lord Barstow said. His thin white brows knitted. "Such untoward doings! I would speak frankly—but I would dislike to offend you."

"You could not offend, my lord."

"Could I not? Then allow me to observe that you do not wear the bridal glow. Perhaps the road has tired you? You must look on Manston as your own home, and me as a kind of father. Certainly I do hope, my lady, that I may be of some use to you."

With his liver-spotted jowls and his hunched posture,

he looked more the grandfather to her. But some instinct pulled her suddenly to distrust his kindness—entreating her to break from his hold and wait for Adrian.

She looked again over the yard. A group of newcomers had joined her husband and his men. In the dying light Adrian's pale hair shone bluish and his back was turned to her, straight and tall.

The pang of tenderness that speared through her closed her throat. Was not love a terrible thing? One thought one had learned to manage it, and then it sprang free again, rattling its claws in one's liver.

God shield us both, for I do love him, beyond aught else.

The twilight was darkening, or else it was her own worries besetting her and closing her away from the light. All at once she felt tired. "I would like to rest," she said.

"Excellent. And there is no call to look so glum, my child, I promise you. Look, my men are even now seeing to your brother's comfort."

Sure enough, they were leading David away by the arm. "Where do they take him?"

"To a comfortable room," Lord Barstow said soothingly. He gave a nod to Lord John, who slipped away toward the stable. "I have no business to pass judgment, my lady; that will be the task of Parliament. While here, he will be housed as a guest—time enough yet for gentle treatments, to steel him against the future."

His gentle voice implied that he found that future a pity.

"That is gracious of you." She cleared her throat.

"I hope Parliament might prove so gracious when my brother's case is put before it."

Lord Barstow clucked and patted her hand. "Only place your faith in the Lord our God and your brother's wits, and all will be well."

The advice echoed her brother's words to her. How odd.

She stepped over the threshold into the house. Her feeling of disquiet suddenly sharpened, although she could see no cause for it. Double doors opened into a moderately sized hall with a low coffered ceiling lit by mullioned windows. Along the walls loitered a handful of men, plainly dressed and idle—peculiarly so, for servants.

Puzzled by the prickle down her spine, she nevertheless heeded it. Turning to Grizel, she said, "Go bid my lord come speak with me—I have forgotten to tell him something."

Lord Barstow took no note of the maid's departure. "My son gives me to understand that your family has known Lord Rivenham since his youth." He guided her past one of the knots of idle men, aiming her toward the staircase. "Is that so?"

She nodded.

"And do you think it likely that Lord Rivenham shared with your brother the names of his many friends in France?"

Again a sense of ominous familiarity seized her. She came to a stop, her skirts swinging around her. Something was wrong here. Lord John laughing with her brother on the road—his father asking the same questions that Lord John had put to her that night at dinner, now so long ago, which had opened her eyes to his dislike of Adrian . . .

She pulled free of Lord Barstow's grip. He gave her a puzzled, frowning smile, but she did not wait to hear what he would say. Turning on her heel, she strode back toward the door, a rectangle of glowing blue light amidst the gloom of the hall.

Steel scraped without.

She picked up her skirts and ran.

At the doorway she grabbed onto the frame, the scene outside imprinting itself with paralyzing vividness:

Some strange man held his sword to Adrian's throat.

Twenty paces away from him, too far across the yard, his men had realized the trap. Their swords were drawn but they were encircled.

Grizel cowered against a wall.

A hand closed on her arm. "You will want to step out of the way, my dear," came Barstow's kindly voice, and then he matched action to advice, pushing her aside as plain-clothed men tumbled past, brandishing swords.

For a moment that seemed to freeze and then grow more complex, like the formation of an ice crystal on glass, blooming before her eyes, Nora divined how it would go:

Lord John and David, in pursuit of a common enemy, had reached some private accord.

The cost, somehow, would be Adrian's life.

She would profit by her brother, but lose her husband in the bargain.

The stillness shattered. Adrian threw himself backward and came up with blade in hand; his opponent lunged and Adrian twisted away, raising his sword to stop a blow that otherwise would have beheaded him. Across the yard, swords clashed as his men gave fight.

Freed of her dread vision, she saw the truth in her own heart. To have her brother at the cost of Adrian was no bargain at all.

The fight raged across the yard, drawing more men from hidden corners. What horses had not been stabled were shying as swords danced past and nicked them. One broke free to make a frantic gallop around the edges of the yard.

Adrian and his men were more than outnumbered. They were being fought two to one. "What is the meaning of this?" she cried to Lord Barstow.

He was watching the melee with a faint smile. "Why, justice for your brother." He cut her a sly glance. "And for you as well. For was it not your husband who persuaded your brother to adopt James Stuart's cause?"

She shook her head wildly. "You speak nonsense!"

"Ah, but think before you speak," Lord Barstow said. "I pray you, lady, *think*—for a man seduced against his better nature to commit evil is a far easier man to pity—and more deserving of mercy—than the man who authored the evil plot. Was it not Lord Rivenham who urged your brother to go abroad? Was it not your husband who oversaw the placing of the poison the night his men slept, and the gunpowder was planted at Hodderby?"

"No! No, that was I! And the gunpowder—"

"Think," he said sharply, glaring at her. "Think of your brother's welfare, madam! If some other man is responsible for the gunpowder, then perhaps that same man also arranged the shipment of weaponry. Indeed, the only sin which might be proved of your brother is his ill-timed holiday to France. And you, my lady—you will soon find yourself freed of an unfortunate connection that gives you no cheer!"

A man fell beneath Adrian's blade, his blood spurting across her husband's face. His savage focus twisted his features past recognition as he hacked forward to his new opponent.

Her hands curled into fists. She stepped forward but Lord Barstow restrained her.

"You must not be slain," he said mildly. "We will require your full support in this undertaking, and your testimony, too."

Her nails cut into her palms. Savagely she turned on him. "You will not have it! I will not—"

Lord John's bounding approach interrupted her. "More men!" he gasped raggedly. "Where are the damned archers—"

"What archers?" Barstow scoffed. "What are you, a woman? Go out and command your men!"

On a sudden hope she looked out. It was true: Adrian and his men were making advances. The dust of the yard was blood-soaked, a picture lifted straight from illustrations of hell; men groaned and writhed and she was god-forsaken, for their misery left her untouched. She had bloodlust inside her, too, now; she cheered inwardly and viciously when Braddock struck down another man, and rejoiced as he reached Adrian's side.

"I will end this," Lord John said. He grabbed her and dragged her backward. Her slippers fell away; gravel scraped her soles.

A knife bit into her throat.

"Rivenham!" he roared. His arm banded her ribs to prevent her struggle. "Throw down your sword or collect the head of your wife!"

David's roar was the first reply. Breaking from his engagement, he bounded toward them.

"Rivenham!" screamed Lord John.

This time Adrian heard. Though it risked her life, she could not restrain her cry as his attention broke from battle to fix on her, and his opponent landed a blow to his arm that staggered him.

Braddock leapt to his master's side, answering the insult with one sharp slice that felled the enemy. "Hold!" Lord John yelled. "Hold, Gardiner!"

His men, hearing, began to retreat in tight formation toward the steps.

When Adrian's men rushed to follow, Adrian said in a carrying voice, "Hold, Ferrers!"

David had reached the steps now, but Lord Barstow unsheathed his sword and held it out to bring him to a stop. "What madness is this?" he demanded of his son. "We will require her testimony—"

"Watch," Lord John bit out. "Lay down your swords," he shouted, "or else I gut her like a sow past her prime!"

Adrian stood too far distant for his expression to come clear to her. But she saw him turn toward Braddock. Whatever he said caused that man to shake his head in fierce denial.

Adrian ignored this. He stepped forward, and Braddock, after a brief hesitation, fell back.

"Open the gates to my men," Adrian called. "They are of no interest to you."

"That is not yours to decide!" Lord John retorted, but his father cuffed him hard.

"Open the gates," Barstow bellowed. "You fool," he snapped to his son. "What idiot refuses to part an enemy from his men?"

Disbelief crawled over her like a swarm of bees. Adrian meant to surrender himself. He did not know that Lord John bluffed. He would be killed for her sake—and why? Even her love for him had served him ill!

"No!" she cried. "Adrian, go—"

Lord John's palm smothered her mouth. It stank of foul sweat and deceits, and made her gag.

"Gently!" David yelled at him. "You whoreson, gently!"

The gates began to creak open.

Adrian threw down his sword.

What overcame her then she could not say, only that it felt larger than herself and seemed to descend from above in a great wave that reddened the world and slowed time, providing her a new vision with which to see opportunities.

She clawed the hand from her face and cried, "David, by your love, help—"

He mounted the step and Lord John took it as provocation, releasing her to answer the new threat—as did his father, who never thought to worry for her. She threw herself into Barstow, a solid smack that shoved him into his son and caused Lord John to stumble to his knees on the steps. She leapt down the stairs and David held out his arms, but she ducked past, screaming as she flew, "Run!"

"Grab her!" screamed Barstow, and she heard her brother's quick curse and his footsteps behind her, while ahead Adrian had recovered his sword and the battle broke open again. But he was coming toward her now and she knew in her gut that this time he would not leave her brother alive.

David was nearly upon her, screaming, telling her she did not understand—

She dropped mid-step to her knees. Her brother, moving too quickly, slammed into her, his boot striking a fire of agony through her hip as he thudded over her and fell to the ground.

Head ringing, she forced herself to crawl forward, past him.

A hard grip caught her arm and hauled her up. Her fear soared and then blinked out, for her husband paid no heed to her brother; his face bloodied, he pulled her to him, bracing her hard beneath her arm, and then retreated backward, his grip suffocating her as he swung her from side to side, his sword outstretched, looking for opposition. Around her the clash of swords became deafening. Her vision blotted out by Adrian's chest, she had no idea how far they progressed, but his sudden whirl made her stumble and then he was taking her under her arms and hauling her up across a horse that sidestepped and stamped as he mounted behind her.

Bodies littered the yard, six, eight, ten—

Lord John was crouched over her brother, screaming into his ear, shaking him—

The horse wheeled beneath Adrian's direction; she caught sight of Braddock, mounted with Grizel behind him, fleeing through the closing gates.

"Hip!" came Adrian's scream in her ear. His mount responded, bolting forward toward the narrowing exit. They were passing through—passing—

The gates slammed shut behind them.

They rode hard for speechless hours as the sun peaked and began to set. In those brief times when they slowed the horses for necessity's sake, to give the beasts proper breath, her lord husband made no effort to fill the silence. But his grip on her remained as hard as though she were still menaced by dangers, and he made no complaint when, by the light of the rising moon, she ripped her petticoats and urged him to his knees by a stream so she could clean and dress his wound.

He was not the only man in need of such aid. By the time she had tended to the last of them, her petticoats were tattered and the moon was setting. Bare-legged beneath her skirts, she retook her seat on Adrian's mount.

They made no further stops, riding straight into town

in the true darkness before dawn. London's streets were ghostly, the horses' hooves clattering over the cobblestones and echoing off the closed shutters of narrow houses. Soho Square slept beneath a fitful breeze that rattled the dying leaves in their branches, and it took several rounds of hard knocking before Adrian's startled, sleepy staff roused to accommodate the unexpected visitors—not only master and mistress but dusty soldiers besides.

Nora barely registered the details of her new home: it was large, and cold, and magnificently appointed. Adrian left to confer with his men, and his chambers echoed around her. Bathwater, lukewarm, came with unlikely speed. Some housemaid substituted for Grizel, who was near to swooning with fatigue, but Nora was content, for the girl scrubbed her with vigor.

Once she was tucked beneath the quilts, she could not sleep, and waited dry-eyed and numb, staring at the fire, until Adrian appeared in the doorway.

She shoved herself upright then. He leaned against the door frame, watching her. So many questions tangled in her throat that she hardly knew where to begin. She found herself strangely abashed. The light of the fire playing over his face lit a shifting expression, now like anger, now like sorrow, and finally, as he stepped toward her, like simple weariness.

"My love," he said as he came to sit on the edge of the bed, "do not think your brother free. The Gardiners are no Jacobites."

On an indrawn breath, she realized that he did not

understand what had passed. He thought it a simple attempt at assassination.

"Adrian"—she leaned toward him to grasp his wrist—"they struck a deal with him. With David."

He hesitated. "A deal."

"My brother was to indict you for the gunpowder—to say you had done his deeds, and dispatched him to France in your stead; that he was only your peon, and you the designer of his plots."

Some grim, terrible smile crossed his lips. "I see. And to what purpose? Did they say?"

Was not the answer obvious? "To shift the blame to you. Lord John is no friend to you—I suppose his family thought they would profit by your downfall. And my brother, too—by the somewhat clearing of his name. Lord Barstow said he might find mercy this way, if he were your dupe rather than his own agent."

The smile faded. "A harebrained plan," he said with calm contempt. "They could never prove my involvement to the satisfaction of my peers."

"Yes, but—" She swallowed. How odd it felt to expose her brother's schemes to him. At last she was at peace with her role, but the lingering feeling of dishonor remained, a useless reflex. "They assumed I would support them with my testimony."

His silence churned her innards. It seemed to smack to her of skepticism. Though this plot was not her doing, she felt her face warm. "I know it was harebrained," she blurted. "Who would care for a woman's word, or trust it where it served her brother? Only—I suppose they depended on the fact that I am married to you. Most women would support their husbands before their brothers. It would have lent credibility to my claim, had I done otherwise."

"Yes." The word came out softly. He laid his hand over hers. "So it would have."

"But I did not agree to it," she said helplessly, for she was increasingly confused by his strange pauses. She wished to make certain he was clear on this point.

"I know," he said. "I was there. I know you had no hand in it." And then he pulled her into an openmouthed kiss.

It caught her by surprise. He took hold of her waist and pulled her up against him, and the skillful aggression of his mouth began to kindle parts of her she had imagined too weary for interest.

When he pulled away, he studied her closely. "You did not accept this bargain," he said—as though the other phrasing had not been sufficiently clear.

"No." She sounded breathless. Wetting her lips, she tried for a more confident voice. "I never considered it. My brother's mistakes are his own. I could not let you pay for them."

"But if he pays with his life?" Now his forehead touched hers, so they were eye to eye. In the dim light, his irises seemed to have a light of their own, an impossible green, the color of new life, of hope. "You knew it might mean his death."

Her hand fluttered to his cheek. The prickling of a new beard lightly abraded her palm. "I cannot bear to think on that," she whispered. "But when it came to your life, my path seemed . . . very clear." Suddenly she could not hold his eyes, and her heart leapt and battered at her ribs. "I had no way to save you both," she said, very low.

"And so you saved me."

She forced herself to look at him again.

There was tenderness on his face, and in his lips as he pressed them, very softly, to hers.

"I love you," she said against his mouth. "You must know you have my heart."

"Yes," he whispered. "So I do."

Aching, she closed her eyes and yielded to his kiss. She welcomed it; she hoped it would concuss her, wipe away awareness of aught but them, here, in this moment. If only the world consisted of the meeting of their mouths, and his gentle grasp of her face, and the beauty between them, subtleties of love made into a communion of the flesh.

Long minutes later, as they lay entwined, he spoke in her ear. "I promise you," he murmured. "I will make this right."

The smile that turned her lips felt infinitely sad; she was glad for the darkness that veiled it from him.

Here was the first promise he had ever spoken to her that she knew, immediately, he would not be able to keep.

22

Nora stepped out of the sedan chair, then put extra coins into the hands of the chairmen. Red and breathless and cross, they hefted the poles over their shoulders, then turned and trotted down the cobblestone lane, past inclining trees with gold and scarlet leaves. Overhead, the sky glowered a livid, cloudless blue.

She stood watching their departure for a long minute, breathing deeply of the biting wind that swept the square. Here, in the verdant quarters of London, the air smelled of sweet decay and wood smoke. What a sharp contrast it made to the stench of the tangled streets where she had stood not half an hour ago. In the oldest part of the city, the breeze was acrid with piss and shit and rotting vegetables, and the breeze lapped against one's face like the breath of a feral dog.

Her lungs were clearing. But her ears would not. The sound of screams still rang in them. *Hang him!* they had cried. *Split his gullet! Entrails to the dogs!*

On a hard breath she made herself mount the stairs.

In the echoing marble-floored entry hall, the butler was waiting. Pike divested her of her cloak and informed her that his lordship was still at the Court of St. James's. Nora thought she detected, in the slight emphasis Pike gave his words, a conspiratorial note—a subtle offer of friendship. Pike had no idea where she had gone today, but he must know, as all London did, of her brother's predicament. The servants would have discussed it amongst themselves: her ladyship's letters to all and sundry, entreating them to use their influence on her brother's behalf; and his lordship's gentle insistence that she wasted her time in beseeching strangers to intercede.

She wondered if the servants took her part in it. They must find it strange that her husband, a favorite of the court, did not use his own influence. But last night he had agreed to do so. He had agreed to speak to the king for her. His majesty's recommendation of clemency, if Adrian could win it, might sway Parliament to be merciful.

She made her way through pocket doors that opened into a salon of tasteful beauty, paneled in gold and cream, with vaulted ceilings and large Italian oils of mythological scenes. A tight-woven silk rug demarcated the sitting area by the bay window, where she took her seat to await her husband's return from St. James's.

A footman appeared with paper, quill, ink, and lap desk. The house was coming to know her routines. But while she took up the quill dutifully, her hand soon fell still, allowing ink to puddle into a blot mid-sentence. *My lady, if you be so kind as to find pity in your heart . . .*

Pity. What a weak commodity on which to build her strategy! Adrian was right: London had found her a mockery once, and in these desperate, imploring letters, it would find fresh cause for derision.

She laid down the quill and gazed out the window. The blank faces of the houses across the square looked untouchable by violence, their windows shining boldly, as though nothing could break them.

"String him up by the gibbets!"

Before today, she had never seen a mob.

Adrian had told her how it would go when David was brought into London. As soon as word had come that Barstow and Lord John had "recovered" her fugitive brother and intended to deliver him to the Tower, Adrian had warned her of the reception her brother might expect.

Of course, he had not dreamed that she would countermand his edict and slip out to witness it for herself.

She had needed to witness it. She could not let her brother endure it alone. Ten minutes after Adrian had left to answer the king's summons, she had stepped from the house and flagged a sedan chair on the high street. For a small fee, the chaplain at St. Magnus had permitted her access to the tower that overlooked the area.

For two hours she had perched by the small window, watching the narrow lane through which David must pass. Low-hanging street signs had rocked uneasily in the wind, the gilt on their facings striking sparks that speared the eye like daggers. Below these signs, and out the windows above them, and even atop the roofs, the waiting crowds had gathered.

Long before her brother's appearance had come the noise. It swelled from the distance like the sound of the ocean breaking against rocks, or the rumbling of great wheels. When the procession had finally appeared, the people below had joined their voices to it, and she had recognized, at last, the bone-breaking howl of the mob.

Her brother had ridden in shackles amidst a circle of masked soldiers. He had not looked up, even when children had dashed into the road to dangle his effigy in his face. Had they fashioned these effigies with their own small hands? Had they knotted the nooses that strangled the dolls' necks? Who were the mothers that permitted such games?

He had not looked up at them. He had not looked up as rotten fruit rained down on him. He had not flinched at the curses or the clods of dirt. As she had watched him, her horror had been overlaid by something fiercer . . . something akin to pride.

She had berated him for his reckless treatment of Hodderby, but in that narrow lane, he showed the part of himself she could never despise. In his honor, he reminded her what it was to be a Colville.

And how the crowd had loathed him for it! How they had howled when he denied them their fun! That gut-curdling din had killed the last of her hopes. After the disturbances in the north, London was furious for recompense. Only her brother's blood would satisfy it.

David had passed onward, out of sight, half of the crowd trailing him, the rest dispersing sluggishly, discontentedly, having hoped for a better show.

She had stayed in the bell tower for a very long time, waiting for her nausea to subside and her heart to slow.

But now, when she put a hand over her breast in the luxurious quiet of this gilded room, her heart yet raced. Could a heart wear out from grief? Could it beat itself to death, like a bird snared in a trap?

"He reached the Tower safely."

The quiet remark startled her; her fingers curled into a fist. She swallowed past the lump in her throat and turned to behold her husband.

Full dress became him. His long, curling wig highlighted the stark angularity of the bones in his face. The powder emphasized the full line of his lips and lent an impossible vividness to his green eyes.

He held himself differently in the maroon brocade suit, more languidly, the height of his heels shifting his balance, putting him taller than nature designed any man. There was great skill to cutting an elegant figure in such heavy embroidered costumes, to maneuvering gracefully in a full-skirted coat. Adrian had mastered it. He came toward her in long, easy strides, his skirts swinging, the brawn of his calves flexing beneath dark silk stockings.

A short distance away, he stopped, perhaps alerted by her lack of greeting to the mood that troubled her. He studied her for a long moment, and she held his gaze, hoping, unfairly, that he might divine the truth and spare her the need to speak it. She would not keep secrets from him any longer, but if she tried to say now what she had seen this morning, she feared she would weep . . . or scream.

It was not his fault.

It was not his fault.

But oh, God, it would be so easy to blame him for it! His actions had set in motion the course that led her brother to London today.

Her own actions at Manston House had ended her brother's hope of escape.

She would never regret it. She would have made the same choice again and again. But it would haunt her. It haunted even this vast and fathomless love that overwhelmed her when she gazed on her husband.

Mayhap her face did speak for her, for Adrian took a long breath before he asked, "Are you well, love?"

His concern undid her. She rose, drawn across the silk carpet toward him. How to answer him? Was she well? Would *they* be well? This love was a miracle, but she was no saint; perhaps she was inadequate to its grace. Could their love have a happy destiny, when its second life had been authored by the events that ensured her brother's death?

Very carefully she touched the gold braid that trimmed Adrian's coat. The warmth it carried from his body made her acutely aware of the chill deep within her. For so long, in their separation, she had gazed across rooms at him, watching from the corner of her eye or beneath her lashes, and the sight of him, turned out so splendidly, golden as an angel, had sawed like a knife in her heart.

Now she could touch him, for he was hers—could touch every part of him, even roughly if she liked, these gold-plated buttons, this intricate Valenciennes lace that spilled from his upturned cuffs. He had stripped off his gloves before coming to find her. His wrist was warm and hard, lightly dusted with hair. She laid her fingers atop his knuckles.

When his hand turned in hers, closing in a hard grip, she knew the answer he must give of what had happened at court. "He says he cannot interfere in these matters," he said evenly. "Parliament must be allowed to proceed as it sees fit."

"Ah." She swallowed hard, but his grip seemed to squeeze her next words from her. "I went to see him. I watched him be brought into the city."

The signet ring on his fingers pressed hard into her bones, an accidental pain that somehow satisfied. It matched the ache inside her. So much happiness to be had from his touch—and so much grief to countermand it. She felt physically torn, as though her soul were breaking.

"Shall we prosper?" she whispered. "After he is . . . dead?"

"Nora," he murmured, the word less sound than breath, but she heard in it so many things: a chiding scold; loving affection; and, hardest to bear . . . compassion. He had no hope to offer in regard to her brother.

She closed her eyes as he drew her against him, satin and lace rustling between them. He smelled of court, of musk and cloves and sweat, for it was always crushed in the state rooms, sweltering from the press of ambitious bodies.

Had there only been a levee, she would have gone with him. But the German king was not sociable, and his next levee was not scheduled until December. One could not impose oneself on a king—particularly one said to hate public displays. Yet if David still lived in December, she would make her own tearful plea for clemency, and be damned who saw her, or what they thought; she would fall to her knees and beg the German . . .

Adrian's lips touched her temple. She turned her cheek into his throat. A light dusting of powder fell across her temple.

"That was rash of you," he said softly, "and dangerous, to go alone into the city. Had you told me you needed to see the procession, I would have taken you."

These kind words sharpened the ache in her. Did she deserve such kindness from him? She grieved for a man who had tried to kill him.

On a hitching breath, she schooled her mind to his concerns. "Did the king say aught of Barstow's deeds?" Ugly rumors were circulating—a broadsheet that spread foul lies, no doubt of Barstow and Lord John's devising. It made the same claims they had asked her to support, and new ones besides: Adrian had conspired with her brother; David's escape from his custody had been no accident; Adrian, too, thus belonged in the Tower.

"There is no worry on that account."

"But all the talk—"

Adrian set her away from him slightly, to show her the dark edge of his smile. "Lord John persuaded his father into a poor gamble. He supposed their friends would approve an attempt to see me laid low. No doubt they would have, in other times. But with the public mood so vicious . . ." His smile faded. "No one wishes to enlist in a bargain that might spare your brother a traitor's end. Not even if it ensures my downfall."

"Of course." To her own ears, her voice sounded scraped raw. She tried to smile. "That is fortunate for you. For us, I mean."

He gathered up her hands again. "Will you be all right tonight?"

She grimaced. He had committed them to some private assembly before they had learned that her brother would enter the city today. "I fear not," she said. She had yet to make a social appearance, but she remembered well what compassion awaited her in court circles. "I would not be fit company—"

"I think you must," he said gently.

The edict seemed odd and cruel. She pulled her hands free of his. "You expect me to laugh and dance while the town screams for my brother's head?"

His expression turned grim. "Nora, you *must*. With the broadsheets on the street, and Barstow's failed conspiracy, it is crucial that we be seen. Your absence would feed rumors that might yet trouble us. But your tears— they would not be so harmful. Rather the opposite, for some would think them owed to my opposition to your family."

How fluently he understood the twisted logics of political society. "Yes, of course. They would relish my tears." She heard how bitter she sounded, but she did not care. London had ever been cruel to her. To face it now, when she was little better than an open wound—

"Trust me, love." He tipped up her chin, catching her in an intent, somber gaze. "I promise you will not regret it."

Nora remembered her old lessons of London. She smiled through the veiled insults to her brother, and through jokes of executions. Though Adrian abandoned her to speak with a minister, leaving her at the mercy of the laughing group that enclosed her, she kept a smile fixed on her lips. She was still smiling when she turned on her heel and walked away from them and him both, desperate to escape the staterooms.

The great heat generated by the crush was as wet and thick as steam. Candle smoke combined unpleasantly with the sweet stink of cologne and sweat and powder, so that each breath felt harder to draw than the last. She dodged around silk-clad hoops and jabbing elbows, gesturing hands and sloshing glasses of wine. A large knot of women, their plumed headdresses waving, unwittingly concealed her passage from Adrian, who stood in deep conversation with the Groom of the Stole.

She would find him again soon enough. For now, what she needed was a private corner in which to steel herself again to this task.

Chatter jammed the space of Lord Fairfax's double-story hall, clashing with the ring of crystal and the frenetic lilt of a harpsichord. But the air was purer here. As she took a deep, grateful breath, a sudden clarity fell over her, as though she were coming awake.

Trust me, Adrian had told her. He had earned her trust a thousand times over. But why must she be here tonight? All London knew her brother had been imprisoned today. Next week, or the week after, *then* she would put herself to this test. But why tonight?

At the far end of the hall, a couple was dancing, or attempting to; their lurching movements suggested that wine had overset them. No one spared her more than a passing glance as she brushed past them toward a darkened hallway.

She did not stop until she was well down the corridor, and then only because the silence revivified her senses. Holding very still, she listened to the sound of her own breathing. Her head was calm now, but it seemed that her body was not. She was panting like a cornered dog.

Her knees folded under her. In astonishment, she observed herself collapse.

The stone tile felt cool beneath her palm.

This is real, she thought. *I am sitting on the floor.*

She took a hard breath through her nose and tried to marshal her resolve. She was a practical woman, and this behavior did not become her. Adrian had explained the advantage in attending this party, and she must honor his wishes. She would be a good wife to him. She loved him. This was horrifically scrubby behavior, not becoming of Lord Rivenham's wife. If somebody saw her, the gossip would lacerate her afterward.

Besides, her skirts would be crushed.

But a weird lassitude was spreading through her. She felt as though she could sit here forever.

"Nora."

Adrian's quiet voice came at her ear. When she summoned the will to turn, she found him crouching beside her, the skirts of his emerald silk coat spilling carelessly across the tiles.

"I cannot do it." She meant to speak calmly but her voice was choked, angry. "You knew it when you wed me. You knew it long before that! You knew I was no hand at these affairs—society, and court, and politics, and polite company. And I cannot pretend! Not when he is so nearby, and suffering—"

He caught her hand and kissed it. "I know," he said. "I knew. And it matters not."

"Then *why*?" She let him keep hold of her hand, but now that her anger was uncovered, it flooded her like a toxin, making her vicious. "Why this charade? To torment me?"

He made no reply to that. "Who offended you?" he asked instead.

"It makes no matter!"

"It matters," he said flatly. "I am a man who keeps careful tally of such things. Tonight is for a different purpose, but tomorrow, I will settle scores."

"*What* purpose? And if I tell you a dozen names, what then? For I cannot recall all the people who scorned me before, and I have no cause to think that the list will be shorter now I have returned!"

His eyes narrowed. "Do you not? Then come," he said, rising, still keeping hold of her hand, forcing her to scramble to her feet. "Let me instruct you differently."

"I do not require it," she said through her teeth, but his hold on her was implacable; with his other hand at the small of her back, he urged her back into the entry hall. "Find a person," he said at her ear when they neared the staterooms. "Any person whom you recall treating you rudely before. We will see how they greet you now."

His goad panicked her. "No! Adrian, I know they respect you. I do not require you to parade me like a possession!"

"But that is what you are." His voice was hard. "A precious possession. Whether you choose to make them see you differently, to respect you as your own woman, will be your choice. But, by God, they will respect you as my wife."

"You cannot *make* them—"

"I can."

Looking into his face, she saw the seriousness of his intentions. For her sake, he would use all his power to bring London to her feet.

A curious shock moved through her.

When last she had been in this town, she had been alone. Someone's wife, yes, but alone all the same.

No longer. She would never be alone again.

A breath escaped her, and her anger seemed to go with it. She reached up to touch his cheek. "You needn't," she said softly, and could not stop herself, despite the public setting and the eyes surely upon them, from stroking his lower lip with her thumb.

How could she let the slings and arrows of vapid fools

wound or deter her? None of these people mattered. She
had *him*.

A muscle still ticked in his jaw. "Tell me who insulted
you," he said.

She surprised herself with a laugh. "You are like a dog
with a bone," she said. "I won't tell a thing to you. But
take me back into the staterooms." She knew her duties
to him. "We have yet to greet our host."

As he led her back into the sweltering, smoky warmth,
she marveled at her sudden calm. Adrian was beside her.
His loyalty was to her, as was hers to him. Who could
touch them? The sidelong glances, the glimpses of teeth
as smiles flashed over her, did not cause her heartbeat
to stutter. So often as a girl she had felt in such settings
removed from herself, distant and numb and out of her
own control, but now, in this moment, she felt fully present, self-possessed and strong.

The test was not long in coming. Their own host delivered it. As Adrian turned away to speak with someone,
Fairfax laid a hand on her arm and purred, "Families are
so troublesome, don't you find?"

She was conscious of painted faces inclining to watch
her, glittering eyes and carmine lips. In the flickering
candlelight, the salon's cinnabar walls looked the shade
of dried blood. "I suppose they can be," she said calmly.
"Do yours trouble you, my lord?"

"Ah, whose does not? But then, you are fortunate,"
Lord Fairfax said smoothly. "Your troubles are nearly
over, I believe."

For a moment, the cruelty left her as stunned and

blank-witted as a doll. A titter went up from a lady nearby—perhaps at some other remark. But perhaps not. *La la la, what a clever joke.*

Nora cleared her throat. "I was about to compliment you on your marvelous hospitality. But I see you have other lessons to teach me."

Her husband's hand closed around her elbow as he turned back. "What are we speaking of?" he asked.

She met his eyes. "Family. Lord Fairfax finds it quite troublesome, and envies my impending happiness in being rid of it."

His brow lifted. "I have no wonder that his mind travels in the domestic direction." To their host, he said with a slow smile, "His Majesty informs me that your cousin is close friends with the Swedish ambassador—and that you recently had him to dine. Evidently you are most faithful to the bonds of blood."

Nora blinked. Earlier in the year, London had been full of rumors that claimed a group of Tories had approached the Swedish ambassador to test his country's support for an uprising against the new king.

The reference rightly caused Fairfax to stiffen. "Indeed not," he said sharply. "I have washed my hands of my cousin, and the whole kingdom knows it."

"Ah, yes," Adrian murmured. "Forgive me, I am confusing my news. It was not the ambassador you had to dinner but the much-heralded oracle, Mr. Smithson—although I believe his talk against our king has seen his popularity much reduced—"

"That was my wife's business!" The paint on Fairfax's

face could not conceal his rising flush. "I had nothing to do with it! And how do you know these things? What damned spies—"

"I begin to understand your distaste for family," Adrian interrupted. "It seems yours quite outstrips your ability at governance."

Fairfax's scowling reply was interrupted by the appearance of a footman, whose whispered message much improved his mood.

"What ho," he said to Adrian. "Governance domestic, eh? I would say your difficulties far outstrip my own, sir. I have just had very interesting news." But it was to Nora, not Adrian, that he directed his next remark: "David Colville has escaped."

Through the ringing in her ears she heard Adrian laugh. "Never say it."

"I would not look so cheerful," Fairfax snapped. "One wonders who accomplished it."

"Indeed." Adrian shrugged. "Were the Gardiners about when it happened? They do seem to enjoy misplacing him."

A dumbfounding intuition struck her. She looked sharply at him, and received a lifted brow in reply. "But this news overwhelms Lady Rivenham," he said. "God save us if the knave comes crawling to our door. Fairfax, you will have to put up with us for another few hours at the least—we must give the Watch a chance to recover him."

Taking her arm, Adrian steered her firmly away—and then pulled her to a stop by a footman bearing a tray of wine. "Drink," he said in an undertone, "and then think before you speak."

The canary was thick with sugar. She applied herself to it, staring at him wide-eyed. Was this some fevered specimen of her imagination? Or did these tidings leave her husband peculiarly composed?

The last sip of the wine set the whole world to spinning. She handed him the empty glass. "Do I now know," she whispered unsteadily, "why we needed to be seen publicly tonight?"

His lips came up against her temple, disguising his remark in the guise of a kiss. "I told you that I would fix this."

23

Two weeks later, Nora and Adrian disembarked in the yard at a coaching inn in Immingham, a port town that lay on the road to estates that once had been the Colvilles'. Those northern holdings, along with Hodderby and the other properties forfeited by her father's and brother's attainders, would soon be invested in her husband. It was fit to inspect them. But the journey northward had been long, and the inn offered welcome respite from another jostling hour in the coach.

What idle onlookers loitered in the damp, rain-riddled yard no doubt remarked on the unlikely coincidence that this modest inn should play host to two equally impressive guests: not only the Earl of Rivenham, but also the recently recalled Swedish ambassador, whose household was sailing to Stockholm with the next tide.

What, with luck, nobody would ever guess, was that the peaceful nature of his recall was owed to the discretion of Lord Rivenham, who, in return for a favor, had burned papers that might otherwise have proved this gentleman's involvement in the kind of political meddling that could incite kings to declare war on formerly friendly nations.

Adrian escorted Nora directly to her rooms. If Grizel was surprised when Nora dispatched her downstairs to the taproom to take ale at her leisure, the maid was too grateful to question the order.

Manners dictated that Adrian pay his respects to the erstwhile ambassador, so he left her alone—and locked the door behind him, shutting her in.

Shortly thereafter, on a deep breath, she walked to the door that opened into the adjoining room. A test of the latch showed that it had been left unlocked. She did not knock before stepping inside.

David wore the ambassador's blue-and-gold livery. He had been prowling the windowless room, but at her footfall, he stopped and turned with such composure that she knew he had been forewarned to expect her.

For a long moment they gazed upon each other through the gray, rainy light. He looked rested and well treated, though still too thin. The distracted fidget of his fingers over the empty sword belt at his waist betrayed anxiety, or perhaps—though she hoped against it—anger. His gaze broke from hers, and he looked over the near-empty room, the narrow cot, with a twitch of his lips that might have been an attempt at a smile.

"So," he said, "I was right to tell you the Tower would not be the end of me."

She found her own smile difficult to call up. "I have thanked God for it every day."

He nodded once and started to push his hand through his hair—pausing when he encountered the curled wig, unfashionably long and heavy, that marked him as the ambassador's footman. "I still think it a trick," he said tightly. He lowered his hand to his side, fisting it, and then paced a short measure to the window. In his restless movements, the dismissive flick of his fingers against the dusty shutters, she saw the discomfort of a man who had been done a favor he knew he did not deserve.

"No trick," she said. "You will go free. From Stockholm, you may find your way to wherever you please."

He sent her a narrow glance. His color was high. "But why? This will cost Rivenham his life."

"He would hardly risk his neck for your sake, David. Suspicion has fallen on Barstow's son, Lord John. One of his rings—a very distinctive diamond ring, which once went by the name of Lady Sarah—was found in your cell. And the men who freed you—"

His snort interrupted her. "*Men*, were they?"

Now her smile came easily; after a moment she laughed. To free him, Adrian's men had undertaken a strange ruse, bringing with them two women and clothing for a third. Her brother had fled the Tower in the guise of a crone in skirts. "Surely you cannot object to how it was accomplished!"

"I object to the author," he said. "You may trust him. But if I go missing on the high seas—"

"Oh, David." She sighed. "Is it so strange? You go free for my sake. What other reason could there be? It is not as though you gave my husband cause for friendship."

Now he faced her fully, and his intent regard smacked of surprise. "He told you," he said. "Of course he did."

"Told me what?"

He shook his head, as though words evaded his service.

She stepped toward him. "Now is not the time to bite back truths. Told me *what*?"

"I cannot understand it," he muttered. He ran a hand down his face. "I put him to the sword once before. But he would not fight! The day he asked to marry you—so many years ago, now—why did I not end him? Father told me to do it—and I was close, *so close* to cutting his throat—only he would not *fight*!"

She felt sick. Her father had ordered Adrian's death? "No," she said. "He never told me that." To think he had returned to that place—what memories must have hounded him—and yet, he had never revealed to her the true extent of her family's cruelty. "God have mercy on you." On her own soul was the sin of ill charity, for she could not include their father in her prayer.

David's answering silence seemed stunned. He cleared his throat. "When he laid down his sword at Manston," he said haltingly, "it was so much . . . so much like that other time. And I remembered again how I had spared him—to my regret; I regretted it so bitterly. All these years, each time I found his eyes on you, leering at you across those crowded rooms at court—but again, at Manston, I was reminded of . . . that day."

He sank into a chair and gave a hoarse, unhappy

laugh. "Shall I say it? I was reminded of honor! Honor and Rivenham: God save me, I must have the brain fever to pair those words. But I tell you, when those men came for me in the Tower—they said they were sent by Barstow, and my idiot brain believed it. Why, my first thought was, *I will find that dog. I will finish what I lacked the guts to do before.* And then, to discover that the same man I aimed to kill was the one who had spared me . . ."

"Some lessons take a very long time to learn," Nora said softly. "Sometimes I think that kindness is the hardest lesson of all."

Certainly it had taken all her courage to learn to trust kindness again—to learn that the world might not be nearly so cruel or colorless as she had once resigned herself to endure.

To learn that love might last, and deserve all her faith and none of her doubts, still seemed a miracle that merited wonder.

"But it was not kindness that led him to save me," her brother said slowly. "As you say, it had nothing to do with me at all." He looked up at her. "So I will go free. But not you. What of *you*, Leonora? What of your choice in this matter?"

She fought to restrain her impatience. "I *had* a choice, David. At Manston House, I chose him."

"Yes." He laughed, a short, unhappy sound. "So you did." He shook his head. In his evident wonder she saw how little he still understood her. "It must have been . . . a heady thing," he said, "to encounter him raised so high, a peer of the realm, a proper Christian, yet still so enamored of you, a widow of no great account—"

Of no great account. She knew he did not speak these words to harm her. David loved her. But brotherly love easily accommodated his other understanding of her, as the woman the world saw: a plain widow, who had done her duty by marrying a man whose last actions before dying had saved the family estate, but whose future prospects would be hounded by barrenness, and shyness, and a lack of social charms.

Only, none of this seemed to touch her now. Adrian allowed her to see an entirely different picture of herself.

He had always seen her differently.

"I love him," she said. "I always have. I loved him when he was a second son and a Catholic. You knew this."

His hand dropped from his eyes. The astonishment on his face struck her as a false, offensive show.

"You *knew* this," she said.

"By God," he said roughly, "but I did not."

"Be honest!" Anger took her a step toward him. "Be honest with yourself if not with me. Where is the use in deceit now? Recall to yourself how I pined for him! How I refused to marry Towe, how I turned down food and water—"

"A girl's foolishness," he said. "You were so *young*, Leo! So young and so sheltered from the world! You had never met an eligible man—my God, can you blame me for trusting my own judgment, our *father's* judgment, over yours? What did you know of the world then—or men—or what trials such love might inflict on you? Nothing!"

"And yet my love endured," she said flatly, "through trials of your own making, and our father's, and several more besides."

He came to his feet. "I wanted only the best for you!"

That, at least, was the truth. "And do you still?"

He made a frustrated noise. "Can you doubt it?"

"Then do me this favor," she said, "and trust *me* now. For I am no longer a sheltered girl."

He folded his lips together and blew a hard breath through his nose. At last, his reluctance obvious, he said, "I wish you the best. But—by God, I wish you might come with me!"

"So be it." She shrugged. "Wishes are harmless, I think."

He gave her a slight smile, effortful in appearance. "So I believe. And . . . you do speak true: you're a woman grown. If your choice be Rivenham . . ." His smile twisted, as though the very name soured his mouth. "So be it. He has proved, at least, that he will be worthy to you."

"Yes," she said. "He has more than proved it. Why, he has done right even by you."

He stared at her a moment longer, then nodded. "So. My love and best blessings to you, sister."

Here was the remark she had awaited. She held out her arms to him, taking him into a hard embrace.

With her face buried against his chest, she closed her eyes, permitting herself to savor this moment, perhaps the last she would ever share with him.

"David," she said very softly—wary of shattering this

brief accord. "Do not follow our father down every path he assigns to you."

His grip tightened briefly. "Yes," he said in a low voice. "I will think carefully on my future now."

But the answer did not satisfy her. She stepped back to look into his eyes. "The world is larger than England and France—larger than the question of a single throne and who must sit on it. Not all Father's causes need be yours. Some, I think, are best given up for lost."

A twinkle of his old humor lit his face. Lightly he flicked her cheek, a brother's taunt. "My wise little pessimist," he said. "You never were cut out for rebellions."

That flick demanded recompense. She caught his ear and twisted it. "And you never truly knew me, if you think that the case. For what is love but a great rebellion against caution and sense?"

His smile widened, tipping into ruefulness. "Very well, then," he said, lifting his hands in a mock concession. "In that rebellion, at least, I concede that you seem to have won."

She let go of his ear. "Dispel your last doubt," she said. "I vanquished all comers."

He sketched her a bow. "As you say, Lady Rivenham."

She found Adrian below, in the taproom. He was speaking with Grizel, whose cozy position beneath Braddock's arm made Nora lift her brow. She was not averse to a wedded tirewoman, but by the looks of it, the arrangements for the wedding would need to be speedy.

As she slid onto the bench by her husband's side, he said quietly, "Was it well?"

"Yes." She looped her arm through his. "It was well."

His lips touched her temple briefly. She smiled, though a strange melancholy was settling over her—the inevitable result, she supposed, of farewells.

By the hearth, a flutist and fiddler launched into a merry tune. Chairs and tables scraped as commonfolk cleared space for a dance. She watched idly as men and women paired up to twirl. After so much worry and wear, the prospect of such simple happiness seemed strange to her, a thing more witnessed than felt.

"They prepare to leave even now," she murmured. "They sail by moonlight, he said."

His hand found hers beneath the table. "He is safe, Nora."

"I know." She called up another, wider smile for him. "And I am so grateful." But her heart would not truly ease until David was well clear of England's shore. Perhaps not even then. Could one unlearn such a long-standing habit of worry overnight?

Adrian lifted her fingers to his lips, calling her back to the moment. "No call for gratitude," he said. "The only aim is to see you happy."

"I *am* happy," she said. And it was true. Only she wished she could *feel* this truth more vibrantly. Happiness once had animated her, had leapt inside her like a song, but this quiet inside her felt more like relief than true joy. "I could ask for nothing more," she said, as much to herself as to him.

"Oh?" His brow lifted. "Then allow me to ask you—nay, to order: in future, you will make no entries to taprooms unless in my escort. I was about to come fetch you."

She caught the light note in his voice, the invitation to playfulness, and tried to match it with her own. "I will endeavor to remember that rule, my lord, if only so I may forbid *your* entry to them unless I am on your arm. Behold this fair strumpet you've discovered—already she has slain one man in your company."

Grizel, blushing, wiggled out from Braddock's hold. "Beg pardon, my lady—"

But Nora laughed, and the maid, visibly relieved by this, offered her an abashed smile.

The moment passed. She watched the dancers again, willing their spirit to infect her. David was safe. Her love was by her side. All was well. When would her body accept it, and leave off this dreadful tension?

Adrian's palm pressed the small of her back. "He will prosper, Nora."

She looked up into his face and saw in his thoughtful expression how well he had followed her thoughts. "Yes," she said. "He will prosper."

"Though I promise you," he said, his smile roguish, "it pains me to predict it."

Her laughter now surprised her. It felt like a balm to the still-bruised places in her heart, and so she surrendered to it, and laughed again, and then covered her mouth with her hand, for suddenly, all of this—the dim, warm, smoky room; the events of the past days and weeks and months; the smell of ale and sweat and her love's strong hand at her back, and his green eyes fastened upon her—felt more than real. As though a mask had peeled from her face, the world suddenly felt so immediate and pressing that her skin seemed to buzz.

Life. Here was life. And she had no idea what it held for her. Not any longer.

Only she could believe it would be sweet. For with this man by her side, what could she not conquer? And she knew now, with a certainty that felt as wholesome and honeyed as the warmth of the summer sun, that he would always be with her. For as long as they lived, they would neither of them allow anything to come between them again.

She released her breath and felt, as she did, as though she had been holding it forever. "We could ride on tonight," she said. It was a whim, spoken without premeditation, but it appealed to her: the full moon and frosty stars; the cool wind, and the promise of home on the horizon.

"Yes," he said, and now he touched her face, drawing the outline of her cheek. His eyes swallowed her. She felt enclosed by them, wholly seen, loved in every way. "But first, I think, we must dance."

"Dance?" She glanced in surprise toward the rough-spun crowd. "Here, in . . . such a place?"

He rose, grinning. "I believe I made a promise to you once," he said. "That we would dance for all to watch, with no pretense of secrecy. Behold: the music is merry; the crowd is considerable; half the eyes are already fastened upon us. And what fortunate eyes they are, to behold you."

Her cheeks warmed at this compliment. She pulled a face at him but could not help the silly smile that seized her. His mood enchanted her; he seemed light, unburdened, the boy she had first known and loved. As he made her a courtier's flourishing bow, she giggled. Taking his hand, she let him draw her to her feet.

"There was more to that promise," she said. He had promised to kiss her in public.

He lifted her hand to his mouth. "Ah, but my memory is not what it once was. Perhaps you will remind me?"

Her smile felt as though it might grow forever. As they proceeded around the table, the other dancers hesitated in their steps, and the crowd grew muted. But then came the bright, ringing sound of Grizel's delighted laugh, and this splintered the hush, allowing the hubbub to rise again, and the dancers to resume their figures. The musicians, no doubt encouraged by such lofty patronage, attacked the tune with new vigor.

Adrian put one hand behind his back and cocked his knee, then stepped forward with unlikely lithe grace. She was reminded with a sudden pang of the last time she had seen him dance these figures. They had been at court, pretending to be strangers to one another, and all she had longed to do was race across the floor to him, to touch him—

Good heavens. "I have forgotten the steps!"

He grinned. "Then we will have to invent new ones, you and I."

"Yes, I like that idea. But what I do remember—" She hesitated, clearing her throat, her face flaming at the shamelessness of her impulse. "The rest of your promise, sir—"

"Ah, yes." His teeth flashing, he took her by the waist and leaned down to speak against her mouth. "Rejoice, my love," he said.

"I do," she whispered.

And then, heedless of the hooting cheers around them, he fulfilled his promise by putting his lips to hers.

They danced mouth to mouth as the fiddler played on.